A HANDFUL OF STARS

An enthralling story of poverty, passion and survival

Janet MacLeod Trotter

On **the Tyneside Sagas**: Gripping and impassioned stories set in
m   us times – votes for women, world wars, rise of fascism – with the
b   of vibrant Tyneside and heroines you won't want to leave behind.

Published by MacLeod Trotter Books

New edition: 2012

ISBN 978-1-908359-19-3

www.janetmacleodtrotter.com

(The photographs used on the cover are of Janet's mother and father)

About the Author

Janet MacLeod Trotter was brought up in the North East of England with her four brothers, by Scottish parents. She is a best-selling author of 16 novels, including the hugely popular Jarrow Trilogy, and a childhood memoir, BEATLES & CHIEFS, which was featured on BBC Radio Four. Her novel, THE HUNGRY HILLS, gained her a place on the shortlist of The Sunday Times' Young Writers' Award, and the TEA PLANTER'S LASS was longlisted for the RNA Romantic Novel Award. A graduate of Edinburgh University, she has been editor of the Clan MacLeod Magazine, a columnist on the Newcastle Journal and has had numerous short stories published in women's magazines. She lives in the North of England with her husband, daughter and son. Find out more about Janet and her other popular novels at: www.janetmacleodtrotter.com

By Janet MacLeod Trotter

Historical:
The Jarrow Trilogy
The Jarrow Lass
Child of Jarrow
Return to Jarrow

The Durham Trilogy
Hungry Hills
The Darkening Skies
Never Stand Alone

The Tyneside Sagas
The Tea Planter's Daughter
The Suffragette
A Crimson Dawn
A Handful of Stars
Chasing the Dream
For Love & Glory

Scottish Historical Romance
The Beltane Fires

Mystery:
The Vanishing of Ruth
The Haunting of Kulah

Teenage:
Love Games

Non Fiction:
Beatles & Chiefs

To Charlie, my marching companion, with special love.
Thanks for bringing us music and your humorous take on life.

***

Praise for A Handful of Stars:

'A vivid and compelling read ... If you like books that reflect a particular point
in history then you will find this one fascinating.'
Derby Evening Telegraph

 'Weaving vivid history with a heart-breaking love story, A Handful of Stars, is
an outstanding depiction of the tensions and turbulence of life in the 1930s. Janet
is often compared to Catherine Cookson, but she is a true original – and an
author you'll take straight to your heart after just one chapter!'
World Books

'MacLeod Trotter writes with confidence and conviction, weaving together a
panorama of inter-connected incidents, all charged with feeling and emotion.
 It's another good read and it proceeds to a dramatic climax.'
The Newcastle Journal

'An enjoyable read giving a vivid picture of the Depression years.'
Bradford Telegraph and Argus

Chapter 1

1928

Clara woke abruptly. There was a muffled explosion and a cry. She was halfway out of bed, one foot on the wool rug, when she realised what it was. It came again, this time with a loud shout of satisfaction. She sank back, amusement overtaking her fear. Her father was sneezing in the shop downstairs. Harry Magee would be up, shaved, dressed and having his first snort of Prince Royal snuff with his early morning pot of tea.

'Helps the sun come up over the yardarm,' he always declared, still stuck in the idiom of his Navy days. She waited for the third sneeze, stretching and yawning in the dawn light that spilled round the edges of the brown velvet curtains in her narrow bedroom.

Brown and beige: her mother's favourite colours. The doors, floors and window sills of their flat were painted chocolate brown, while the wallpapers were various shades of cream. The parlour furniture was upholstered in tan brocade or faux leather and the kitchen linoleum was the colour of toffee. The tea set was ivory, the teapot mahogany, the table linen off-white fringed with cream lace. Patience Magee adored the new Bakelite switches and fittings, installed when the street had been electrified.

'The colour of Fry's chocolate,' she sighed. 'Don't you just want to eat it?'

Clara and her younger brother, Jimmy, liked to tease her. They danced around the kitchen when they should have been washing up the dishes.

'Look at the colour of Dad's snuff,' Clara would swoon.

'Don't you just want to eat it!' Jimmy would shout and double over laughing.

'You've got no sense of fashion.' Patience would waft a hand at them with a jangle of bracelets, trying not to smile. 'And no taste.'

Patience frequently told her children how she had acquired 'taste' while working as a cashier in a children's clothing department in Newcastle by observing the style of the well-to-do women who shopped there.

'When I worked at Lawson's ...' or 'Before your father swept me off my stockinged feet. . .' were household phrases that preceded words of wisdom about fashion or commerce. Clara and Jimmy only half listened to their mother's dreamy words but their father would pull at his greying moustache and nod with vigour.

'Never a truer word, bonny lass. You've the brains and the beauty,' he would declare, catching her round the waist and squeezing her to him.

Clara's mother thought no one matched up to her strict aesthetics, least of all their customers and neighbours in Byfell-on-Tyne. That was why their millinery and fancy goods shop was stuffed with the gaudiest of trinkets: green and gold sugar bowls, rose-covered china pots for the dressing table, figurines dressed in blue and purple, ribbons of red and yellow, turquoise hatpins and orange frosted-glass tumblers and jugs.

Clara had learned from her mother how to flatter their clients, ask about their families, discuss changes in fashions and encourage them to buy the bright treasures of Magee's to adorn the mantelpieces and dressers of their modest terraced houses.

From below, the third sneeze came, gentler, followed by a long sigh. Clara padded over to the dressing table and poured chilly water into the china

1

washbowl. Although they had a proper bathroom of which her parents were immensely proud (Prudence had had to compromise on black tiles), Clara liked to throw back the curtains, splash her face and hands in cold water and gaze at the sun coming up over the rooftops and cranes of the shipyards, the River Tyne briefly polished with golden light.

But the day was grey and drizzly with hardly enough light to dress by, despite its being August. Clara felt a pang of disappointment. The day after tomorrow was the bank holiday and for once her parents were going to shut the shop, for they were invited to the wedding of a local boxer. Clara had hoped to go to Whitley Bay with her best friend Reenie Lewis, and even though they had been landed with taking Jimmy along they planned a great day out at the beach.

Clara glanced at herself in the mirror. She looked older than her fourteen years, even when her slanted dark blue eyes were puffy with sleep, her long hair tangled. She pulled her fingers through it. 'Like dark honey,' Patience often murmured when she brushed her daughter's hair at night. Her mother loved to brush Clara's hair and still insisted on doing a hundred strokes before bedtime, even though her daughter had left school.

'My mouth's too big,' Clara complained to her reflection, wishing she had a neat button mouth like Reenie's. Reenie also had a new permanent wave in her soft blonde hair, which made her look like a young starlet. But then Reenie was a year older and her family ran a barber's-cum-hairdresser's in the next street and her mother, Marta, had done it.

Once a week, Patience deigned to have her hair washed and dried by Marta Lewis, and every two months she had it bleached. Yet, despite this intimate relationship, Clara's mother could not hide her dislike of the other woman.

'You would think after all these years here,' she often complained, 'Mrs Leizmann would've lost her Kraut accent. She doesn't even seem to try.'

Patience still insisted on referring to the Lewises as the Leizmanns, even though Oscar and Marta had changed their name after the Great War when anti-German sentiment was still riding high.

'Call them Lewis, my bonny,' Clara's father would chide good-naturedly. 'We must be neighbourly.'

'Well I knew them before the war and names stick,' Patience would sniff. 'Strange lot, if you ask me. Communist posters in the windows and gingham checks.' She shuddered. 'Too much *red*!'

When Clara jumped to the defence of her best friend, Patience reluctantly conceded, 'Maybe Reenie's not so bad. But then she's been mixing with the likes of us — good manners rub off. Not like those wild lads.'

Wild lads. Clara caught herself smiling. Reenie's noisy brother Benny was three years older but with half the sense of his sister. He had his mother's dark looks, was too impatient to be a good barber and idolised their eldest brother, Frank.

Frank; a man at twenty-one with a flop of fair hair that fell across his forehead when he played his violin. Clara always wanted to reach up and push aside the wayward strands so she could see the intensity of his blue eyes. When he was making music raw passion showed in his handsome face and Clara had a terrible crush on him. On Monday, Frank would be playing at the Cafe Cairo on the promenade and maybe she and Reenie would get to dance. In the mirror, Clara saw her fair skin darken in a blush. She ducked quickly and plunged her face in cold water as if she could numb her thoughts of Frank Lewis. Besides in his eyes, she was just his little sister Reenie's chatterbox friend.

Clara forced herself to think of the day ahead. She would be needed to open up the shop and keep an eye on Jimmy while her parents went to the warehouse to buy stock. Usually, they did this on a Monday, but with the bank holiday the warehouse would be shut. Climbing the steep back stairs to the long attic room, she went to wake her brother. He shared it with a neglected stack of boxes and crates full of ornaments and caps that Harry had once rashly acquired without consultation with his wife. They were cheap, he had enthused. They were for tinkers, she had laughed, pecking him on the cheek and consigning them to the loft. Jimmy was curled up like a hibernating mouse, taking up only a fraction of his bed. At twelve, her brother was still small and skinny and looked much younger. She teased him when he insisted he was going to be a boxer like their dad had been in the Navy. Jimmy liked nothing better than being taken down to Craven's boxing hall, a converted warehouse by the river, to watch the men training.

Clara called him awake, but when he did not stir she rummaged around in an open box, pulled out a huge grey flat cap and pulled it down over her eyes.

'Roll up, roll up,' she bellowed, 'come and see the champion feather-featherweight of the world — Mr James Magee! Matched with Charlie Chaplin.' She dived into another box and pulled out a bowler hat, quickly replacing the cap. She waddled across the room impersonating the silent movie star, pulled back the bed covers and started to tickle.

'Gerroff!' squealed Jimmy.

'And Chaplin lands the first tickle with a long left,' Clara laughed. 'Magee's putting up no resistance ...'

Jimmy rolled out of reach and swung a foot at his sister.

Clara caught it and tickled the sole. He giggled and shouted, 'Stop it!'

'Magee desperately tries to kick out, but is disqualified. Chaplin wins again,' Clara declared, letting go the foot and holding up her arm in victory. Jimmy reared up and punched wildly, knocking the bowler hat off her head.

'No he doesn't,' he cried, aiming another fist at her stomach.

'Ouch!' Clara stepped back, clutching her midriff. 'That hurt.'

Jimmy gave her a guilty look from under dark eyebrows, a miniature version of their father's. 'Divn't start what you cannot finish,' he muttered.

Abruptly, Clara laughed. 'Is that what Vincent Craven tells you? Sounds like something he'd say.'

Jimmy could not help a smirk. 'Maybe.'

Clara sat down and gave him an affectionate hug. 'You'll be a boxer yet. Make Mr Craven lots of money, I bet.'

Jimmy's look was eager. 'He doesn't do it for the money, he does it for the fight, for the glory. Says there's nowt better than seeing two men in their prime matched one against the other, giving it all they've got, till the best man wins.'

Clara felt a small twist of unease. 'Can't see the attraction myself. I'd rather see you being a promoter or a matchmaker like Craven than scrapping in the ring.'

Jimmy shrugged her off impatiently. 'You can't be one of them till you've proved yoursel' a canny boxer first. And I'm ganin' to be the best. Cannot wait to leave school.'

'Don't let Mam hear you,' Clara snorted.

'She's let you leave at fourteen,' Jimmy pointed out.

'Aye, but they've always wanted me to help in the shop. Mam has grander ideas for you than being Mr Craven's punchbag.'

Jimmy pushed her away. 'Nick off, I want to get dressed.'

Clara descended the stairs to see her mother coming out of the bathroom draped in a silk kimono, her hair in pins. Patience yawned a good morning and disappeared into the spacious bedroom she shared with Harry, with its corner bay window overlooking both Tenter Terrace and the High Street.

Down further, Clara found her father in the shop polishing the counters and singing 'If You Were the Only Girl in the World', out of tune.

'What do you want for yer breakfast, my bonny?' he beamed, stopping in mid-song. 'Porridge or scrambled eggs?'

'Both.' Clara grinned and gave him a kiss on the cheek, knowing this was the right answer. Her father was an early riser and always cooked breakfast, taking a tray of tea and toast up to Patience in bed. On Saturdays and Sundays he always cooked eggs or bacon as well as the daily porridge, washed down with tea so strong it made the tongue tingle.

Together, in the back kitchen, they assembled the tray for Patience, Clara stirring the porridge while her father talked animatedly about the fight at Craven's the following week.

'Samson — that pitman from Bedlington — he's been matched with Danny Watts.'

'Thought Watts was getting wed on Monday?' Clara queried.

'Aye, but he's not fightin' till Saturday,' Harry replied.

'Not much of a honeymoon,' Clara said.

'Seamen don't get well paid, pet, and weddings cost money. His missus will understand.'

Clara was sceptical. 'I'm going to have a grand wedding and a long honeymoon — touring round the country in a Riley.'

Harry laughed. 'Well, you'll either have to marry a rich lad, or I'll have to win a lot more at the betting.'

'Rich lad.' Clara was adamant. She did not like her father betting, however small the wager. He never won on horses or dogs, only sometimes on boxers. But he claimed it was his only vice apart from the snuff and one day, he declared, he would surprise them all with a bonanza win and buy Patience a department store in Newcastle.

Harry disappeared with the tray for his wife as Jimmy came in. Clara served them breakfast and then argued with Jimmy as to who should collect their mother's tray in a bid to escape the washing-up.

'It's my turn,' Jimmy shouted. They both loved to linger in the warm bedroom with the coal fire, sprawled on the beige cashmere bedspread chatting to their mother or watching her reflection in the dressing-table mirror as she applied creams and make-up from delicate glass and silver pots.

Clara relented quickly. She did not want a moody Jimmy for the morning and it occurred to her that her mother might question her too closely about her bank holiday trip. She had mentioned nothing about Benny's coming along with Reenie, or their hope of dancing at the Cafe Cairo on the promenade.

An hour later, Clara opened the shop as Patience appeared in a cream rayon suit with pearl buttons, opaque stockings, buckled shoes and a neat cloche hat. A waft of spicy musk followed her and Clara felt a sudden lump in her throat to see the adoration on her father's face.

'Isn't your mam a picture?' He grinned. 'Keeps the suppliers on their toes when they see they're dealing with quality.'

Patience pulled on her gloves with a brisk laugh. 'And extends our credit terms.' She kissed her children. 'We won't be long. Mrs Shaw's coming in for a corset fitting at eleven, but I'll be back for that.'

Jimmy followed them out into the street and watched them climb into the van. It was old and belched black smoke, but they were proud to have it. One day, Harry was always promising, they would drive around Byfell in a saloon car like Vinnie Craven. Patience, always the pragmatic one, assured him the van was what was needed to run a successful retail business.

The morning passed quickly with a steady stream of customers coming in to buy needles and ribbon, children's caps and socks, and to browse the new ornaments and giftware. Clara had Jimmy up the ladder to fetch down a box of buttons for Mrs Laidlaw, who was knitting a baby coat for her newest grandchild.

'These yellow butterfly ones are just in,' Clara assured her. 'No one else round here will be wearing them yet. And I can match them up with some ribbon. That pattern needs some ribbon sewn in — make it that little bit different, don't you think?'

Mrs Laidlaw agreed. Clara knew that if you did not advise her what to do, she would be in the shop half an hour dithering over small purchases and would leave empty-handed. The woman had six children and fifteen grandchildren and was constantly unravelling old jumpers to knit new ones for the youngest. The Laidlaws were a hardened brood who readily used their fists, but Patience said even thugs needed socks and underwear. Patience knew all their names and ages, but Clara found she had to write them down in the back of her diary or else she forgot.

'Is the christening soon?' Clara asked. 'Cos I've got just the thing.' Before Mrs Laidlaw could answer, Clara was round the counter and leaning into the shop window, picking out a baby spoon set made of horn. 'Aren't they beautiful —?'

As she straightened, Clara came face to face with a man staring in at her from the pavement. The sales patter dried in her throat. He gazed with eyes that sagged behind cracked spectacles, his long face gaunt. But he was staring, not at the goods in the display, but straight at her, as if he had been waiting for her to come to the window. She felt a jolt of alarm and turned abruptly away.

Unnerved, she gabbled too much about the spoons and Mrs Laidlaw decided they were too expensive. Clara wrapped up the buttons and ribbon and took the woman's money. She served two other customers before glancing again at the display window. With relief she saw that the man had gone. It was nothing to get fussed about. He had just been passing and happened to glance in when she looked up, that's all.

As eleven approached, there was a lull in business and Clara dashed into the kitchen to make a pot of tea. She heard the bell above the door tinkle and called Jimmy to the back shop to mind the kettle. He pulled a funny face as he came through the curtain.

'Odd-body,' he giggled.

Clara stepped into the shop and saw the strange man again. He took off his cap and clutched it, revealing greasy strands of receding black hair. He wore a heavy coat, though it was damp and muggy outside. The loose skin round his chin was nicked with shaving cuts from a blunt razor. She was aware that he smelled. Her insides squirmed.

'Can I help you?' she asked, trying to hide her distaste.

He hesitated, then stepped closer, never taking his eyes from hers. His look was mystifying, as if he was sad or angry with her. But what had she done? She could not remember ever seeing him before. He licked his dry lips as if he would speak, but instead just stood there staring and shaking his head. Perhaps he was simple, she thought.

'Are you lost?' she asked, as if to a child.

For a moment, the trace of a smile touched his colourless lips and he did not

5

look quite so old. Then his shoulders sagged under the weight of his oversized coat and his face tensed again.

Maybe he was a lunatic with a knife in his pocket, Clara thought wildly, an out-of-work soldier sent mad in the trenches. She dreamed up such storylines about customers for her diary, but this seemed horribly possible.

'Would you like to speak to my father?' she asked quickly. 'He's just in the back.'

The man looked aghast. Suddenly he blurted out, 'What is your name?'

'Clara,' she gulped.

He shook his head again as if this was the wrong answer.

'And your name is, sir?' Clara asked. 'Just so I can tell my dad.'

He grew agitated. 'Your father — let me speak to him.' His accent was strange; maybe foreign.

Behind them the door opened with a jangle and Mrs Shaw bustled in. Clara waved her over with too loud a voice.

'Oh, come in, Mrs Shaw. Mam's expecting you. Jimmy's just making tea; would you like a cup while you're waiting?' She spun round, flapping at the curtain behind. 'Jimmy! Quickly!'

A moment later, the door was jangling again and Clara turned to see the stranger bolting out of the shop, the heel of one shoe slapping loosely on the tiled floor. Her heart thumped in relief.

'Mam won't be long, Mrs Shaw,' she sighed, as Jimmy appeared, slopping a cup of tea.

He grinned at her and she knew he had been listening behind the curtain.

'And your name is, sir?' he mimicked under his breath.

She laughed and stuck out her tongue at him, before turning to show Mrs Shaw into the tiny fitting room. There was hardly room for both her and the portly customer. Harry thought they should use the space for displaying more hats, but Patience did a steady business in lingerie among those too busy or too frugal to walk the mile up to Byker High Street or travel into Newcastle. She flattered them and listened to their worries. Corsets might have been out of fashion since the early '20s, but Patience had both loyal customers and faith in corsets making a come-back. To Clara's relief, her mother swept in to take over the sale before Mrs Shaw had a chance to derobe.

At closing time, Harry fished out half a crown from the till and told Clara to treat herself and Reenie to the best seats at the Coliseum to see the new Greta Garbo film, *A Woman of Affairs*, and pie and peas on the way home. Jimmy had already disappeared out to play. Clara changed into a new pink blouse and rushed round to Drummond Street to find Reenie sweeping up in the hairdresser's. Although her friend had stayed on at school and was hoping to train as a nurse, her parents relied on her to help out on busy Saturdays. Reenie beamed at her in relief.

'That's grand,' she cried, on hearing of the treat, abandoning the broom and pulling off her apron.

Marta, a small, neat woman with a cascade of dark wavy hair, appeared with a flurry of questions.

'Clara, come in. Will you have tea with us? How are you doing in shop today? Busy, *ja*? Come in, come in.'

'Shop's been canny.' Clara smiled.

'We haven't time for tea, Mam,' Reenie said quickly, grabbing her friend by the arm.

'But you must eat something,' Marta remonstrated.

6

'Later or we'll miss the newsreel.' Reenie was adamant.

'Don't you want to change?' Clara asked, regretting her friend's haste. She did not care much for the news and could not understand why Rennie and her brothers found it so interesting. She craned now for a glimpse of Benny or Frank over the partition that divided the small booths of the hair salon from the even smaller barber's. But all she could see was Oscar Lewis's bald head bobbing up and down as he limped around tidying his shop. He was a quiet man with one leg shorter than the other, which was partly compensated for by wearing a large, specially made boot. He was dextrous with scissors and often cut the hair of women customers too. Oscar caught sight of Clara and nodded with a cautious smile, then carried on with his task.

'Bye, Papa!' Reenie called out as she pushed Clara to the door. 'Bye, Mam.'

Marta pursued them into the street. 'I'll keep something hot for you. Behave yourselves and don't talk to strange boys, *ja*?'

'No, Mam,' Reenie agreed, adding under her breath, 'not strange ones.'

Clara suppressed a laugh as arm in arm they hurried towards the High Street. They chattered about their day.

'I hate having to wash their hair.' Reenie grimaced. 'One woman had lice, but Mam wouldn't let me say anything in case she got offended and didn't come back. I think she should be told, then she can do something about it. Now her whole family will have them.'

'Yes, Nurse Lewis,' Clara grinned.

'Well, you're all right,' Reenie snorted, digging her in the ribs, 'you have nice things to sell — useless but nice.'

Clara bridled. 'What do you mean, useless?'

Reenie smirked. 'Who needs a set of frosted cocktail glasses or a jug in the shape of a fat monk?'

'Who needs a permanent wave?' Clara sparked back.

Reenie coloured and laughed. 'Some of us want to look good for the Revolution.'

'Is that why Benny is growing a little beard like that Russian on the film — what's his name?'

'Trotsky.'

'Aye, him.'

Reenie gave Clara a sideways look. 'So you've noticed our Benny's new look. That'll please him.'

It was Clara's turn to blush. 'Why should it?'

'Cos he's got a soft spot for you. Haven't you noticed how many collar studs he's been buying from your shop lately?'

Clara shrugged. 'He does seem to lose them easily.'

'Aye, right.' Reenie laughed, her blue eyes teasing. 'He's got a drawer full of them.'

'Give over!' Clara gave her a shove. She felt a nervous thrill despite her embarrassment. It made her feel grown up to hear that Benny Lewis fancied her.

Still laughing, they rounded the corner into the High Street, two blocks down from Magee's. Under the romantic cinema posters of John Gilbert embracing Garbo, a queue was growing for the early evening performance. Just as they were about to cross the road, Clara stopped and gasped.

'What's wrong?' Reenie asked.

Clara's insides clenched. 'Over there. It's that man again.' She recognised the scruffy coat and the strangely shaped cap, not a style they had ever sold. He was eyeing the queue from a shop doorway as if watching out for someone. He had not yet seen them.

'What about him?' Reenie asked impatiently.

Clara would not move. 'Today. He was staring into the shop at me — then he came in.'

'And?' Reenie demanded.

Clara felt foolish. 'He asked me my name. Didn't buy anything.'

Reenie rolled her eyes. 'What a little capitalist. It's not a crime to look in a shop and buy nowt. Look at him; he's just down on his luck. Probably wanted a cup of tea.'

Clara felt a pang of guilt. 'Aye, probably.'

'Haway,' Reenie said, steering her off the pavement, 'leave the poor man be.'

They crossed the road and joined the queue, shuffling forward with the others. Clara determined not to look towards the stranger, though all the time she stood waiting she had the overwhelming feeling that she was being watched. It made her spine prickle. She was relieved when they reached the top of the steps and entered the large red and gold painted doors. Her spirits lifted in anticipation of the film ahead, the plush seats and the creamy block of ice cream between wafers they would treat themselves to with the pie money.

But she could not resist a last glance behind. Her stomach lurched. The strange man had moved away from the shop door and was standing at the bottom of the steps, looking up. Looking directly at her.

She wanted to tell Reenie, pull her back and show her how the man was staring. But her friend was already inside the foyer. Well, he looked too poor to be able to follow her inside, she told herself, quelling her panic. Then she felt bad about such a thought. He was harmless, and besides, he was watching everyone go in, not just her.

Quickly she turned away and escaped inside.

Chapter 2

Sunday was wet, so no one noticed that Clara was avoiding going outside. Her parents were not churchgoers, preferring to sleep in on their precious day off, eat well, then take a tram in the afternoon and walk in one of the city parks, observing the fashions. Until recently, Clara had taken Jimmy along to Sunday school at the Presbyterian church to keep him out of the way while her parents slept. But these days he liked to take himself down to Craven's and watch the boxers practising in the gym.

Despite the rain Jimmy was determined to visit Craven's. 'Danny Watts will be down the day,' he said excitedly.

'Be back for dinner at twelve,' Patience said, blowing him a kiss with a wave of silk kimono.

'Aye, Mam,' he agreed, though they all knew food never reached the table before one o'clock on Sundays.

'Should Clara walk him down?' Patience asked Harry, unsure.

'No point the pair of them gettin' wet,' Harry grunted. 'Lad knows the way blindfold.'

'But it's rough down there.' Patience was worried.

'It's fine, Mam,' Jimmy said impatiently.

'Straight there and straight back,' Harry instructed.

Clara had a momentary pang of disquiet. What if that man was lurking around outside again? He had been there when they had come out of the cinema. He had not followed them home, but even Reenie seemed unnerved by him and had insisted Clara go home with her.

'I'll get Frank or Benny to walk you round,' she had said. Frank had been out, but Benny had offered at once.

By then the vagrant had disappeared and Clara hoped Benny did not think they had made it all up just to get him to walk with her. She had been unusually bashful with him after Reenie's comments about the collar studs. They had walked apart, but at her front door he had winked and said, 'See you Monday.'

While still wrestling with her thoughts, Clara heard the front door bang shut. Jimmy was gone.

'I could go down and fetch him later,' Clara offered.

Harry's laughter was short. 'Lad'll never grow up with you two fussing over him like a bairn. At his age I was working on the ferry.'

'Was that before slavery was abolished, Dad?' Clara teased.

He leaned over and tweaked her nose.' Less of the cheek,' he chuckled. 'Good honest hard graft. Made me strong. Able to look out for myself. Only thing I was soft about was your mam.'

'You weren't half as hard as you like to make out.' Patience smiled, ruffling her husband's thinning hair. 'You hated the ferries.'

'No, I just hated being away from you and the lass,' Harry protested. 'Wanted you away from that boarding house, an' all.'

'What boarding house?' Clara asked, intrigued. They hardly ever talked about the past, except her mother's brief glamorous job in a department store.

Patience waved a hand. 'A place in Shields,' she said vaguely. 'I ran it with my aunt before you were born.'

'I thought you worked at Lawson's?' Clara was puzzled.

'Before that,' Patience said, colouring.

9

'Time for a cup of tea,' Harry said swiftly.

Clara was on the point of telling them about the strange man hanging around the neighbourhood, then decided against it. They would only worry and maybe prevent her from going to Whitley Bay the next day. She left her parents in peace and went to her bedroom to write up her diary. Lying on the bed, she recorded all the useful bits of information about yesterday's customers on the back pages before she forgot. Then she wrote in detail about the film and how she and Reenie had done Greta Garbo impersonations in the Lewises' kitchen and made Marta and Oscar laugh. She described Benny's new look, his wispy beard and moustache. It made him look older but Clara decided it did not suit him.

She hesitated a long moment, pencil tapping on teeth, then wrote about the odd man who appeared to be following her. Was he just a vagrant or really a spy? Perhaps he was one of those dangerous men her mother warned about who preyed on young girls, snatched them off the street and sold them into slavery abroad. Or maybe he was a long-lost shipmate of her father's who had been captured by pirates and only just released and was now trying to find his old friend.

In the end, she settled for a tragic story of a man who had lost his family in a fire and was so mad with grief he had lost his memory too. He was roaming the land trying to find them and to remember who he was. This way she could feel sorry for him rather than be frightened.

Clara closed her diary, wrapped it back up in its piece of muslin and placed it carefully in a hatbox under her bed on top of the two diaries she had kept for 1926 and 1927. Going to the window, she saw that the rain had stopped and the sky was lightening. On a whim, she decided to go out.

'I'm off to fetch Jimmy,' she called outside her parents' door.

'Straight there and straight back,' Patience replied.

Clara rolled her eyes. Her mother could be over-protective at times. She grabbed a jacket from its peg in the porch, glanced at herself in the hall mirror, ran her fingers through her hair and set out. The rain had cleared the air and it felt fresher, a light breeze coming off the river. To her relief there was no sign of the stranger. Clara sang to herself all the way as she zigzagged down the maze of terraced housing that led to the riverside.

The boxing hall looked unprepossessing from the outside, a drab brick warehouse with a corrugated iron roof, yet inside there was a rough glamour to its lofty gym with tiered seating and high swinging lights. When they were children, Harry had often brought them down after school to watch the men training at the punchbags and to chat to fast-talking Vinnie.

Vinnie's shiny black car was parked outside the gym with two boys minding it. Old Stan Craven had been the first person in Byfell to own a motor car, Harry had told her. Now he was dead and Vincent had inherited the boxing hall and his father's Albion. Clara was aware of a stab of envy. One day, when she was the owner of a string of shops, she would drive a car like that, or maybe a bigger one, and perhaps even employ a chauffeur.

Smoothing back her hair, she smiled at the boys and walked into the hall, confident and straight-backed. Old Mrs Craven was sitting in the kiosk smoking a cigarette and flicking ash into a metal ashtray that she always carried around. Her hair was dyed as black as coal and coiled into a severe bun with not a wisp out of place. Her wrinkled face was powdered china-white and her lips were coated in ruby-red lipstick that bled into the lined skin round her mouth. Clara had once been frightened of this woman with her deep booming voice, but not anymore.

'Morning, Mrs Craven,' she smiled.

'Clara,' Mrs Craven rasped in her gravelly voice. 'Thought you'd forgotten us, or got too grand to be seen round here.' She winked to show she was teasing, before taking a long draw on her cigarette.

'Too busy in the shop more like,' Clara replied.

Dolly Craven coughed. 'How are your mam and dad? Jimmy tells me nothing — dashes through here like a train — he's that keen to see the boxing.'

'Both grand,' Clara said. 'Looking forward to the wedding tomorrow. Mam's had her outfit bought for weeks.'

'I'll see you all there then — chance to have a good natter,' Dolly said, picking a flake of tobacco off the tip of her tongue.

'Oh, me and Jimmy aren't ganin'. We're off down the beach with Reenie.'

Dolly squinted at her through a cloud of smoke. 'Reenie Lewis?'

'Aye.'

Dolly flicked ash in the direction of the gym door. 'Her brother's in there. Hasn't been down for years. But Danny's that popular.'

'Benny's here?' Clara asked in surprise. 'Didn't know he boxed.'

She could feel herself colouring under the older woman's scrutiny. 'Like him, do you?' Dolly chuckled as Clara denied it. 'Anyway, it's not that little tearaway. The other one.'

'Frank?' Clara exclaimed.

'Don't sound so surprised. Has a handy pair of fists on him. My Stan used to say he'd make a champion flyweight one day. Gave it up just to play his fiddle and cut lads' hair. Crying waste if you ask me. You can make a good living at the boxing if you've brains as well as brawn; like my Stan and Vinnie. But some lads won't be told.'

Clara was amazed. Reenie had never talked about Frank being a boxer, but maybe it had been before they had become good friends.

'Is Jimmy inside?' she asked quickly. 'I've come to get him.'

Dolly nodded. 'Not that you'll be able to drag him away until Danny Watts goes for his dinner.' She laughed throatily.

It was crowded in the hall. A few young men were hammering punchbags in the corner, but most of them had gathered to watch local hero Watts, sparring in the ring with a training partner. She caught sight of Jimmy standing on a stool next to Frank, their heads close together as Frank made some comment and Jimmy nodded in agreement.

As she moved towards them, Frank looked round at the swinging door and smiled at the sight of her. Clara's stomach somersaulted. She swallowed and gave a small wave. He beckoned her over. Clara wished she had taken more care over her appearance before coming out, brushed her hair at least. It was stuffy in the hall; she took off her jacket as she crossed the room.

'Hello, Clara,' Frank said, making room for her beside them. His tousled hair was still wet from the morning downpour, his chin newly shaven, smelling of soap.

'I'm not ganin' home,' Jimmy said at once. 'Not till training's finished.'

Frank grinned at Clara. 'Won't be long,' he assured her.

She nodded, ridiculously tongue-tied. They were standing so close she could feel his shirt sleeve brushing her bare arm, the warmth of him. She gulped and slid him a look.

'Didn't know you liked boxing,' she said.

'I don't.' He smiled, his vivid blue eyes appraising her.

Clara blushed. 'Mrs Craven said you used to be a canny boxer - could've been

11

a champion.'

Frank laughed. 'She spins a good tale. I used to box a bit, kept myself fit in case there was any bother, but that was all.'

'Any bother?' Clara queried.

His face tightened. 'After the War. Some folks picked on the likes of me parents — for being German. I reckoned learning to use me fists might stop the number of bricks that got hoyed through our shop window on a Saturday night.'

'That's terrible. Rennie never said anything.'

'Hasn't happened since we moved to Byfell,' Frank said quietly.

Clara observed him. 'Still don't see you as the fighting kind.'

His smile returned quickly. 'I'm not. But I've learned to defend myself.'

Clara could not help noticing the broadness of his chest under the open-necked shirt, the muscular arms. She had never stood this close to him before. She felt almost sick, her heart was banging so fast. She forced herself to look away.

'So why are you down here the day?' she asked.

'Come to see Watts like everyone else — he was me hero when I was a lad.'

Clara forced herself to ask, 'Will you be playing at the Cairo the morra?'

Jimmy turned round and shushed her. 'Stop asking questions, our Clara, and let Frank watch.'

Clara blushed deeper. 'Sorry. I'm always doing that,' she laughed.

Frank smiled and leaned closer, whispering in her ear, 'I don't mind. And yes, I'm playing at the Cairo tomorrow.'

She grinned back, hoping he could not feel her heart knocking in her chest like a hammer. She turned and tried to concentrate on the sparring match, all the time acutely aware of Frank beside her and the tingling sensation left by his lips where they had brushed close to her ear. In front, on his stool, Jimmy was yelling and cheering as loudly as the older boys around him.

Soon it was over and Watts was stepping out of the ring, swamped by young fans who wanted to speak to him. Jimmy hung about on the fringe, ignoring Clara's attempts to get him to leave.

'I'll walk back up the road with you,' Frank offered. 'If you come now Jimmy, I'll let you try on me boxing gloves.'

'Can I?' he asked in excitement.

Frank nodded. Coming out of the gym into the foyer again, they ran straight into Vinnie Craven. The boxing hall owner was immaculately dressed in a navy blue suit and stiff collar and tie, with spats above his shiny shoes. His dark hair and thin moustache were well groomed. He was shaking the rain off his trilby hat.

'Frank, man,' Vinnie greeted him with a clap on his shoulder. 'Good to see yer. You all right?'

Frank shook his hand. 'Aye, canny.'

'Jimmy lad,' Vinnie grinned and gave the boy a friendly jab, 'you picking up some tips from Danny, eh?'

Jimmy nodded and grinned back. 'I want to stay but me sister says I have to gan home.'

Vinnie pretended to look shocked. He winked at Clara. 'What a cruel sister you have. Pretty but cruel. We can't have you leaving without a word with the great man. Haway, and I'll introduce you. A few minutes won't hurt, eh, Clara?'

Clara tried to protest. 'We have to get back for dinner.'

'It's raining cats and dogs out there; you'll get a drenching,' Vinnie persisted. 'Tell you what; let Jimmy have a word with Danny and then I'll run you back in

12

the car. How about that?'

'Oh, canny!' cried Jimmy. But Vinnie's dark eyes were watching Clara, waiting for her agreement.

She nodded, at once excited by the thought of driving through Byfell in a motor car.

'Grand.' Vinnie smiled and touched her cheek with casual intimacy. 'Come with me.'

As he led them back inside the hall, Frank stepped away. 'Ta-ra then.' He nodded in farewell. Clara stopped in dismay. She had assumed he would stay too.

'Aye, ta-ra, Frank.' Vinnie waved him on as he held the door open for Clara and Jimmy. 'You're welcome down here any time.'

Jimmy seemed to have instantly forgotten Frank's offer of the boxing gloves and was dashing back into the hall without a backward glance. Clara gave Frank a look of apology. He smiled briefly and turned away. Vinnie let the door swing shut and Frank was gone.

Vinnie steered her by the elbow and a moment later both she and Jimmy were being introduced to Danny Watts as Harry Magee's daughter and son. Danny greeted them kindly. As Jimmy was just standing there in bashful awe, Clara gabbled a good luck for his forthcoming wedding. Then Vinnie was guiding them both away, promising the boxer he would be back in a few minutes.

Dolly watched in surprise as Vinnie took them out to the car. Clara waved goodbye. It was raining lightly, nothing more, and Clara wondered if the promoter simply liked showing off his car and giving lifts. She did not care, for she was as eager as Jimmy to ride in the Albion. Vinnie held the back door open.

'You hop in there, bonny lad,' he told Jimmy. 'Clara can sit up front with me like a proper lady.'

She felt a ridiculous thrill at his words and the way he held open the door for her with a flourish. She sank on to the soft leather seat, inhaling its expensive smell. There was something else mixed with the leather; Anzora Viola - Vinnie's hair oil. Her stomach fluttered. Soon he was sitting beside her and starting up the car. Jimmy perched excitedly on the edge of his seat, peering over Clara's shoulder.

'It's just like it is at the pictures,' Clara blurted out as they picked up speed along the street. 'All them big cars in London on Pathé News. Eh, I wish Reenie was here an' all!'

'Who's Reenie?' Vinnie asked in amusement.

'Me best friend,' Clara said. 'Frank Lewis's sister.'

Just as she said his name, they passed Frank strolling up the street, hands in pockets, collar turned up against the rain. Clara felt a pang of regret and wondered if Vinnie would stop for him. But he just tooted and waved as they sped by.

'So what do you and Reenie like to do — go dancing?' Vinnie asked.

Clara laughed self-consciously. 'Not much chance of that.'

Vinnie glanced at her and for a brief moment put out a hand and touched her knee. 'We'll have to change that,' he declared. 'Why don't you bring your friend Reenie along to the wedding party tomorrow? We're holding it at our place and we've hired a band.'

Clara said hastily, 'Oh, no, we're not invited to the wedding.'

'Not invited? Course you're invited,' Vinnie cried. 'I've just invited yer.'

'But me and Jimmy are ganin' to Whitley Bay with Reenie — it's all

13

planned,' Clara explained.

Vinnie laughed. 'You can go to Whitley any day of the week — it's not every day you get the chance to go to a posh wedding and dance, is it? And there'll be plenty for you to eat, Jimmy. We need to fatten you up if you want to be one of me fighters, eh? What's your favourite food, lad?'

'Yorkshire puddin',' Jimmy answered.

'There'll be puddings the size of dinner plates.'

'And will I get to speak to Danny again?' Jimmy asked eagerly.

'Speak to him?' Vinnie laughed. 'You'll sit at his table — I'll make sure you do.'

'Oh, champion!' Jimmy cried.

'No,' Clara said stubbornly, 'you can't. It's Mam and Dad are invited, not us. They want me to keep you out of harm's way, Jimmy. That's kind of you, Mr Craven, but it's all been arranged.'

Vinnie drove into Tenter Terrace saying nothing and Clara worried she had caused offence. She was rather in awe of him; he was so much older and sophisticated in his expensive clothes. It made her uncomfortable the way he had touched her knee. He pulled up at the kerb outside the shop, turned off the engine and got out. Clara sat there wondering what to do.

'Spoilsport,' Jimmy muttered from behind. 'I want to gan to the weddin'.'

'You were happy with the beach till two minutes ago,' Clara replied.

Vinnie was swiftly round to her side and opening the door. She stepped out, aware of him watching her.

'Ta, Mr Craven, and sorry, you know —' she said, feeling awkward. 'It's just—'

He put a hand on her arm. 'No need to feel sorry.' He smiled. 'I like a lass who knows her own mind.'

She met his gaze. He had very dark eyes. His look was lively, knowing. This was a man who knew about life. She felt a small shiver. Was it excitement or fear that a man of his age should look at her like that, as if she were grown up? Then he stood aside and turned his attention to Jimmy.

'Never mind, bonny lad.' He patted his head. 'You come down the hall any time you want. How about I save a couple of seats for you and your dad at the match next Saturday?'

'Really?' Jimmy gasped. Vinnie nodded. 'Oh, ta very much, Mr Craven. That'd be grand.'

'Done!' Vinnie laughed and pushed Jimmy towards his sister.

Just as Clara turned to make for their front door, she saw the strange man. He was standing across the street, trying to shelter in a shop doorway, watching them. She stopped, catching her breath.

'What's wrong?' Vinnie asked at once, following her look.

'Nothing,' Clara said quickly.

'Is it that man?' he demanded. 'Do you know him?'

'No, it's just — he's been hanging around here — came in the shop,' she stuttered.

Jimmy laughed. 'It's that Mr Odd-Body again.'

'He been bothering you?' Vinnie asked.

The man stepped away from the sheltering porch towards them, raising a hand.

'He's coming over here,' Clara said in alarm.

Vinnie grabbed both her and Jimmy by the arm. 'Get yourselves indoors out of the rain — I'll sort him out.' Clara hesitated. 'Go on, lass, look after your brother.'

14

Clara hurried to the door with Jimmy and bundled him inside. She shut the door and they clattered up the stairs to the first floor, running to the sitting-room window to peer out. Patience looked up from reading the newspaper, startled. Jimmy gabbled about the funny man.

'Mr Craven's ganin' to sort him out,' he cried with glee.

Patience hurried over too, calling to Harry to come out of the kitchen and look. Vinnie was standing in the middle of the street confronting the stranger with a jabbing finger. The man had his hands half raised in a defensive gesture.

'Just some silly drunk,' Patience said dismissively.

'He's not a drunk,' Clara protested.

'How would you know?' Patience asked.

'Cos he's been in the shop,' Clara confessed.

'Who has?' Harry asked, joining them, his face red from cooking in the small hot kitchen.

They pointed out of the window at the confrontation in the street. The old man was standing his ground, arguing back. Vinnie pushed him backwards with the flat of his hands, his voice raised.

'Looks harmless enough,' Harry said. 'What did he want in the shop?'

Clara shrugged, uneasy at the memory. 'Just asked me what I was called. Didn't stop to buy anything. I pretended you were in the back — so then he asked to speak to you.'

'Me?' Harry demanded.

'Aye, but luckily Mrs Shaw came in and he scarpered.'

'Did he say anything else?'

Clara shook her head. 'Seemed to have difficulty speaking — like he was foreign or something.'

Harry gave her a sharp look. 'Come away from the window,' he instructed. 'Vinnie's dealing with it. Probably just a beggar.'

'So you don't know him?' Clara asked. 'Thought maybe it was someone you knew from the Navy who was down on his luck.'

Just at that moment, the old man looked up and saw them staring at him from the window. Patience gave a small gasp, her hand flying to her mouth. Vinnie shoved the man backwards. Caught off guard, he staggered and fell. Vinnie stood over him, but the man scrambled to his feet. He glanced up again, then turned and hurried away.

'I said come away,' Harry said more sharply. 'It's a fuss about nothing.'

Patience put out a hand, saying tensely, 'Harry, go and speak to Vincent. Find out what he said.'

Clara was struck by the look that passed between them. Did they know something about this man? Harry left the room without another word and hurried downstairs. Clara wanted to see what he said to Vinnie but her mother stopped her.

'Do as your father says,' she said. 'And the table needs setting.'

The table was set and the plates of food served up ready on the table before Harry returned upstairs. Patience shot him a look. He shook his head.

'It was nothing, just like I said.' He sat down. Patience let out a sigh of relief.

'Then why did you take so long?' Clara asked.

He gave her a sharp look, then smiled quickly. 'Talking about the wedding, my bonny, that's all.'

'Mr Craven invited us too,' Jimmy piped up, 'but Clara said no.'

'Did he?' Patience said in astonishment.

'He didn't really mean it,' Clara was dismissive.

'Yes he did,' Jimmy contradicted her. 'Promised there'd be big Yorkshire puddings and I'd get to sit with Danny Watts and Clara could dance and Reenie could come.'

Patience laughed. 'Goodness me, what a lot of promises!'

'It's all true!'

'Sounds like a good idea to me,' Harry said abruptly.

They all stared at him.

'Harry?' Patience laughed in disbelief. 'Clara wants to go to the seaside with Reenie.'

'It might not be safe,' he said, 'and we don't know what they'll get up to. Whitley will be packed with strangers from miles around — and they might lose Jimmy in the crowds.'

'Dad! Course we won't,' Clara protested.

Harry cut her off. 'No, no. Two lasses and a bairn on their own.'

'We won't be on our own — Benny's ganin' too and he's no bairn.' Clara put down her knife and fork.

'Benny?' Patience echoed. 'You never said he was going. He's as daft as a brush.'

'That's settled then,' Harry decreed. 'You're both coming to the wedding.'

'But what about Reenie?' Clara asked in dismay.

'If Vinnie's invited her then she can come too,' Harry answered.

Clara pushed away her plate in annoyance.

'And don't give me that sulky lip,' Harry reproved her. 'It's for your own good.'

Clara glared at him. 'Is this all because of that old tramp? It is, isn't it? You know something about him you're not telling.'

Harry stabbed his meat with his fork. 'It's nothing to do with him. Now, I've said what's happening and that's an end of it.'

Patience intervened. 'Clara pet, just eat your dinner. We'll all have a walk in the park later.'

Clara bit back words of protest. Harry avoided her look. Only Jimmy seemed pleased and, with a grin of triumph at Clara, tucked into his food.

That afternoon, they took a tram to Heaton and walked around the park until the rain came on again. Clara found no enjoyment in her parents' banter about the passers-by or in listening to the brass band playing under the bandstand. She was full of annoyance that her planned day out had somehow been spoiled by the argument between Vinnie and the stranger. On the way home, she insisted on calling at the Lewises' to tell Reenie of the change in plan.

'Don't be long,' Harry warned.

To her disappointment only the parents were in the tiny upstairs flat.

'Reenie and her brothers are out — what you call — the hiking, *ja*? Marta explained. 'They went on bus with YS.'

'YS?' Clara frowned.

'Young Socialists. Walking, picnic, talking.' Marta laughed. 'They come back late, I think. Here,' Marta pulled her into a seat, 'you sit down and I fetching cup of tea.'

Oscar put down the book he was reading and nodded in greeting. Soon Marta was back with tea and biscuits. Clara told them about the wedding invitation. There was a quick-fire conversation between the parents in German, then Marta shook her head.

'It's not right, I think. Reenie cannot go. The Watts are not sending the invitation?'

'No,' Clara admitted, 'but Mr Craven says they are laying on the spread.'

'The spread?'

'The wedding meal,' Clara explained. 'Danny Watts is one of his boxers and he's marrying a lass from the south, so her family cannot arrange it. Danny's mam's a widow so she cannot afford a big party; that's why the Cravens are doing it all.'

Marta looked perplexed. 'But Danny and his fiancée — they choose who comes, *ja*?'

'Aye, but if Vinnie Craven says we can go, then Danny's not ganin' to say no,' Clara answered.

Marta had another exchange in German with her husband, this time more heated. Finally Marta shrugged. 'It is up to Reenie, I think. If she wants, she can go.'

Clara felt relief. 'Please tell her to come. It's at half past eleven — St Michael's. Then dinner at the Cravens'. She can come round to ours first. And if she needs a hat, I can lend her one out the shop.'

Oscar went back to reading his book while Marta and Clara drank tea and chatted. Realising she could not sit there until the others got back, Clara reluctantly got up to leave.

'Ta for the tea, Mrs Lewis, and tell Reenie I'll see her the morra.'

Marta insisted that she take their umbrella against the rain to protect her hair. 'You don't want frizzy for the wedding,' the woman laughed.

Clara hurried on down the street. With the umbrella low over her head, she did not see the man until she almost bumped into him. She gasped to see the tramp standing in her way. Up close, he looked a fraction younger, his blue-grey eyes through the cracked spectacles intelligent and alert.

'Clara.' He spoke her name slowly, deliberately, as if he needed practice.

'What do you want?' she asked sharply to mask her fear. 'Why are you hanging around here?'

He stared at her for what seemed like an age, then put out his hand to touch her arm. She jumped back, shaking the umbrella at him, showering them both with spray.

'Leave me alone!' she shouted.

He backed off quickly. 'Yes, yes, I'm sorry.' Again she detected a foreign accent. He sounded a bit like Oscar Lewis.

Clara stepped off the pavement and edged round him.

'Please, Clara,' he said more urgently, 'tell your father I need to speak to him.'

'What for?' Clara asked, still moving away.

The man seemed lost for words, shaking his head. Clara turned and began to hurry into her street. He called after her. 'Tell him the clock-mender wants to see him. He has something of mine — I want it back. Tell him, Clara!'

'Go away!' she called over her shoulder. She ran the rest of the way home. Pausing in the doorway to the flat she glanced round, expecting the man to be pursuing her.

But the street was empty and he was gone.

Chapter 3

Late that night, Clara lay awake listening to her parents arguing. She could not make out their wrangling, but she had never heard them like this before. They hardly ever disagreed and if they did, it would end swiftly in teasing and laughter. But this was serious. Her father was denying something, her mother was tearfully accusing. Snatches of suppressed shouting vibrated through the wall of her bedroom.

'. . . I blame you!'

'. . . won't come to that.'

'What if he's said something?'

'. . . your fault too!'

'You promised me . . . have to sort it out!'

'All right, all right. . .'

'. . . turns up at the wedding . . . never forgive . . .'

'Stop crying, woman!'

'Don't touch me!'

Clara wished she had said nothing about the man's confronting her in the street earlier. Her parents had been quite upset. Harry had wanted to rush out and look for him, but Patience had shouted at him not to go and make things worse. When Clara had asked her mother to tell her what was going on, Patience had snapped, 'It's none of your business! That nebby nose of yours will get you into trouble.'

It was so unlike her mother to rebuff her that Clara had retreated to her room and stayed there. But Patience had not come in to make up or explain.

Clara could not sleep. The door to her parents' bedroom opened then banged shut. She heard her father rushing downstairs and slamming out of the house. Next door she could hear her mother weeping. What could have caused such upset between them? Had her father done something shameful? What was it that Patience wanted Harry to sort out? The only thing she could imagine her mother being so angry about was finding out that her father had been unfaithful.

The terrible thought hit her. What if her father had had an affair with another woman? Maybe the foreigner was something to do with this woman — a father, a husband? He had come back for vengeance, to make her father pay. Clara sat up in alarm. She had to know.

Tiptoeing out of the bedroom, she knocked on her mother's door.

'Mam,' she called quietly, 'are you all right?'

She heard sniffing, then, 'Yes. Go back to bed.'

Instead, Clara pushed open the door and slipped through. Patience was sitting in the dark at the window in her kimono, staring out, her face ghostly pale in the glow of a street lamp.

Clara went to her. 'What's the matter?'

'Nothing!' Patience hissed. 'I told you, go back—'

'I'm not a bairn anymore,' Clara interrupted. 'I heard you and Dad arguing.' Patience hung her head. Clara put her arms round her. 'Has he done something wrong?' She hesitated then pressed on. 'Is it about another woman?'

Patience gasped. She grabbed Clara's wrists and dug in her fingers. 'What do you know? Has that man told you more than you're letting on?'

'Ow, Mam!' Clara winced, trying to pull away. 'That hurts.'

'Sorry,' Patience said at once, letting go. 'But you must tell me.'

'I've told you everything,' Clara insisted. 'It's you that's keeping things in the dark.'

'Your father's done nothing wrong,' her mother answered quickly. 'It's all a mistake.'

'But it's to do with that man?' Clara questioned.

Patience cried, 'No! I don't want you to mention him again, do you hear?'

Clara stood back. Her mother quickly relented and grabbed her hand.

'Oh, my darling, I'm sorry. I don't blame you for asking. But your father will sort it out — he always does, doesn't he? So you mustn't worry.'

'Worry about what?' Clara asked in confusion. 'If Dad's taken something belonging to this man—'

'But he hasn't!' Patience cried. 'No, the man was lying.'

'Who is he, Mam? Tell me that at least.'

Patience let out a long, shuddering sigh. She wiped her face on her silk sleeve and forced a smile.

'Oh, he's just a vagrant like your father said. Trying to get money out of us to pay off a gambling debt or some such story. Your father's too soft by half — wants to pay him off. That's probably what he's doing right now.' Patience held out her arms to Clara. 'You mustn't worry about it, pet. We were being silly arguing over it.'

Clara was not sure she believed her mother, but was happy to accept her embrace. They held each other and Patience rocked her back and forth, smoothing her hair. Clara could feel the dampness on her mother's cheeks from her tears and squeezed her tighter. She hated to see Patience unhappy.

They stayed there, hugging in the chair, watching the clouds breaking up in the night sky.

'Look, there's the moon,' Patience murmured, breaking off from her soft humming. 'Bright as a new penny. And the stars. I love stars the best. Don't you just want to grab as many as you can and keep them?'

Clara nodded, reassured by her mother's change of mood.

Patience went on. 'It'll be good weather for the wedding after all. Everything's going to be just fine.'

Clara yawned. 'I hope Reenie comes too.'

'You're sleepy. Go back to bed,' Patience told her.

'Can I stay in your bed till Dad gets back?' Clara asked. 'Please.'

Patience relented and they snuggled down together. Despite her efforts to stay awake, the next thing Clara knew was her father bending over and kissing her forehead. It was the middle of the night, and moonlight was streaming directly into the room like a searchlight. Both her parents were smiling down at her.

'Dad?' Clara said, stirring.

'Everything's all right,' he assured her.

'The man?' Clara asked.

Harry nodded. 'He'll not be back, don't you worry.'

'But—'

'Time to go back to your own bed, pet,' Patience whispered. 'We've all got a busy day ahead.' She leaned over and kissed her daughter too.

Clara climbed sleepily out of bed and padded across the room. At the door she heard Harry say, 'Sleep tight, my bonny.'

Back in her own room, Clara felt fully awake between the chilly sheets. She got out again and reached for her diary. Taking it to the window and pulling back the curtains, she could see to write by the bright moon without putting on

19

the light. She began to write up the day's events, then stopped.

She felt awkward describing the moment she had stood next to Frank, her heart banging like a blacksmith's hammer. And she did not know what to write about the foreign vagrant. Part of her feared him and the hold he seemed to have over her parents, and part of her felt sorry for him. She had looked into his tired eyes and seen a yearning there, a flash of human spirit that seemed at odds with his neglected appearance.

She closed the diary. She would fill it all in later, the details of this strange day, when she was not so tired. In the margin of the exercise book she wrote, *Tonight there was a penny moon and a sky full of stars.* That would remind her of it all.

Taking the diary back to bed, she fell asleep clutching it under the covers.

Chapter 4

To Clara's delight, Reenie turned up in her best Sunday frock just before eleven on the bank holiday. The early morning mist had cleared into a bright hot day. Clara wore her favourite china blue dress and Patience had helped pin up her long hair.

'Makes you look all grown up,' her mother had said, smiling tearfully and kissing her head.

Her father was singing sea shanties in the bathroom while he shaved, as if nothing had happened the night before. Patience too seemed in such a good mood that she took little persuading to let Reenie choose a hat from the display in the shop.

'I don't need a hat,' Reenie protested in embarrassment.

'Yes you do,' Clara insisted with her mother, as they dragged her downstairs.

After trying on half a dozen, Reenie said, 'Enough. I'll have the red one.'

'No, not red,' Patience cried. 'A straw hat with a nice ribbon like Clara's is what you want.'

Reenie submitted to the straw hat.

'You look really bonny in that.' Clara admired her friend.

'Turn heads, you will.' Patience winked. 'Proper little Mary Pickford.'

Harry called to them to hurry up or they would be late. He linked arms with Clara and Reenie and did not stop talking all the way down the High Street towards St Michael's. To Clara he seemed over-exuberant. She caught a whiff of whisky on his breath. He never drank in the morning, ever. Clara wondered what had really happened the previous night. Despite all his assurances, perhaps her father still feared that the stranger would turn up at the wedding and cause a scene.

He caught her eyeing him and smiled. 'This is going to be a grand day for us all,' he announced. 'Vinnie Craven's fixed everything.'

'Harry!' Patience warned.

'What, my bonny? I'm just saying, Vinnie's seen to it that our children have been invited after all. And the lovely Reenie. Quite right too!' He laughed loudly. 'Yes, Vinnie's the man.'

Clara saw the look of alarm Patience gave him and wondered if her father was drunk. Jimmy ran ahead, scuffing his newly polished shoes as he kicked a stone up the street, excited at the thought of seeing Danny Watts again. Clara dismissed her father's strange remarks as over-excitement too. Soon they were filing into church, feeling important as the crowd of onlookers outside cheered and pointed at the wedding guests.

Vinnie was standing in the entrance, greeting people and shaking their hands as if he were the father of the bride. Clara noticed that the smartly dressed boys who were showing people to their seats were the lads who hung around his gym.

Vinnie gave Clara and Reenie an appreciative look. 'What beautiful young ladies.' He grinned. 'Harry, you'll have to keep your eye on them today.'

Harry grasped Vinnie by the hand and held it longer than was necessary. Vinnie nodded. 'Everything's sorted. Take it easy, have a grand day.' He slapped Harry on the shoulder and gently pushed him forward.

Clara thought she saw tears glinting in her father's eyes, but maybe it was just the reflection from the candlelight in the cavernous church. It was suddenly cool and dim after the glare of sunlight outside. She shivered. Vinnie put out a hand and rubbed her arm.

'Not too cold, Clara?' he asked. 'Mam can lend you a shawl.'

'No, I'm canny,' she said quickly, surprised that he had noticed.

'You are that.' Vinnie smiled and squeezed her arm briefly before letting go.

Reenie sniggered as they took their seats and Clara jabbed an elbow at her friend. 'Got his eye on you,' Reenie whispered.

'Don't be daft, he's an old man,' Clara hissed. 'Twice our age.'

It was a short service, the bride in a shell-pink satin dress and Danny looking twice as pink with pride. He was not a handsome man, his features flattened by boxing, but they both looked so happy that Clara thought them attractive. There were very few sitting on the bride's side, while the groom's pews were full of local friends and boxing associates of the Cravens'. Dolly Craven was dressed in a profusion of cream lace and a large black felt hat with a red feather pinned in front.

Reenie nudged Clara. 'Look at Mrs Craven sitting up front. You would think it was her lass getting wed. And who's that next to her with the fur coat?'

'Vinnie's latest?' Clara guessed, trying not to stare at the thin woman with the dark bobbed hair and vivid lipstick, sleek as a cat in her expensive coat. The woman caught her gawping and a smile flickered across her face as if she was used to attention.

Clara blushed and looked away. Miss Fur-coat was not a patch on her mother. Patience was the best-dressed woman in the church in a coffee-coloured dress, a matching jacket and a pillbox hat with a half-veil that gave her a chic, mysterious look. Her mother walked and held herself like a film star. Still, she could not help wondering who the young woman was. When Vinnie came to sit close beside the newcomer and give her his dazzling smile, Clara tried not to speculate about her relationship with Vinnie. Every time she saw him out with a woman it was with someone different.

Afterwards, the wedding party made its way to the Cravens' semi-detached house on Larch Avenue. It was a good twenty-minute walk from the High Street to the new estate on the northern boundary of Byfell, which looked on to fields of ripe corn. Vinnie to-ed and fro-ed giving lifts in his Albion. The Magees and Reenie were halfway there on foot and perspiring in the heat when he stopped and ordered them all to pile into the car. Harry sat in front with Jimmy on his knee while the women got in the back, and Vinnie roared up the street tooting at the staring passers-by.

Clara and Reenie were eager to see the house, having never been to the new estate. The houses were large and spaced out with saplings planted at the edge of the broad pavements; the Cravens' had green-painted doors and window sills, leaded windows and an ostentatious stained-glass window above the entrance. Inside, the polished floors were carpeted and there were separate rooms for dining and sitting in. Food was laid out on two solid oak tables in one room and the carpet rolled back in the other for dancing.

Vinnie's youths were taking coats and hats up to a bedroom and assembling presents on a table in the hallway.

'Drinks in the garden,' Dolly called as she ushered guests through the sitting room and out through a glass doorway into a small, neat garden with a steep rockery. 'It's called a French window,' Dolly said proudly, catching sight of Patience's admiring look.

A maid dressed in uniform came out of the kitchen with a tray of drinks. 'Sherry, ma'am?' she offered.

Patience took one. 'The lasses can have one too, seeing as it's a wedding.' She nodded at her daughter and her friend.

'Don't worry, there's a barrel of beer in the kitchen.' Vinnie appeared and clapped Harry on the back. He called to one of the boys to bring Harry a pint.

Soon the garden was full of guests chatting noisily, laughing and toasting the newly-weds. Vinnie made a short speech and Danny gave a bashful reply, thanking the Cravens for their generosity in holding the wedding party.

Vinnie laughed and swung an arm round him. 'That's all right, bonny lad. Just make sure you win your match on Saturday, eh?'

Then Dolly ordered them to go and eat. 'Fill up your plates and find somewhere to sit,' she encouraged them. 'Go on, little Jimmy, you tuck in.'

Clara and Reenie could not believe the choice of meats and pickles, sandwiches and cakes. They took their food back outside and perched on a stone wall. Jimmy joined them with a plate piled high.

'They did Yorkshires specially for me,' he crowed. 'Have you been upstairs? They've got a toilet in the bathroom. I've been three times.'

Clara and Reenie burst out laughing. 'Beats hopping across a cold yard in the middle of winter, that's for sure,' Reenie said.

Music struck up from inside the house from a fiddler and a concertina player hired by the Cravens. Vinnie came out. 'Come on, girls, someone has to start the dancing.' He held out a hand to Clara. Feeling awkward, she took it, with a warning look at Reenie not to tease her.

The bride and groom were waltzing round the small dance space. Vinnie pulled Clara close to him. She blushed.

'I can't waltz, Mr Craven.'

'Nothing to it,' Vinnie assured her. 'Just let me lead you.' He placed her hand on his shoulder, held her firmly in the back and set off after the newly-weds. 'One, two, three — that's it — step back when I step forward — two, three. Good lass. Easy, isn't it?'

Vinnie was not much taller than her, but he had a wiry strength; she could feel it in his arms. He was immaculately dressed with expensive gold cufflinks and tiepin that had not come from Magee's. He had a full mouth under the neatly groomed moustache, and dark mesmerising eyes. She had never been this close to him before and never noticed that his brown eyes were flecked with gold.

'You have beautiful eyes,' he said suddenly.

Clara flushed deeper to think he had mirrored her thoughts. She glanced away and concentrated on their feet.

'One day you'll be even bonnier than your mother,' Vinnie murmured, 'and that's saying something.'

Clara laughed. 'Is that why you've got so many lady friends — cos you flatter them all the time?'

Vinnie grinned. 'Have I lots of lady friends?'

'Well,' Clara said, 'that's what I've heard.'

He chuckled. 'Shouldn't listen to gossip. I'm just waiting for the right lass to come along. Nothing wrong with that, is there?'

Clara did not reply. She did not know how to respond to Vinnie's flirting, for she knew that was all it was. It puzzled her why he paid her any attention when there were plenty women there nearer his age — especially the slim woman in the fur coat who had watched them take the dance floor while she sipped sherry. Earlier, the woman had let Vinnie slip off the fur coat and hand it to one of his boys. She wore a pearl-grey dress that shimmered as she moved. He had leaned close and whispered something that had made the woman laugh and brush his cheek with a long pink fingernail. All this Clara had noticed.

'Who's the lady in the grey dress, Mr Craven?' Clara asked, curiosity getting the better of her.

Vinnie gave her a quizzical smile and followed her look. 'Ah, that's Joanie; Joanie West, the actress. She's appearing at the Essoldo this month. Lovely dancer. Would you like to meet her?'

'Eeh, she wouldn't want to talk to me.' Clara coloured. 'But I bet Mam would.'

'Consider it done.' Vinnie smiled, and squeezed her hand. 'No need to go all shy about Joanie. She doesn't bite — and you can more than hold your own.'

'Not on the dance floor,' Clara giggled.

Vinnie chuckled. 'Maybe not — but give it time. You're just a young 'un.'

Clara felt a twinge of annoyance at this reminder of her age. She felt gauche and immature compared to the likes of Joanie West; she yearned to be older and seeing more of life. She and Reenie and Jimmy were the only young guests there. Vinnie's flattery meant nothing; he was just trying to make her feel at home. The dance finished and Vinnie gave her one last twirl. He kissed her hand and then led her back to Reenie.

'Haway, Miss Lewis, would you like a dance?' He bowed to Clara's friend.

She hesitated then nodded. Clara watched them do the Military Two-step, noticing that Vinnie talked just as much to Reenie, even though she was a good dancer and did not need telling what to do.

Afterwards, the friends watched him move around the room, chatting and laughing with his guests, never staying longer than a minute; except with Joanie West. He lit cigarettes for her which she smoked in a long tortoiseshell holder and danced with her more than anyone else. She slipped her arm through his when they stood chatting too. Vinnie steered Joanie over to meet Patience. Clara watched her mother's animated face as she talked to the dancer. Clara told Reenie what she knew.

'Do you think she's famous?' Clara whispered, fascinated by the woman's languid poise compared to her mother's gushing questions.

Reenie shrugged. 'I've never heard of her. Just a chorus girl, I wouldn't wonder. Speaks with a southern accent — London maybe.'

It grew too hot in the stuffy sitting room, so they went outside only to find it even hotter in the sheltered garden. It was two o'clock.

'Wish we were on the beach now,' Clara sighed. 'I'm boiled.'

Reenie nudged her. 'Why don't we go?'

Clara stared in surprise. 'Go to Whitley?'

Reenie nodded. 'Aye, it's still early. And it's boring here — they're all getting drunk and talking daft.'

Clara glanced around. No one was dancing anymore; it was too hot. Her father was in the middle of a group of men drinking beer and ordering the fiddler to play their favourite tunes. Patience was probably still holding forth about corsets to a bored Joanie in the dining room. The bride and Danny looked ready to leave.

'Let's wait till we wave them off,' Clara suggested. 'Vinnie's taking them down to the station — says they're spending the night in Hexham.'

'Ooh, Vinnie, is it?' Reenie sniggered.

Clara dug her in the ribs and laughed. 'Give over!'

Soon after, Danny and his bride left in Vinnie's car with the guests waving them off and showering them with rice. Clara picked that moment to tell her mother she was walking back with Reenie.

'Want to get out of these clothes,' Clara said. 'Can I stop over at Reenie's the night?'

'No,' Patience answered. 'I'll need you to open up in the morning, judging by the state your father's in.'

Clara was going to argue, but Reenie intervened. 'That's all right. Clara will be back later this evening.' She pulled her friend away. 'Let's go before she makes us take Jimmy with us,' she whispered.

They slipped out of the house, after a quick thank-you to Dolly. Clara had a pang of guilt about leaving Jimmy, but he was earning halfpennies collecting up glasses and refilling drinks. Joanie saw them go and gave a disinterested wave, blowing out smoke rings.

They found Benny mooching around on the corner of Tenter Terrace, waiting for them to return. His face lit up immediately.

'Didn't think you'd be back so soon,' he said.

'Surprised you're still here,' Reenie remarked.

Benny gave a bashful grin. 'Thought I'd wait for you. How was the party?'

'Got boring,' Reenie said dismissively, 'and too hot to spend the day indoors. Can't wait to get out of this dress.'

'Leave it on,' Clara urged. 'We've missed half the afternoon as it is. Let's just go for the train.'

'Aye, Clara's right,' Benny agreed, 'and you both look that bonny in your frocks and hats.' He winked at Clara. 'And Mam's made a picnic. Haway, we've got everything we want.' He linked arms with the two girls, and they went down the street singing raucously, '"Oh, I do like to be beside the seaside!"'

Half an hour later, they were emerging from a stuffy train on to the platform at Whitley Bay and soon afterwards were joining the throngs on the beach. Men sat perspiring in jackets, their trouser legs rolled up; others had stripped to shirtsleeves and younger ones went bare-chested, turning pink in the heat.

Clara kicked off her shoes and tucked the skirt of her dress into her knickers.

'First in the sea wins a coconut,' she challenged and hopped across the hot sand to the water's edge.

Hurling off his shoes and jacket, without waiting to take off his socks or roll up his trousers, Benny ran after her. He plunged in fully clothed, ignoring Reenie's protests. Clara screamed as he splashed her with icy salt water. Recovering, she laughed and splashed back, kicking up spray. Benny grabbed at her straw hat and pulled it off. He filled it with water and chucked it back.

'Me mam'll kill you for that!' Clara gasped. In a flash she scooped up water in the hat and threw it over Benny. He seized her round the waist, picked her up and dumped her in the water.

Clara shrieked at the cold. Gasping for breath, she stood up and lunged after him. He dodged out of the water. She chased him. Benny tripped, trying to avoid a small boy with a bucket, and Clara shoved him into the sea. He pulled her after him. They sat in the shallow water, panting and helpless with laughter. All the tension of the past two days over the strange man and her parents' rowing melted away. They were both thoroughly soaked and neither cared an inch.

Reenie stood on the wet sand, clutching Clara's discarded hat and shaking her head. 'You're both as daft as each other. You've ruined your trousers, Benny. And look at this hat.' She waved it at them.

Benny came out of the water, dripping, and took the battered hat, plonking it on his cropped black hair. He stretched out a hand to Clara.

'I'm not falling for that one,' she snorted.

'Truce,' he said, leaning closer. She took his hand and he hauled her out of the water. Her best dress clung heavily; hair coiled round her neck, half out of its pins.

'What a sight I must look,' she giggled, squeezing the water out of her skirt.

'The bonniest sight.' Benny grinned. Before she could dodge away, he planted a kiss on her cold cheek, brazen as could be.

'Give over!' she said, blushing, giving him a shove.

They found a patch of beach to sit on and dry out, though the whole strand was still crowded, families reluctant to start the journey home. Only the returning tide would make them move. Clara let down her wet hair and pulled salty fingers through it.

Benny shared out the food he had brought, unwrapping a parcel of bacon sandwiches from their greaseproof paper and handing them round.

'No, ta. I'm still full of dinner,' Clara said.

Reenie took one. 'I'm always hungry. Mind you, the food was lovely. Roast beef and pork and cold ham — and salads and pickles.'

'And cream buns.' Clara rolled her eyes in delight. 'And a maid to serve it all out.'

'Very posh,' Benny smirked.

'Aye, it was. They've got two inside toilets — one up, one down.'

'Bet Craven's got a servant to wipe his arse, an' all,' Benny grunted.

'Don't be crude,' Reenie scolded.

Benny laughed as he munched his sandwich. 'Ooh, one weddin' dinner with the middle classes and you're beginning to sound like them, our Reenie,' he teased. 'Vincent Craven turned your head, has he?'

She gave him a withering look. 'No, he was too busy working his charm on Clara.'

'No he wasn't!' Clara protested. 'He danced with you too.'

'Aye, but he waltzed with you,' Reenie teased, 'cheek to cheek.'

'We didn't. . .' Clara went crimson.

'Ladies!' Benny cried. 'Are you falling out over Vincent Craven? How can I compete?' He jumped up and walked round them, imitating Vinnie's energetic swagger. He flicked the end of an imaginary moustache and gave Clara a knowing smile. 'Can I have the last waltz, Miss Magee?' he asked in a deep voice that mimicked Vinnie's.

Both Clara and Reenie laughed.

Benny continued in a low voice, 'I've just got time before the next fight, which is going to make me a git big amount of money. Haway, Miss Magee, and make an old man happy.'

'That's very good.' Clara clapped.

'Horribly like him,' Reenie agreed. 'Say no, Clara, or you'll regret it.'

Benny narrowed his eyes at his sister, 'Hey, Bolshie Lewis, I wasn't asking your opinion. I'll get my lads on to you and shut you up good and proper.'

Clara remonstrated. 'Vinnie's not a thug — he's a real gentleman.'

Benny winked and pulled on his moustache again. 'That's my lass.' He bowed and helped Clara to her feet. They shuffled around in the sand, tripping over each other.

'Benny, you're getting sand on the picnic,' Reenie cried.

Clara flopped down. 'Aye, and he can't dance for toffee.'

Benny sank to his knees beside them. 'I can't compete with Craven. Shall I throw mesel' in the sea now?'

Clara said, 'Not yet — buy us an ice cream first.'

26

'Heartless lass.' Benny groaned and sank on to the sand clutching his chest. 'All you care about is your stomach.'

Laughing, Clara lay back in the sun and closed her eyes. She listened to Reenie telling Benny about the wedding and the guests. She dozed off. Reenie shook her awake.

'Tide's coming in.'

Clara sat up. The beach was emptying. She shivered, her dress still damp.

'Take this,' Benny said, wrapping his jacket round her shoulders.

'Ta. How long have I been asleep?'

'An hour,' Reenie said.

'Never!' Clara exclaimed, standing up and brushing off sand from her dress and legs.

'Must have been the sherry,' Reenie said, smirking.

'You were dreaming.' Benny looked earnest. 'Calling out in your sleep.'

'Was I?' Clara eyed him.

'Aye. Sounded like a nightmare. You kept repeating the same name - Vinnie, Vinnie; oh, Vinnie!'

Clara whipped him with his jacket. 'Benny Lewis, you liar!'

He laughed and grabbed the jacket from her, dodging out of her reach. When he offered it back, she pushed it away.

'Don't want your scabby jacket,' she pouted. 'I don't fancy Vincent Craven and he doesn't fancy me, so stop going on about it.' She bent to retrieve her battered hat.

Reenie said, 'Enough teasing. Let's go and listen to Frank's band.'

'I can hardly go like a drowned rat,' Clara said in dismay, rueing her spontaneous run into the sea. Hastily, she began to twist and pin up her hair.

'We'll dry off in the tea room,' Benny declared, wrapping his jacket firmly round her. 'Gan on, take it till you warm up. It may not be as posh as some, but it's earned by my own sweat, not like some who make money out of the hard graft of others—'

'Benny!' Reenie warned.

'I don't care how Mr Craven makes his money,' Clara retorted. 'He's a hard worker and he doesn't have any airs and graces, and he's canny to everyone.'

'Regular St Vincent,' Benny mocked.

'Why you so against him? Your Frank's a friend of his,' Clara pointed out.

'That's true,' Reenie conceded. 'They met in the Young Socialists.'

'Aye, hard as that is to believe,' Benny grunted. 'He's an Old Capitalist now.'

'Didn't think Mr Craven was interested in politics,' Clara said in surprise.

'Used to be,' Benny admitted. 'Old Stan Craven led a strike at Byfell pit before the War, and Vincent ran a soup kitchen at the boxing hall during the General Strike.'

'Oh, yes.' Clara nodded. 'I remember that.'

'So Clara's right.' Reenie nudged her brother. 'Mr Craven's heart is in the right place. It's just he doesn't have time to come down to the YS now he has to run the business himself.'

'Aye,' Benny grinned, 'and even if he could, he'd be too old.'

'That we can agree on,' Clara laughed.

Benny swung an arm about her shoulders. 'Comrades?'

'Friends,' she agreed.

They made their way to Cafe Cairo, but it was crowded and the doorman looked at them askance.

'It's a tea dance this afternoon,' he said with a look that implied they were not

27

welcome.

'That's what we've come for.' Benny smiled. 'Our brother is in the orchestra.'

'We dance here regularly,' Reenie added with her no-nonsense look.

The man let them in, Clara trying to suppress a giggle. 'Regularly, do we?' she whispered as they passed through the foyer into the glass-domed tea room.

She gasped at the sight of potted palms arranged round gilded pillars, the walls depicting ancient Egyptians and exotic beasts in gaudy colours. Tables were covered with dazzling white cloths and silver cake stands. The room was filled with the hubbub of chatter and clinking china cups. They squeezed on to a table with an elderly couple who introduced themselves as Lockwood and offered them some of their sandwiches.

'We can't eat all this,' Mrs Lockwood insisted. Reenie and Benny tucked in, but Clara declined. Her stomach had knotted up at the sight of Frank on the raised dais in a black dinner suit, hair groomed, face frowning in concentration.

The dance came to an end and the band leader announced a tango. Clara sat in frustration that she could not do it. A waitress came over and Benny ordered a pot of tea. Clara watched the dancers carefully and peered over their heads for a glimpse of Frank, wishing they could sit closer to the band. Reenie and Benny chattered to Major and Mrs Lockwood about the bank holiday crowds and the recent weather, until the band struck up a quickstep.

'I can do this!' Clara exclaimed. 'Mam taught me. Come on, Benny.'

Benny grinned with pleasure. 'Modern lasses, eh?' He winked at their surprised companions. Out on the dance floor he said, 'Am I not supposed to do the asking?'

'I'd have fallen off me perch and died waiting for you to ask,' Clara snorted.

They careered round the room knocking into other dancers on the crowded dance floor. As they passed the orchestra, Clara glanced up at Frank, but he was too absorbed in the music to notice them.

'You've got two left feet,' she complained as they rejoined their companions.

'Thought I was supposed to lead,' Benny countered.

'Might have helped if you knew the dance.'

A waltz struck up and the elderly Major Lockwood pushed back his chair and got to his feet. 'Allow me,' he said with a short bow to Clara.

She accepted at once, while Reenie dragged Benny off to dance with her. The Major glided spryly round the floor holding Clara at a respectful distance and soon she was moving with the same assurance. The romantic music filled her with longing. They swept past Frank and this time she thought she caught his attention. She smiled and saw his eyes widen in surprise. The dance came to an end all too soon.

'Thank you,' she said to her elderly partner. 'That's the best dance I've ever had.' He chuckled with pleasure. Not to be outdone, Benny pulled her on to the floor for another waltz.

'What is it with these older men?' he teased.

'Maturity, style, good manners,' Clara answered, suppressing a smile.

'Is that all?' Benny replied. 'Then I've nothing to worry about.'

'Ability to dance — ouch, my foot!'

Benny spun them against the flow of the other dancers without seeming to notice. 'Will you be my lass?' he asked abruptly.

Clara's insides lurched. She caught sight of Frank over Benny's shoulder, the light catching his strong features and blond hair. To her he was perfection, as handsome and unattainable as a Greek god. She tried to laugh off Benny's offer.

'I'm too young to be courting. Dad would have a blue fit.'

'Your da likes me,' Benny insisted. 'Always asks for me to cut his hair when he comes in.'

'Mam thinks you're wild,' Clara told him.

'I am.' Benny laughed. 'Wild about you.'

'Very funny,' Clara said, pushing him away at the end of the dance. 'But the answer's still no.'

Benny shrugged good-naturedly. 'I can wait.'

The tea dance ended and the elderly couple left. Benny went off to pay for the pot of tea. To Clara's delight, Frank came across to greet them, carrying his violin case.

'Thought you weren't coming,' he said with a wry smile. 'A wedding and a posh party not enough for one day?'

'Not for us.' Reenie grinned. 'We would've come sooner if Clara and Benny hadn't soaked each other in the sea.'

Frank gave Clara a direct look that made her turn crimson.

'Daft, I know,' she mumbled, 'but we were that hot and bothered. . .'

'Glad you've had a good day.' Frank smiled, running a finger under his tight collar. 'I'd have done anything for a dip in the sea.'

'Can you come home with us now?' Reenie asked.

'Aye, I'm finished,' Frank said. As they walked across to Benny, he added, 'You're a grand dancer, Clara, especially with Major Lockwood.'

She smiled in delight. 'Ta, Frank. You know the old gentleman?'

'He and his wife come in every Saturday afternoon. You get to know the regulars.'

'You looked that caught up in the music, didn't think you noticed the dancers.'

'Only the good ones.' Frank smiled and touched her briefly on the arm. Clara flinched.

'You still cold?' Benny asked in concern. 'Take me jacket again.'

'No, I'm fine,' Clara said quickly, hugging her arms and moving away to walk beside Reenie.

The heat had gone from the day as they made their way back on the crowded train towards the city. The men stood while Reenie and Clara squeezed in next to a couple with a tired and wailing baby. With relief they scrambled off at Byfell and walked up the street. People sat out on stools, chatting and drinking while their children chased each other up and down the lanes.

As they neared Tenter Terrace, Clara slowed her pace. She did not want to go home; she wanted this day of freedom to go on for ever. Reenie sensed her mood.

'Come back to ours for an hour or so,' she suggested. 'Mam will want all the details of the wedding and you notice much more than I do.'

Oscar and Marta were sitting on a bench in their back yard listening to their gramophone. A recorded voice soared out of the back door, hauntingly beautiful. Clara stopped and caught her breath. Frank turned and for the briefest of moments they held each other's look. The music swelled and died back.

'Makes the back of me neck tingle,' Clara whispered. 'What is it?'

'Songs of the Auvergne,' Frank answered, still watching her.

'The music of angels,' Marta sighed.

'Prefer Count Basic, mesel'.' Benny made a trumpet noise and broke the mood.

'Come, children and tell us everything!' Marta bustled around getting them drinks and handing out pieces of meat pie and boiled eggs. Oscar put on another record and wound up the gramophone.

29

'Schumann,' he beamed proudly, limping back to his seat.

As Reenie had predicted, Marta quizzed them on all the details of the wedding. When she asked about the trip to the beach, no one mentioned Clara and Benny's high jinks in the sea.

'You have a good day, *ja?*' She smiled.

'Very,' Clara nodded, swapping a look with Reenie. 'Wish we could've danced more.'

'Consider it done.' Benny mimicked Vinnie's deep drawl as he sauntered over to the back door. They heard him shuffling through the box of records. There was a scrape and a hiss. Oscar sucked in his cheeks in alarm.

'Don't scratch it!'

Benny came out dancing with an imaginary partner to a lively polka. He grabbed Clara's hand and they swirled round the back yard, Clara giggling with embarrassment. Frank held out his hands to Reenie.

'Let's show them how it's really done,' he challenged. Brother and sister polkaed round in perfect time. Oscar chuckled and Maria insisted on their dancing too. They shuffled round at a sedate pace. When Benny went to put on another record, his mother called for a waltz. Over the call of children's voices in the street beyond, the music of Strauss filled the warm evening air.

Swiftly, Frank reached for Clara's hand. 'I'm not Major Lockwood, but I won't crush your toes as much as Benny.'

Clara could not believe her luck as Frank swept her into the waltz, his hand cupping hers, holding her close. She almost forgot to breathe. She stared at their feet, concentrating too hard on the steps.

'Look up,' he murmured, 'and trust your partner.'

In a minute they were moving as one, flowing together with the music. Clara's heart thumped at twice its usual speed. She glanced up into his face. His blue-eyed gaze went through her like an electric shock, but she could not look away. Frank smiled and warmth flooded through her like sunshine. She had never felt so alive. She wanted to dance right out of the cramped yard, down the street and off into the unknown. If only this one dance could go on for ever.

But it stopped all too soon. For a moment they stood holding each other, smiling, and Clara wondered what Frank was thinking, longed to know if he felt anything at all for his sister's friend. Then he gave a mock bow and let her go. Clara turned to see the rest of his family watching them.

No one said anything. Then Benny abruptly laughed.

'Don't let Vincent Craven see you dancing with Clara like that.'

Clara blushed. Reenie tutted. 'Stop going on about Mr Craven — you're like a stuck record. Clara doesn't find it funny.'

Benny looked contrite. 'Sorry.'

'*Ja,*' Marta nodded. 'He means nothing, Clara. Just always joking, joking.'

Benny brightened. 'Who's for a game of cards?'

As the shadows lengthened, they went indoors. Oscar lit a lamp and got out the chess board, challenging Frank to a game. The others played cards and the conversation flowed backwards and forwards between the two tables.

Clara was reluctantly thinking she should be going home when a noise erupted in the street below. A man was shouting incoherently. There was a hammering on the shop door. The chatter stopped. Reenie and Clara exchanged looks of alarm; their first thought was the vagrant.

'. . . come out! . . . Leizmann! . . . in there?' The man let out a stream of drunken abuse.

The battering on the door began again. Clara saw the fear on the faces of

30

Reenie's parents and remembered Frank telling her of attacks on their shop. Was this how the attacks started, with some drunken reveller causing a disturbance in the street on his way home? Benny went to the window and peered out.

'It's Mr Magee,' he said in astonishment. 'Can hardly stand up.'

Clara froze. Her father's belligerent voice rang out.

'. . . got my bonny? Leizmann! . . . fight yer . . . Boche!'

She went hot with shame. What on earth possessed him? She stood up quickly. 'I'd better go; I'm sorry.'

'I'll see to it,' Frank said at once.

'Me an' all.' Benny rushed to follow him.

From the top of the stairs, Clara watched Frank unbolt the door. Harry swayed in front of him. Frank caught and steadied him, but he shook him off.

'Where is she? Where yer hiding her?'

'No one's hiding her, Mr Magee,' Frank said evenly. 'Clara's with Reenie. They've had a grand day.'

'No right! Should've been with me — with her own people,' he raged. 'Clara! Get down here now! You don't belong here.' He pushed at Frank. 'Get out me way.'

Frank blocked his attempt to enter. 'Not in your state, Mr Magee. We'll bring Clara home.'

'Aye,' Benny said hotly, pushing forward, 'don't speak to us like that — and in front of the lasses.'

This maddened Harry more. 'Don't you tell me . . !' He took a swing at Benny.

Frank caught Harry's arm and shoved him off the doorstep. Harry swore foully, cursing the Lewises, and came at him again. Frank dodged the swinging punch and jabbed Harry on the chin. He buckled at the knees and crumpled to the ground.

Clara dashed out. 'What have you done to him?'

Frank looked as surprised as she was. She bent over her father. He reeked of whisky and beer.

'Dad, are you all right?' Clara shook him. He groaned and his eyes flickered open.

'We'll get him home,' Frank said calmly. 'Benny, give me a hand.'

The two brothers hauled Harry to his feet and hoisted his arms round their shoulders.

'Canny punch, Frank,' Benny said in admiration as they staggered forward.

Clara followed, engulfed by shame. She could not blame Frank for his action, but it just compounded her father's humiliation and hers. If she had not stayed out so long, none of this would have happened. Now terrible things had been said that could not be forgotten. She had no idea her father harboured such feelings towards the Lewises.

Halfway down the street, a car turned the corner and dazzled them in its headlamps. It stopped, engine still running. Patience jumped out of the passenger side and rushed towards them.

'Harry! My God, what's happened?' she demanded.

'He's had a few too many, that's all,' Frank grunted.

'Our Frank sorted him out,' Benny boasted. 'He was mouthing off about me dad — calling us all Boche.'

Patience looked aghast. 'You hit my Harry?'

'He was saying terrible things, Mam,' Clara defended Frank.

'You're the cause of this,' Patience berated her. 'You should have been home hours ago. You know how we worry.'

31

Vinnie appeared. 'Put him in the car, lads. I'll get him home. Sure he meant nothing by it. Just a little worried about young Clara,' Vinnie smiled. 'I told him not to worry, but Clara's very precious to him.' He turned and held out a beckoning hand to her. 'Come on, lass, come to your mam. You missed a good party, running off when you did.'

Harry was helped into the passenger seat; Patience pushed Clara into the back and climbed in after her.

'Thanks, lads.' Vinnie shook the brothers by the hand. 'No hard feelings, eh?'

Frank nodded.

'Come to the fight on Saturday; I'll give you ringside seats if you like.' He slid behind the wheel and waved them off.

As they turned and drove off down the street, Clara regretted that she had not said a proper goodbye or apologised for her father. She waved, but it was probably too dark for them to see.

'Your dress is stiff with salt,' Patience fretted. 'And look at the state of your hair. Where's your hat? What have you been up to? I tell you, Clara, I don't want you spending so much time with those people. What's wrong with your own family? Aren't you happy with us?'

Her mother sounded so tearful that Clara bit back her protest. She was too tired to argue. To her surprise, Vinnie spoke up for her.

'Don't be too hard on the lass, Patience,' he murmured. 'She's just young.'

Clara's gratitude at his defending her was tinged with annoyance that he still saw her as an immature girl.

Her father stirred in the front seat. He gulped as if he would be sick. Then, abruptly, he began to weep.

'I did it for you, lass,' he sobbed, 'I did it for you.'

'Did what?' Clara asked, upset by his weeping.

But nobody answered.

Chapter 5

Summer, 1931

Clara got up at first light and dressed quickly in her hiking trousers and shirt. She had a rucksack already packed the night before with a picnic and a waterproof jacket (a second-hand one from the market). She did not want to wake anyone. Patience would plead with her to stay and keep her company.

'Your father will be off down to Craven's drinking half the afternoon,' she would complain. 'We can take a trip up the park or Jesmond Dene if you want to walk.'

Clara splashed her face with cold water. She used to love Sundays at home — best day in the week. But that was before the terrible slump when her father had started drinking heavily and betting on anything that moved. It was madness, of course, with nearly three million people on the dole. But the worse business got, the more Harry chased the impossible.

'Just takes the one big win,' he would insist when Patience begged him tearfully to stop.

There had been a terrible row the night before. Harry had been brought home hardly able to climb the stairs after a big match at Craven's. Two of Vinnie's men had hauled him up to the flat and dumped him on the landing.

'Don't think I'm going to tip you,' Patience had cried at them, prodding Harry with a disdainful toe. 'Ask Vinnie who's going to pay me rent next month if he takes any more money off *him*!'

'Shurrup, wom'n,' Harry had slurred, trying to rouse himself but failing.

The men had gone without a word while Patience and Harry had a slanging match. Finally Patience had stormed into her bedroom, slammed the door and locked it. As she had done countless times before, Clara had gone and fetched Jimmy down from the attic and together they had helped their father on to the sitting-room sofa, taken off his boots and covered him with a rug. He was snoring in seconds.

'It's not Mr Craven's fault,' Jimmy said defensively. 'Dad just makes a fool of himself.'

At fifteen, Jimmy was taller than Clara though still lean. His fresh-faced looks were marred by spots, his blue eyes watchful. He had left school the previous year and worked as a paper boy for a shop that sold to the shipyard workers. The job had lasted two months. The shipyard was closing, the newsagent had gone bust and Jimmy was out of work along with increasing numbers of Tynesiders.

Yet Jimmy baulked at working in Magee's. 'Lass's work,' he called it, preferring to hang around the boxing gym cadging cigarettes from the older boys. Craven's was the one business that seemed to be thriving in Byfell. Not only did it attract large numbers to big fights, it also showed talking films. Craven Hall provided a few hours of escapism for the hard-pressed locals. In fact, Vinnie Craven was doing so well he had bought a bankrupted garment factory and started up a local garage.

Half the time, Clara did not know where her brother was. She was too busy trying to keep the shop going with her worried mother. These days they would sell anything: cheap, cut-price clothing and second-hand goods. Magee's was more like a pawnshop than a fancy goods store now.

'Why do you always stick up for Mr Craven? He could stop Dad betting money he hasn't got,' Clara sparked back.

'He tries,' Jimmy declared. 'He thinks the world of me dad — get sick of hearing him say how he was a war hero and one of Byfell's best boxers. And look at him now — a useless drunk.'

'Don't speak about him like that,' Clara said.

She looked pitifully at Harry snoring on the sofa, his face bloated and purplish with drink, the rest of his body shrinking like wizened fruit. Her father was looking old. He had changed so much over the past three years, turning moody and argumentative, taking offence where none was meant. Gone was the cheerful man who had beaten them up in the morning to cook their breakfast and sing lustily while stirring the porridge.

Her parents' love for each other had withered too. There was a constant tension as if they could hardly bear to be in the same room. Very occasionally, if Patience coaxed Harry to stay at home and not drink, there were days when they laughed again and went to bed early. Despite their private war, they both managed to keep up a cheerful appearance in the shop to their dwindling number of faithful customers.

But then Harry would go back on the drink and disappear all day. One time he had gone for two days. Patience, frantic with worry, sent Jimmy to ask Vinnie to look for him. Vinnie had brought Harry back in his car, cuts all over his face. Clara wondered if her father was seeing another woman again — for she was convinced that had been the source of the trouble three years ago — but could not imagine that anyone would put up with him in the state he was in now.

With the worry that the shop might not survive till the end of the year, life in Tenter Terrace was bleak. Clara's one escape was hiking on a Sunday with the Lewises and their friends in the Young Socialists. She was not the least bit political, but she enjoyed their company more than ever. Even when Reenie was working and could not join the hike, Clara went.

It was the cause of frequent arguments with her mother. Ever since Harry's drunken outburst at the Lewises', Patience had discouraged Clara from visiting there.

'Reenie can come round here if she wants,' she had said, 'but I don't see why you have to go there at all. You might upset your father again.'

'Why should it upset him? He said sorry for all that long ago,' Clara protested.

'Cos when he's had a drink in him, he doesn't think straight. And besides, the Lewises are not really our type of people.'

'Why? Because they're German and Socialist?' Clara retaliated. 'Or because they run a better business than us?'

'Don't speak to me like that!'

That was how arguments with her mother always ended, with Patience shouting and Clara slamming out of the room.

Clara was determined not to give up her friendship with the Lewises. The incident three years ago had made her all the more resolute in sticking by them. Her parents were prejudiced because Britain had once been at war with Germany. But that had nothing to do with the Lewises. Benny was good company and there was always the possibility that Frank might be there. Lately, a young teacher called Lillian seemed to be his companion.

'She's dotty about him,' Reenie had said, 'but our Frank doesn't seem to notice.'

Clara brushed out her long dark blonde hair and tied it back in a red ribbon. She wished she was intelligent like Lillian and able to say clever things about the state of the world to impress Frank. But she knew that she never would. Still, she could make Reenie and her brothers laugh, which was more than could be said of the serious, dark-haired Lillian.

Clara tiptoed out of the flat, holding her rucksack and stout shoes in her hands. The shoes were old ones of Jimmy's and decidedly unfashionable. But worn with thick socks they were protection against muddy paths. She put them on at the bottom of the stairs.

Just as she was opening the door as quietly as possible, a figure loomed at the top of the stairs.

'Clara! Where you going?' Harry was swaying in last night's clothes, his sparse hair sticking up like barbed wire, his eyes bleary.

'Shoosh, Dad.' Clara waved at him. 'Don't wake the others. I'm off hiking.'

He grabbed the banister rail and staggered down a couple of steps. Clara dashed back up to steady him. 'Haway, Humpty-Dumpty, sit down.'

He smiled ruefully. 'Remember how I used to teach you nursery rhymes?' He plonked down on the step. 'And I sang to you, didn't I?' Suddenly his head sagged and he let out a sob.

'Dad?' Clara perched beside him, putting an arm about his shaking shoulders. He stank of stale drink. 'Don't upset yourself. You weren't that bad at singing.'

Harry gave a half-laugh, crying at the same time. He shook his head. 'I've been a terrible father, a terrible man.'

'Don't be daft, course you haven't,' Clara comforted him. 'There's not a mean bone in your body. If only you could stop drinking so much . . .'

Harry sniffed. 'Stops me thinking.'

'Aye, it does that all right,' Clara sighed. 'But you mustn't worry about the shop - we'll manage somehow.'

He groaned and buried his face in his hands. 'The shop! I don't care tuppence for the place. I'd go back to sea tomorrow. But losing it will finish your mother. I only ever did it for her — it's what she always dreamed of, stuck in that filthy boarding house with a tyrant of an aunt.' He broke off, shaking his head.

'Mam won't let it fail,' Clara insisted. 'We'll get by selling cheaper goods.'

He gave her a haggard look. 'I did it for her — it was all for her,' he said in agitation. 'She blames me now, but she was happy enough at the time.'

'Blames you for what, Dad? You're not making sense.'

'No,' he said bitterly, 'none of it makes sense anymore.'

Clara placed her hand over his. It was clammy and shaking. 'Tell me what's really the matter. I'm seventeen and know the business backwards. But if there are debts I don't know about. . .'

He gave her such a harrowed look that Clara faltered.

'Some debts,' he whispered, 'can never be repaid.'

Clara's insides churned. His mood and baffling words were frightening her. She squeezed his hand. 'We'll get through this together,' she encouraged him.

Harry pulled out a dirty handkerchief and wiped his face. He nodded. 'Off you go. Don't be late.'

'Will you be all right, Dad?' Clara asked, uncertain.

'Right as rain,' he sniffed.

Clara stood up and kissed him on the forehead. 'Have a wash and change and get Mam her breakfast, eh? That'll start the day on the right foot.'

He nodded and watched her as she descended the stairs and picked up the rucksack.

35

'I love you, my bonny,' he said. 'You're the best of daughters.'

Clara was taken aback. It was a long time since he had said anything affectionate. She smiled. 'And you're a canny father — most of the time.'

She heard him give a rueful laugh as she closed the door behind her.

Chapter 6

All the way up to the summit, Frank and Benny had been arguing about Oswald Mosley's New Party.

'I don't blame him for turning his back on the Labour Party,' Benny declared. 'Call themselves Socialists, but what are they doing for the working class? Bugger all. Three million on the dole and they cut unemployment benefit! They're sitting on their backsides in London — they're not the ones ganin' hungry.'

'And Mosley's a Socialist, is he?' Frank was scornful. 'He's a Tory toff in Labour clothing. Gives a few angry speeches, stirs up trouble, then nicks off to the south of France.'

'Well at least he's trying to do some'at,' Benny protested. 'He's got ideas — public works — making jobs for lads.'

'Then why didn't he push harder for them when he had the chance?' Frank demanded.

Lillian, who was walking between them, agreed. 'Yes, he was in the Ministry for Employment.'

'No one in government was listening to him,' Benny cried.

'He should've stayed and fought his corner.' Frank stayed calm. 'Mosley's on a big ego trip and it's damaging the party.'

'Yes, Frank's right.' Lillian nodded vigorously. 'He's splitting the Labour vote and letting the Tories in.'

'Well I'm tempted to vote for him mesel,' Benny said hotly.

'You can't mean that?' Lillian said, shocked.

'I do!'

'Oh, Benny.' Lillian shuddered.

Behind them, Reenie rolled her eyes at Clara. Clara made a gesture of pretending to strangle someone.

'You'll have to start a hiking group for Mosleyites then,' Lillian said stiffly.

'All marching in step behind their leader, of course,' Frank teased. He put a hand on his brother's shoulder but Benny shook him off.

Clara threw down her pack in the heather. Today, their arguing grated on her nerves. 'Let's stop here. Might be too windy at the top.'

'Agreed.' Reenie followed suit, spreading out a piece of tarpaulin for them to sit on.

Others settled around them in small groups and shared out food.

'Benny, what you got in your sandwiches?' Clara asked, hoping to divert him from further wrangling. 'If it's more exciting than fish paste, we're swapping.'

Benny nodded and plonked himself down next to her. The moor spread out for miles ahead, broken only by the snaking curve of the Roman Wall. Clara breathed in deeply, letting the peaceful surroundings calm her. She was not really hungry at all, her stomach still knotted after the strange conversation with her father. She could not work out why it so disturbed her.

'Pork and pickled beetroot,' Benny said, peering into his sandwich and offering it to Clara.

'Heaven!' She handed him one of hers.

'Glad to please you,' Benny grinned, his good humour quickly returning.

Reenie poured out tea from a flask that had been bought from Magee's and handed a cup to Clara. 'Amazing what the Romans did,' she mused, 'building that huge wall in the middle of nowhere. Must have taken hundreds of men -thousands maybe.'

'Aye, plenty of employment in those days,' Benny grunted through his sandwich.

'Cheap labour more like,' Reenie remarked, 'and no unions to protect them.'

'And a military dictatorship running everyone's lives,' Frank added. 'Dictatorships get walls built, but they treat life cheaply.'

Clara watched Lillian nodding vigorously and her heart sank. The teacher was sitting close to Frank.

'That's what Mosley would be like in power. He's a demagogue, like Mussolini and his *fascisti* in Italy. They talk about giving power to the people but they only want it for themselves.'

Clara looked at Reenie in dismay, wondering if Lillian was deliberately rekindling the argument to impress Frank.

'Mosley's on the side of the working classes,' Benny said at once.

'He may think he is,' Frank said dryly. 'But he's not going to give up his country house and his upper-class lifestyle for us.'

'Why should he?' Clara piped up. They all turned and stared at her. She blushed. 'Well, why can't you be rich and support the workers too? If people work hard for their money, they're entitled to spend it.'

The brothers looked nonplussed. Reenie snorted with laughter, but Lillian clucked in disapproval. 'Sometimes I wonder why you ever joined the YS, Clara. You don't seem to have grasped the fundamentals of Socialism at all.'

'No, I'm just a simple shopkeeper's daughter,' Clara quipped. 'Wouldn't know a fundamental if it came up and bit me on the bottom.'

Benny and Reenie spluttered with laughter. Lillian went red.

'I didn't say you were simple,' she replied, 'just surprised why you come.'

Clara waved a sandwich nonchalantly. 'Even shopkeepers can appreciate a dose of fresh air once a week, Lillian. Besides, we need a break from counting all that money.'

'Admit it, Clara,' Benny chuckled, 'you really come for the lads.'

'In your dreams,' Clara replied.

Lillian let out an impatient sigh. 'Everything has to be a joke with you,' she muttered and turned back to Frank. At once she started questioning him about the situation in Germany. Clara hid her annoyance, pretending not to listen to their conversation about Hitler and the National Socialists. As usual, Lillian was trying to show her up.

Clara felt a small pain in her chest at the sight of Frank leaning back on his pack, blond hair tousled by the wind, frowning into the distance as Lillian debated the emergent Nazi party. Clara swallowed her resentment. Lillian had a good job at a school in Newcastle; she could afford the luxury of debate. She did not have a brother out of work or parents who were tearing themselves apart over a nearly bankrupt business. But she would not give the condescending teacher the satisfaction of seeing how much she cared about such things. Instead, she chatted to Reenie and Benny about the fair that was coming to the town, and when they packed up and moved on she walked ahead, setting a fast pace.

Only when they descended to the valley and were approaching the station did Lillian and Frank catch up. Lillian and Reenie went off to the ladies' cloakroom. Benny was talking about football to another lad.

Frank took Clara by the elbow. 'Anything wrong, lass?'

She jerked as if stung. 'No, nowt.'

He quickly let go. 'You mustn't mind Lillian — she's very committed and

38

doesn't see when others are joking.'

Clara smiled. 'Who was joking?'

He looked unsure. 'Maybe I'm wrong, but I think it's your way of hiding what you feel.'

'Dr Freud! You've found me out,' Clara teased.

'Is everything all right at home?' Frank persisted. 'I know business is bad . . .'

She longed to unburden herself about their debts, her father's drinking and gambling, his guilt about something he could not tell her. He seemed to be on a road to self-destruction. But these were private affairs. She would not betray her parents by airing their troubles in public. It was something she could only confide to her diary.

Clara glanced away from his intense look. 'I come here to forget all that,' she said lightly. 'Monday morning comes soon enough.'

'Of course,' Frank agreed. 'I didn't mean to pry.'

Moments later, the others were joining them again. Sitting on the train home, watching Lillian and Frank discuss a new left-wing bookshop in Newcastle's West End, Clara regretted her wasted opportunity to confide in Frank. But she felt so immature and gauche in his presence, like a tongue-tied schoolgirl. All she could do was say something flippant to cover her nervousness.

Benny started a sing-song in the carriage which everyone joined in. At Newcastle Central Station they dispersed.

'Would you like to come to our house for tea?' Lillian asked Frank. 'Mam's doing roast mutton.'

Clara's mouth watered at the thought. The Magees would be having thin slices of cold ham and pease pudding.

Frank gave a bashful smile. 'Thanks for asking, but I'm playing at the Rex later. Can't turn work down these days; not when most of the picture houses don't have bands anymore.'

Lillian nodded. 'Another time.'

Clara walked back with the Lewises to Byfell, saving on the tram fare. The nearer they got to home, the slower she walked.

'Come back to ours,' Reenie insisted, sensing her reluctance.

'Well. . .' Clara hesitated.

'Gan on,' Benny encouraged her.

She smiled. 'Just for a bit, then.'

Marta and Oscar welcomed her in as if they had expected her and they all sat round the kitchen table eating brisket and vegetables while Marta questioned them on the day. There was lively conversation again about Oswald Mosley. Benny, outnumbered by the others, resorted to teasing his brother about Lillian's adoring attention.

'"Frank's always right,"' he mimicked the teacher. '"Oh, Benny how could you! And Clara, you just don't take anything seriously, do you?"'

Reenie and Clara hooted with laughter and even Frank chuckled.

'Don't listen to him,' Marta said. 'I like the sound of this Lillian - sensible, good job. Next time you bring her here for tea, Frank, *ja*? It's time you find a sweetheart.'

'Frank's sweetheart is that violin,' Benny smirked.

Frank pushed back his fringe, his fair face colouring. He glanced round and caught Clara watching him. She laughed. 'Lucky violin.'

His eyes widened in surprise. For a moment they all looked at her. Clara wanted to sink under the table. What on earth had made her say such a thing? She could feel herself go hot. It was Benny who broke the silence with a suggestive whistle.

'Watch out, Frank, our Clara's got a secret crush on you,' he crowed.

'No, I haven't!' Clara protested.

'Don't embarrass her,' Frank said. 'We all know when Clara's joking.' He stood up. 'And talking of the sweet violin, we have a date. Ta for the tea, Mam.' He kissed his mother in passing and flicked Clara a glance. 'Ta-ra, Clara.'

She nodded, unable to meet his look. She wanted to run out after him and explain that it was true, she had not been joking. But she would only make a bigger fool of herself. Instead, she helped Marta clear the table and wash up. Afterwards, Benny offered to walk her round to Tenter Terrace.

'You don't need to, it's not dark,' Clara said.

'I'd like to.' Benny smiled and grabbed his cap.

Reenie gave her a look as they went. Clara knew her friend would like Benny to court her. She was always making remarks about how much her brother thought of her and how alike they were in outlook. 'He's never looked at another lass but you,' Reenie had once told her. 'Put him out of his misery and go out with him.'

Out in the mellow evening light, Benny walked by her side.

'Clara,' he began hesitantly, 'have you — do you really care for our Frank?'

Clara's heart thumped. She must make light of this.

'I care for all your family,' she answered truthfully.

'You know what I mean.' Benny stopped, hands plunged in pockets. 'Just tell me.'

Clara took a deep breath. 'I do care for Frank,' she admitted. 'I suppose I've always looked up to him — admired him.' She stared at the cobbles. 'But Frank doesn't seem interested in lasses, does he? And I didn't mean anything by the comment — I was just being daft.'

They looked at each other. Benny gave her a quizzical smile. 'So I'm still in with a chance?'

'Maybes.' Clara laughed and gave him a playful punch. 'Now will you walk me home?'

'My pleasure, ma'am.' Benny bowed and held out his arm. Clara hesitated, then took it.

They turned the corner into Tenter Terrace to see Vinnie's car parked outside the shop. Clara's heart lurched. It probably meant her father was so drunk that Vinnie had given him a lift home. So much for making breakfast and keeping Patience company, she thought crossly.

'Craven's here?' Benny queried. Clara nodded. Suddenly she did not want to be left to face the situation alone.

'Will you come up with me, just for a minute?' she urged. 'Me dad might — not be well. And Mr Craven struts about the flat like he owns it and we should all be grateful for what he does. But he does nowt to stop me dad drinking and throwing good money after bad.'

Benny squeezed her arm. 'Don't worry, lass. Course I'll come up.'

When they walked into the sitting room, Vinnie was standing over Patience, still in his coat and hat. Patience flew at her.

'Where've you been?'

'Hiking. You knew I was going,' Clara defended herself. Her mother's face was strained.

'What's he doing here?' she asked rudely.

'Clara asked me up, Mrs Magee,' Benny said at once.

'Mam, what's going on?' Clara demanded.

40

Patience stood there, clutching her hands to stop them shaking. It was Vinnie who answered, stepping towards Clara and Benny.

'Clara, pet,' he said calmly, 'have you seen your father today?'

Clara nodded. 'This morning, just as I was leaving. Why?'

'I'm sure it's nothing to worry about,' Vinnie said, placing a hand on her arm, 'but we don't know where he is. Jimmy's out looking round the town with some of my lads.'

'He's missing,' Patience wailed. 'Hasn't been here all day. I thought he'd gone back to Craven Hall — but Jimmy came home and said he'd not been there all day.' She covered her face and let out a howl.

Clara pushed past Vinnie to put her arms about her. 'Don't, Mam. We'll find him.'

'Course we will. 'Vinnie encouraged her. 'Probably fallen asleep somewhere.'

Patience cried angrily, 'The daft man! I'll string him up. Making us worry like this.'

'Let me gan and look,' Benny volunteered.

'No,' Patience sniffed. 'I don't want the whole world to know what a fool he is.'

'That's kind of you, Benny lad,' Vinnie murmured, steering Patience into a seat. 'Clara, did your father speak to you this morning?'

Clara nodded. 'He wasn't making much sense.'

'Can you remember anything that might give us a clue where to look?'

Clara struggled with the uncomfortable memory. 'He was feeling sorry for himself,' she began. 'Kept going on about debts — debts he couldn't pay.' She glanced awkwardly at Benny, but he just nodded in encouragement. 'Dad seemed full of regret about something. Said he'd done it for Mam; he'd done everything for you, Mam.'

Patience gasped. Vinnie asked, 'Did your father say what that something was?'

Clara shook her head. 'He wouldn't say.'

Patience buckled, weeping loudly into her hands. Vinnie put an arm about her but she pulled away. Vinnie stood up and nodded to Clara to comfort her mother. Clara went at once to hold her. Patience clung on to her daughter.

'Dad did say something else,' Clara said. 'He talked about going back to sea — said he'd prefer that to the shop. I don't think he was serious, though.'

Patience's head went up. 'Do you think that's possible?' Her tear-streaked face lit with hope.

'Didn't he used to work on the ferries at Shields?' Clara asked.

'He worked all over,' Patience nodded.

Vinnie added, 'And he was in the Merchant Navy during the war. Folk talk about Flanders heroes, but the merchantmen were the bravest of all.'

Benny piped up. 'We could look down Shields; see if he's tried to board a ship. Someone might have seen him.'

Vinnie nodded. 'We'll go in my car.'

Clara jumped up. 'I want to come too.'

Vinnie beckoned her over and said in a low murmur, 'I think you should stay with your mam; she's in a bad way. You can tell Jimmy what's happening.' Clara was about to protest when Vinnie put a strong hand on her shoulder. 'Bet your dad will be here by the time we get back.' He smiled. 'God willing.'

He turned and went swiftly from the room, not waiting for her to argue. Benny followed with an encouraging smile. Clara was left to wait with her distraught mother.

41

Chapter 7

It grew dark before anyone returned. Clara sat watching in the window. 'Someone's coming. I think it's Jimmy.' Footsteps came thudding up the stairs and the women crossed the room.

'Have you found him?' Patience demanded.

Jimmy shook his head. 'Nowt. Clarkie sent me home. I wanted to stay out.'

'You've done enough,' his mother said, holding out her arms. But he stood still, shoulders drooping. He looked exhausted.

'I'll make us some more tea,' Clara said, touching him on the shoulder as she passed. 'Good lad, you've done your best. Vinnie s gone to look down Shields, see if he's hanging around the boats.'

'He should've taken me with him,' Jimmy muttered.

'Benny's gone to help,' Clara said.

'Benny? Why him?'

Patience sniffed. 'He came back with your sister, though I don't know why a Leizmann has to get involved.'

'Mam,' Clara chided, 'he's only trying to help. He likes me dad.'

When she returned with a fresh pot, Jimmy was curled up on the settee next to his mother, both with their eyes closed. The tea grew cold while Clara sat in the window, frustrated at doing nothing. She should have insisted on going with the men. Her mother had said little beyond scolding her for leaving her all day and taking tea at the Lewises'.

Clara wanted to say it was more friendly at Reenie's house. Marta would not dream of treating Jimmy with the frostiness Patience showed to Benny. But her mother was overwrought with worry, so she bit her tongue and did not argue back.

A knock on the downstairs door roused them, Clara peered out, but a mist had stolen up from the river and everything glowed mysteriously in the lamplight.

'I'll go,' she said, hurrying across the room and clattering down the stairs.

Her heart jolted at the sight of Frank stepping forward from the mist. He looked at her awkwardly from under his cap.

'Sorry to bother you, Clara, but Mam's fussing. Is Benny still with you?'

Clara flushed. 'Oh, no! I'm sorry. He's gone with Mr Craven.'

'Vinnie?' Frank frowned.

Clara quickly explained what had happened.

'That's bad.' Frank looked concerned. 'What can I do to help?'

Clara shrugged helplessly. 'There's nothing to do but wait.'

'Then I'll wait with you,' he offered. 'Just let me tell them at home first.'

The window opened above them. 'Clara!' her mother called down. 'Who is it?'

'Frank Lewis,' Clara replied. 'I'll be up in a minute.'

'Frank,' Patience spoke to him directly, 'please go home. We really don't need any more of your family involved.'

Clara squirmed at her mother's rudeness. Frank gave her a questioning look and she nodded for him to go.

'Goodnight, Mrs Magee,' Frank answered. 'You can send Jimmy for me if you change your mind.'

'Yes, thank you,' Patience answered. 'Come inside, Clara. It's turning damp and you'll catch cold.'

'I'm sorry,' Clara apologised. 'She's not herself.'

Frank put out a hand and touched her shoulder. 'No need to say sorry.'

Clara wanted to clutch his hand and put it to her face, feel the warmth of his palm. She swallowed. 'How was your date at the pictures?'

He laughed softly. 'Grand.'

'Hurry up, Clara,' Patience fretted above.

Clara gave an exasperated sigh. When would she next have a chance to be alone with Frank? But he was stepping away.

'I'm sure your father will be home soon. Goodnight, Clara.'

She watched him disappear back into the silvery mist. She stood there for several minutes staring at the place where he had been, breathing in the cool damp air. She tried to clear her head of thoughts of him. Noises came clearly from far off: a foghorn, a barking dog rattling on its chain, someone putting out milk bottles. She should let Frank know how she felt about him. At least then she would find out his own feelings, which were as blanketed in mystery as the street in fog.

Clara turned indoors, her spirits lifting at the decision. Soon, when her father was back and things had calmed down, she would tell Frank she loved him. His brief appearance had already given her optimism. Her father would return. This was not the first time he had taken off for the day. The only difference was that Vinnie usually knew where to find him and this time he seemed as in the dark as they were.

'Why didn't Frank stay?' Jimmy asked on her return.

'Ask Mam.' Clara yawned, throwing her mother a look.

'We don't need the Leizmanns knowing our business,' Patience snapped.

'Frank's canny,' Jimmy said. 'Always gives me a tanner when I see him.'

Clara smiled. 'That's kind.'

'You shouldn't take money off him,' Patience reproved him. 'We're not a charity case yet.'

Clara gave Jimmy a look that said don't argue back.

'Why don't you go to bed, Mam, try to rest?' she coaxed.

'I couldn't sleep,' she fretted.

'Just lie down. I'll take it in turns with Jimmy to stay awake.'

'What do you think's really happened to me dad?' Jimmy asked when she had gone. 'What if he's never coming back . . ?'

Clara tried to quell the same unease that her brother was feeling. She would have dismissed Harry's disappearance as the usual drinking spree if she had not had that disturbing conversation with him that morning. She had never seen him so melancholic. Yet as she had left the flat she had heard him grunt with laughter. That was not the sound of a man at the end of his tether.

'No point thinking the worst,' she said wearily.

'I tell you one thing,' Jimmy said sternly, 'when he comes back, he's ganin' on the wagon. Mr Craven says alcohol's a poison. Makes you unfit and daft in the head. He doesn't let any of his lads drink and I'm never ganin' to either.'

Clara eyed him in surprise. 'Good for you. I didn't know Mr Craven was so strict. There was plenty drink at Danny Watts's wedding, I seem to remember.'

Jimmy shrugged. 'Didn't want to spoil a party. It's all right in moderation, he says. But you can't be a fighter and a drinker. Lads that do end up in a lot of bother. He hoys them out if they turn up drunk.'

'So why does he let Dad drink the way he does down at the hall?' Clara pointed out.

'Cos Dad's well beyond fighting,' Jimmy answered. 'Mr Craven's different with him - sees him as this great war hero. Won't let anyone say owt bad about me dad.'

Clara mused. 'He really does like Dad, doesn't he? That's why he's spending so much time looking out for him.'

Jimmy nodded. 'Aye, Mr Craven thinks the world of him - his second father, he calls him. Clarkie says Mr Craven took it really bad when old Stan Craven died.'

In the early hours of the morning, Vinnie and Benny returned.

'Sorry.' Vinnie shook his head. 'There's no sign of him down Shields.'

'He'll be sleeping it off somewhere,' Benny tried to comfort them.

'We must go to the police in the morning, Clara,' Vinnie instructed, 'and report him missing.'

Clara nodded, her hopes dashed.

'You get yourself off home now, lad,' Vinnie told Benny. 'You look done in.'

'We could look some more,' Benny suggested.

'Thanks, Benny,' Clara smiled, 'but you've done more than enough. And Frank's been round looking for you - your mam's worrying.'

Benny flushed. 'I'm not a bairn.'

Vinnie put a hand on his shoulder and steered him towards the door. 'There's nothing more can be done till the morning. Go home.'

Benny left and Vinnie looked ready to settle down.

'There's no need to stay, Mr Craven,' Clara insisted. 'If Dad comes back, me and Jimmy can deal with him.'

He gave her a look of surprise. 'I don't like to leave the pair of you alone,' he said in concern.

'We're not alone; Mam's with us.'

'But Patience is hardly in any state to cope—'

'She's coped with me dad's drinking and disappearing before,' Clara interrupted. 'We've had three years of this.'

Annoyance flashed across Vinnie's face, then he was smiling as usual. 'You're a grand support to your mother, I can see that.' He picked up his trilby and gloves from the nest of tables. 'I'll call round tomorrow.'

Jimmy followed him down the stairs and let him out. Returning, he scowled at his sister. 'Why did you send him away after all the help he's been?'

'I just didn't want him round the flat,' Clara sighed, not quite sure why she felt uncomfortable in Vinnie's presence. 'And there's nothing more we can do tonight. Let's get some sleep.'

She lay under her covers, half dressed, ready to spring up if she heard her father return. Perhaps he had walked out on them, turned his back on all the debt and wrangling and walked right out of town? Perhaps one of his gambling creditors was after him and he had gone into hiding? Perhaps he was lying in a back alley somewhere, having fallen down drunk and knocked himself unconscious? Clara lay exhausted but sleepless, tortured by the not knowing.

At six in the morning, she got up and washed. The shop would have to be opened like any other Monday. She would get her mother breakfast and go to the police station to report her father missing before opening for business.

She glanced in on Patience. Her mother was curled up on top of the bed sleeping, her breathing noisy. Clara tiptoed out again and went downstairs, through the shop to the back kitchen. Filling the kettle, she lit the gas jet and put it on to boil. Yawning, she reached into the bread bin for the end of the loaf. It made her think of yesterday's paste sandwiches and the hike on the moors.

Maybe if she had not gone, her father would have stayed around all day too. But regretting the past was a futile pastime. She cut three slices. Jimmy could have the large crust.

While she waited for the kettle to boil, Clara went into the shop and pulled up the blinds. She thought she would sweep the floor for something to do, and went into the small changing room where they kept the brush. As she turned on the light, she tripped on something in the doorway. An empty bottle rolled away from her. Puzzled, she looked up.

Her father was hanging from a hook in the ceiling.

Stunned disbelief seized her. Her chest constricted. She could not breathe, could not cry out. He was still in the crumpled clothes she had last seen him in, his face pulled into a terrible grimace. Clara grabbed at his dangling hand. It was stiff and cold.

She gulped and retched, then found breath again.

Clara's screaming woke Patience in an instant and had Jimmy racing down the stairs from two floors up.

Chapter 8

Clara woke up sweating, her pulse racing. She had not slept more than two hours at a stretch for over a week. The hideous sight of her father hanged in the downstairs closet haunted every waking moment and pursued her into her dreams. It did not look like him. It was a bloated, grotesque parody of Harry's craggy, lively face.

She could not enter the shop, nor talk about it, except to the police officer who came to take a statement. There was a post-mortem, an inquest that was adjourned for a fortnight and a reporter from a local newspaper who came asking questions until Vinnie ordered him away. Nevertheless, there was a write-up in the Tyne Times telling of Harry's suicide and describing him as a 'former merchant seaman and down-on-his-luck businessman' with 'a lot of debts'. Some neighbour who would not be named was quoted as saying that Harry Magee had 'turned to the bottle'.

Patience railed, 'What neighbour? Bet it was that nebby Mrs Shaw. They've no right to print such stories.'

'But they're true,' Jimmy pointed out.

'Don't speak about your father like that,' she said tearfully. 'Isn't it bad enough we have police brought to our door and all the town know of our private affairs?'

Patience would not eat. She existed on black tea, sitting around in her kimono with the blinds drawn not bothering to get dressed.

The shop remained closed. People came to offer their condolences but were turned away.

'Mam doesn't want to see anybody just yet,' Clara had to explain, 'not till after the funeral.'

Marta and Reenie came with a meat pie, fresh bread and a basket of apples. The friends hugged and Clara cried. Benny and Frank called round with flowers, but Clara did not dare let them in.

'Thanks, both of you.' Clara tried to smile, her face pale and eyes dark-ringed.

'It must've been terrible,' Benny blurted out, 'him being there all the time and you not knowing—'

Frank elbowed him to be quiet. 'Is there anything you need?' he asked.

She wanted him to hold her, keep her safe from the nightmares. She shook her head, swallowing down tears.

'You just have to ask,' Frank said gently. 'Anything at all. It's no bother.'

Clara nodded, unable to speak for fear of weeping in the street.

The only visitors Patience would allow were the Cravens. Dolly sat with her, filling their sitting room with cigarette smoke and keeping up a mournful commentary.

'I know just how you're feeling. My Stan's been dead nearly eight years but it seems like yesterday. There's not a day goes by when I'm not thinking about him. They say time heals but don't you believe them. You never get over it, Patience,' she sighed, 'you just learn to bear it.'

Patience hardly seemed to notice Dolly, but Clara could not bear to listen. She went to her room and pored over her diary, yet could not bring herself to write in it. The last entry had been the night before her hike to the Roman Wall. She kept herself busy by cleaning; obsessively scrubbing, sweeping, dusting and polishing. While the flat had never been so pristine, the shop below gathered dust.

Vinnie helped them plan the funeral. He suggested a service at St Michael's, but Patience doubted the vicar would allow it. 'Might be problems with burying him in holy ground — the way he died,' she said bitterly.

They decided Harry would be cremated in a quiet ceremony, just family and close friends.

'I'd like some of my lads to carry the coffin.' Vinnie said. 'A mark of respect from me, like.'

Patience was pathetically grateful, but Clara worried about the cost. 'Will we have to pay them, Mr Craven?'

Vinnie looked offended by the idea. 'Course not. I'll see to that. And we're more than happy to hold the wake at ours, aren't we, Mother?'

Dolly nodded and blew out smoke. 'I'll get caterers in.'

'No, thank you,' Clara said firmly. 'We'll manage here, won't we, Mam?' She shot her mother a nervous look. Patience seemed a world away and might agree to anything. But Clara was certain they could not afford caterers and her father would not have wanted to be beholden to the Cravens.

'Are you sure?' Vinnie said, his look almost challenging.

'Quite sure.' Clara held her ground.

The day before the funeral, Clara steeled herself to go into the shop. She took Jimmy with her.

'We need to take the money from the till to pay the undertaker and buy food for the party.'

It was eerily quiet, the hats suspended in the window like stuffed birds in a museum. Jimmy switched on the light. With a deep breath, Clara crossed the room, avoiding a glance at the door to the closet. She opened the till. It was empty but for a handful of copper coins. She spread them out on the counter. One and a ha'penny.

'Jimmy, have you been—'

'No! I'm not a thief,' he said hotly.

'Sorry … it's just… on that last Saturday there was over five pounds.'

Jimmy grunted. 'Remember Dad went out that night and got himself in a right state.'

Clara's heart sank. 'Mam keeps a secret supply in a box in the closet,' she said tensely.

'Do you want me to look?' Jimmy asked.

Clara shook her head. It would be just as traumatic for her brother to go back in the room. She must not be a coward. She walked towards it, swallowing bile. The smell hit her: a fusty mix of clothing, sweat, dust and a trace of her father's odour. She clamped a hand over her mouth while frantically grabbing a box from behind a roll of material. When she tipped it open, a tangle of hairpins and ribbon fell out. At the bottom was a cloth drawstring bag. Clara threw it at Jimmy by the door and bolted from the room.

'Open it,' she gasped, taking deep gulps to calm herself.

Jimmy loosened the tie, pulled it open and delved inside. 'Nowt,' he said.

Clara grabbed it off him and shook it upside down. It was empty. At that moment, Patience walked in, arms clutched round her, shivering in her dressing gown. She glanced between them and at the bag.

'He stole it all, didn't he?' she croaked.

Clara felt panic rising. 'What about the bank? You've got an account, haven't you?'

Patience gave a mirthless laugh. 'Haven't used it for months — never

47

anything to put in it.'

Clara licked dry lips. 'Well, at least the funeral costs are covered by insurance. Dad always talked about his burial fund.'

They searched the shop and turned the flat upside down looking for the insurance policy but could not find it.

'We must have it to pay the undertaker,' Clara cried.

Patience, galvanised by her daughter's alarm, got dressed and went to visit the broker who had taken their payments. She returned, looking drained.

'Your father cashed it in three months ago,' she said, sinking into a chair.

Clara was stunned. Why had he never said things were so bad? 'We need to buy food for tomorrow, Mam,' she fretted. 'What'll we do?'

They stared at each other in silence.

'Gan to the pawnshop,' Jimmy suggested. 'There's plenty of fancy things in the shop we could sell.'

They looked at him aghast. The Magees were the ones who had given credit to their poorer customers. They had never had to stoop to using the pawnshop. Clara had never been inside one in her life.

'We can't; that's stock,' Patience said in agitation. 'Some of it's not paid for yet. And we've got creditors; we have to keep the shop going.'

Clara steeled herself. 'Our things then,' she said. 'You can have my silver brooch and christening mug.'

'And there's all that junk in me bedroom,' Jimmy reminded her. 'Caps that Dad bought years ago.'

Clara watched her mother struggle with the idea. 'It's so shaming,' she whispered.

'It's just temporary,' Clara said gently. 'We'll soon get the things back when the shop's open again.'

Eventually Patience nodded. She stood up. 'Your father's things go first. He's got us in this mess, he'll bail us out.'

She strode into her bedroom and pulling open his wardrobe began to fling clothes on to the floor. His best suit, two white shirts, collars, studs and ties, an old Homburg hat that Clara had never seen him wear, his dressing gown, pyjamas, socks and shoes.

Patience whipped off the bedcover and bundled everything inside it. She marched to the washstand and picked up his brush and comb, a button hook and a shoehorn and threw them into the pile.

Clara had never seen such white fury on her mother's face. 'Mam, you don't have to get rid of it all.'

'Oh, yes I do!' she hissed. 'I don't want to see any of it again as long as I live.' She gathered the corners of the cover, yanked them into a tight knot and hurled the bundle at the open door. 'Go on; take it down the pawn shop and good riddance!'

Clara threw Jimmy a warning look and pushed him out of the room, dragging the bundle behind her. She closed the door. Behind it, they heard muffled sobbing and Clara imagined her mother crying into the stripped bed. She wanted to rush back in and comfort her, but her mother had been so angry she feared she would make things worse.

'Help me with this lot,' she murmured to her brother. 'Let her alone for a bit.'

Brother and sister carried the bundle between them down the street, praying they would not meet too many people they knew. They chose a pawnshop on the edge of Byfell, away from the High Street and shops where they were known. Clara dumped down the parcel, out of breath.

The pawnbroker was not interested in most of the goods, but he saw the tears in Clara's eyes and relented.

'I'll take the brush set and the suit for six pounds,' he offered.

'Six pounds? But they're silver!' Clara cried. 'Please, Mr Slater, we have to pay for me father's funeral as well as eat. I cannot go back without ten pounds or me mam will be ill. It's hard enough for her having to part with her dear husband's cherished possessions.'

'Eight,' he said grudgingly.

'Take the hat too,' Clara pleaded, 'and the shirts are best quality. Ten pounds for the lot.'

He agreed with a sigh. 'Ever thought of coming to work for me?'

She watched tensely as he counted out the money. She pocketed it, then reached for the bedcover. The pawnbroker put out his hand to stop her. 'I've paid for that; you said the lot.'

Clara decided not to argue. She could not risk the man changing his mind. Back outside she slipped her arm through Jimmy's.

'Not so bad, eh?' he asked.

'No,' Clara sighed. 'But I'd hate to do this week in week out like some folk.'

'It won't come to that,' Jimmy promised.

'How you so sure?'

'Mr Craven won't let it — he'll look after us.'

Clara faced him. 'Jimmy, why should he? The Cravens aren't even family.'

'Aye, but they're as good as,' Jimmy answered. 'Mr Craven's told me not to worry. He'll do anything for Harry Magee's family, that's what he said.'

Clara gave an impatient sigh. 'It might have been better if he'd tried to help Dad while he was still alive.'

Jimmy scowled. 'Dad wouldn't let him. He was too proud.'

'Well so am I.' Clara was short. 'I'll not be beholden to the Cravens, no matter how well-meaning they are.'

They walked home in silence.

Chapter 9

Despite the family's attempt to have a quiet funeral, dozens of people turned up to pay their respects to Harry at the simple service. Vinnie organised where people sat and he and Dolly walked in with the family behind the coffin. Jimmy helped carry it, along with Clarkie and two others from the boxing hall whom Clara knew by sight. She glimpsed the Lewises near the back, but Patience had baulked at the suggestion that they should greet mourners at the door, so there was no chance to thank them.

Back at the flat, there was a modest tea laid out in the dining room. The Cravens donated two bottles of sherry and one of whisky, which Vinnie dispensed to the handful of guests: a few neighbours and shopkeepers who had been specially asked by Patience. Clara surveyed them. Which of them had gossiped to the reporter? she wondered.

At least Reenie was here to keep her company, she thought gratefully. Together they handed round homemade scones and sponge cake. Patience had not wanted the Lewises invited, but Clara had been stubborn in her insistence that Reenie come. Of all their neighbours, the Lewises had been the kindest, leaving plates of food at the door, and little notes of encouragement. Clara wished Reenie's brothers were there too, but she put on a brave face and kept busy seeing to the guests. Patience sat in a corner, handkerchief in hand, while people approached her in ones and twos to give their condolences.

Eventually, Reenie said, 'Sorry, Clara, but I have to go. I'm on night shift.'

Clara went downstairs with her friend. 'Thanks for coming. Don't think I'd have got through the afternoon without you.' She looked at Reenie forlornly. 'I still can't believe Dad's gone. It's the daft little things I miss, like him sneezing in the morning. If I hear someone sneeze in the street, I look out to see if it's him.'

Tears welled in her eyes. Reenie hugged her.

'Come round when you want; Mam would like to see you.'

'I'd like that too,' Clara sniffed. 'Please thank her for all the food — and the lads for the flowers — they're still lovely.'

They said goodbye and Clara steeled herself to return upstairs. She glanced into the dining room to see Jimmy playing cards with Clarkie and his friends. In the sitting room, Dolly sat with Patience. Vinnie was holding court among a small group of businessmen reminiscing about Harry and what a popular man he was. Their laughter grated on Clara's nerves. She wondered how much money they owed to the people in the room. Her father had always done the bookkeeping, leaving the ordering to Patience. Tomorrow or the day after, she would have to sit down with her mother and sort out their finances. Was there a will? Patience had refused to talk about such things.

Clara walked back out again. She sat on the kitchen step watching the sun inch its way across the yard until it was all in shadow. It grew quiet upstairs. Eventually, Jimmy found her.

'What you doing here? We've been worried.'

'I couldn't stand being jolly any longer. Have they all gone?'

'Aye. Mam's lying down.'

Clara stood up and made for the stairs. She was clearing the plates when a noise behind startled her. Whipping round, she saw her father sitting in his large armchair, his dark head just visible over the top. She felt winded.

'Dad?' she whispered.

The man stood up and in that instant she saw it was Vinnie. She had not noticed how alike the two men were from the back.

'Sorry. I didn't mean to scare you.' Vinnie smiled.

'That's Dad's chair,' Clara said angrily.

He raised his hands in apology. 'My mistake. Forgive me.'

She did not believe it was a mistake. He knew it was Harry's chair and for some reason this offended her.

'Why are you still here?' she demanded. 'Jimmy said everyone had gone.'

He came towards her. 'Wanted to make sure you were all right — and your mother. It's been a tough day for both of you.'

'Yes,' Clara agreed. She took a deep breath to calm down. He was trying to be helpful, that's all. He meant nothing by sitting in the chair. She forced herself to add, 'Thanks for all you've done today. Mam appreciates it.'

'It's no bother,' he said, leaning close. 'I'm here to help whenever you want me.'

He smelt of musk, of hair oil. The way he looked at her made her nervous. She nodded and stepped away.

Vinnie went. Clara cleared away and washed up the dishes. She took a glass of water in to her mother, but she was sleeping so soundly, Clara left it and tiptoed out. She went to bed early and lay listening to the sounds in the street below. She worried about what tomorrow would bring and how they would cope. She wondered if Vinnie wanted her mother to be more than just his friend's widow. He was being very attentive. Before she could work out if this would be a good thing or a bad thing, Clara fell into an exhausted sleep.

The next day, she galvanised her mother into addressing their future. Patience remembered Harry talking about a will. They went to the bank, which had always dealt with the legal side of the business too. The manager, an old boxing friend of Harry's, sat them down.

'I'm so very sorry,' Mr Hopkins said, 'but Harry died intestate.'

Patience looked at him blankly.

Clara asked, 'What does that mean?'

'It means there is no will. I was always on at him to make one. You will have to apply as his nearest beneficiary, Mrs Magee. We can arrange a solicitor to handle it all if you like.'

Clara looked at her mother and then at Mr Hopkins. 'Can we afford one?' she asked, feeling awkward.

Mr Hopkins cleared his throat. 'Judging by your bank account, no. But there will be other assets, I assume. Stock, personal goods, insurance policies, perhaps?' When they did not answer, he ploughed on, 'Well, Harry owned the lease on the shop, I know that.' He attempted a sympathetic smile. 'I know this is hard to talk about at such a time, Mrs Magee, but there is much to sort out. Of course you can handle matters yourself, but I wouldn't recommend it. Probate can be a complex matter.'

'Probate?' Patience echoed in bewilderment.

'You have to list Harry's assets and his debts before you can claim the remainder as yours. Then you apply for a grant of probate.'

'How long will that take?' Patience asked.

'If he had made a will, it could all have been sorted out in a couple of months. But it may take considerably longer.'

'Months?' Patience gasped. 'But I've a family to keep.'

The manager's look was pitying. 'Would you like me to appoint a solicitor?'

51

'Aye, a cheap one,' she answered bitterly.

The following day, they reopened the shop. Some of their regular customers called in to give a word of encouragement, but nobody was buying.

'It'll pick up,' Clara reassured her mother, 'once word gets round we're open for business again.'

But the rest of the week was almost as bad. By Saturday, they had taken only four pounds six shillings and threepence ha'penny. It was barely a fortnight since Harry had died and no one was demanding money from them yet. The landlord's agent, Mr Simmons, had told them they could leave payment till the end of the month. Yet they needed money from somewhere. Jimmy was sent back to the pawnshop twice more with clothing and china.

On the Sunday, Clara and Jimmy tried to persuade their mother to take a walk in the park, but she would not leave the flat. The blinds remained drawn and she stayed in her room. Jimmy disappeared off, Clara did not know where, but she stayed to keep an eye on Patience. For the first time in two weeks she wrote up her diary, pouring out her feelings of loss for her father and his senseless death. She lay on her bed crying quietly and thinking of Reenie and her brothers hiking somewhere up country in the mellow September sunshine. If only she could turn back time two weeks and prevent her father's suicide. She would never forgive herself for walking out that morning and leaving him to face his final day without her.

Her tortured thoughts were interrupted by a knock on the door below. Looking out, she saw Vinnie's gleaming black car parked in the road. Her heart sank, and she dodged out of sight. Perhaps her mother would answer. He knocked again, louder this time. She waited. Of course her mother would not answer; she was unable to face anyone in her present state of mind. To Clara's shock, she heard the downstairs door open and Vinnie's heavy tread coming up the stairs. The cheek of it! He was coming in uninvited.

'Anyone at home?' His deep voice rumbled along the corridor.

Clara's heart thumped. Should she pretend to be asleep or face up to him?

'Patience? Clara?' he called, walking into the sitting room.

Annoyance flaring, Clara strode out of her room to confront him. 'Mr Craven, what are you doing here?' She meant to sound cross but her voice came out croaky after all her crying.

'Wanted to make sure you were all right,' he said in concern. 'You've been crying.' He whipped out a white handkerchief from his breast pocket and handed it to her. She hesitated. 'Go on, take it, please.'

Clara blew her nose. The handkerchief smelled of starch and cologne. She noticed the monogram, VC, embroidered in dark blue thread.

'Thank you,' she said, handing it back.

'Keep it.' He smiled. 'I've plenty others.'

Clara felt foolish standing in her stockinged feet and crumpled dress, hair loose, clutching his handkerchief.

'Mam's resting. So was I.'

Vinnie arched his dark eyebrows. 'Sorry. I thought I saw you at the window.'

Clara blushed. 'You shouldn't just walk in like that, without being asked.'

He gave an indulgent laugh. 'I'm a friend, aren't I? Friends come in and out of each other's houses where I was brought up.'

'Even in posh Larch Avenue?' Clara questioned.

Vinnie looked more serious. 'I came with an invitation. Mam would like to invite you all to tea.'

'Thank you but no,' Clara said stiffly. 'Mam won't go anywhere just now. It's much too soon. And I've no idea where Jimmy is.'

Vinnie said casually, 'Oh, he's at our house already.'

'Your house?' Clara was disbelieving.

'I found him hanging around near the river with a gang of older lads. Didn't want him getting in any bother, so I took him home. Maybes you should take more interest in where the lad goes.'

Clara was stung. 'You should have brought him straight home if you were so worried.'

He was quick to answer. 'Looked like he needed a good dinner. Mam's been feeding him up.'

'There was no need,' Clara said in irritation.

Vinnie eyed her. 'Doesn't smell like anything's cooking here, lass. So why don't you come back with me? We can fetch your mam something for later. Haway, get your coat.'

Clara was sorely tempted by the thought of a big tea in the Cravens' comfortable house. She herself was no cook and they had lived on bread and tinned meat all week because her mother had lost interest in food. But she resented his high-handed manner.

'I said no thank you,' she said firmly. 'I'd rather stay and look after Mam.'

'You're very stubborn,' Vinnie said with a shake of his head. 'Don't be too proud to ask for help.' He added in a murmur, 'Your father wasn't.'

Clara's stomach lurched. 'What do you mean by that?'

He gave a shrug and made for the door.

'Tell me,' Clara demanded, going after him. 'Do we owe you money, Mr Craven? We need to know. Everything's in such a mess.'

He turned and came back, resting his hands on her shoulders. 'Let me help you.'

She shrugged him off, at once regretting her words. 'We can manage.'

He gave her a long, penetrating look. 'I won't be coming after Harry's family for money owed,' he said sternly. 'But there are others who will. Take my advice, Clara, and don't throw goodwill back in the face of a friend. You're going to need me.'

He marched out with a squeak of new leather shoes, leaving behind the scent of Anzora Viola. Clara stood still, her pulse pounding. She felt a mixture of indignation and fear. He made his offer of help sound like a threat. And who were these shadowy people who would be after them? Money sharks, illegal bookmakers? Or was Vinnie trying to scare her so she would run to him for help and grovel in gratitude? Not content with all his money-making ploys, he seemed to want to be running everyone else's business too.

Well, they would manage without him. Her father had been foolish to borrow money from others and let the Cravens indulge him instead of getting him to stop. From now on the Magees would be indebted to no one.

When Jimmy finally came home, bearing a box of food, Clara upbraided him.

'I don't want you scrounging off the Cravens like that again.'

His triumphant expression turned to a scowl. 'You can't stop me.'

'You'll stay and help out here where I can keep an eye on you,' she ordered.

'Mr Craven's right, you're pig-headed,' he accused her. 'Says lasses take more time to see sense.'

Clara flushed. 'How dare he!'

Jimmy walked out.

Clara's fury lasted until the following day, when hunger got the better of her and she shared out the food parcel for their tea. Patience fretted that her daughter might have caused Vinnie and Dolly offence.

'You mustn't get on the wrong side of them,' she said anxiously. 'You'll go and apologise.' When Clara refused, her mother sent Jimmy round instead.

It made Clara all the more determined to keep the shop going, but all the following week hardly anyone came in and Clara really began to worry. It was as if people were deliberately avoiding the shop. She asked around the neighbouring shops if they were finding trade as slack, but she was met with shrugging shoulders and embarrassed looks. Harry's unnatural death seemed to have jinxed Magee's and no one wanted anything to do with it.

One afternoon, a young boy dashed in and asked breathlessly, 'Missus, can I see the room where the man hanged hissel'?'

Patience let out a gasp of horror and clutched the counter. 'Get out!' she hissed.

Clara dashed to support her mother as her knees buckled. The boy stood gawping at the effect he had had.

Clara said sharply, 'Go on, scarper.'

The boy fled. Clara heard a shriek of laughter outside: 'See, I dared!' Then the boy and his friends ran off.

After that, Patience refused to serve in the shop. 'My nerves can't take it,' she said, retreating to bed. 'Get Jimmy to help you.'

But Jimmy went out early in the morning and stayed away all day long. He did not heed a word that Clara said. One day he came back with a couple of fish and said he had caught them with Clarkie in Byfell burn. Clara knew the burn was so polluted that no one fished in it.

'Since when have mackerel been a river fish?' she demanded. 'Have you pinched them?'

'Clarkie give us them,' Jimmy muttered and refused to say any more.

One evening, Clara forced herself to sit down with the shop ledgers. Patience said reading figures gave her a headache so it was no good asking her. Clara discovered a box full of bills, none of which looked as if they had been paid.

Some were handwritten notes in Harry's writing, promising to pay the bearer sums of money.

'I can't make head or tail of all this,' Clara told her mother in frustration. Patience was slumped in bed reading a penny romance. The second sherry bottle left over from the funeral was on the bedside table, almost empty. She looked drawn and ill.

'Ask Vinnie to take a look,' she said tiredly.

'Mam, we have to sort out our own mess.'

Patience's chin trembled. 'I'm sorry, pet, I know I'm next to useless. It's all too much for me.'

Clara went to hug her, not wanting to see her cry again. 'Shall I fetch the doctor? You've not been out of bed for days. And I wish you would eat more.'

'No,' she protested weakly, 'I just want to be left alone.'

'Tomorrow I'll get a tonic from the chemist,' Clara promised. 'You just need pepping up.'

Despite the tonic, Patience showed no interest in getting out of bed. The next evening, Clara took the books round to the Lewises' and knocked at their door. Marta welcomed her with a big hug that reduced her to tears. Benny gave her one too.

'I told Mam we should have fetched you round sooner,' he told her, 'but Da said we had to show respect and let you alone till you felt up to it.'

Clara felt indescribable relief being held by the kind Benny. She blurted out all her troubles about the shop and her mother's withdrawal, the legal problems and the mounting debt.

'I can't manage on me own and Jimmy's just a law unto himself,' she cried.

Marta soon had her sitting at the table with a bowl of hot broth and chunks of homemade bread in front of her. Oscar sat at the other end, placed his spectacles on his nose and began to look through the ledger and papers that Clara had brought round. Benny sat across the table watching her, grinning every time she looked up.

'Is Reenie working?' Clara asked once her meal was finished.

'Aye.' Benny nodded.

Marta fussed, 'We hardly see her. She is like the owl — sleeps all day and works all night.'

'She loves it, Mam,' Benny said.

'And Frank?' Clara asked shyly.

Benny smirked. 'Out with the Head Mistress.'

Marta clucked. 'He is at the meeting with Lillian. She is not headmistress.'

'Not yet,' Benny answered, 'but give her time.'

'Oh.' Clara tried to hide her disappointment. 'I thought he might have been playing at Cafe Cairo or the Rex.'

Marta shook her head and frowned. 'You not know? They both close down. No need for musicians in picture house. No one want to see silent films now.'

'But Cafe Cairo as well?' Clara was shocked.

'Aye,' Benny sighed, 'those places are closing overnight. People aren't ganin' out as much as they did. Not to posh places, at least.'

'How is your business doing?' Clara asked cautiously.

'Canny,' Benny said brightly. 'Hair never stops growing and Da says they can pay when they can afford it, if he knows the means test men have been in.'

Clara's insides churned at the mention of the new means test. She had heard customers gossiping in the shop about those who had suffered the humiliation of having officials prying round their houses to see if they had anything worth selling before they would give them a penny of relief. It was unthinkable that things would get that bad for her family.

She sat chatting happily for another hour, giving occasional glances at Oscar who was deeply absorbed in the paperwork.

Benny winked at her. 'If anyone can sort it out, Da will.'

They played a game of draughts while Marta sewed. Clara dreaded the moment she would have to return to the mournful flat and its unlit fire. Finally, Oscar took off his spectacles and rubbed his eyes. He stood up and limped over to Clara. He looked down at her with eyes as startlingly blue as Frank's. It made her chest ache.

'My dear,' he said, placing a hand on her shoulder, 'the books are bad, very bad. We will try to help, but we do not have much money to spare.'

'No,' Clara protested. 'I'm not asking for money.'

'I know,' he said, patting her shoulder.

Marta asked in concern, 'How bad, Oscar?'

He let out a long sigh. 'Mr Magee has not kept the books for months, so it is difficult to say. But there are many bills unpaid and no money to pay them. It is a matter of how long some of these creditors will wait. I'm surprised the bank has allowed it to go on so long.'

Clara went hot with shame. 'The manager is an old boxing friend of Dad's — I think he's been turning a blind eye.'

Oscar sat down beside her. 'And the shop — how is it doing?'

Clara shook her head. 'Badly.'

'You pay rent for it?' he asked quietly.

'Yes. But the bank manager says me dad bought the lease for it. So that must be worth something, musn't it?'

'Yes,' Oscar agreed. 'At least you could sell it and take on somewhere smaller, perhaps. But in the present slump, there aren't many who want to take on a lease. Is it a long one?'

Clara shrugged, feeling foolish for not knowing. 'Me and Mam should've taken more interest in that side of things. Mam's always been more interested in the buying — she's a good spender — and I just never thought to ask.'

'Why should you?' Oscar comforted her. 'You are young. This is not your fault. But the capitalists — they will not wait for your business to pick up again.'

'Aye,' Benny said indignantly, 'anything that doesn't make an instant profit has to gan to the wall. I bet your landlord is some rich bastard sitting in a country house somewhere.'

'Benjamin!' his mother remonstrated. 'Watch your language.'

'Well, it's true,' he said. They'll be in hock to some toff who's never been anywhere near Byfell in his life.'

'Benny is right,' Oscar grunted, 'but that doesn't help Clara.' He scratched his bald head as he thought. 'I have a friend in the Party — a lawyer, Max Sobel. I will ask him to take on the sorting of your father's will if you like.'

'That's kind,' Clara said, feeling awkward, 'but how can I pay him?'

'He will do it for free if I ask,' Oscar insisted. 'We all help each other.'

'He gets free shaves for life,' Benny said with a wink, moving round the table towards her.

Marta looked puzzled. 'But Max Sobel — he has the beard.'

Benny rolled his eyes. 'It was a joke, Mam. Didn't want Clara feeling beholden.'

Clara's heart squeezed at his kindness. Impulsively, she threw her arms round Benny and gave him a tearful hug.

Chapter 10

When Patience discovered that Clara had been to the Lewises for help she was livid.

'How dare you hang our dirty washing out for others to see? You had no right.'

Clara sparked back. 'What else was I to do with you lying in bed not bothering what day of the week it is? You may have given up, but I haven't.'

Patience choked back tears. 'How can you speak to me like that?'

'I'm sorry if it upsets you, Mam, but we're in real bother. You can't shut your eyes to it anymore.'

Patience pulled at her hair. 'I'll not have you going to this Bolshie lawyer. They hate business people like us.'

'Don't be daft—'

'No,' Patience said in agitation. 'We'll stick with Jack Hopkins's man.'

That Sunday, Clara rounded on Jimmy before he sneaked out.

'You're going to help me take all those caps and scarves from the loft and hawk them down Newcastle,' she ordered. 'So don't think you can skive off to the Cravens'.' Her brother was about to protest. 'Listen, Jimmy,' she cut him short, 'if we don't get some money soon, we'll be on the street. Just think what that'll do to Mam.'

Jimmy nodded sullenly and retreated to the loft.

They filled two boxes and lugged them on the tram down to Newcastle's quayside and the Sunday market. Clara walked with a box balanced on her head, to the amusement of some sailors.

'What tribe are you from, love?' one jeered.

'Geordie tribe,' she sparked back. 'And I'll have a headdress to suit you — unless you're too swell-headed.'

She dumped the box down near some railings and opened it up. The sailors drifted over to look.

'Hang the scarves over the railings,' she murmured to Jimmy as she turned to banter with the men. She persuaded one to buy a tweed cap and another a tartan scarf. In the next half-hour, Clara had sold half the contents of one box. But the prices the cheap goods were fetching were low. Scores of people roamed up and down the makeshift stalls, all on the lookout for bargains.

At the end of the morning, they had less than eight shillings to show for their hard selling. They packed what was left into the smaller box and returned home. Clara tried to be optimistic but she knew they could not live hand to mouth like this for much longer.

The following week, Mr Simmons turned up for the rent. They were a month in arrears and needed to pay for October too. Patience could not face him and stayed upstairs.

'If you could just give us a few more days,' Clara pleaded. 'My father's affairs still have to be sorted out.'

The portly agent huffed. 'I've been very patient with you, Miss Magee, and I don't wish to see you upset, but this is business. My clients are not running a charity.'

Clara nodded. 'Just another week, please.'

'The end of the week then,' he sighed, 'but no longer.'

When the agent left, Clara flew upstairs to confront her mother.

'What have you got that's worth selling?' she asked, hands on hips. 'Cos if we don't find the rent by the end of the week he'll send in the bailiffs.'

'They can't,' Patience gasped. 'Jack Hopkins has told all our creditors they must wait till after probate.'

'Fat Simmons isn't going to wait for such niceties,' Clara retorted.

That afternoon, Clara paid a visit to a local auctioneer. The following day, a man came round to assess their furniture. Patience sat, white-faced, while he made a list of her possessions. He sat down in Harry's wing-backed chair.

'I like this,' he said cheerfully. 'Not worth much, but I could fancy this mesel'.'

Clara tensed. She wanted to cry out that he could never have it; he was not worthy of sitting in her father's favourite chair. But she remained tight-lipped while he offered for it, along with the mahogany dining-room table and chairs, the teak sideboard and Patience's walnut wardrobe and dressing table. The amount would just cover the two months' rent, but no more.

'But we paid good money for these,' Patience said indignantly.

'They're second-hand, missus.' The man shrugged. 'You can try another auction, but you'll not get a fairer price.'

'We'll sell,' Clara said quickly. 'What about the pictures?'

'I'll give you five bob for the one of the sailing ship,' he grunted, 'and the same for the big mirror with the gilt frame.'

'Not the sailing ship,' Patience protested.

'The mirror then,' Clara compromised.

There and then, the auctioneer removed the furniture with the help of two men who had been waiting downstairs. They looked underfed, their clothes threadbare. Clara wondered how long they had been out of regular work. There were dozens like them loitering around the town eager for casual work like this. She must save Jimmy from such a fate. While the men staggered downstairs with the table and chairs, she steered Patience into the bedroom.

'Come on, Mam, I'll help you empty the wardrobe,' she coaxed.

She transferred her mother's clothes into her father's now empty wardrobe, a cheap piece of furniture that Patience had once painted dark brown. When it came to dismantling the dressing table, her mother sat on the bed and wept.

'You can have my washstand,' Clara promised. 'I'll find something in the store room.' She swallowed down unexpected tears at the sight of her mother's most personal possessions — her underwear and stockings, the dressing-table set and jewellery boxes — heaped on the floor.

When Jimmy turned up at teatime, he stared open-mouthed at the space where the dining table had been.

'No, we haven't been burgled,' Clara retorted. 'It's sold.'

He gave her a look of panic, as if he had not realised quite how bad their circumstances were.

'Help me carry up the table from the kitchen,' she said quickly. 'Once it's got a cloth on, we'll not notice the difference.'

That evening, they sat round the rough wooden table on an assortment of chairs; one from the shop, one from the attic and a kitchen stool. Clara served them up scrambled eggs and fried potato, but Jimmy complained that he was still hungry. He went out again muttering that Clarkie would buy him a bag of chips.

'I thought I might pop over to Reenie's,' Clara mentioned.

Patience looked up in dismay. She was hunched on the sofa. 'Please don't leave me,' she whimpered. 'Not tonight.'

Clara sighed. 'All right.'

She switched on the radio and turned it till she found some dance-hall music. 'I'll be back in a minute.' Clara returned with her mother's pearl-handled hairbrush. That would be their last possession to be pawned, she vowed. Sitting down, she coaxed, 'Let me brush out your hair, Mam. I've seen smarter scarecrows.'

Patience let her take out the pins and brush through the tangles. The music filled the quiet room and Clara brushed in time to the easy rhythms just as her mother had so often done for her.

'That's lovely, pet,' Patience murmured, eyes closed, face relaxing for the first time in days.

Clara wondered when it was that she had slipped into her mother's role and Patience into hers. As she brushed gently at the dyed hair that was beginning to show grey roots again, she was almost overwhelmed by the weight of responsibility she carried for her family.

'Things'll get better,' she said, as much to reassure herself as her mother.

***

Two days later, they were roused early by a banging on the shop door. Clara stumbled out of bed and peered down. There was a van parked in the empty street.

'Open up,' a man shouted, hammering on the door again.

She pulled on her clothes and ran downstairs, through the darkened shop, and opened up. A man with a grey moustache waved a piece of paper at her. Another burly man and a boy about Jimmy's age stood behind him.

'I've come for the goods,' the front man grunted, stepping close.

'What goods?' Clara asked.

'Stock,' he said. 'Silverdale's want it back; it's all in the letter.'

Clara looked at him aghast. 'You can't have it. It's paid for.'

'I'm just doing me job, miss, and boss says fetch back the stock. Outstanding bills, he says. Shop's ganin' to close.'

'No it's not,' Clara cried.

'Just read the letter, miss,' he said brusquely, nodding at his mates to follow him. They barged past Clara. She stood shaking, trying to make sense of the letter in her hand. Silverdale's, the fancy goods warehouse, were taking action after repeated invoices had gone unpaid. It appeared none of the stock belonged to them: it was all on credit. Fear rose in Clara's throat. She thought she would vomit.

She ran back upstairs, screaming, 'Mam! Jimmy! They're taking everything!'

Jimmy came leaping down the attic stairs. Patience appeared in her kimono, looking dishevelled and confused.

'The men from Silverdale's,' Clara gabbled. 'We've got to stop them.'

Patience looked terrified. 'We can't—'

Jimmy sprang past Clara without a word. She followed him back down.

'What you think you're doing?' Jimmy shouted. The men hardly glanced up from methodically packing up boxes and carrying them out. Jimmy lunged at the boy. 'Stop it, I said.'

The boy staggered backwards and Jimmy took a swing at him. The burly man turned and stopped the boy from falling. He faced up to Jimmy, shoving him back.

'Any trouble and I'll knock yer teeth out, son.'

Jimmy went red with fury. 'I'll get Vinnie Craven on you!'

The man snorted, 'Never heard of him,' and carried on working.

Jimmy stood clenching and unclenching his fists. Clara went to stand by him, but he ran out of the shop in humiliation. She could do nothing but watch the men dismantle the shop, helpless to stop them. When one of them lifted the coat stand displaying winter hats, she grabbed hold of it.

'That's not Silverdale's,' she hissed, 'that was me dad's.'

He shrugged and left it. They went without a word, slamming the doors of the van and chugging off down the street with a belch of blue smoke. Clara bolted the doors and let out a sob. There was nothing left to sell apart from some cheap clothes and boxes of buttons. She found her mother in the sitting room, rocking back and forth in front of the dead fire, crying.

Clara crouched down beside her. 'Someone's put the word out the shop's closing,' she said angrily. 'Now they'll all be after their money. We'll have to go back and see Mr Hopkins, beg him for a loan.'

'Where's Jimmy?' Patience wailed.

'Ran off,' Clara answered. 'The men showed him up.'

'He's no fighter, poor lad,' Patience whispered.

'Maybe he's going to have to learn,' Clara said grimly.

***

'It's out of the question,' Mr Hopkins said, when Clara asked for a temporary loan. 'I'm in trouble from head office as it is, allowing your father so much credit. You've nothing to offer as security.'

'There's the lease,' Clara reminded him.

Mr Hopkins looked uncomfortable. 'Assigning the lease to someone else is the only way you are going to pay off the debts you already owe, Miss Magee. You must look for someone to take it over as soon as possible. In the present climate I know that will be difficult, but I can approach my clients to see if anyone is interested.' He cleared his throat. 'Otherwise . . .'

'Otherwise what?'

'We'll have to take measures to recoup our money.'

'Meaning?'

'You'll be declared bankrupt and the bailiffs will be sent in,' he said, going very red.

Clara's look was withering. 'They'll find nowt worth having now.'

'I'm sorry,' he said, with a helpless wave of the hands. 'Your father was a good friend, a popular man. I wish I could help more, but we have to be businesslike.'

Clara rose and said in a bitter voice, 'Aye, if everyone was friends with Harry Magee who say they were, we wouldn't be in this bother, would we?'

That evening Jimmy returned with bruises and cuts to his face and hands.

Patience cried, 'Jimmy pet! Where've you been?'

'Who've you been fighting?' Clara exclaimed.

Jimmy tried to look defiant, but his chin trembled as he said, 'Lads set on us.'

'Who did?' Clara demanded.

'The Laidlaws.'

'But why? They're customers,' Patience gasped, while Clara filled a bowl of clean water to clean his cuts.

'Said me dad owed old man Laidlaw money at the betting,' Jimmy gulped, 'and we had to pay or else. Said they'd waited long enough out of respect, but they'd not wait any longer.'

Clara's stomach turned. This was just the start of it. It was going to be like Vinnie said, men from Harry's past chasing them for money.

'They must've heard about the clear-out,' Clara said. 'They'll be queuing up to get what's left.'

'But we've nothing to pay them with,' Patience wailed. 'What are we to do?'

Clara carried on bathing Jimmy's cuts. 'Go back to the pawnshop, what else is there? When people see we've got nowt left, they'll stop bothering us.'

All that week, Clara and Jimmy went backwards and forwards to Mr Slater's and another pawnbroker's in Newcastle that specialised in jewellery. Trinket boxes, photograph frames, cutlery, linen, a fur stole and their best shoes all went. The lads who were harassing Jimmy were paid off and Clara put a notice in the shop window advertising a closing down sale on the Saturday. She was called back to the bank on the Friday. Mr Hopkins had found a buyer for the lease.

'He's offering twenty-five pounds.' Mr Hopkins smiled.

Clara's face fell. 'Twenty-five pounds for a five-year lease? But that's not even enough to clear the debts, is it?'

The manager pursed his lips. 'No, but it's a fair offer in the circumstances.'

'You mean they know we're desperate, so can push down the price?' Clara was scathing. 'Who is it?'

'I can't say.' Mr Hopkins frowned. 'But he's a reputable businessman. I know this is distressing for you, Miss Magee, but as executor to your father's estate I strongly recommend you accept,'

Clara sighed. 'Give us till next week to decide.'

Word got back to the Lewises and Reenie came rushing round. 'You never said things were this bad,' she cried.

'It's all happened that quick,' Clara said in bewilderment. 'We have to get rid of the lease, or else they'll make us bankrupt. So far we've had a stingy offer of twenty-five pounds. Our debts are fifty.'

'But what'll you do?' Reenie was full of concern. 'It's your home.'

Clara's eyes glittered with tears. 'We'll find somewhere smaller. I'll get a job.' Really, she had no idea. She lay awake at night frantic with worry, imagining the worst - Jimmy caught thieving, her mother in the workhouse. What had seemed like pure nightmare a few weeks ago now seemed possible.

'Come round tonight and have your tea with us,' Reenie urged. 'All of you.'

Clara accepted gratefully, exhausted by the efforts of the day. But Patience refused, so Jimmy would not go either.

Clara snapped, 'Well I'm going; they're the best friends we've got.'

To her delight Frank was also at home and not out with Lillian. They all made a fuss of her, showing no offence at being snubbed by Patience. After tea, Oscar reached for his newspaper while the others sat round the fire. Marta encouraged Frank to play his violin. Clara watched him while he bent with concentration over his instrument and the bow soared back and forth. She loved him when he played, the intensity of the music matched by his look, his handsome face stirred into passionate nods and frowns.

The music was so beautiful, tears caught in the back of her throat and she could not speak for several minutes after he finished. Frank glanced over and smiled. Clara burst into tears.

'Look what you've done,' Benny cried, rushing to fling an arm round her. 'And we're supposed to be cheering her up.'

'Sorry.' Frank blushed.

Clara shook her head. She could not explain how moved she had been.

'Play a polka,' Marta ordered. 'Dance, dance! That will make Clara happy.'

The next moment, the table was being pushed back and the Lewises were on their feet. Benny pulled her into his arms and they barged around the cluttered room. Clara laughed for the first time in ages.

Afterwards they sank into chairs and Marta fetched them glasses of water. 'Now is the time, Oscar.' She nodded at her husband. He stood up and came over to stand with his back to the fire, facing them as if to give a speech.

'We have a proposal to make, Clara,' he said sombrely. 'Our premises here are very small.'

'Squashed like sardines, *ja*? Marta interjected.

'We could do with bigger premises,' Oscar went on. 'Frank has always wanted to sell books as well as cut hair.'

Frank smiled. 'Barber's shops are like debating societies - so we can sell them radical books as well as a short back and sides.'

Oscar scratched his bald head nervously. 'We would like to make your mother an offer for Magee's shop.'

Clara stared. 'You - you want to buy the lease off us?' she stammered.

Oscar nodded. 'We will pay sixty pounds for the lease.'

Clara's eyes flooded with tears again. She glanced at Reenie, knowing she must have told her parents what was needed to cover their debts. She was overcome by their kindness. 'But you've hardly had time to think about it,' she said, blinking back tears.

'We've been talking of moving for ages,' Reenie assured her.

'It's not charity,' Benny was blunt, 'it's solidarity.'

'You must talk it over with your mother first, of course,' Oscar said.

Clara nodded. 'Thank you,' she said, her voice quavering. She glanced around at their compassionate, smiling faces and wished she could tell them how much she loved them. 'All of you — thanks.'

Chapter 11

It was the end of the year before the affairs were finally sorted. By then, Clara was working as a part-time cleaner in the offices of lawyer Max Sobel. He was a jovial, plump man in his fifties with a booming laugh, who littered the office with half-smoked cigarettes and half-drunk cups of tea. Once Clara could not resist tidying the piles of papers that were scattered across the room as if by a storm, and this was the only time she saw him lose his temper.

'Now I can't find anything!' he shouted. The next day he apologised and asked her to clean his flat once a week too.

Hopkins was amazed at the offer from the Lewises, but urged Patience to take it. Clara knew her mother resented her hairdresser's taking over her beloved shop. She muttered about upstarts and foreigners, but had no stomach for resistance. She was growing thinner and more fragile, crying at the slightest criticism.

Vinnie, who had been toing and froing between Tyneside and London for much of the autumn, began turning up in his sleek car, with an errand for Jimmy, or to whisk Patience away to have tea with Dolly. He offered Clara a part-time job in his small garments factory but she turned it down. Patience scolded her.

'Why didn't you take it?'

'I can't sew for toffee,' Clara was dismissive, 'and it looks a dump. I'd rather work for Mr Sobel any day. He's got contacts — I'll get some'at better soon enough.'

'Just don't go getting on the wrong side of Mr Craven, that's all,' Patience fretted.

'I'm not,' Clara said impatiently. 'Anyway, why are you so worried what Mr Craven thinks?' But her mother had no reply.

It was Clara who trailed around finding somewhere cheaper for them to rent. Reenie went with her when she could. Many of the rooms were filthy, leaking and crumbling with mould. In the end, it was Max who told her that the one-bedroomed flat above his was unexpectedly vacant because his neighbour had done a flit. It was next to the railway station and the windows rattled loudly every time a train went past, but it was weather-tight and Clara accepted at once.

Dolly Craven did her best to put Patience off, and when Vinnie came back from another business trip he reproached Clara for acting too hastily. Vinnie had the knack of praising Clara for her independence and common sense, while all the time undermining her decisions.

'I admire you, lass.' He smiled all the way up to his gold-flecked eyes. 'You don't let anything get you down. But those streets round the station are rough. Have you thought about coming home in the dark?'

'I worry about that too,' Patience fretted.

'Let me lend you a little bit,' Vinnie offered, 'so you can pick somewhere more . . . respectable.'

'No thank you, Mr Craven,' Clara said stoutly, 'we're borrowing from no one. Flat's canny — and if it's good enough for the likes of Mr Sobel then it's good enough for us.'

Vinnie shook his head regretfully. 'Promise me you'll ask for my help before rushing into things next time.'

'Thank you,' Clara said warily. 'If we need it, we'll ask.'

Though she would never tell the Cravens, Clara knew that she had to find more work if they were to be able to afford the rent on the tiny flat in Minto Street. They had nothing spare after clearing Harry's debts and nearly all their possessions had been pawned. Even her mother's pearl-handled hairbrush. It had been a bitter day when Clara had taken a last small bagful to Mr Slater's, battling a raw easterly wind just before Christmas. The print of the sailing ship had gone too.

But at least they had avoided the means test and parish handouts, and she felt fiercely proud of that. They would start again and owe nobody anything from now on. They had a table and chairs, a double bed which she would share with her mother and a put-you-up for Jimmy to sleep on. Jimmy was her main worry.

All autumn he had been a law unto himself. He came home wearing clothes that did not belong to him, often with small parcels of food or a pocketful of coins. When she challenged him, he swore he earned them doing casual jobs for people she had never heard of. Patience had taken up smoking to calm her nerves and sometimes he would turn up with a full packet of cigarettes and flourish them at her.

'Are they paid for?' Clara would snap.

'I've earned them,' he always replied. 'Stop yer fussin'.'

She agonised whether to ask Vinnie to take her brother in hand, but decided against it. In the New Year, Clara began cleaning at other businesses in the same building as Max's on his recommendation; an accountant's and, more importantly, the offices of the Tyne Times. She preferred to go in very early rather than after they closed, so she could be back to look after Patience who grew morose if left too long on her own.

One evening, Max knocked at their door and asked for a word. Clara invited him in. He stood warming his hands at the fire, chatting pleasantly to Patience and offering her a cigarette. He refused a cup of tea. Clara waited to hear the reason for the visit.

Max blew out his cheeks, looking embarrassed.

'I wondered if you'd noticed — whether you've seen anyone going into my flat at all in recent weeks? While I'm at work, that is.'

Clara shook her head. 'Why do you ask?'

'Well.' Max puffed and blew. 'I know I'm not the tidiest of men, but things appear to be going missing.' Clara looked at him aghast.

Patience said querulously, 'You're not suggesting Clara's taking things?'

'No, not at all!' Max cried. 'I trust her completely.'

Clara flushed. 'But I'm very careful to lock up after I've been in, Mr Sobel. And Mam's here nearly all the time. She'd have heard if anyone was downstairs. Wouldn't you, Mam?'

Patience nodded. 'Unless I had the wireless on, I suppose.'

There was an awkward pause, then Max said cheerfully, 'Not to worry. I just thought I'd ask.'

Clara followed him to the door. 'What sorts of things are missing?'

'Oh, well, nothing major. Cigarettes, loose change.' He gave a baffled laugh. 'And socks.'

'We'll keep a look out,' Clara promised and closed the door behind him. She came back frowning. She went to check under the mat by the fire. The key to the downstairs flat was there, in its usual place.

'Mam?'

'What?' Patience eyed her.

Clara shook her head. 'No, nothing.'

Two days later, Clara hurried her work and returned home earlier than usual. Patience was still in bed. Clara slipped downstairs and crouched in the tiny understairs cupboard, opposite Max's door. She waited. Cramp seized her legs and she was on the point of giving up when the front door opened. She heard footsteps start up the stairs, then stop. Softly they turned and came back down again. A man's tread stopped outside the downstairs flat door. Clara heard the scrape of a key in the lock. Was it Max? The door closed quietly.

She emerged, stretching her stiff limbs. Someone was in the flat, but was it her employer? She had to find out. If it was a stranger, she would run out into the street and shout for help. Heart beating fast, she tried the door. It opened directly into Max's sitting room. A figure bending over his desk jerked round. They stared at each other in mutual horror.

'Jimmy!' Clara gasped, her worst fears confirmed. 'What are you doing in here?'

He recovered quickly. 'Door was open — came in to check nowt was wrong.'

'Don't lie,' Clara said, furious, 'I heard you unlock it. Give me that key.'

'What key?'

She dashed forward and seized his hand, prising the key out of his grasp. It was new and shiny. 'You've had your own cut,' she cried in disgust. 'How long you been stealing from Mr Sobel? Don't deny it. Those cigarettes you've been fetching Mam — and the money — they're all from here, aren't they? You haven't been working for anyone. You're a common little thief!' Clara was so angry that she slapped her brother on the cheek.

He pushed her back. 'Leave off us,' he cried. 'He won't mind. You said yourself he's that untidy, he won't even notice.'

Clara looked at him aghast. 'That's not the point. And anyhow, he has noticed. He came up to tell us two nights ago. I was that ashamed he might have thought it was me.'

'Well, we need it more than he does.' Jimmy was defensive. 'It's just a bit extra on your wages.'

Clara was livid. 'Don't you dare bring me into this. I earn those wages through hard graft. What you're doing is stealing. And just cos it's from a good man who might not condemn you doesn't make it any less wrong.'

'I'm sorry.' Jimmy swallowed. 'It's these lads. They make me take things — say they'll give us a hiding if I don't.'

'What lads?' Clara said worriedly. 'Not the Laidlaws?'

'Aye,' Jimmy admitted. 'They've never let us alone since you paid them that money.'

Clara hunched in dismay. 'Oh, Jimmy lad. You mustn't let them threaten you.'

'How can I stop 'em?' He looked forlorn.

'You'll have to learn to stand up for yourself more,' she sighed.

After a moment, Jimmy whispered. 'You don't have to tell Mr Sobel about this, do you?'

'No,' Clara said, forcing herself to be firm with him, 'but you do.'

'He's a lawyer,' Jimmy protested. 'He'll nick me.'

'That's up to him. But I tell you this for free; you stop your thieving right this minute or I'll throw you out the house.'

He scowled. 'Mam wouldn't let yer.'

'Mam doesn't pay the rent,' Clara snapped.

That evening, Clara marched Jimmy downstairs to confess to Max. He handed over the forged key, crimson-faced, and muttered an apology.

Max nodded, embarrassed. 'Well, it was brave of you to own up. Thank you.'

'And that's not all,' Clara prompted her brother.

Jimmy mumbled, 'Aye. I'll pay you back by doing jobs — clean yer shoes, yer windows, fetch stuff.'

Max shrugged, but Clara said, 'Don't you let him off, Mr Sobel.'

Later, in bed, Clara talked it over with a shocked Patience.

'What we going to do with him?' Clara sighed.

'I blame myself,' Patience whispered. 'I should've kept an eye on what he was up to. Our Jimmy a thief! I'm sorry, pet. I'm no use to you anymore. It's just since your father died — my nerves. . .' She broke off.

Clara cradled her in the dark. 'Don't upset yourself. You'll get better.'

Patience cried into her shoulder. 'I'm that lucky to have you, lass. I don't know how I'd manage without you.'

'You won't have to, Mam,' Clara promised, cuddling her like a child.

***

The next day, Clara came to a decision. After cleaning at the offices, she washed, brushed out her hair, put on her best clothes and went down to Craven's boxing hall. Dolly gave her a condescending smile, but told her Vincent was in a meeting with another promoter from London. Clara hung around waiting. When he eventually emerged, he was escorting a buxom, well-dressed woman and laughing about some fight.

Spotting Clara, he smiled with surprise and introduced them.

'Madame Gautier's up from London,' he explained. This is Clara — daughter of Harry Magee. You remember Harry, welterweight champion before the War?'

The women nodded at each other. Clara said, 'Sorry. I can come back later.'

'No, no.' Vinnie stopped her. 'We're having a late lunch in town, before Madame Gautier's train. I've a few minutes.'

He called his mother over to look after the promoter and ushered Clara into his office.

She had never been in before. It was immaculately furnished with comfortable chairs, a roll-top desk and a large cabinet holding silver trophies. The walls were lined with photos of boxers and their coaches. A deep red carpet deadened the noise of their shoes. It was like an oasis of peace and comfort amid the noisy, draughty hall and its warren of rooms. Vinnie steered her into a seat. The room smelled of polish and hyacinths. There was a bowl of the white and blue flowers on a stand in the window. The glass beyond an iron grille was frosted, allowing no view of the drab riverside street beyond.

Clara stopped staring around her and came to the point. 'It's Jimmy. He's been in a bit of bother.'

Vinnie was full of concern. 'Is he hurt?'

'Not that kind of bother. Stealing,' she said, glancing away, 'for other lads.'

'I see. Do you need money to pay someone off?' he asked.

Clara looked at him in surprise and shook her head. 'I want — I wondered if you could find Jimmy a job? Not just hanging around with lads outside here, waiting for the odd errand.' She eyed him boldly. 'I mean a proper job; an apprenticeship or something. You have contacts, businesses. He won't listen to me or Mam, but he will to you, Mr Craven. He looks up to you. And there must be something he could do. Even if it's for hardly any pay. It's not the money that's important; it's keeping him off the streets where he's getting into mischief. It's giving him something to do. Toughen him up so he won't keep getting picked on by older lads. Cos sooner or later our Jimmy's going to get caught stealing for them. The shame would kill Mam.'

For a long moment he gazed at her with his shrewd dark eyes. Suddenly he reached out and covered her hand with his. Hers was trembling, his was warm and reassuring.

'He's a lucky lad, having such a caring sister,' he murmured. 'You've got guts coming here and asking. Do you know how many times I get people knocking on me door asking favours for little Tommy or Jimmy or whoever? Just cos they were friendly with me dad and think the world owes them a living.'

'I'm not asking favours,' Clara bristled. 'It's just you said to come to you for help if we needed it.'

'And now you do?' Vinnie fixed her with his unblinking look.

Clara found it impossible to look away. She nodded.

He smiled. 'Of course I'll try to do something for Jimmy. He's a canny young 'un.'

'Yes. He just needs steering in the right direction,' Clara agreed.

Vinnie nodded. 'Bit discipline and hard work, it's amazing what it does to a lad. But only if they're led right. Got to have loyalty. Got to have the right man at the top — firm but fair.'

Clara watched him. She had not seen this side of Vinnie, the firm taskmaster. She was used to the suave businessman, the charming ladies' man, the show-off. She was encouraged by this more serious outlook. It was just what her brother needed to keep him from petty crime and the influence of wilder lads.

'We'll see what we can do,' Vinnie said, patting her hand. 'Send Jimmy down here tomorrow and I'll have a word.'

'Thank you.' Clara smiled and stood up. She allowed him to take her by the elbow and guide her out.

Within the week, Jimmy was boasting proudly that he was going to be working at Craven's garage.

'I'm just cleaning cars and running errands to start with,' he said excitedly, 'but any free time, I'm allowed in the gym. Mr Craven says I'll be a champ like me dad some day. And he's giving me a bit pocket money. Tide me over till he sees how I go.'

Clara glanced at Patience. She had sworn her mother to secrecy over the visit to Vinnie. Her mother smiled back.

'That's grand news, son, really grand.'

'Aye,' Clara agreed. 'Good for you.' Silently, she prayed that this might be the turning point in their fortunes. Though she would never admit that to Vinnie Craven.

Chapter 12

It was on one of the walking trips with the Lewises that the suggestion of journalism first came up. Frank fell into step beside Clara as they walked along a coastal path north of Whitley Bay. She glanced back nervously at Lillian, but she was deep in conversation with Reenie. The spring air was bracing and Frank had to lean towards her to be heard. Clara's heart thumped with familiar excitement.

'How is work?' he asked.

'Regular but dull,' she admitted. 'Mr Sobel's canny, but it's lonely working in the early morning when no one's around. Sometimes I stay on at the newspaper office and make them cups of tea; just to have a bit chat before I go home. Mam's started going down the boxing hall of a morning - making coffee for Dolly Craven and helping out. Sometimes she does a bit at the garage so she can keep an eye on our Jimmy. It's grand that she's feeling better and we need every extra penny—' She broke off, blushing. 'Sorry, I'm gabbling as usual.'

He smiled. 'I like you gabbling.'

Clara laughed, feeling suddenly tongue-tied. They walked on in silence, side by side, Clara searching for something to keep him in conversation.

'I wish I could be a reporter at the paper and not just sweep up their mess,' she blurted out. Immediately she regretted speaking her thoughts. Frank would laugh at her for having such pretensions.

'Why don't you?' he replied. She eyed him but he looked quite serious.

'It's just a daft dream,' she said. 'I can't even write.'

'You keep a diary, don't you?'

Clara's eyes widened. 'How do you know that?'

'You mentioned it once after you'd had some bother with a tramp,' Frank answered. 'Said you put all your thoughts down and it helped you work things out.'

Clara covered her face. 'Did I?'

'Aye.' He smiled. 'And you said you'd kept a diary since you were twelve and Reenie couldn't get over it - she didn't even know you had one.'

'Fancy you remembering.' Clara laughed. 'Well, it's true, but it doesn't mean I can write things in a newspaper.'

'No,' Frank agreed, 'but you don't need to be a great writer for that. What matters more is an eye for a story — being inquisitive about things, about people.'

'Being nosy, you mean? I can do that all right.' She grinned. 'But where would I start? They're never going to ask the cleaner for stories.'

'Do you read the *Tyne Times*?' Frank asked her.

Clara nodded. 'I fish the old copies out the bin and take them home for a read.'

'So you know the kinds of stories they like,' he went on. 'Local news and sport mostly, a bit of gossip about well-known people, the odd disaster.'

'Yes,' Clara agreed, 'they love a hard-luck story or man-makes-good type of tale.'

'Look for your own stories,' Frank encouraged her. 'Use the contacts that you have which the staff reporters don't. Boxers, for instance. You could get an interview with Danny Watts or one of the young lads coming through under Vinnie Craven. For a lot of these lads it's the only way out of poverty and unemployment.'

'They don't like anything too political, mind.' Clara was doubtful.

'That's where your skill as a reporter comes in,' Frank told her. 'You tell them a story but underneath the message is clear; the working class bear the brunt in any slump. Capitalism has failed.'

Clara snorted. 'Not sure my writing's up to all of that. The Admiral's very sensitive to words like capitalism. "Dash it, Magee, we're not writing a Bolshevik manifesto,"' she mimicked.

Frank chuckled. 'Who's the Admiral?'

'The editor, Lance Jellicoe,' Clara explained. 'It's his nickname.'

'After Lord Jellicoe, the admiral?' Frank guessed.

Clara nodded. 'They're not related, but he loves people to think they are. And he loves sport, so a boxing story might be a good idea.' Clara's interest quickened. 'Or I could write about this hiking group — the new craze for fresh air and exercise — couldn't I?'

'Aye.' Frank nodded. 'Tell them how the Socialists are looking after the bodies as well as the minds of ordinary people.'

Clara nudged him. 'You don't give up, do you?'

'Never,' he murmured, 'and neither should you. Keep writing, Clara, till the Admiral takes your stories.'

He met her excited look. Her insides lurched at the intense blue of his eyes. She never had summoned up the courage to tell him how she felt. They were so rarely alone like this and even now she could hear the others gaining on them, as the path widened into a field of sheep.

'Hey.' Benny caught them up. 'What you two plotting? Revolution?' He threw an arm possessively round Clara.

'Nothing less, Benny lad.' Frank smiled and slowed his pace. The next moment, Benny and Clara were ahead and he was dropping back to wait for the others.

'Tell me what you were saying.' Benny grinned, putting his head next to hers. 'You were that close you looked sewn together. Lillian was so worried, she sent me to spy on you.'

Clara felt annoyance. 'There was no need. Frank was just asking about work. He thinks I should try my hand at newspaper stories.'

'You be a journalist?' Benny sounded astonished.

Clara pulled away. 'And why not? Do you think I'm not up to it cos I'm a Magee and not a brainy Lewis?'

Benny was quick to reassure her. 'No, it's a grand idea. You'd make a canny reporter. I'd spill the beans to you, any day.'

'I'm serious,' Clara huffed.

'So am I,' Benny said, 'and I'll do anything I can to help; keep me ears open at the barber's for any news. You'd be amazed what people tell you.'

'Aye, that's what I need,' Clara enthused, 'a big story to make them sit up and notice me at the paper.'

'That's my lass,' Benny said proudly, kissing her swiftly on the cheek before she could dodge away.

At the end of the hike, Clara was so euphoric about the idea of writing for the newspaper that she agreed to go with Benny to the pictures the following Wednesday. He teased her during the newsreels, keeping up a low commentary about reporter Magee until someone behind told him to be quiet. He plied her with chocolates and made her laugh. Afterwards he walked her home all the way to Minto Street, their chatter about the film never stopping. She had the key in the lock and the door half open when he pulled her back into the dark and kissed her roundly on the lips.

Clara should not have been surprised. Benny had been angling to walk out with her for ages. Yet it was a shock to feel his lips on hers; moist, enthusiastic, playful. Her first proper kiss. Momentarily, her pulse quickened. She felt grown up, excited. But then she looked at his boyish good looks, his eager face, and remembered that this was Benny. She felt the same mix of affection and irritation that she had for her brother. She was not in love with him. Right up until this moment, Clara had not been quite sure. Now she was.

When he bent towards her again, she pulled away. 'Night, Benny,' she said firmly, stepping through the door. 'Thanks for a canny evening.'

'Can we do this again?' he asked.

'Go to the pictures, you mean?'

'Aye, that's what I mean.' He grinned. He looked so hopeful.

'Maybes,' she half agreed.

'Champion!' he said, as she closed the door.

That probably would have been the end of it, if Patience had not made such a fuss. Jimmy had been out in the street that night and seen the kiss in the doorway. He had told his mother out of amusement, but the next evening Patience rounded on her daughter.

'Kissing in the street,' she said in disgust. 'What came over you, Clara?'

'I'm nearly eighteen,' Clara exclaimed. 'I've been earning a wage for years and keeping our heads above water. Don't treat me like a bairn.'

'But with that lad!' Patience scolded.

'What's wrong with Benny?'

'What's right with him?' Patience cried. 'He's the worst of that Leizmann lot, always out to cause trouble with his placards and his leaflets. Dolly says he tries to stir up the lads at the hall about going on hunger marches. I wonder he has time to cut anyone's hair. Course, his parents have no control over him.'

'Probably agree with what he's doing,' Clara answered.

'Exactly my point,' Patience said. 'They're a strange lot and he's a troublemaker. The Cravens agree with me. You deserve a better lad than him.'

Clara was stung. 'You've told the Cravens about this?'

'They care about you. Dolly says—'

'I don't care what she says,' Clara said crossly. 'And Mr Craven's hardly one to talk. He's courted half of Tyneside according to the *Tyne Times*.'

'Can't believe what you read in the papers,' Patience said, flustered. 'Especially that one. I'll never forgive the things they said about your father . . .' Her voice quavered.

The criticism riled Clara even further. The paper was going to be her way out of drudgery whether her mother liked it or not.

'Benny's canny,' she said defensively, 'and I'll see him if I want.'

'Clara!'

'And by the way, I'm going to write for the *Tyne Times*. I've had enough of cleaning to last a lifetime.'

Clara turned her back on her mother's shocked face, glared at Jimmy for making trouble and marched into the bedroom, slamming the door. That night, she sat up late, writing an article on hiking on scraps of brown paper. The next day, after work, she went straight round to the Lewises' to interview them about the hiking club. Frank was out delivering a second-hand book to a housebound customer, but Benny was more than keen to give his comments. Reenie appeared yawning, having come off her shift.

'There's a meeting in town of the Women's League of Health and Beauty,' she told her friend. 'They're keen on exercise. You could cover that for your story too.'

'When?' Clara was eager.

'This evening, seven o'clock at the Hippodrome.'

'Can you come?' Clara asked.

'I'd like to but I'm working,' Reenie sighed.

Clara regretted that she saw so little of her friend these days. But they were both lucky to have jobs at all and she knew Reenie's steady income was a great help to her family.

As she left, Benny followed her out. 'Can I see you Saturday? There's a dance on at the town hall. Fundraiser for the Minority Movement.'

'What's that?'

Benny rolled his eyes. 'Thought you were supposed to be a reporter?' he teased. 'The Movement supports the unemployed. Do what the big unions should be doing for their members but aren't.'

'Sounds political.' She frowned.

'It is,' Benny replied. 'But we can just dance and talk about health and beauty if you like.'

Clara laughed. 'Now you're talking. What time?'

'I'll come and fetch you at six; you can have your tea here first.'

Clara nodded. She felt a small twinge of guilt that her ready acceptance had more to do with the chance of seeing Frank at Saturday tea than dancing with Benny.

Clara walked all the way into Newcastle to save on the tram fare and attended the meeting at the Hippodrome. The downstairs was half full, mostly of young women in their twenties. She exchanged names with the well-dressed, dark-haired woman sitting next to her. Willa Templeton laughed nervously when Clara asked her why she was there.

'My husband thinks it will do me good. Get my figure back after having Baby.'

Clara glanced enviously at the woman's shapely figure. She felt scrawny in comparison. 'You don't look like you've just had a baby,' she exclaimed.

Willa looked pleased. 'Well, Baby's nearly two and I still can't get into most of my wedding trousseau. George has a point, but he's a bit of an exercise fanatic, if you ask me. Takes cold baths and long runs. Ex-army. What about you?'

Clara paused while this torrent of information sank in. 'I'm here to write about it for the local paper,' she said boldly.

Willa arched her plucked eyebrows. The hand she put on Clara's arm was well manicured, the nails immaculately polished in pink.

'You're a journalist?' she gasped. 'How exciting. Will I be able to read about myself? George would like that. He's always got an eye out for publicity. Thinks it's good for business. That's why he likes me to be involved in charity work too. Dogs' homes and veterans' clubs are his favourites.'

'What sort of business?' Clara asked.

Willa waved a hand. 'Some sort of manufacturing — machine tools. I'm not very up on it all. George doesn't talk about it with me, of course.'

'Is that Templeton's at Wallsend?'

71

Willa looked impressed. 'You've heard of it?'

Clara did not like to say she had overheard Frank and Benny fulminating over the firm's refusal to allow in the unions. 'Oh, yes, it's well known.' She smiled.

'My, my.' Willa preened. 'George will be pleased.'

After that, the presentation began, followed by a fitness display to music. The cheerful organiser promised both better health and sociability to those who joined. Their regime was a mix of remedial exercises, Indian yoga and Greek dance, she enthused, which would aid 'graceful deportment and figure training'.

'Movement is life,' she said eagerly, 'and as you see, we have exercises suitable for all women no matter what their age or ability.'

Clara scribbled down her words as best she could in the darkened auditorium. Afterwards, she spoke to two or three others for their opinions. On the way out, Willa caught her up.

'Clara, will you join?'

Clara was frank. 'Can't afford to at the moment.'

'That's a shame.' Willa looked disappointed. 'Listen, I could lend you the subscription if you like.'

'That's very kind, but I couldn't accept it,' Clara replied. 'I might join later in the year.'

'I hope so,' Willa said. 'I'm rather nervous of joining on my own.' She rummaged in her handbag and handed Clara a card. 'Here's my number. Telephone me if you decide to go for it.'

Clara took it with a smile. 'I will, I promise.'

It was only later, on the tram home, that she studied the card more closely. The Templetons lived in Jesmond, one of the most well-to-do areas of Newcastle. Their home was so grand it had a name not a number: Madras House. The nearest Clara had ever been to Jesmond was walking in the steep-sided dene that lay at its foot. Carefully, she tucked the card inside her notes and thrust them deep into her pocket.

That night, she could not sleep for the excitement of the evening. She lit a candle at the kitchen table and wrote her impressions of the meeting. In the morning, she waited impatiently at Max's office to show him the article.

'What do you think?' she asked anxiously. 'Is it good enough for the *Tyne Times*?'

He frowned. 'Some of it's good - the quotes from people - that's lively. But it's a bit jumbled.' He waved the scraps of brown paper at her. 'And it's in a thousand bits.'

Clara sighed in disappointment. 'It's rubbish, isn't it?'

'No, not at all,' Max encouraged her. 'Look, why don't you rewrite it on fresh paper — you can have some of mine. Then we'll get Miss Fisher to type it up for you.'

'Ta, Mr Sobel. That's grand.' Clara grinned.

'And why don't you make it into two articles - one on the hiking, one on the Women's League of Health and Beauty? Keep them short. Jellicoe can't read long sentences,' Max said dryly.

Clara set to rewriting. With smiles and pleading and offers to make the tea, she persuaded Max's secretary, Miss Fisher, to type up the articles.

As she was on the point of rushing off, Miss Fisher asked, 'Would you like to borrow my coat and hat? Smarten yourself up, eh?'

Clara was grateful. Her own coat was a shabby second-hand one and her best felt hat had been pawned. The secretary's style was a little old-fashioned, but smart, and they were a similar size. Miss Fisher helped her pin up her hair under the plain black hat.

'Gloves,' Miss Fisher said as a final suggestion.

Clara pulled on a pair of black gloves over her work-roughened hands and went straight round to the newspaper offices. She asked to see the editor. Neither Miss Holt, the secretary, nor Adam Paxton, the reporter in the main office, appeared to recognise her.

'What name shall I say?'

'Miss Magee,' Clara said, dry-mouthed.

Miss Holt squinted at Clara. 'You're the cleaner! I'm sorry, Mr Jellicoe s very busy—'

'Just a few minutes,' Clara urged. 'Please.'

'If you're after more pay, you'll not get it.'

'It's nothing to do with that. I've got information.'

The woman gave her a disbelieving look, but went and asked. She came back saying, 'He'll see you for two minutes, no longer.'

Clara rushed into the inner office, pulling her typed articles out of Miss Fisher's coat pocket and thrusting them across the desk of the craggy-faced editor.

'Afternoon, Mr Jellicoe. Would you take a look at these? I know you're interested in sport.'

He scowled at her from under shaggy grey eyebrows.

'Miss Holt tells me you're the cleaner. What's all this?'

Clara took a deep breath. 'They're articles. I wrote them. I think your readers will be interested.'

He jammed on his spectacles, took the sheets of paper and glanced over them suspiciously. Clara held her breath.

'Hiking? Health and Beauty? This isn't sport, Miss Magee,' he said dismissively, dropping them on the desk. Clara gulped.

'They're very popular pastimes,' she answered, 'growing in numbers all the time. The Hippodrome was nearly full.' She knew he was not listening, had already gone back to reading something in his lap. 'Mrs Willa Templeton wants me to join the League. You know Templeton's of Wallsend, don't you, Mr Jellicoe?'

He looked up. 'Templeton's?'

'Yes. The League is full of interesting people like Mrs Templeton. I thought I could write a few articles about pastimes and hobbies; things that interest younger lass— ladies like Mrs Templeton.'

He looked dubious, but picked up the articles again and read them more closely.

'Did you type these yourself?'

Clara hesitated. 'I'm learning to type.'

'They're not bad,' he said grudgingly. 'I like the chatty style.' He eyed her over his spectacles. 'But I don't need another reporter. Can't afford one.'

Clara said quickly, 'I'm not asking for a job — just the chance to write bits and pieces now and again.'

'Freelance?' he queried.

Clara nodded, not quite sure what he meant. 'And I've other contacts in the sporting world,' she added. 'I know Danny Watts and the Cravens.'

He looked at her with more interest. 'How do you know them?'

'My father was a welterweight. Vincent Craven's an old family friend.' Clara felt herself blushing as she used Vinnie's name to her advantage.

Jellicoe scrutinised her. 'How is it that someone with business friends like you is working as a daily help?'

Clara held herself with dignity. 'I'm a businesswoman by training. But things have been a struggle since my dad died last year.'

Realisation dawned on his jowly face. 'You're Harry Magee's daughter?'

She nodded.

He looked away. 'Terrible business.' He shuffled the papers and cleared his throat. 'I can't offer you anything at the moment, but I'll hang on to these. I'm sorry about your father. He was a popular man.'

Clara clenched her hands. The editor did not look up. The interview was obviously over. 'Thank you, Mr Jellicoe,' she forced herself to say as she left.

As she crossed the main office her spirits plunged. Adam the reporter called over, 'Clara, pet, make us a cuppa before you go.'

'Make it yourself,' she muttered and marched out.

Chapter 13

On Saturday, Clara's battered spirits revived at the news that Reenie would be able to go to the dance with them and Frank would be playing in the band. At Saturday tea, Frank was encouraging.

'Jellicoe hasn't turned you down. He's a hard-nosed boss testing you out to see if you'll stick at it. Keep pestering him with articles. And don't let him publish them without paying.'

Clara gave him a grateful smile. She had felt like giving up on the whole idea.

'But what else could I write about?'

'What about something really important,' Benny enthused, 'like uncovering the scandal of low pay in Craven's garment factory? You could gan and talk to the lasses, hear their side of the story. Find out why Craven won't let them join a union.'

'Yes,' Reenie agreed. 'You said yourself you would never work there.'

'I don't know...' Clara felt uncomfortable. 'It's not Jellicoe's kind of story.'

'It would be if it was news,' Benny argued.

'But it's not,' Clara pointed out.

'Well, maybe it will be,' he muttered.

Marta served them more meatloaf and vegetables and the conversation turned to other issues. Oscar was worried about news from his brother Heinrich in Germany. The right-wing Nazi party had made big gains in the March elections.

'Heinrich said it was a farce,' Oscar said in contempt. 'Most of the polling booths were in public houses.'

'Not respectable,' Marta tutted.

'And Hitler's bully-boys could throw their weight around,' Oscar growled.

'At least they don't have a majority in the Reichstag,' Frank pointed out.

'That's right,' Benny agreed. 'And Uncle says the Communists have made gains too. The Left will hold together and keep the little bastards out.'

'Benjamin!' Marta scolded.

They talked on about family in Germany and the situation there as if it was really important. To Clara it seemed too far away to matter very much. Britain had its own problems. She did not want to think about such depressing things and tried to catch Benny's attention.

'Clara's gone very quiet,' Reenie teased. 'She's trying to tell you she's bored, Benny.'

Clara blushed. 'I don't want us to miss any of the dance, that's all.'

Frank glanced at the clock and jumped up. 'I should be there.' As he grabbed his jacket and pushed back his wayward hair, he told Reenie, 'Keep an eye out for Lillian. She said she'd meet you at the entrance.'

Clara's face fell. 'Oh, is Lillian going?'

Benny laughed. 'Don't worry, I'll keep you safe from the Head Mistress.'

'Benjamin,' Marta clucked. 'Lillian is a nice girl.'

Benny winked at Clara. 'Course she is, Mam. Just right for our Frank.'

***

The town hall ballroom was packed, but then the entrance was by donation and many people had streamed in for free. The band was made up of volunteers and an anonymous wealthy Socialist had donated pie and peas suppers that were being served in an upstairs room.

Lillian stood waiting for them with two others from the YS. Clara noticed that the young teacher had put waves in her straight hair, and was wearing lipstick and a new dress. Her insides clenched. Benny was right. How could Frank not fall for Lillian's dark looks and intelligence? Clara slipped her arm through Benny's, determined to make the most of this precious night out. She felt his answering squeeze.

'Haway, lass,' Benny grinned, 'time for some Health and Beauty.'

They danced non-stop until the interval when there were speeches and buckets were passed round. To Clara's surprise Frank got up to speak.

'I have news from our comrades on the Continent.' He got straight to the point.

'Speak up!' someone shouted from the back. 'Can't hear you.'

Frank's fair face reddened. He raised his voice. 'In Germany the Socialists and trade unions are uniting in an "Iron Front" against the Nazis. Even the Catholics are worried enough to join. The fascists are on the rise with their swastika signs. They claim to be pure Aryans, but it's just an excuse to spread hatred of anyone who's different or disagrees with them. Their main targets are the unions and the Left, just like the fascists in Italy. And Hitler is their new Mussolini.'

'The Nazis have a fascist salute, *Heil* Hitler. The Iron Front has a freedom salute, *Freiheit*!' Frank raised his arm straight in the air and clenched his fist. 'When Nazis threaten them in the streets, our comrades shout, "*Heilt* Hitler *vom Grossenwahn*!" Cure Hitler of big-headedness!'

A ripple of laughter went around the room. Then someone shouted, 'Speak Geordie, man.'

Another heckler joined in. 'Hurray up. The pies are gettin' cold!'

Clara saw Frank's agitation. Hot-faced, he ploughed on.

'Some of you think it can't happen here,' he shouted, 'but it can and it will. Look at Mosley, breaking up the Labour Party, promising a kind of socialism like Hitler. But fascists aren't interested in socialism; they're only interested in grabbing power and rounding up those who stand in their way.'

Around them, people began to talk restlessly. Clara told them to be quiet but the noise grew.

'They exploit the poor and the unemployed — turn them against each other. In Germany—' Frank tried to shout above them.

'Thank you, comrade,' one of the organisers interrupted, starting to clap. 'Vote for Socialist revolution! Put what money you can spare in the buckets. Thank you.'

There was a ripple of applause. Frank shook his head and sat down. Clara wanted to push her way through the crowd and comfort him. But the others were just like her; they did not see what Germany had to do with life in Byfell. What mattered was making ends meet and finding work.

Benny steered her upstairs to join the queue for food.

'Not like Frank to speak out in public,' she said. 'Folk could've had the decency to listen.'

'He's like me dad,' Benny snorted, 'always more interested in what's happening on the Continent than here. But it wasn't the place to say it. Tonight's all about trying to get lads unionised.'

'Still, I feel sorry for him,' Clara said.

'Don't.' Benny squeezed her hand. 'He's got Lillian to fuss over him.'

When they returned to the dance hall, Clara was astonished to see Vinnie

Craven talking to the band. Joanie West was beside him, smoking. She must be back performing in Newcastle. The smell of Turkish cigarettes wafted over. Surrounding them was a group of young men.

'There's Jimmy!' Clara gasped to Benny. 'What's he doing here?'

She pushed her way towards them and confronted her brother. 'I thought you were keeping an eye on Mam tonight?'

Jimmy gave her a sulky look. 'I'm workin'.'

Clara laughed. 'At what?'

Vinnie turned from speaking to Frank. 'For me.' He smiled, his eyes appraising. 'Evening Clara; evening Benny. You make a lovely couple on the dance floor. You remember Joanie — Joanie West?'

Clara nodded at the dancer. She had not aged in the four years. Joanie gave a cool smile that did not light her eyes.

'Joanie's on tour at the Palladium. Great show. You should take Clara to see it, Benny.' Vinnie bantered.

Benny gave him a suspicious look. 'No disrespect to Miss West, but I haven't much time for music hall.'

'No, you wouldn't,' Vinnie sneered, 'not with you trying to get my lads out on strike and busy turning England into a Bolshevik colony.'

Benny squared up to him. 'A fair day's pay for a fair day's work, Mr Craven. That's all the lads want.'

'Hear that, lads?' Vinnie chuckled. 'Benny Lewis knows just what you want.' The youths laughed loudly and closed in. Their posture was menacing. Clara saw Jimmy aping the older boys, legs apart, arms folded like in a team photograph.

Benny was scathing. 'I know they want more than slave wages.'

Frank stood up. 'Benny lad, take it easy.'

'Aye, listen to your big brother for once. My lads are happy,' Vinnie went on, 'cos they have a boss who looks after them better than any shop steward. Union men just care about themselves and the sound of their own voices — like politicians. Who needs them?'

'Aye, a right little Hitler, aren't you?' Benny said hot-temperedly.

Vinnie laughed, but the look in his eyes was deadly serious. 'You've got more in common with Adolf than me, Benny,' he said softly. 'Isn't he a fellow Kraut?'

At once, Benny was thrusting a hand towards Vinnie, pushing him in the chest. Three of Vinnie's entourage jumped forward. Two shielded Vinnie while a third, Clarkie, punched Benny away.

Frank sprang between them. 'Haway, lads, that's enough!'

A fist swung at him, but Frank dodged and struck back instantly, knocking his attacker sideways. Lillian screamed. Vinnie got in amongst them.

'Lads, lads!' He pulled one of his youths off Benny. The others backed off as some of the stewards muscled forward.

'We'll have no trouble in here,' one of them shouted.

Vinnie reached out a hand to help Benny to his feet. Benny ignored it and stood up unaided, clutching his stomach.

'Settle it outside,' the steward said gruffly.

'Nothing to settle,' Vinnie said, 'just a difference of opinion.' He held out his hand to Benny. 'No hard feelings?'

Benny stood looking furious. Clara said tensely, 'Shake on it, Benny.'

Suddenly Frank spoke up. 'Perhaps if you apologise for what you called him, Vinnie, he'll be able to shake your hand as an equal.'

Vinnie gave him a sharp look. 'It was just a joke.'

'Name-calling is the first weapon of the fascist bully,' Frank said, tight-jawed.

Vinnie's eyes narrowed. For an instant, Clara thought she saw real anger. But she must have been wrong, for the next moment Vinnie was laughing and clapping both Frank and Benny on the shoulder.

'My deepest apologies, lads. You know I meant no harm by it. Frank, I can see you haven't lost any of your punch. You must come down to the hall and give my lads a lesson or two.' He turned and nodded at his men to follow, holding out an arm to Joanie. He dropped his voice as he passed Clara. 'Keep that hot-headed lad of yours out of trouble, eh?' He touched her arm. 'The last thing I want to see is you getting hurt.'

Clara watched them swagger out of the hall, Jimmy striding to keep up with Vinnie. Her heart stirred with unease.

'What did he say to you?' Benny asked angrily.

'Said to keep you out of trouble,' Clara said, facing him in annoyance. 'Why can't you keep your temper?'

'He started it,' Benny protested.

'No, you did,' Clara pointed out, 'by being rude to that actress.'

'He was itching for an argument,' Benny answered. 'What was he doing here anyway? Ask yourself that. Recruiting ground for more of his bully boys, shouldn't wonder.'

'Our Jimmy's not a bully.' Clara was indignant. 'At least Mr Craven's keeping him off the streets.'

'Teaching him to rule the streets, more like,' Benny ridiculed. 'Lad should be learning a trade.'

'Well, there aren't any,' Clara snapped.

Benny looked at her helplessly and let out a big sigh. 'Aye, I know. Sorry, lass. We shouldn't be arguing. I'll not let Craven spoil our night out.'

But for Clara the evening had been spoiled; both Vinnie and Benny had seen to that. It was her first real tiff with Benny. Reenie noticed and left some nursing friends to come and sit with them. After a while, they danced again and at the end of the evening Benny walked her home. By then, Clara had forgiven him and let him kiss her goodnight at the end of the street. But she did not linger, just in case her brother or someone else was watching.

Chapter 14

The next week, Clara forgot all about the unpleasantness at the dance. Adam Paxton waved a new copy of the weekly *Tyne Times* at her as she finished cleaning.

'Admiral's using your piece on Health and Beauty. Congratulations.'

'Never!' Clara rushed over. There, covering a column and a half, was her story of the meeting and the quote from Willa Templeton. Her very own words in print for the first time. Clara gazed at them in delight.

Emboldened, she knocked on the editor's door.

'Just wanted to thank you very much for using my article, Mr Jellicoe,' she said in her most well-spoken voice. He nodded in acknowledgement. She asked if she could write something else.

'Doesn't mean I'll print it,' he grunted. 'Depends if it's good enough.'

'It will be,' she said confidently. 'And sir? How much do I get paid?'

He shot her a warning look. 'That was just a trial article. I had to rewrite most of it. You might get paid for the next one.'

Clara swallowed her disappointment, determined to win his praise next time.

An opportunity arose soon afterwards when she heard from Jimmy of a big fight in the offing. Danny Watts was back from sea and Vinnie was putting him up against a champion from London.

'It's ganna be massive,' Jimmy said in excitement. 'There's that much interest, Mr Craven's hiring the Hippodrome.'

Clara went straight to Jellicoe and asked to cover it for the paper.

'Women don't do boxing,' he said shortly. 'Paxton can cover it.'

'I can give it a different touch.' Clara would not be put off. 'Not just the fight, but the social occasion; who's there and what they're wearing.'

He looked at her as if she was mad.

'And I can get interviews with Danny and the other lad,' she said eagerly. 'I've met the London promoter. Please, Mr Jellicoe, say yes.'

She took his sigh and nod as agreement.

Clara knew if she was to make a success of this, she needed Vinnie's co-operation. She went to see him and asked if she could interview Danny and any of the punters. He looked as astonished as her editor.

'Since when have you been writing for the *Times*?' he asked, intrigued.

'Last week.' Clara smiled proudly. She was not going to say she had yet to be paid for her work. 'Did you not see the article on the Women's League of Health and Beauty?'

Vinnie's smile was sardonic. 'Must have missed that one.'

'Well, I wrote it.'

'Good for you. And you've got another commission?'

'Well,' Clara said with less conviction, 'I have to prove myself first. That's why I want to do a good job on the fight.'

'I'd be happy to help.' Vinnie smiled. 'Maybe I can guide you on the technical details.'

Clara nodded with enthusiasm. 'And I was wondering if you could suggest who I might interview.'

Vinnie tapped his nose conspiratorially. 'I've heard word about something that could put your story on the front page.'

Clara's pulse quickened. 'What's that?'

Vinnie beckoned her to come closer. He lowered his voice. 'Some very distinguished visitors are coming. Got a call this morning.'

'Who?'

'Brigadier and Mrs Bell-Carr of Hoxton Hall.'

She stood open-mouthed in wonder. 'Bell-Carr?'

Vinnie chuckled. 'You've heard of them?'

'Dad used to talk about him. Said he was a canny boxer — amateur. It was the first time I'd heard there were boxers who didn't have to fight for money.'

'Aye,' Vinnie said. 'Alastair Bell-Carr used to box at school. He's right keen on the sport. Used to come down from Hoxton regular when me father was alive and when the brigadier was still a bachelor.'

'Oh yes! He married an Irish heiress, didn't he?' Clara exclaimed.

He gave her a quizzical look. 'How do you know that?'

'It was in the Sunday paper once; they were opening some fete. I remember Dad reading it out to Mam, and Mam saying we could do with one of them heiress types. She was a Fitz Johns. The names stuck in my mind. I never forget a name.'

'Well, well,' Vinnie said, smiling in admiration. 'You are the little journalist.'

She left full of excitement.

When the night came, there was such a crush of people that Clara struggled to get near enough to see the Bell-Carrs. They came with a party of friends, laughing and chattering loudly as they were ushered upstairs to the front of the grand circle. Clara glimpsed a tall, balding man with a trim moustache in full evening dress and a petite woman wrapped in furs with a flash of an ice-blue sequinned gown beneath.

Vinnie got Clara to the side of the stalls for a good view of the fight and she scribbled madly in a notebook Max had given her. She had already been to the Watts' home and interviewed both Danny and his wife, as well as speaking to Madame Gautier, the London promoter, about her charge. She observed Vinnie sitting close to the woman and making her laugh.

Watts and Kain were equally matched and to Clara there seemed little between them. Then in the thirteenth round, with two more to go, Watts felled Kain. A left hook caught him off guard and the Londoner dropped to the floor. There was a huge roar from the home crowd. The referee stood over the fighter, counting him out. At the count of six, he struggled back on his feet. There was a counter-roar.

The men battled on for two more rounds. At the end, the referee held up Watts's knotted arm as the winner. The din was deafening. Above, Clara caught sight of the Bell-Carrs and their party rising to leave. She dashed to the door, and as they came sweeping downstairs she rushed forward.

'Brigadier Bell-Carr, excuse me, sir. I'm from the *Tyne Times*,' she said breathlessly. 'What did you think of the fight?'

He carried on past her without a glance in her direction. The others followed, talking loudly over her questions as if she did not exist.

'Mrs Bell-Carr!' Clara called out as they disappeared through the wide doors.

Unexpectedly, the small, sandy-haired woman turned round and smiled. She reminded Clara of a very sleek kitten.

'Did you enjoy the fight?'

'I did.' She smiled. 'And the best man won.'

'Where are you going now?' Clara asked.

'To dinner, dear girl.'

'At Hoxton Hall?'

'No.' She gave a throaty laugh. 'To the Sandford Rooms, darling.'

Then she was gone and Clara was left trembling at her audacity and wondering where the Sandford Rooms were.

Lance Jellicoe was pleased with her work and the article appeared in the next week's edition. From him she learned that the Sandford was an exclusive dining club, frequented by gentry and well-to-do businessmen.

'They sometimes have debates and visiting speakers,' the editor told her. 'The food is first class.'

'You're a member too?' Clara asked, wide-eyed.

'No,' Jellicoe admitted, 'but I was a guest of the Italian consul once.'

Clara had a yearning that one day she would dine at the Sandford Rooms, but she kept it to herself. After that, to Clara's amazed delight, Jellicoe began to give her small events to cover that Adam Paxton was happy to avoid: the opening of a new dress shop, a talk on childhood diseases and inoculations, spring gardening tips, Easter events for the family. Quickly, Clara began to build up her own contacts and suggest articles of interest to their female readership. She began a recipe column, which made Reenie laugh.

'But you never cook,' her friend snorted.

'No, I'm just passing on information,' Clara said breezily. She published several of Marta's simple, wholesome recipes.

Clara spoke to butchers and bakers, gardeners and cooks to discover their tips on preparing food as cheaply and easily as possible. It was so popular that Jellicoe gave her a Women's Page and put her on a part-time weekly rate. She covered everything from new labour-saving devices in the home to the healthy properties of honey. She did film reviews but was also quick to volunteer for dull meetings or local society events, knowing that the more she learned about the area and the more people she met, the more indispensable she became to her editor. She also insisted on keeping her coverage of the local boxing, knowing that if she was ever to be taken on full time, she would have to learn as much as possible about sport.

Whereas once she would have been awkward going into Craven's boxing hall alone, she now became a regular visitor. Clarkie and the other young men who hung around doing odd jobs for Vinnie gave her a warm welcome and tipped her off if there was a visiting boxer or music hall comedian.

Vinnie knew so many people in both the sporting and the entertainment business that there was a constant coming and going of visitors and promoters there to do deals. Yet he always seemed to have time to spare for a quick chat and to introduce her to whoever was around. Often Patience was there, helping Dolly with the front of house or helping feed the young men who gathered at the hall. Vinnie seemed to be providing an unofficial soup kitchen for dozens of the Byfell youth. In return, Clara saw how much they respected and adored him.

Gradually, Clara began to earn enough from her journalism to give up cleaning at the newspaper offices and the accountants'. But she kept on at Max's office and flat, partly for the money and partly because of his kindness to her during the bad times. She was determined to buy back as many of her mother's possessions from the pawnbroker's as she could afford. While Patience and Jimmy were getting their meals at Craven's hall and free cigarettes from Dolly, they were earning little more than pocket money for the most basic necessities.

So busy was Clara with her new-found work that she saw increasingly little of Reenie and her family. She had no time to go hiking. Sundays were spent covering church parades, writing up her articles or sleeping off the exhaustion of the week. Patience encouraged her to stay away.

'That Benny's causing trouble for Vinnie,' she told her with disapproval. 'Stirring things up at the garment factory.'

'In what way?' Clara asked.

'Trying to get the lasses to strike,' Patience said querulously. 'He'll not be happy till there's revolution and blood on the streets. That's what comes of letting foreigners into our country. They bring in all these outlandish ideas that aren't right for us English.'

'Don't be daft,' Clara said impatiently. 'Benny's as English as I am.'

Patience gave her a sharp look. Clara left before her mother worked herself up into another rant about the Lewises. She suspected Dolly had a lot to do with Patience's hardening attitudes. 'Outlandish' was the sort of word Dolly would use. They spent too much time gossiping together and finding fault, in Clara's opinion.

Clara, equally stubborn, allowed Benny to continue to court her into the early summer. But even though the times they could meet up were infrequent, they were not always harmonious. They argued over Jimmy, who Benny thought was spying on them. They argued over Patience. Clara was often too tired to smooth Benny's hurt feelings.

'The old wife can't stand me, can she?' Benny accused.

'You could be more friendly yourself,' Clara pointed out.

'She gans out the room whenever I come up!'

'Only 'cos you ignore her in her own home.'

'Cos I'm not lickin' her boots enough,' Benny ridiculed.

'You know Mam's not been the same since Dad died,' Clara sighed impatiently. 'You should be more understanding.'

'No,' Benny said with a tempestuous look Clara was beginning to know well. 'She's always looked down her nose at us — specially me mam. Still calls her Mrs Leizmann in the street like it's an insult.'

'Well don't bother coming up if it's such a trial.'

'I won't!'

Sometimes they would stop speaking for days. But neither of them could stay angry for long and they always made up, Benny contrite for losing his temper and Clara apologising for her family's unfriendliness. He would pull her into his arms and give her an affectionate kiss. Clara's fondness for Benny would be rekindled. And their friendship seemed to please Reenie and Marta, whose opinion she valued more than her own mother's.

On one of the few occasions the two friends managed to get together for a stroll on the High Street, Reenie said, 'Mam's that happy about you and Benny courting. She thinks you're good for him —know how to calm him down.'

'Doesn't seem like that to me at times,' Clara said, rolling her eyes. 'He gets that steamed up about the slightest thing. And he'll argue black is white till the cows come home.'

'That's Benny; always been passionate about things,' Reenie agreed.

'So's Frank,' Clara commented, 'but he doesn't mouth off all the time like his brother.'

'Frank's an idealist,' Reenie said. 'He's got all these notions about how the world should be, but he'll never do anything about them. He and Lillian think you just have to educate people and everything will change for the better. Pair of dreamers.'

Clara felt a pang whenever Frank and Lillian were mentioned together. 'Maybe Frank's right.'

Reenie snorted. 'If you've got a hundred years to spare. Me and Benny believe you need action, not words. Things need to change here and now.'

'Like stirring up trouble at the garment factory?' Clara challenged her.

'The lasses there have no rights,' Reenie replied. 'Craven could sack them all tomorrow if he felt like it.'

'But he won't,' Clara said.

'He's threatened to if they join a union,' Reenie told her indignantly.

'Maybe they're better off not bothering then,' Clara shrugged.

Reenie gave her a shocked look. 'Imagine it was you or me working there. For a reporter you show a strange lack of interest in what's going on at the factory. Are you scared of what Vincent Craven might say?'

'Course not,' Clara flashed.

'Go and ask him about it then,' Reenie urged. 'Find out for yourself what's really going on.'

Clara decided to investigate. She went to the factory, an old warehouse down by the river, and asked to see the manager. He was busy. She came back at the end of the day to catch the women on their way home. But when she mentioned the newspaper, no one would talk to her. Only one woman stopped long enough to say, 'You that Clara Magee? Thought you'd be much older. That recipe page is canny helpful.'

The janitor, locking the gates behind them, told her she was not welcome and to clear off. When she told Benny, he grew angry.

'What did I tell you? Craven's hiding a can of worms in there. Come with me tomorrow while I hand out leaflets.'

They arranged to meet there when the buzzer went at the close of work. By the time Clara arrived Benny was already there with two helpers from the YS, shouting at the top of his voice as the women streamed past him.

'You have to stand up for yourselves, lasses,' he cried. 'No one else in there will. Stick together.'

'I'll stick to you any day of the week, bonny lad,' an older woman called out, making the younger ones laugh.

Benny grinned and shoved a leaflet at her. 'Join the union; they'll stick up for you. Come to the meeting of the United Clothing Workers' Union next Friday. Behind the town hall.'

A few took the leaflets, stuffing them into pockets. Others passed heads down.

Another woman brushed him off. 'Aye, the minute we join, they'll have us on strike and we'll be out on our ear.'

'Not if you all stick together,' Benny argued.

'They'll just bring in other lasses who'll work for less,' she said sourly. 'These jobs are like gold dust.' She pushed past him.

'Are you managing on what Craven pays you?' Benny shouted after her.

Others passed him, glancing over their shoulders at the factory behind. Clara saw the manager striding towards them, followed by the janitor. The women hurried on, dropping any leaflets they had taken.

'Benny, it's no use,' Clara warned, 'the boss is coming over.'

Benny carried on. 'Nothing will change for the better unless you change it,' he boomed out. 'The union will help you fight for a decent wage — one you can feed your families on. Don't let Craven and his henchmen bully you with their threats of sacking and docked wages. Now is the time to act!'

'Clear off!' the manager bawled. 'I've warned you before about harassing my workers. I've called the police.'

Benny ignored him. 'Don't be frightened,' he urged the women. 'All you're asking for is a fair day's pay for a fair day's work. It's your right. It's what your families deserve. Don't let the bosses grind you down. Fight back, lasses! Remember the meeting: Friday, seven o'clock.'

A whistle blew further up the street and two constables came running down. But the appearance of the manager was all that was needed to disperse the crowd. The policeman told Benny and his comrades to move on. The other two nodded, but Benny stood his ground.

'This is a public street,' he argued. 'We've just as much right to be here as anyone.'

'Not if you're disturbing the peace,' the constable replied.

'What's happened to free speech?' Benny demanded.

'Move along, lad, or I'll have to arrest you.'

Clara took Benny by the arm. 'Come on, you're not helping anyone by getting nicked.'

'That's right, miss,' the policeman encouraged her. 'Don't I know you from somewhere?'

'Clara Magee, *Tyne Times*,' she smiled. 'Spoke to you last week about a missing puppy. It's PC Hobson, isn't it? The family couldn't have been more grateful for you finding their pet.'

'Happy to help,' he preened. 'Now you talk some sense into your gentleman friend here. We don't want any more trouble outside the factory.'

Clara nodded. 'The truth is, there wouldn't have been any trouble if the management had agreed to see me yesterday.' She shot the manager a look. 'You see, I'm doing a piece for the *Times* — Women in the Workplace. Benny here was only trying to help me speak to some of the lasses.'

'He was doing no such thing,' the manager retorted.

The policeman raised a conciliatory hand. 'I'm sure Mr Reid would be happy to help.'

The manager scowled. 'I suppose I could see you next week,' he muttered.

'Thank you.' Clara smiled. 'Would Tuesday suit? I'd like a look round the factory and to talk to some of the employees. An hour would be fine.'

Mr Reid shot her a furious look. 'Half an hour's all I can spare. Ten o'clock sharp.' Then he retreated back into the factory, the janitor at his heels.

Benny's friends left, promising to help at the meeting on Friday. Benny and Clara walked towards Minto Street.

'You could talk the hind legs off a donkey,' Benny said in admiration. 'I nearly believed all that Women in the Workplace stuff.'

'It's true,' Clara retorted. 'If I get inside, that's what I'm interested in. What it's like for the lasses - not just their pay. How they manage with their families. Do the men help out at home.'

Benny laughed ruefully. 'My, you sound like our Reenie.'

'It's like you said,' Clara quipped, 'us lasses should stick together.'

'Do you want your tea at ours?' he asked, looking hopeful.

Clara shook her head. 'Sorry, I've got a history society meeting. Industries of Byfell in the Nineteenth Century.'

'Aye, the good old days,' Benny grunted, 'when they had some.'

She smiled. 'Bye, Benny.'

'Come to the meeting on Friday, won't you?' Benny pleaded. 'Then you can talk to the women without Reid breathing down their necks. You'll not hear the truth otherwise.'

'I'll see,' Clara said, not wanting to commit herself either way.

She watched him stride off, hands plunged into the pockets of his ill-fitting suit, wiry dark hair sticking out at angles. He was becoming more and more the eccentric revolutionary. Clara had a pang of misgiving that the meeting might be an explosive one, with Benny right in the heat of it.

Chapter 15

Two days later, while Clara was still pondering whether to turn up to the union meeting, she had a surprise visitor to the flat. She was working at the table in the window, the May sunshine streaming in through the soot-smudged panes. Patience and Jimmy were out.

She opened the door to find Vinnie standing there in a dark suit and starched white shirt, ebony cane in hand. There was no sign of his car in the street. He touched his trilby in a respectful nod and gave her his lop-sided smile.

'Afternoon, Clara.'

'Mam's not in,' she said, suddenly nervous.

'I know; she's at the hall. It's you I've come to see.'

Her stomach churned. 'It's about the factory, isn't it? You don't want me asking questions. You've come to stop me, but I'm not easy put off.'

The way he eyed her only increased her alarm. Abruptly, he asked, 'Fancy a walk? I've heard how much you like hiking.'

She stared at him, baffled. 'I — I'm working.'

'Half an hour,' he bargained. 'We both need a break from work now and again. Your mam says you never stop.'

'Someone's got to earn our living,' Clara said pointedly.

Vinnie chuckled. 'I love that fighting spirit. Haway and get your coat.'

Upstairs, Clara pulled a comb through her hair and grabbed her jacket, a green tweed one she had spotted in a second-hand shop and sewn blue buttons on to make it less dull. Alarm bells were going off in her head telling her not to go with Vinnie, yet she was too intrigued to resist. It gave her the same rush of excitement that following a story did.

Vinnie walked her round the corner to where his car was parked and flicked a coin to a boy minding it.

'That's for you, Denis, not your old man.' He winked.

'Ta, Mr Craven,' the boy gasped and ran off gleefully with his easily earned treasure.

'I thought we were walking?' Clara hesitated as he held the door open for her.

'We will,' he promised.

They drove out of Byfell towards the coast. In fifteen minutes they were in open countryside, pulling into a quiet village with the sea shimmering away on the horizon. Inland, the hazy smoke from a distant pit village was the only interruption to a cloudless blue sky. Clara had not realised what a beautiful day it was until now. They parked beside a squat stone church, half hidden in a canopy of lush green leaves. Vinnie opened the door for her.

'Come on, I want to show you something.' He held out his arm.

Cautiously, she put a hand on it. He walked her through the old lych-gate and into the shade of the trees. Clara felt her misgivings return. What was all this about? Beneath their feet, the last of the late spring blossom lay like a fading carpet. There was a fresh, earthy smell. She shivered in the dankness. Vinnie put an arm about her and rubbed her shoulder. 'You're cold?'

'No, I'm fine,' she said, pulling away.

He led her round the side of the church, through the damp grass to a plain headstone. He read aloud.

William Craven, stonemason. Born 1842. Died 1872.

Also Sarah, daughter of William. Born 1869. Died 1872.

Gone but not Forgotten.'

Vinnie took off his leather gloves and caressed the stone. His jaw clenched. Clara waited for him to explain. When he turned to her, his dark eyes were bright with tears. It shocked her to see him so vulnerable. Finally he spoke, his voice a low rumble like the distant tide.

'He's me grandfather. Me father used to bring me here once a year, just to remember. Not that he ever knew his own father — he was just a bairn when he died. Typhoid fever. Took the pair of them. Sarah was me dad's sister. Never knew her either.'

'Just three years old,' Clara whispered. 'Poor wee pet.'

'And William was only thirty — younger than me. A good life cut short,' Vinnie continued. He seemed to want to unburden himself. 'Me grandma had to gan into service. Me father was sent to a married aunt in Byfell. She did her best for him, but she had five others. Me dad went down the pit when he was twelve. He learned bare-knuckle fighting during a lay-off at the pit. Small, stocky, hard as nails he was. He began winning good prize money. Bought the old hall off this cinematographer that went bust in 1910. That's how the boxing started. Made a good living in the end. But he never forgot where he came from.' Vinnie tapped the headstone. 'This stonemason. A man who worked with his hands. A craftsman who died too young to pass on his skills to his son. Died of a poor man's disease, Clara.' He fixed her with an unblinking look. 'But I'm not ashamed of where I come from. I'm proud. I look around this village and I know where I belong.' He dug his polished shoe into the soft earth. 'This is the soil of my ancestors,' he said, eyes alight.

Clara was moved by his words yet still puzzled. 'It's a sad story, Mr Craven. But why have you brought me here?'

Vinnie stepped close, his look intense. 'To show you that I care for the common man — 'cos I'm one of them. Me father championed the underdog — stood up for the working class all his life — and he taught me to do the same. I look around Byfell at the lads kicking their heels on street corners, at men grown old at thirty, and it makes me blood boil. And what does the Government do for our people? Nowt, that's what! A Labour Party that cuts benefits and throws more lads on the dole than ever before. That's not sticking up for the working class. That's joining the bosses; the big corporations, the money-lenders that bleed us dry.'

He kept his voice controlled, but his eyes blazed. 'I went to hear Oswald Mosley when I was in London and he's the only one with any vision. He opened my eyes, Clara, made me see how weak our rulers are. And they're to blame for all the small businesses that have gone to the wall — decent folk like your parents. The politicians don't care about them. Neither do the unions.'

Clara swallowed. 'My dad brought his troubles on himself with his gambling. You can't blame the politicians for that.'

Vinnie took her by the arm. 'They did nothing to put lads back to work. If they had, their families would have had money to spend in your parents' shop and Harry would still be alive today.'

'Don't say that,' Clara gasped.

'I didn't mean to upset you,' Vinnie said, holding her firm.

'Then why bring me here? Why lecture me?' she demanded.

'I want to convince you that I'm not some money-grabbing boss who thinks nothing of the people I employ. I give jobs to lads round the hall just to keep them off the street and give them some self-respect. Half the time I don't need them.'

'Like Jimmy, you mean?' Clara's eyes stung.

'Aye, like Jimmy.' Vinnie was blunt. 'You came to me for help and I did what me old dad taught me to do: stick up for my own kind.'

'Me and Mam are very grateful,' Clara gulped.

'I don't want your gratitude,' Vinnie exclaimed. 'I didn't do it for that. I did it for Jimmy 'cos he's just like me or me dad. Lads need work like they need air to breathe. It gives them respect. Without it they give up and die — die inside.'

'And what about lasses?' Clara demanded. 'We need work and respect too.'

'Aye, and that's why I keep the garment factory going,' Vinnie insisted. 'Some of those lasses are the only wage-earners in their families. They would rather be at home looking after their bairns, but if they were they would starve.' His voice rose. 'Do you know what I think when I see those lasses stitching? I think of me grandma having to gan away to London into place and never being a proper mam again. I give these lasses jobs so they can stay close to their bairns and still be proper mothers and wives. No one else is giving them work.'

Clara wriggled out of his grip. 'So any job is better than no job, even if you pay them a pittance?'

His face tensed in anger. 'I pay them lasses what I can afford. The factory nearly went bust last year cos of a boycott by Indian cotton workers, stirred up by foreign agitators. I could double the wages the morra and in two months the factory would be bankrupt and they'd all be out of work again. That's what agitators like Benny don't understand. Is that what you want?'

Clara would not be intimidated. 'I just want to have a look round and speak to the lasses myself. Mr Reid's giving me half an hour on Tuesday.'

'I can do better than that,' Vinnie declared. 'I'll take you round myself. You can speak to who you like for as long as you like. Then you can judge if a Craven is true to his word.'

Clara turned away, clutching her arms to stop herself shaking. Talk of her father's death and Vinnie's passionate outpouring had upset her more than she cared to admit. She felt his hands cup round her shoulders, more gently.

'Dear Clara,' he said, his tone softening, 'forgive me. I had no right to try to sway you like this, no matter how strongly I feel about things. You must make up your own mind. It's just. . .' His hands dropped from holding her.

She turned to face him. 'Just what?'

A muscle in his cheek worked as he clenched his jaw. What was it this usually talkative man was finding so difficult to say? When he spoke, it was almost with the bashfulness of a youth.

'I admire you, Clara. A lot.'

'Me?' she said in amazement.

'Why is that so strange?' He smiled. 'You've shown so much spirit. You're just a young lass, yet you're the strong one; the one who'll do anything to stop your family going under. Not for one moment have you let up. It's driven me mad the way you won't accept any help for yourself, I won't deny it. But by heck, Harry would be proud of you.'

Clara let out a small sob. It seemed to come from nowhere. At once Vinnie had his arms round her, cradling her head on his shoulder. She dissolved into tears.

'There, there, lass,' he crooned, 'have a good cry. I know how much you miss him.'

She leaned into him and let out the sorrow that had lain like a weight inside her for so long. She had never really mourned her father properly. His suicide had been so fraught with shock and shame, the aftermath too tied up with worry about the sea of debts and how to cope. She had had to keep strong for her mother, for Jimmy, pretending to the outside world that she was not beaten by any of it. Even with her closest friends, Reenie, Benny and Frank, she had been unable to unburden herself fully. Until today.

How could she have guessed that it would be tough, suave, man of the world Vinnie who would slide underneath her defences and unlock her grief? It was as if he knew her better than any of them. No one else had understood her so easily, except her father. And Vinnie was the only one to have said Harry would be proud of her. Everyone else, including her mother, avoided any mention of her father, as if he was for ever tainted by what he had done. Vinnie was alone in talking about Harry as if he was still a good friend. She clung on to him gratefully, soothed by the way he stroked her hair, comforted by his strong arms and the smell of expensive cologne.

Eventually, her weeping subsided and she pulled away, growing self-conscious at the way she had so quickly succumbed to her feelings. Vinnie produced a fresh handkerchief from his breast pocket and wiped her tear-stained face. She took it and blew her nose.

'Keep it,' he said.

She laughed through her tears. 'You'll have no hankies left at this rate. I've still got your other one.'

'Good.' He smiled.

'I'm sorry about—'

'Don't be.' Vinnie cut her off. 'There's nowt wrong in a lass crying.' He touched her face briefly. 'Now I'm ganin' to cheer you up.' He bent to retrieve his gloves and stick. 'Come along, Miss Magee. It's tea time.' He ushered her forward.

Out of the boot of the car, Vinnie lifted a wicker picnic basket and a tartan rug. He led Clara to the end of the churchyard wall and round the corner to a sheltered village green. A large manor house stood opposite and a scattering of cottages bordered it on the other two sides. He spread out the rug on the rough grass under the dappled shade of a young willow tree. Opening the basket, he produced a Thermos flask and two neat boxes.

'Go on, see what's inside,' he encouraged.

While he set out two china plates and linen napkins, and poured tea into china cups, Clara investigated the food.

'Salmon sandwiches?' she gasped. 'And chocolate cake! Mr Craven, you shouldn't have gone to all this bother.' She was overwhelmed.

'No bother.' He smiled. 'It's you who's doing me the favour.'

'How come?'

'It's just the excuse I need to get out in the fresh air and away from all me problems.' He winked. 'And how better than in the company of a pretty young lady?'

Clara felt herself blushing, even though she knew this was typical Vinnie flattery.

'Not pretty,' Clara snorted, 'red-faced from all that blubbering.'

Vinnie handed her a cup of tea. 'No, you're right, not pretty,' he said, with a scrutinising look. 'Just plain beautiful.'

Clara threw back her head and laughed, spilling tea on her skirt. She put down the cup and dabbed at the stains with his handkerchief, still laughing. 'Now look at me!'

'Umm.' Vinnie grinned. 'I can't help it. I could look at you all day.'

'Stop it,' Clara said, going crimson. He had her quite confused as to how she

89

felt. 'The lengths you'll go to just to make me write a nice article about your factory!' she quipped.

He laughed out loud. 'That's my girl; back to the knock-out punch.'

Clara dived for one of the sandwiches and took a large bite. Safer to eat and say nothing. It tasted delicious and she realised how hungry she was. He urged her to eat a second and a third. In the end she demolished most of them and followed up with two pieces of rich chocolate cake.

'Can't remember the last time I had cake this good,' she sighed, licking the sticky icing off her fingertips.

Vinnie smiled in satisfaction. 'I'll tell Ella, our cook.'

'You have your own cook?' Clara asked, impressed.

'Ella's been with us for years,' he explained. 'Does a bit of housework and most of the cooking. With Mam working in the business, Ella came to help out. Now we couldn't do without her.'

Clara leaned back on her elbows, enjoying the sun on her face and the feel of a full stomach. They spoke about their families and Vinnie talked a lot about his boxing business. He alluded to interests in property and exports. He was part of some consortium with other businessmen called Cooper Holdings.

'Is that why you went to London last year?' Clara asked.

'That was mainly the boxing. I was helping to set up a new venue with another promoter. But I made some good contacts while I was there.'

'So you're in business with Madame Gautier?' Clara asked, sliding him a look.

Vinnie shook his head. 'It didn't work out.' He poured out the last of the tea. 'And you, Clara,' he said, eyeing her, 'what do you want out of life?'

She sat up and gazed across at the old manor house behind its rusting gates. 'I want to live in a house like that,' she murmured, 'to move away from the railway tracks. For Mam never to have to worry about money again. For Jimmy to be a prize fighter.' She laughed at herself. 'And I'm going to be editor of the *Tyne Times* one day. Not asking much, am I?'

Vinnie did not laugh. 'It's good to have goals in life. I like to see ambition. There are too many people in this world who have no imagination, no vision of the future. Weak, small-minded people who allow themselves to be pushed around. We're not like that, Clara, you and I.'

She looked at him in surprise. It sounded strange to hear him talk of them as being similar. She thought they had nothing in common. He lived in a different world. It was exciting to be included as one of his kind, no matter how far-fetched.

'And Benny?' Vinnie asked abruptly. 'Is he a part of your future?'

Clara went puce. 'Benny? I don't know — I mean — we're not. . . Goodness, I haven't thought about it!' She covered her cheeks with her hands.

'Well, I bet he has.' Vinnie said, his smile sardonic.

Clara shook her head. 'Benny's more like a brother, really.'

Vinnie said, 'He's a canny lad, but he'll ruin your life if you let him. Can't control that temper of his. And he's not interested in the good things in life like you are — in bettering himself.'

Clara felt suddenly disloyal for talking about Benny like that. 'He's got more in common with you than you think. I remember him arguing with Frank about Mosley. Benny admired him till his New Party fizzled out.'

'That's just it,' Vinnie declared, leaning closer. 'Benny blows hot and cold. He doesn't know his own mind.' He held her look. 'Now Frank's different. There's a man who thinks deeply about things. He's got brains and brawn. He's too attracted to the Communists for his own good - they're not the answer. But he could go far. Could make an ambitious woman happy.'

Clara gawped at him in astonishment. She could feel the blood rushing to her cheeks. How could he possibly know how she felt about Frank? She did not know what to say. Vinnie watched her. Clara glanced away.

'Frank lives for his music more than anything,' she said, trying to keep her voice from shaking. 'For his sake, I hope he can go far with his playing.'

'Yes,' Vinnie said quietly, 'I agree. He needs to get away from that family. They're holding him back. Their ways of thinking are different from ours.'

Clara gave him a sharp look. 'The Lewises are the kindest people I know. I won't hear a word said against them.' She shook the cake crumbs from her skirt and began packing up the basket. She did not dare glance at him again in case she had caused offence with her sudden rebuke.

They walked back to the car. Vinnie carrying the basket. A fresh breeze was blowing off the sea. It was later than Clara had thought. On the drive back to Byfell Vinnie chatted about Lance Jellicoe's being a friend and a business associate. No mention was made again of the Lewis family. When they pulled into Minto Street, Clara's spirits flagged. The short time in the country away from the tightly packed, smoky streets, had left her yearning for more.

'Thank you very much, Mr Craven,' she said, climbing out of the passenger seat. 'I really enjoyed that.'

'Maybe we can do it again sometime?' he suggested.

Clara nodded. 'And the visit to the factory?' she reminded him.

'How about Friday? Ten o'clock, say. I'll pick you up in the car.'

She raised her eyebrows. 'Turning up in the boss's car? Doesn't look very impartial. I'll walk, thanks all the same.'

As she moved past him, he put a hand on her arm. 'Clara. I've just remembered. I've got two tickets for the new Garbo film at the Paramount cinema. Would you like to come?'

Her eyes widened. 'The new place on Pilgrim Street?' Reenie and she had talked about going. It was a huge, American-style cinema, but Clara could no longer afford such a luxurious night out. 'I'd love to go.'

'Good.' He smiled. 'Friday night, seven-thirty performance. We could go for a bite to eat at Fenwick's tea room beforehand.'

Clara's face fell. 'Oh, Friday. I'm sorry, I can't. I promised Ben — I — er — have to cover a meeting.'

Vinnie shrugged. 'Not to worry.' He stepped away. Clara felt a rush of disappointment. She could hardly believe she was giving up the chance of going to the Paramount just to be at Benny's wretched union meeting.

'Thanks anyway,' she said, watching him walk round to the driver's side.

Vinnie touched his hat to her. 'Ta-ra, Clara. Don't work too hard. All work and no play makes a dull girl, as they say.'

He drove off down the bumpy cobbles. Clara stood looking after him, her feelings in turmoil. Why had Vinnie really taken her on the picnic? How could a man of his age and experience be interested in someone like her? Yet he seemed to enjoy her company, flattered her unnecessarily, and wanted to take her out again. She had to admit the thought excited her too. He was good-looking and glamorous. He had wealth and social contacts. She could not help admiring his brash self-confidence.

Clara sighed and made for her grimy front door. A train rattled past on the embankment above, deafening her and shrouding her in sooty smoke. She coughed and slammed the door shut. The ground shook beneath her until the long goods train had thundered by. She must dismiss thoughts of Vinnie. He was only trying to win her over so she would give his factory good publicity in the newspaper. She suspected every move that Vinnie Craven made was calculated. Springing up the stairs, two at a time, Clara determined she was not going to be a pawn in one of his games.

Chapter 16

Walking around the factory on Friday morning, Clara had expected something worse. There was a long, brightly lit room with rows of sewing machines on benches. It was noisy with the clatter of machinery, but the women looked intent on their work, their hair confined in blue mob caps. Below was the cutting room, stacked with bails of cheap cotton and worsted cloth. Here there was a male foreman in charge of half a dozen women.

It was Vinnie who showed her round, not the taciturn Mr Reid, who stayed in his office behind a firmly shut door perhaps annoyed that her meeting with him had been superseded. Vinnie stopped now and again to introduce Clara to one of the workers. He knew all their names and asked after their families. Their faces lit up when he spoke to them. This was not a loathed employer, Clara had to admit.

She had gone determined to unearth tales of woe. But she was completely disarmed by the friendly women and Vinnie's teasing banter. She could hardly believe they were the same anxious faces that she had seen leaving the factory a few days before. Perhaps they had cares and worries, but they did not seem to be about work.

There was Cathy who had three children to support and could not be more grateful to Mr Craven. There was bubbly Margaret who was in her first job and could not wait to get to work every morning.

'It's warm here in the winter and the other lasses are canny. I look forward to me work,' she insisted.

Vinnie left Clara to interview Vera, a supervisor. 'We're shipping clothes to the Continent. Pound's weak so our exports are cheap.'

Clara raised the issue of joining a union. Vera was dismissive. 'We don't want trouble. The lasses aren't political. We trust Mr Craven to look after our interests.'

'So he's warned you not to join?' Clara questioned.

A flicker of uncertainty crossed Vera's face. She said hastily, 'No one wants to. Like I said, Mr Craven takes care of us.' Clara could get nothing more out of her on the subject.

Afterwards, Vinnie asked her, 'Satisfied? Or are you going to show me up as a wicked boss who keeps his employees chained to their machines?'

Clara gave him a look. 'Mr Jellicoe wouldn't print it, would he? You being such a mate of his.'

Vinnie chuckled. 'How cynical for one so young.' He walked her to the gate. 'Can I give you a lift anywhere?'

'No thank you.'

'What are you doing now?'

Clara hesitated. She had intended to go to the office to write up her piece about the factory girls. Suddenly, she realised she had lost interest. There was no story to tell, no scandal to unearth. They were just ordinary women muddling along in a mundane job like scores of others. Maybe unionisation was an issue, but not for her. Jellicoe did not employ her as a political correspondent. He paid for warm-hearted stories about people's lives or articles on homemaking.

Vinnie saw her indecision and said, 'Fancy lunch out? I know a nice restaurant in Tynemouth which does the best Dover sole on Tyneside.'

How did he know that fish was her favourite? With difficulty Clara said,

'That's kind of you, Mr Craven, but I can't. I've work to do.'

He did not hide his disappointment. Clara wondered again why he was showing her such attention. She had flattered herself that it was the power of her pen that concerned him. But she saw now the foolishness of her conceit. Her article would not make the slightest difference to the way people viewed his business, even if it got published at all.

He gave her a sad smile as he raised his hat in farewell. He turned towards his car.

Impulsively Clara called out, 'Mr Craven!'

Vinnie stopped. She stepped towards him. 'I was thinking — wondering if you still had those tickets for the pictures tonight.' He stared at her and her heart hammered with nervousness. She gulped. 'Maybe you're taking someone else now. But if you weren't — I'd like to come.' She went red with embarrassment. He made her feel so gauche, surveying her with his dark, knowing eyes. What had made her blurt it out?

Then he smiled and her insides somersaulted. 'No, I'm not going with anyone else. Nothing would give me greater pleasure than taking you, Clara.'

'That's grand.' She grinned.

'I'll pick you up at six. We'll eat first.'

Clara was so excited she had to stop herself skipping along the pavement as she made for the office. She composed a light-hearted piece about young women at work and talked over an idea with Jellicoe for an article on the latest in furnishings. On the spur of the moment, she sent a letter to Willa Templeton asking to meet up. Willa might be useful.

As Clara hurried to get ready for her trip to the Paramount, she quelled her guilt about Benny. She had never promised she would go to the meeting. And the trip to the pictures would be partly for work; she had told Jellicoe she would review the film and do a piece on the new giant cinema. It was not a date with Vinnie; he just happened to have a spare ticket.

Yet, as she ironed her only smart dress, pinned up her coils of dark blonde hair and applied some of Patience's red lipstick in the cracked mirror, Clara knew she was taking more care than if she was meeting Reenie or Benny. Her mother was openly approving.

'It's a great honour, you know,' she said, hovering over her daughter, smoking frantically. 'Don't go saying anything cheeky to put him off.'

'Mam,' Clara cried, 'it's just a trip to the pictures. He means nothing by it.'

'Still, Vinnie Craven showing my daughter some attention.' Patience preened. 'That'll make the neighbours sit up - all the Mrs Laidlaws and the Mrs Shaws of the world who think they're above us since we lost the shop.'

Clara shot her mother a worried look. 'Don't hang your hopes on anything, Mam. Like I said, there's nothing in it.'

'You and Vinnie, eh?' She smiled and blew out smoke.

Vinnie came promptly at six to collect her, dressed in a smart suit with a lilac shirt and dark tie. His hair was immaculately styled and she could tell from the smoothness of his chin that he had just been shaved and had his moustache trimmed. He smelt of expensive soap and cologne. His smile and bow of the head made her insides flutter. She sank into the leather car seat, clasping her hands to stop them shaking. Vinnie did all the talking. He parked outside Fenwick's prestigious department store on Northumberland Street and guided her inside.

The tea rooms were full of chattering well-dressed customers. Clara tried not to stare. She had no idea the place was so popular. There was certainly money in some quarters of Newcastle. They were shown to a reserved table in the corner, near to a concert band. With a pang, Clara thought of Frank and how he would love to be playing like this, instead of scratching a living trying to sell second-hand books to people with no money.

'What's wrong, Clara?' Vinnie disturbed her thoughts. 'You're very quiet.'

She forced a smile. 'Nothing. I'm just taking it all in.'

'You're off duty,' he chided. 'Relax, Miss *Tyne Times*.'

She gave him a guilty glance. 'Actually, I'm not. I said I'd do a piece on the new cinema.'

Vinnie let out a loud laugh that made people glance over. 'I should have guessed. And here I was thinking Miss Magee was here because of me, not old Jellicoe.'

Clara smirked. 'Well, Greta Garbo first. Then you and Mr Jellicoe.'

He leaned across and grasped her hand. 'As long as I come before Jellicoe.' He grinned.

To Clara's consternation, he held on to her hand until the waitress came to take their order. She wanted to pull away, yet part of her thrilled at his easy possessiveness in front of the other diners. The way he gazed across at her made her feel desirable and it was a heady feeling.

Vinnie ordered fish pie and peas for them both, followed by a huge glass of ice cream and fruit for Clara and a pot of tea. He watched her scrape the bottom of the glass with a long spoon.

'They won't need to clean that,' he teased. 'Have another one.'

Clara sat back in contentment. 'That was heaven. Couldn't manage any more.'

Vinnie paid and they made for the entrance. A voice stopped them.

'Hello over there! It's Clara, isn't it?' A dark-haired woman in a yellow hat and dress put out a hand as they passed. She was sitting with a red-haired man and an older woman in uniform with a small boy on her knee.

'Mrs Templeton!' Clara exclaimed. 'How nice to see you.'

'You've never got in touch,' she said reproachfully.

'I've just written to you.' Clara smiled. 'How's that for coincidence?'

Willa introduced her husband, nanny and son. Clara said bashfully, 'And this is Mr Craven — er — a family friend.'

'Vincent,' Vinnie said at once, grasping the hand of George Templeton.

'George,' he said in reply.

'Templeton's the engineers?' Vinnie asked.

George nodded. 'And are you anything to do with Craven's boxing hall?'

'The very one.' Vinnie grinned. 'Do you like boxing?'

'Oh, George is mad about any sport,' Willa cried.

'You must come as my guests,' Vinnie offered at once, 'both of you.'

'Willa won't be interested,' George snorted, 'but I'd be happy to.'

'Of course I'm interested,' Willa declared. 'I've never been inside a boxing hall. I think it would be fascinating. Clara, do you go and watch?'

'Sometimes,' she admitted. 'I cover fights for the paper.'

'Clara's a journalist, darling,' Willa told her husband.

'So be careful what you say,' Vinnie winked. 'She misses nothing.'

They parted, the women agreeing to meet up soon. As they walked down to Pilgrim Street, Vinnie took her arm in his. 'Here I am trying to impress you, and you're the one with friends in high society. You are full of surprises, Miss Magee. How do you know Mrs Templeton?'

'We met at a League of Health and Beauty meeting. It was my first try at journalism. I may have given Mrs Templeton the impression I was already working for the *Tyne Times*,' Clara grinned.

'You certainly left an impression,' Vinnie said admiringly, 'but that doesn't surprise me at all.'

Clara was enchanted by the vast Paramount cinema with its art deco interior, sweeping staircase, plush carpets and row upon row of velvet-upholstered seating. It was like stepping into a Hollywood film set. Vinnie bought the biggest box of chocolates they had and escorted her to the front of the balcony. So captivated was she that Clara forgot to take any notes until the film was over and they were joining the throng of people leaving the cinema. Outside it was still light and she felt disorientated, as if stepping back from another world. Still wrapped in the emotion of the story's climax, she chattered about the film to prolong the experience.

On the drive back, Clara fell silent as the afterglow of her evening of luxury began to fade. The familiar terraces and shabby high street of Byfell closed about her once more. As they passed the town hall, Clara glanced away, a stab of guilt reminding her that she had failed to meet up with Benny. She would make time to see him tomorrow and explain. But the thought was like a chilly draught. How could she admit that she had had one of the best evenings of her life?

She glanced over at Vinnie's angular profile and felt sudden panic. What was she doing with this older man? It would come to no good. He was well known for his philandering and no doubt saw her as an easy conquest. By the time they pulled into Minto Street, Clara had decided that she must encourage Vinnie no further.

As soon as they stopped outside the flat, Clara had the door open.

'Thanks for taking me, Mr Craven. I've had a grand time.'

Vinnie reached across and stopped her. 'Me too, Clara.'

He took her hand, raised it to his lips and kissed it. She was acutely aware of how rough and callused her hand must feel. The hand of a drudge. For all her journalistic ambitions, she was still a cleaner for Max and a maid-of-all-work for her melancholic mother. She snatched her hand away.

'Should've worn gloves,' she joked. 'I must taste of carbolic soap.'

'Don't be ashamed of working hands,' Vinnie said. 'They're beautiful.'

She climbed out quickly before he could walk her to the door or make a further assignation. The kiss, however gentlemanly, had unnerved her. It implied something greater than casual friendship. Clara rushed inside without looking back. On the stairs, she heard him driving away with a toot of his horn.

Her heart was still hammering when she entered the flat. Patience and Jimmy both rose to greet her.

'How was your evening, pet?' Patience asked anxiously.

'Canny—'

'He's been arrested,' Jimmy said excitedly. 'There was a big punch-up.'

'Clara doesn't want to be bothered with all that now,' Patience said, trying to hide her agitation. 'I want to hear about her night out.'

Clara stared from one to the other. Her stomach lurched with dread. 'Who's been arrested? Tell me.'

'Benny,' Jimmy answered. 'The police came. Him and two others got nicked at that union meetin'. I saw it all.'

'What were you doing there?' Clara gasped. Jimmy shrugged.

'It's just as well you didn't go,' Patience said. 'You could've got hurt.'

'Was Benny hurt?'

'Got a bloody mouth,' Jimmy said.

Clara turned round at once and made for the door.

96

'Where do you think you're going?' her mother asked querulously.

'To Reenie's — see what's happening.'

'You can't!' Patience cried. Clara hesitated.

'Tell her, Mam,' Jimmy muttered.

Patience fumbled for a half-smoked cigarette, smouldering on a saucer. She inhaled deeply. 'Benny came round earlier,' she said, not meeting Clara's look.

Clara's heart lurched. 'Did you tell him where I was?'

'He already knew,' Jimmy answered. 'Vinnie went round to Lewis's for a shave and trim. Told Benny he was taking you to the pictures.'

Patience faced her. 'He came round here shouting his head off, demanding to see you. I told him he was too late and to stop bothering you. The things he said about Vinnie don't bear repeating. I told you that lad was nothing but trouble.'

Feeling faint, Clara clutched a chair and sat down. 'I should've been there,' she groaned. 'This is all my fault.'

'No it's not,' Patience said, coming to put an arm about her. 'If anyone deserved a trip to the pictures it was you, pet. You're not responsible for Benny's losing his head over the matter. It's not as if you were properly courting. And now you've got Vinnie—'

'I haven't got him,' Clara said angrily, shaking her off. 'I'm not such a fool as to be taken in by a film and a fancy box of chocolates. He's done that for plenty of lasses.'

'You're different,' Patience said stoutly. 'Dolly says so and she should know. She's seen them come and go.'

'Aye, our Clara,' Jimmy agreed. 'He's always asking me questions about you.'

'But why?'

'Cos he sees you've got breeding,' Patience said proudly, 'no matter what your circumstances. He knows you're going to make something of yourself.'

Clara covered her face in her hands. She did not know what to think.

'What of Benny's family?' she whispered. 'Were any of them there at the meeting?'

'I saw Frank,' Jimmy answered. 'I think he was trying to calm it down. Didn't see him after.'

Clara bit her lip. What would Frank think of her now? She could not bear the thought of his disapproval. It would be worse than Benny's anger.

'How did the fighting start?'

'What does it matter?' Patience sighed. 'What's done is done.'

'I want to know,' Clara insisted.

Jimmy said, 'Some of the husbands and fathers of the lasses what work at the factory turned up. Didn't like their women being told what to do. Chased the speakers. Benny wouldn't shut his gob.'

Clara groaned. How like Benny.

'Nothing you can do about it tonight,' Patience pointed out. 'Come to bed. I want to hear all about your evening.'

Clara could not sleep. She worried about Benny in a police cell and about what had happened to Frank. She dreaded to think what Reenie and her parents now thought of her for going out with Vinnie. Vinnie Craven! He had deliberately provoked Benny by going to Lewis's for a shave. She would have sharp words with him when she saw him next. But however much she tossed and turned with her tortured thoughts, she ended up blaming herself.

Early the next day, Clara went up to the police station. PC Hobson told her that Benny was to be held over the weekend and appear before magistrates on

Monday morning. To Clara's relief, Frank was not one of the other men arrested.

'I warned you to keep that lad out of trouble,' the constable frowned.

'Can I see him?' Clara asked.

'Best not to. Let him cool off, eh?'

She went round to Max's flat and caught him on his way out. He saw the state she was in and pulled her inside. She explained everything.

'Can you do anything for Benny?' she pleaded.

'I'll go up to the station now,' Max promised. 'See what he's charged with.' He gave her a strange look. Finally, he asked, 'How well do you know Vincent Craven?'

Clara blushed. 'He's just a friend of the family. He and Dad were close.'

'Be careful,' Max said quietly. 'He can be very charming, but he uses people. I've seen it in his business dealings. And I'm told he's a bit of a ladies' man.'

'I'm not one of his ladies,' Clara retorted, 'so don't worry about me.'

Clara stayed away from the Lewises until closing time, knowing they would be especially busy without Benny and no doubt trying to put on a brave face. The news of the fight and arrests was all over town. There were rumours that it had been a co-ordinated attack; men had been paid to break up the meeting. Others said it was a setup by the Communists to reflect badly on Craven's factory and treatment of the workers.

Heart hammering, Clara knocked at the Lewises' door. Frank was sweeping up and answered. Clara's throat dried.

'Do you want to come in?' he asked kindly. She nodded. 'You know about Benny then?' He closed the door behind her. She nodded again and swallowed hard.

'I'm sorry. How is he?'

'Max came round and told us he's all right. Sobered up.'

'He'd been drinking?' Clara gasped.

Frank gave her a penetrating look. 'He was upset before the meeting.'

'Who is it?' Marta called down the stairs.

'Clara,' Frank called back.

There was a silence, then, 'Clara, are you hungry?'

Tears stung her eyes. How could Benny's mother be so forgiving? Her chin trembled as she went to the stairs and looked up.

'No thank you, Mrs Lewis. I just came to say how sorry I was about Benny.'

'Come up,' Marta insisted. 'We drink tea, *ja*?'

Upstairs, Reenie was bolting down a meal of bacon and egg before going to work. She was not so charitable.

'I heard it was Vinnie's men who started it,' she said indignantly. 'He's that scared of his workers joining the union.'

'That's a bit far-fetched,' Clara countered. 'I've seen round the factory and the lasses don't look put upon to me.'

Reenie's look was disdainful. 'He's really turned your head, hasn't he? Just one trip to the pictures and—'

'Reenie,' Frank chided, 'leave the lass be. You can see she's worried about our Benny.'

'Is she?' Reenie was disbelieving. 'Got a funny way of showing it.'

'Don't listen to her, Clara,' Marta said, pushing a cup of tea towards her. 'She is being the loyal sister.'

'Just as well someone is,' Reenie muttered.

Clara put down her cup, stung by her friend's barbed comments. 'I didn't start

98

the fight and I didn't put Benny in the cells! I never even said I'd go to his meeting. I got the chance to see Garbo at the flicks and I took it. Bet you'd have done the same given half a chance, Reenie.'

Reenie flushed. 'If I was courting I wouldn't have gone out with another man behind his back.'

Clara sprang up, indignant. 'Me and Benny aren't courting. We fall out more often than Laurel and Hardy.' She saw the look of dismay on Marta's face. 'I'm really sorry, Mrs Lewis. I like Benny a lot, but there's nothing serious between us. Benny knows that even if Reenie can't see it.'

Reenie rose too. 'Just go, Clara, before your big gob says any more.'

Clara hurried downstairs, swallowing tears. She had made things ten times worse by coming. She had never seen Reenie so angry. Footsteps followed her down. Frank unbolted the door for her.

'Clara,' he said gently, putting a hand on her shoulder, 'Reenie's upset. She doesn't really blame you. She just thinks the world of our Benny and wants you to as well.'

Clara felt herself shaking under his touch. 'But she's right,' she whispered unhappily, 'it is my fault. I should have told Benny long ago I don't love him — not in the way he wants.'

Slowly, Frank pulled Clara round to face him. He lifted her chin. Her heart banged erratically like a caged bird.

'You must put Benny out of his misery, Clara,' he chided gently. She nodded, swallowing down tears. How could she admit her guilty secret; that she had gone out with Benny so she could see more of Frank? He would think even less of her. The warmth of Frank's hand burned into her shoulder. 'Tell me,' he asked, 'do you love someone else?'

Her eyes widened in shock. Had Frank guessed all along how she felt about him? She trembled under his touch. She wanted nothing more than to be enfolded in his arms and never let go. But she could not do it, not with Benny incarcerated at the police station. She had betrayed him once already.

'Clara?' he prompted, his voice a deep vibration between them.

She swallowed hard. 'Yes, I love another man,' she whispered, her large eyes pleading with him to understand.

At that moment, Reenie came clattering downstairs and interrupted.

'Still here?' she said frostily.

Clara jumped back guiltily. 'I'm going.'

'Goodbye, Clara,' Frank said, turning away.

'Goodbye,' she choked. As she hurried out, the word echoed in her head. It sounded so final.

Chapter 17

As Saturday evening wore on, Clara s unhappiness at what she had done and at her impotence to help Benny fanned into anger against Vinnie. She stormed down to Craven Hall.

'He's dining out,' Clarkie told her. 'Rotary Club. Do you want to leave a message, miss?'

Clara let out a sigh of frustration. 'No. No message.'

She trailed home. Her mother was in bed; Jimmy was minding cars for Clarkie. Staggering upstairs with the tin bath from the yard, she boiled up a large pan of water and had a shallow wash. One day she would live again in a house with a proper bath and plumbing and hot running water. She dried her hair with a threadbare towel and pulled on her mother's old kimono. Tiptoeing into the bedroom, she fetched her diary from its box under the bed and returned to the main room to write it up. She had written nothing for three days. Two hours later, she was still writing.

Halfway through describing her trip to the Paramount, she was startled by a knock on the door downstairs. Clara thought about ignoring it. But what if it was Frank with news of Benny, or something had happened to Jimmy? Hastily, she threw a jacket over the kimono.

A dark figure was silhouetted in the half-light.

'You wanted to see me?' It was Vinnie's deep voice.

'It — it's late,' Clara stammered. 'What I have to say can wait.'

'Can I come in?' He stepped towards her. 'I won't stay long. I've news of Benny.'

This took her by surprise, and she stood aside to let him in. He was in evening dress, stiff-winged collar and bow tie. He carried a silver-topped cane and smelled of cigars. He stood very close in the tiny lobby, looking her over.

'I'm sorry. I got you out of bed,' he murmured.

She blushed. 'No, I was up writing.'

He nodded at the stairs. 'You lead the way.'

Clara padded up the steps in bare feet, acutely away of him following behind. In the sitting room she retreated across the floor and stood in front of the empty grate with her arms folded.

'Tell me about Benny,' she said tensely.

He put down his hat and stick. 'Do you mind if I undo this?' he asked, straining at his stiff collar. Clara nodded. She watched him pull off his tie and release the collar, rubbing at his thick neck. He discarded his jacket and flopped on to a chair. 'By, it's hot tonight.'

'Benny?' she reminded him.

'Aye, Benny,' Vinnie said. 'I was told about the trouble this morning. I've been to see the lad.'

'You've seen him? They wouldn't let me,' Clara gasped. 'How is he?'

'He's all right. Don't think there'll be much of a case to answer.'

'What do you mean?'

'The most serious charge was assault on another lad,' Vinnie explained. 'He's the brother of a lass who works for me at the factory. I've had a word and he's prepared to drop the complaint. If you ask me who was at fault, it was six of one and half a dozen of the other.'

Clara gawped at him. 'You mean they'll let Benny go free?'

'Not exactly,' Vinnie cautioned. 'He'll still have to go in front of the beaks on Monday morning for breach of the peace. But it's a first offence. Mostly likely they'll let him off with a caution.'

She stared at him, not knowing whether to be angry or grateful.

'Some folk are saying you paid men to stir up trouble,' she accused him. 'Did you?'

He gave her a hurt look. 'Do you really think that little of me?'

'It doesn't matter what I think.' Clara was abrupt. 'People have a right to join unions if they want — and to hold meetings without being intimidated.'

'I quite agree,' Vinnie replied. 'Do you think I'd concern myself over a handful of hotheads? Everyone's entitled to their own views.'

Clara found him infuriating. She was still angry at him yet he was being surprisingly reasonable. She found it hard to believe Reenie's accusations that Vinnie was behind the violence.

She advanced on him. 'You want me to be grateful for you helping Benny. But none of this would've happened if you hadn't gone and stirred things up at the barber's.'

'What do you mean?' Vinnie gave an incredulous laugh.

'Getting Benny to shave you and telling him you were taking me out,' Clara said hotly.

'But it was true, wasn't it?' Vinnie challenged her.

'Yes, but you knew it would provoke him. Benny went out and got drunk, then got himself arrested.'

Vinnie jumped up and came close. 'So you'd rather have done it behind Benny's back — risk him finding out later?'

'No,' Clara said, feeling confusion. 'It wasn't like that. There was nothing to find out.'

Vinnie reached out and took her hand. 'You wanted to go out with me, I didn't force you,' he reminded her. 'You enjoyed yourself and so did I. I don't have any regrets. What happened to Benny had nothing to do with us — he would have got into trouble anyway.'

She tried to pull away, but Vinnie held her in a firm grip. 'Look at me, Clara,' he commanded. 'Tell me you didn't enjoy yourself last night. Tell me you would rather have been with Benny. Just say it and I'll go — not bother you again.'

She looked into his dark mesmerising eyes. They blazed with emotion — dangerous emotion. She forced herself to look away.

'See,' Vinnie said in triumph, 'you can't say it 'cos it wouldn't be true.' His hold tightened. 'You feel something too, Clara, just like I do. I've been waiting all my life to feel this way about a lass. Now I've found you, Harry's daughter, right under me nose all the time. A war hero for a father, a classy mother. Good Geordie stock. By heck, lass, together we could conquer anything.'

'Stop it!' Clara flung him off. 'I don't know how I feel about you.'

A flash of impatience crossed his face and was gone. He smiled disarmingly, raising his hands in surrender. 'Fair enough. It's early days and I'm not going to push you into anything you don't want.' He retrieved his jacket and tie and jammed on his hat. Picking up his stick, he tossed it in the air and caught it. He fixed her with his look. 'But I know what I want — and I'm prepared to wait for it.'

Clara clutched her arms to stop herself shaking, staring at him in mute confusion as he made for the door. Turning, he swept her with a final look. 'You suit the kimono,' he winked. 'I'll see myself out.'

***

Benny appeared in court on Monday, and was bound over to keep the peace for twelve months and warned to stay away from Craven's factory. Clara was in court, but too embarrassed to sit with his family. To her, Benny had the miserable but defiant expression of a young boy being reprimanded by his elders.

Outside, she hurried over to see him as he left the court with Frank and his parents. Frank nodded a greeting. 'We'll leave the pair of you to have a word,' he said, steering his parents away. 'See you at the shop, Benny.'

Alone, Clara and Benny glanced at each other awkwardly.

'Sorry I wasn't there on Friday night,' Clara said quietly.

Benny grunted. 'No, Greta Garbo's much more important than the revolution,' he mocked.

Clara sighed. 'Do you want to tell me what happened?'

His tone was brittle. 'It was a fix-up. Those lads were waiting for us — all organised. Meeting had hardly started when they began heckling and hoying stones. He put them up to it.'

'Who did?' Clara asked, tensing.

'Craven, who else?'

'I don't believe it,' Clara said. 'He's not going to bother over a few activists handing out leaflets. Said himself everyone's entitled to their say.'

'Course you'd know all about what Vinnie Craven thinks,' Benny said bitterly.

Clara huffed with impatience. 'All right, I deserve that. I'm not proud of the way I went out with him and didn't tell you. It didn't seem important—'

'Not important?' Benny cried. 'But you're my lass.'

'No, Benny, I'm not,' Clara replied. 'I'm not anyone's lass. I'm very fond of you and I want to stay friends. But it's never going to be more than that.'

'It's your mam, isn't it?' Benny said angrily. 'She's put the block on you seeing me.'

'It's not just Mam,' Clara said, 'it's me. Look, Benny,' she appealed to him, 'we're not suited. We're always arguing — look at us now. You've got very strong views about things which I don't share. I'm interested in things that you dismiss as shallow and daft.'

'Like Vinnie Craven?'

Clara lost patience. 'If it wasn't for him, you'd probably be in prison by now. Don't blame Mr Craven for what's happened.'

Benny glared, 'Never thought you'd be taken in by his type. He'll not stop till everyone on Tyneside's working for him or in his debt. Right little Mussolini.'

'If you're jealous of him, that's your problem,' Clara said with a pitying look. 'I'm sorry I've hurt you, Benny. I love your family as much as my own, but I won't pretend any longer that I'm in love with you.'

She walked away from him, digging her nails into her palms to stop herself crying. She felt wretched at his unhappiness, but Frank was right: it would be worse to drag out their fraught courtship any further. Benny did not call her back.

Clara busied herself all day with assignments and worked late into the night. She pushed herself all that week, getting up at the crack of dawn to clean Max's office and sitting at her desk in the newspaper office before anyone else came in. She drove herself with work. She volunteered to cover every flower show, garden fete and society meeting possible. But hardest of all was stifling her longing for Frank. She avoided Vinnie Craven and did not allow herself to dwell on Benny.

Two weeks later, Clara got a call at the office from Willa Templeton inviting her to a charity tea party at Madras House, in aid of crippled veterans. Brigadier Bell-Carr, their patron, would be there and would she like to do a report for the newspaper? Patience was as excited by the news as Clara was and told her she must buy something pretty to wear for the occasion. Since Clara had broken up with Benny and no longer went round to the Lewises of an evening, her mother had perked up considerably. She showed a keen interest in what her daughter was doing and no longer retreated to bed at six in the evening.

Clara went round to Slater's pawnshop and bought a pale blue dress and bolero jacket she had eyed in the window that no one had reclaimed. She wanted to look her best for tea at Madras House.

Mr Slater took her aside and said, 'I've something for you.'

He was growing forgetful and the shop was a chaos of boxes of clothes and household goods. He rummaged around in an old suitcase, then pulled open some drawers in a tallboy.

'I put it away safe,' he mumbled.

'Mr Slater, I'm in a hurry,' Clara said. 'I could call back later.'

'Found it in the lining of your father's coat,' he continued.

Clara froze. 'What did you say?'

That coat you brought in: blue serge, large collar, silk lining.'

Clara remembered the coat. Her father had worn it for best and they had held on to it for Jimmy until two months ago when he had suddenly grown too tall.

'The lining was frayed, so the missus was mending it when the necklace fell out,' he rambled on. 'Must've fallen through a pocket. I said to the missus, I'll not take what I've not paid for. I'll keep it for Miss Magee, it might be sentimental.' He poked inside a faded satin jewellery box. 'Ah! Here it is.'

Mr Slater fished out a chain with his arthritic fingers and held it out to Clara. She took it, full of curiosity. It was a locket. She peered at it in her hand. It was lightweight, slightly dented, the ornate engraving worn thin. She did not recognise it at all. The catch was faulty and the locket fell open easily. On one side was a lock of pale blond hair, almost white; on the other, a fuzzy photograph. Clara looked closer. It was of a woman, her hair parted and tightly bound behind, her eyes solemn but her mouth blurred as if she was breaking into a smile. Clara had never seen her before.

She handed it back with a frown. 'There must be a mistake. It's not one of my family.'

Mr Slater slowly shook his head as if it was just as big a mystery to him. 'It came out of your father's coat, so by rights it's yours.'

All at once, it hit her. This must be the woman with whom her father had had an affair. It was his tawdry secret, a cheap locket probably given by his lover with her hair and picture to remind him of her when they were apart. Revulsion welled up inside her. Clara nearly flung the locket across the room. Her family's problems had stemmed from the moment that angry unkempt foreigner had dogged them and caused her parents to row. He had been some-thing to do with this woman and had wanted her father to pay for his indiscretions. Perhaps he had wanted the locket back too. He'd said that Harry had something that belonged to him. Her father had never been the same afterwards. That's when the drinking and the gambling had started. That's when his debts had begun to mount until they had engulfed him like a tidal wave and shattered all their lives.

Clara stared at the woman's photograph with hatred. She was convinced this stranger was the cause of all the trouble between her parents.

'Keep it,' Mr Slater said, 'or sell it to a collector.'

'It can't be worth anything,' Clara said in disdain.

'It's foreign. I've only seen one like it before — belonged to a White Russian from the time of the last tsar.'

Clara stared at it with indecision. Despite her distaste, curiosity flared again. She pocketed it. Perhaps she would find out more about this woman. Or keep it as a nest egg. One thing was for certain; she would never tell her mother about its existence. Patience's nerves were so fragile, such a revelation would plunge her back into melancholy. Clara thanked the pawnbroker and left.

Chapter 18

Madras House was a solid Victorian villa set back from the street with large bay windows and ornate ironwork balconies at the upper storeys. To Clara's surprise it was austerely furnished in an art deco style of geometric wallpaper and angular furniture. A pair of tall Chinese vases filled with ferns gave a splash of colour in the hallway and a series of modern paintings of muscular figures in bold colours hung on the pale yellow walls of the sitting room.

Clara tried not to stare open-mouthed as a housemaid ushered her through French windows to a large walled garden. A vast tea of sandwiches and buttered scones was laid out on trestle tables. The linen tablecloths snapped in the breeze, dazzling the eye. Behind, a dozen uniformed maids were pouring tea into dainty Chinese-patterned cups. Scores of guests stood around chatting. The majority were well-dressed women; a few were men in wheelchairs or propped up on crutches. Clara felt out of place and quickly pulled out her notebook and pencil to look professional.

Willa Templeton called for everyone's attention. She sounded nervous.

'On behalf of the committee, I'd just like to say - we're all very grateful for this splendid turn-out. Well done everybody. It's a — it's a huge honour to have with us our patron, Brigadier Bell-Carr, and his lady wife, to open our tea party this afternoon.' Willa began an enthusiastic hand-clapping that was quickly taken up by her guests.

The brigadier began to speak, but his delivery was mumbled. Clara eased her way closer through the crowd to hear.

'. . . heartening that in such depressed times as these the English don't forget their wounded comrades ...talking of the true Englishman . . . unbeaten by foreign armies . . . disgrace that our government gives nothing to these brave men . . . left to fend for themselves all these years. It's what happens when you let Bolsheviks run the place.'

Clara saw his wife put out a restraining hand and squeeze his arm. The brigadier cleared his throat. 'Anyway, we must never forget the brave battalions who sacrificed everything to make England great. We're of their blood — we spring from the same soil.' He warmed to his theme, his voice growing stronger with conviction. 'We must stand together against vested powers. We're all in the same boat - instead of a land fit for heroes, we've seen our incomes fall and our investments wiped out, while others have grown rich on other people's misery.'

'Alastair,' Cissie Bell-Carr reproved with a throaty laugh, 'they're here for tea, not a political rally.'

There was a ripple of awkward laughter. Clara could not work out if it was over their patron's speech or his wife's interruption.

'My wife is right, of course,' he said stiffly. 'Give as generously as you can to these splendid chaps — our ex-servicemen — and enjoy this wonderful tea.'

There was polite applause and the hubbub of voices rose again as people began to tuck into the large mounds of sandwiches. Clara had never seen so much food. Her mouth watered. Just as she was on the point of helping herself to a sandwich, Willa pounced.

'Clara, darling, come and meet our guests of honour.' She waved frantically. 'I told them you'd give us a good write-up.'

Clara found herself shaking hands with the tall brigadier who had ignored her at the Hippodrome. He gave her a distracted nod.

'Hope you'll be able to put in everything I said,' he told her gruffly. 'Or does your newspaper suffer the usual Bolshie bias?'

Clara gave him a baffled look. 'We tend to stick to sport and stories about cats stuck up chimneys.'

He grunted at her and turned away to talk to a man with an eyepatch.

Cissie Bell-Carr gave her a warm smile. 'Don't worry,' she whispered, 'his bark's very much worse than his bite.' She had a trace of an Irish accent. 'Haven't we met before, Miss Magee?'

'At the Hippodrome; Watts versus Kain,' Clara reminded her. 'You were off to the Sandford Rooms. Did you have a good dinner?'

'Oh, yes! Marvellous dinner.' She assessed Clara with shrewd hazel eyes. 'And you mentioned my outfit in the article. I believe you called me glamorous. You see, I've remembered. Flattery will get you far.' She laughed.

'And are you still interested in boxing, Mrs Bell-Carr?' Clara asked.

'Oh, yes.' She smiled. 'I just love watching those fit young men and their muscled bodies, don't you?'

Willa squeaked with nervous laughter. 'Cissie, be careful. Clara will quote you.'

'And you, Miss Magee,' Cissie asked, 'what do you like to do for entertainment?'

'Clara adores the cinema,' Willa answered for her. 'Did you enjoy Grand Hotel the other week?'

'Very much,' Clara said. 'I'm a Garbo fan. My friend Reenie and I used to practise speaking as low as Garbo to give us an air of mystery. But lads just thought we had colds.'

Cissie and Willa laughed with her.

'I love Garbo too,' Cissie told her. 'Some day, Clara, you must come out to Hoxton Hall and we'll watch old films. We have a film projector in the library. We don't use it nearly enough.'

'Do you really mean that?' Clara gasped.

'Of course I do. Willa could bring you out. We'll have our own film show.' She lowered her voice for just the women. 'It's deadly dull at Hoxton most of the week now that James is off to boarding school. I can tell you'd brighten it up no end.'

'Super!' Willa enthused. 'Nanny could bring Baby. He loves Buster Keaton.'

'So do I.' Clara grinned. 'Reminds me of my brother Jimmy — he's just as clumsy.'

'And what does Jimmy do?' Cissie asked.

Clara hesitated. 'He works at Craven's boxing hall. Wants to box professionally someday.'

'One of Vincent Craven's young men?' Cissie asked. Clara nodded. 'My husband thinks highly of Vincent and what he's doing for the unemployed boys.'

'Clara's a good friend of Mr Craven's,' Willa said eagerly. 'They went to see Grand Hotel together. Isn't that right, Clara?'

Clara reddened. 'He's a family friend.'

Cissie put a hand on her arm. 'Well, you keep good company. The brigadier thinks Vincent is a man for the future. We need more ambitious young men like him who care about the state this country is in.' She gave a conspiratorial smile. 'Besides, he's quite the charmer.'

Clara excused herself to go and interview some of the men who were the recipients of the charity. Most had been brought from Gilead, a large hospital twenty miles up the Tyne valley.

'Been there since 1920,' an ex-soldier called Bob Grayson told her.

'Don't you ever go home?' Clara asked in astonishment.

He gave her a strange look. 'It is me home. I need nursing all the time. Can't even wipe me own backside,' he told her bluntly. 'Mam couldn't have managed. She's dead now, any road.' He nodded at another man sitting in a wheelchair staring blankly around him, his hands shaking in his lap. 'Some of 'em are gaga.' He lowered his voice. 'Gilead's a lunatic asylum too, you know. They don't like to mention that. Surprised they brought old Percy. Still, it's a day out and we shouldn't grumble.'

Clara was thankful her own father had survived the War unharmed. If Patience had had to fend for herself and her young children, how different their lives would have been. It made her all the more determined to grab every opportunity that came her way. Willa and Cissie's friendship, for instance.

By the time Clara left she had arranged to meet Willa again for a swim at the city pool. Clara silently thanked her father for having taught her to swim as a child at the public baths. Cissie had promised to arrange a trip up to Hoxton Hall over the summer. As she made her way back to Byfell on the tram, Clara's head reeled. How was it that these well-to-do women had befriended her? She had nothing in common with them, except a sense of fun and a love of matinee idols. But she liked them for their openness, their lack of snobbery. And her instinct told her that underneath the light-hearted chatter, they were a touch lonely and bored.

Maybe their interest in her was transitory and they saw her as an exotic species they could cultivate: an ambitious working-class girl they could take under their wing and fashion in their own image. Clara did not care. She would seize the chance that these friendships offered of entering a new and exciting world, beyond the confines of Byfell's smoky streets. She smiled to think how her mother would demand every little detail.

As the tram rattled downriver, Clara also pondered her relationship with Vinnie. It came as a surprise to hear that he was admired by influential people like the Bell-Carrs. She had to admit to feeling a little flattered to be linked with him by Willa. Maybe she judged him too harshly and he did not see her just in terms of a casual affair.

Still, Clara felt uncomfortable with the thought. She did not love Vinnie. Deep down, she hoped that if she bided her time, the opportunity would come to tell Frank that she loved him. No one came close to him in her affections. Yet it was still too soon after the break-up with Benny to declare her feelings. Reenie was not speaking to her and Clara did not have the nerve to go near the Lewises' shop.

***

She began to see Willa on a weekly basis. They would meet in town for a swim or go to an art exhibition. Willa was keen on modernists and liked to patronise local artists. Sometimes Clara would go to Madras House for coffee and they would play outside with Willa's little boy Robert, Clara chasing him in endless games of hide and seek around the large garden. She would entertain him with a trick her father had taught her, making a coin disappear from the palm of her hand and pretending she found it in the boy's ear. Robert squealed with laughter and demanded she repeat it again and again.

Always, Willa would announce when it was time for Clara to go.

'I must get ready for George coming home,' Willa would explain. 'He likes just me and Baby to be here when he gets in. He has such a tiring time at work, with all the uncertainty over trade. Pipe and slippers time, he calls it. Not that he smokes,' she laughed.

Clara marvelled at the Templetons' leisured existence compared to her own upbringing. Her parents had known what a really tiring day at work was: keeping a shop open till the last customer went, staying up late sorting stock or wrestling with figures, endless worries over bank loans, rentmen, creditors and the dwindling demand for fancy goods. They had painstakingly built up their own business over many years, only to see it come crashing down. Vinnie had blamed the government's mishandling of the economy rather than Harry's recklessness with money. Whatever the cause, Clara admired the Templetons for hanging on to their business. Yet, as she left the comfort of Madras House for Minto Street, she could not help envy welling up inside too.

Once, in late July, Cissie Bell-Carr was visiting when Clara called.

'You must forgive me, dear girl, for not arranging your visit to Hoxton.' Cissie was fulsome in apology. 'Alastair and I have been away in Ireland. And now James is back for the holidays and it's almost the shooting season. But I promise you, we'll get together soon.'

Clara was sceptical. But a week later, Vinnie called in at the newspaper offices, waving a gilt-edged invitation at her. Clara saw Miss Holt give her a curious look and ushered Vinnie into the corridor. She had refused several invitations to the pictures since the Benny incident and given the boxing assignments to Adam Paxton.

'Why have you been avoiding me, lass?' Vinnie demanded.

'I've been busy.' Clara was evasive.

'Not too busy to drop everything for Mrs Templeton when she asks you,' he said dryly.

'Who told you that?' she demanded. 'Jimmy Big-mouth, I suppose.'

'I've met George Templeton at a couple of Rotary meetings, as it happens,' Vinnie answered. 'He was asking me about you — whether you were a suitable friend for his wife.'

'Of all the cheek!' Clara exclaimed.

'Don't worry, I told him you were.' He was standing very close, eyeing her keenly. 'So why are you keeping away from me, Clara? What are you afraid of?'

'Nothing.' Clara held his look. 'What have you got there?'

He smiled suddenly. 'A summons from the Bell-Carrs, no less. Dinner at the Sandford Rooms. They're coming to the heavyweight fight next week.'

Clara folded her arms. 'Good for you. What's that got to do with me?'

Vinnie handed her the card. 'They want you there too — as my partner. Look, Mrs Bell-Carr's written it on the bottom.'

Clara took the card suspiciously. It was addressed to 'Vincent Craven and Guest', cordially inviting them to attend a late supper at the Sandford Rooms in Grainger Street on Saturday 6 August after 9 p.m. Written across the bottom of the card in large looped black ink was the instruction, 'I insist you bring Clara as your partner. She must discover for herself how good the chef is at the Sandford! Cissie Bell-Carr.'

Clara stared back at Vinnie. He knew she could not resist such an opportunity.

'I suppose I could do a write-up on the restaurant,' she said.

Vinnie chuckled. 'I'll send Clarkie round to pick you up in the car. Be ready at six-thirty. We'll have cocktails in the office first.' Clara nodded. He stepped towards her and she tensed. Vinnie pulled out a five pound note and pressed it into her hand. 'Buy something canny to wear.'

She gasped at the amount. 'I don't need your money,' she protested, thrusting it back at him.

'See it as a loan then.' He shrugged, refusing to take it back. 'Listen, Clara, it's a big chance for you to mix with the right people — make new contacts for your job. You need to dress up for the part, lass. Believe me, looking smart impresses people like the Bell-Carrs. It's money in the bank.'

Clara was easily tempted. When had she ever had five pounds to spend on clothes? She could buy a whole new wardrobe. 'Just a loan, then,' she agreed.

Vinnie left her with that strange mix of unease and excitement that she was coming to associate with him.

Patience went into town with Clara for the first time since Harry had died. She was shaking with nerves all the way on the tram and Clara insisted on her sitting down in a cafe for a cup of tea before they embarked on shopping. It was Patience who wanted to go round all the town's dress shops and department stores, but she soon tired and had to keep sitting down. Concerned that the trip was exhausting her mother, Clara swiftly chose an elegant dark blue satin cocktail dress, black high-heeled shoes, gloves and a black slouch hat which perched at a rakish angle. In the fitting room her mother became weepy.

'You look beautiful,' she said, choking back tears. 'All grown up.'

She was tearful too when Clara made ready on Saturday night, washing her hair and brushing it out into rippling waves, carefully applying rouge and bright red lipstick that she had bought on their shopping trip.

'Don't, Mam,' Clara said, trying to comfort her.

'I just keep thinking of Harry — how proud he would've—' She broke off, burying her face in her hands.

Clara put her arms round her mother and kissed her forehead. 'I know how much you miss him,' she whispered. 'I do too. But you mustn't upset yourself.'

Patience dropped her hands. 'I'm not upset,' she hissed, 'I'm angry.'

Clara drew back in surprise. Her mother's face was tense with suppressed rage.

'That stupid, selfish man! Why did he go and leave us? We had everything he ever wanted; you and Jimmy, the shop and a canny home. We had standing in the town; people looked up to him. I'm sick of hearing people say what a grand man he was. Well, if he was that grand, why did he do such a cowardly thing?'

'Mam, stop it,' Clara said in agitation. She had no idea her mother harboured such bitterness. 'Dad wasn't a coward. Things just got on top of him.'

'Why do you defend him after all we've been through?' Patience railed.

'Because I loved him,' Clara replied, 'and I know you did too.'

Patience gave her a bleak look. 'He doesn't deserve it. He wasn't the man you thought he was.'

'What do you mean?' Clara demanded.

Patience clenched her mouth shut and shook her head. Clara thought suddenly of the woman in the photograph and understood her mother's angry sorrow. She'd hidden the locket away in an old handbag where Patience wouldn't find it. Harry had let her down badly. But that did not make him a bad father to her and she would not let his memory be tarnished by the affair.

'I think I understand,' she said gently.

Patience shot her a look. She seized Clara by the hand. 'You can't understand. But promise me this: don't turn your nose up at Vinnie Craven. There's a man who knows his mind. He's ambitious and clever in business - more than your father ever was. Stick with him and you'll go far. The Cravens have been good to us since Harry died.'

'So have others,' Clara retorted. 'I'll not be made to feel beholden.'

'You could do a lot worse than Vinnie,' Patience persisted. 'If it wasn't for him Jimmy would probably be in a Borstal by now. Anyway, the man's daft about you.'

Clara gave a derisive laugh. 'I annoy him, more like, 'cos I won't fall at his feet like other lasses.'

Patience sighed impatiently. 'Don't know where you get such stubbornness from.'

Clara smiled, wiping off the lipstick mark she had made on her mother's forehead. 'You, of course.'

A car horn tooted in the street below. Clara's heart lurched. She went to the window and saw Vinnie's car below.

'It's Clarkie.' She put on her new hat and gloves and snatched up a small handbag she had bought in a closing-down sale in Byfell. It held her lipstick, comb, notebook and pencil. The horn tooted again. 'Wish me luck.'

Patience smiled finally. She held her daughter's face briefly between her bony hands. 'Enjoy yourself,' she said, kissing her nose. 'I'll want every detail in the morning.'

Clarkie was dressed in a smart suit, a little too long in the arms. He gave Clara an appreciative grin and held the door open for her as he had seen his boss do. As she sat in the car, Max walked past and did a double-take.

'Clara, is that you?' he called out. She smiled and waved as Clarkie revved the engine and pulled away with a sudden lurch. They laughed at the look of astonishment on his face.

'Why's he looking so surprised?' Clara cried.

''Cos you look like a film star, miss,' Clarkie said.

When she walked into the hall Clara was aware of people staring. Clarkie led her through to the office as if she were visiting for the first time. Dolly was dressed up in a velvet evening gown, busily setting out glasses on the sideboard. None of the guest party had yet arrived. Dolly gasped at the sight of Clara in her new dress.

'What a picture!' she cried. 'Wait till Vinnie sees you.'

'Sees what?' Vinnie asked, breezing in from the far door that led from the training gym. He was immaculately turned out in evening dress, his dark hair smoothed, his chin newly shaven. He checked his step, for a moment not seeming to recognise Clara. Then he continued towards her, taking in every detail at a glance.

'You look beautiful,' he murmured, taking her bare arm and raising her gloved hand to his lips. 'Better than Garbo.' He smiled and planted a lingering kiss on her fingers.

Clara blushed. For a moment she thought of Reenie and how she would have snorted with laughter to hear Vinnie's flattery. Clara had a pang of regret that she would not be able to gossip with her friend about the evening. She no longer knew how Reenie spent her precious few hours off work.

Dismissing such thoughts, she smiled back at Vinnie. He was looking his most handsome. It set her pulse racing. Tonight she was going to enjoy herself. She accepted a cocktail from Dolly.

Soon afterwards, the Templetons arrived with two other local businessmen and their wives. The Bell-Carrs came just before the fight was due to start. They took their seats at the ringside as if they knew they were the star attraction. Clara was light-headed from the two drinks she had drunk too quickly in her nervousness. She felt important sitting on the same row as the glamorous guests with Vinnie beside her. He squeezed her hand before the fight began and she did not pull away.

Caught up in the action in the ring, she shouted encouragement to the local fighter as loudly as the others. The visiting boxer from Middlesbrough was knocked out in the tenth round and the local crowd stamped and roared. Vinnie leaned over and kissed Clara on the cheek in delight. She laughed and applauded.

Still feeling giddy with excitement, she followed the Templetons out of the row. Jimmy was among the young men holding back the press of spectators to allow the special guests to leave first. She swayed, a little unsteady in her high-heeled shoes. Vinnie grabbed her arm and she hung on to him as they left the hall. She was concentrating too hard on walking in the new shoes to notice any of the faces in the dimly lit hall.

Clara had no idea that Frank was standing near the doorway observing her. He pressed closer to see the glamorous young woman in the low-cut blue dress who clung to Vinnie's arm as they went past. From the back of the hall, something had reminded him of Clara: the long pale neck, the toss of honey-coloured hair, the glimpse of red lips in a generous smile. She went by laughing. Realisation punched him in the stomach. It was Clara. Her face under the jaunty hat was flushed, happy.

Then, when she was almost past, their eyes met. Clara faltered. Frank wondered if he embarrassed her, reminded her of the trouble over Benny. He thought she would pretend she had not seen him and walk swiftly on.

'Frank,' she gasped, making Vinnie come to a halt. 'How are you?'

'Champion.' Frank nodded. 'And you?'

She smiled. 'The same.'

Vinnie glanced between them, and then stuck out his hand. 'Good to see you, Frank lad. Enjoy the fight?'

Frank shook hands. 'Aye. Makes me wish I was up there myself.'

'Not too late,' Vinnie said, clapping him on the shoulder.

'Wouldn't do much for my musician's fingers,' Frank smiled wryly.

'Are you playing much?' Clara asked.

Frank shook his head. 'Can't get the work.'

'Maybe you should try a bit further afield,' Vinnie suggested. 'Come and have a chat. I've got contacts down London way.' He steered Clara forward. 'Must catch up with our guests. Nice to see you, Frank.'

Clara kept looking at Frank as Vinnie propelled her away. 'Tell Reenie I miss her,' she called over her shoulder. 'Tell her for me, Frank.'

***

Frank raised a hand in farewell and felt a ridiculous rush of disappointment. He had never seen Clara look so attractive — or so unobtainable. The warm-hearted girl who had blushed and giggled around him with Reenie was grown up. He had thought at one stage that Clara might have a crush on him. He had never taken it seriously; she always seemed too young.

Yet over the past year, seeing her battle for her family and refuse to be defeated by grief or poverty, his admiration for her had soared. He loved her for her spirit and love of life, her curiosity about people and her warmth towards everyone. Tragedy had diminished none of these. How tempted he had been to ask her out. But then Benny had gone charging in, trying to win her affection. Now she was courting Vinnie.

Jostled by the crowd leaving the hall, Frank felt leaden. Yet it was hardly a surprise to see her with Craven. The last time he had spoken to Clara — that moment on the doorstep when he had tried to discover if she still had feelings for him — she had said there was another man in her life. Now he had the proof that it was Vinnie.

Making his way home, he pondered the idea of leaving Byfell as Vinnie suggested. Lillian had talked of hiking in Germany over the summer holidays. A trip was being organised through the Workers' Educational Association where she ran an evening course. He could take his violin, stay with relations. Find out for himself what was really happening now the Nazis were the biggest party in the Reichstag.

By the time he reached home, Frank's vague restlessness had hardened into a plan to go abroad — at least for the summer.

***

Clara was quiet in the car on the way to the Sandford Rooms. She sat in the back with Mabel Blake, whose husband ran a scrap metal business by the river. Ted Blake was in the front chatting to Vinnie about import duties on raw materials.

Clara gazed out of the window at the guttering lights on the river. She was about to eat in a first-class restaurant for the very first time with some of Tyneside's most well-to-do. It should be the most thrilling evening of her life — had begun as such. But seeing Frank had upset all that. Even with his fair hair ruffled and wearing a threadbare jacket, he had looked so handsome. It had stopped her breath to see him again. Their brief conversation had been tantalising and Vinnie had given her no chance to ask after all Frank's family. She realised how much she missed sitting round the Lewises' kitchen table talking about life.

What if Frank took up Vinnie's suggestion and left the area? She hated the idea. Not that she saw anything of him now. But at least she could imagine him a few streets away in Tenter Terrace and there was always the possibility of seeing him, of one day . . .

Don't be daft! Clara berated herself. There was never going to be such a day. Tonight, Frank had looked at her strangely, as if he hardly knew her. He would never feel the same way about her as she felt about him. She turned to Mabel and forced herself to make small talk.

'Tell me about your family, Mrs Blake,' Clara smiled. Women like her always wanted to talk about their husband and children.

For the rest of the drive, her fellow passenger chattered non-stop about her two sons and Clara hardly had to say a word. When they arrived outside the Sandford Rooms, Vinnie was swift to claim her again.

'You all right, lass?' he asked her, linking arms.

Clara nodded. 'Bit nervous, that's all.'

'No need to be,' Vinnie assured her, with a squeeze of the arm. 'I'm here to look after you.'

Chapter 19

Things changed for Clara the night of the supper at the Sandford Rooms. She revelled in the sumptuous surroundings of the restaurant with its dark wood-panelled walls, chandeliers and deferential waiters. Her nervousness at dining with the Bell-Carrs and their friends was quickly dispelled by a glass of champagne and Vinnie's encouragement. Seated between George Templeton and Ted Blake, with Vinnie, Cissie and Willa opposite, Clara found herself holding her own as the conversation ranged from boxing and films to politics and fashion.

Never had she imagined she would dine in such a place or make people like Cissie Bell-Carr laugh at her anecdotes about life as a local reporter. As the evening wore on, she warmed to the brigadier's vivacious Irish wife. In a strange way they were both outsiders and recognised the yearning in the other for fun and new experiences. Only Alastair Bell-Carr, sitting at the head of the table, left her cold. He was middle-aged and humourless, his manner haughty and condescending, especially to the women, and most of all to her. It seemed to annoy him that she had opinions and voiced them.

'Where were you educated, Clara?' he asked, interrupting one of her stories.

She flushed but quipped back, 'In a school, Brigadier. Even Byfell has them.'

Cissie snorted with laughter. 'Good answer.'

Alastair scowled. 'Journalism — odd choice for a young girl like you. Does your father approve?'

Clara's heart squeezed. 'He doesn't know. He died a year ago.'

Alastair shot her a look as if she might be joking again. Vinnie intervened quickly.

'Clara's father was Harry Magee — champion welterweight in his day. And a war hero at sea.'

'Bravo,' said George Templeton.

'I'm so sorry,' Cissie said in concern.

Alastair blustered, 'Yes, indeed. Sorry to hear it.' His stony look belied his words. 'But in these dire times of unemployment, I can't approve of your taking a job from a man.'

Clara would not let the comment pass. 'And I can't imagine many men wanting to write about steamed puddings and stain removal.'

There was an awkward pause, and then Cissie laughed. 'How right you are.'

The conversation swiftly changed to cars and discussion of the new Austin Ten, soon to be launched. Clara exchanged looks with Vinnie across the table. Had she been too outspoken? He smiled back in reassurance.

At the end of the evening, Vinnie dropped the Blakes off at their large terraced house on the outskirts of Byfell. He turned to Clara, who was sitting in the back seat.

'Do you want to come back to Larch Avenue for a nightcap?'

She hesitated. It had been a wonderful evening but she was tired and longed for bed.

'No thanks. I have to be up early. Please just take me home.'

He drove on down the High Street. The Lewises' shop and flat — Clara's old home — was in darkness. She looked away quickly. As they made their way towards Minto Street, Vinnie began to hum 'On the Sunny Side of the Street'. Clara remembered her father whistling it. She leaned forward and put her hand on his shoulder.

'Ta for sticking up for me about Dad,' she said.

'Was pleased to, lass,' he said, glancing over his shoulder.

'That brigadier's a dry old stick,' Clara mused. 'Can't imagine what Cissie sees in him.'

'Money,' Vinnie smiled. 'Don't women love that?'

Clara snorted. 'I heard it was Cissie's family had the money; the Fitz Johns of Dublin. Protestant Irish brewers, Mr Jellicoe said.'

'Power and influence then,' Vinnie suggested, as he turned the car into her street. 'I'm told he's got the ear of certain peers and politicians. Did you know he gave donations to Mosley's New Party? He writes for *The Patriot* too.'

'*The Patriot*?'

Vinnie said, 'It's a right-wing journal; pro the Empire, law and order, religion — that sort of thing. Some of it's common sense, but other views are a bit extreme.'

'Such as?'

'Keep all foreigners out — especially Jews and Communists.'

'Why them?'

Vinnie shrugged. 'Some people think they're trying to take over everything. In a conspiracy together to rule the world. Freemasons are in it too, apparently.'

'To rule the world?' Clara burst out laughing. 'Is that what the brigadier thinks?'

'Aye, I suppose.' Vinnie laughed uncertainly. 'He certainly has a bee in his bonnet about Jews — thinks they're all secretly Bolsheviks.'

Clara rolled her eyes. 'So the brigadier's mad as well as stuffy. Poor Cissie. You don't believe all that conspiracy nonsense, do you?'

Vinnie parked the car and turned to face her. 'Do you ever stop asking questions, Miss Magee?' he teased.

'Why do you ask?'

He was about to protest, then realised she was teasing him back. They both grinned. He reached over and took her hand. 'You look beautiful tonight,' he said softly. Peeling off her glove, he bent and kissed the palm of her hand. It sent delightful shivers through her. He kissed her wrist and the inside of her arm. Clara caught her breath. He met her look.

'Can I take you out again, Clara?'

She gulped and whispered, 'Yes.'

'Good.' He smiled and let go of her hand.

Her heart was still banging when she climbed out of the car and he walked her to the door. He did not attempt to kiss her again. Clara went to bed that night with a twist of dissatisfaction. Reluctantly, she took off her new dress and shoes in the confines of the tiny airless bedroom. They never opened the window because of the noise and soot from passing trains. Patience lay snoring gently, an empty sherry glass on the floor beside her.

As Clara struggled to fall asleep on the hard mattress, her mind whirring with the events of the evening, she was struck by an uncomfortable thought. It was not just the glamour of the company and the restaurant that she had enjoyed; tonight had stirred up new feelings for Vinnie. She was flattered by his attention in front of the others, and felt gratitude at the way he had defended her from the arrogant brigadier. But there was more to it than that. When he had kissed her in the car she had felt a flare of desire. It was different from anything she had experienced before.

114

***

Vinnie's courting of Clara was determined. He sent bouquets of flowers to the *Tyne Times* offices and took her to the cinema twice in one week. On the August bank holiday he drove her to Morpeth to watch their Olympic games and they rowed on the river. He took her to the music hall and the theatre. On the anniversary of Harry's death, a huge bunch of chrysanthemums was delivered to Minto Street from Vinnie. Clara came home from work that Monday, having smothered her grief by keeping busy, and dissolved into tears at the gesture.

'See what a good man he is,' Patience said tearfully.

It struck Clara that there was nothing from the Lewises, not even a note from her old friends. How quickly they had excluded her after the incident over Benny. It saddened her greatly that Reenie could so easily break off their friendship. Perhaps Frank had never passed on her message to his sister. He obviously had no thought for her on such a difficult day. Clara felt the first stirrings of resentment towards them. There they were, one happy close-knit family that did not need outsiders, living in a comfortable flat that by rights should still be Clara's home. They had prospered in the Magees' old shop while making out that they had done them a favour by taking on the lease. She understood for the first time why her mother had turned so bitter.

One Sunday in September, Vinnie collected all the Magees and took them for lunch at Larch Avenue. There were huge Yorkshire puddings for Jimmy and generous glasses of sherry for Patience. Afterwards, they all crammed in the car with Vinnie and Dolly and drove to Whitley Bay for a walk along the promenade.

With a pang, Clara noticed that the Cafe Cairo was closed and boarded up. How distant that holiday trip with Reenie seemed when she and Benny had splashed in the sea and they had danced to Frank's band. She experienced a fresh wave of longing that took her quite by surprise. She thought she had successfully put Frank out of her thoughts these past weeks.

'Isn't that where Frank Lewis used to play, Clara?' Jimmy asked unexpectedly.

Clara was startled, as if her brother had read her thoughts. 'Y-yes, it was. I danced there once.' She knew she was blushing.

Patience gave her a warning look. Clara's mother was frightened she would come out with the tale about skipping the end of the Watts wedding and Benny soaking her in the sea. She hated any reference to Benny in front of Vinnie.

'I haven't seen Frank Lewis around for a while,' Dolly commented. 'Not since you had that chat with him, Vinnie. Did he go down to London?'

Clara held her breath.

'No.' Vinnie watched her as he answered. 'Didn't seem interested in my offer.' He paused. 'He's gone abroad instead.'

'Abroad!' Clara exclaimed. 'Where?'

'Germany.'

Patience huffed. 'Well, that's no surprise. A leopard can't change its spots.'

'Meaning?' Clara demanded.

'Once a Leizmann, always a Leizmann.' Patience was dismissive. 'With any luck they'll all go back where they belong.'

Clara turned her back on her mother in annoyance. 'Has he gone for long, Vinnie?'

Vinnie shrugged. 'Well, he's nothing to rush back for, has he? That left-wing bookstall of his was a lame duck and he's never really liked being a barber.' He

115

smiled at her. 'No, he's gone with his violin and his girlfriend — that teacher he always talked about — Lillian, isn't it?'

Clara went crimson. 'How do you know all this?'

'Oscar told me — last time I was having a trim.'

She stared at him in disbelief. 'You mean you still go to Lewis's for your haircut?'

Vinnie said, 'Once a fortnight. Why shouldn't I? No one cuts hair as neat as Oscar — or gives such a close shave.'

Clara was dumbfounded. She could only imagine what Benny must think of Vinnie's patronage.

'You're too kind by half,' Patience told Vinnie. 'Those people tried to blacken your name over the arrest of that lad and you still give them your custom. You're a true gentleman.'

Dolly peered at Clara. 'Something wrong? Looks like you need a sit down. Vinnie,' she ordered, 'we'll have ice creams all round.'

'Champion!' Jimmy cried with all the enthusiasm of a small boy.

'Come on, lad,' Vinnie said, 'you help me carry. Ladies, take a seat.'

Later, Clara was still plagued by the news of Frank's departure. She had to find out for herself. Perhaps he had only gone on holiday. Lillian's term would be starting again and she would have to come back. She thought about going to the hospital where Reenie worked. But they might not let her see her on duty. She could go round to the shop and have her hair done as brazenly as Vinnie, but her courage failed her. What would she say after all these months of silence? Then she suddenly thought of Max. She had given up cleaning for him shortly after Benny's arrest. Jellicoe had given her an unexpected wage increase and she had been quick to stop the daily chore. Both she and Max kept such long working hours that they seldom saw each other. She knew he had a weakness for strawberry jam and one evening knocked at the downstairs flat with a jar.

'Hello, stranger!' He beamed and welcomed her in. Papers were scattered all over the room.

'Max, the place is a tip,' she chided. 'You promised me you'd get another daily.'

'I know exactly where everything is since you left me,' he insisted, turfing a pile of files off a chair. 'And the papers keep the dust down.'

Clara laughed and sat down. He boiled up a pan of coffee and they drank out of chipped enamel mugs, chatting about their work.

'So you're moving in exalted circles these days,' he said dryly. 'You do know the Bell-Carrs are incorrigible fascists?'

'Is that bad?' Clara asked with a teasing smile.

'Fatal,' Max cried. 'Bell-Carr writes poisonous articles in all the right-wing journals. He's a member of the Imperial Fascist League. God help people like me if his kind ever get into power.'

'Cos you're a Bolshie?' Clara said in mock horror.

'And Jewish.'

'Are you?' Clara had never thought about it.

'Non-practising. But that doesn't matter to bigots like Bell-Carr. He'd have us all done away with.'

'I'll put in a good word for you when the time comes,' Clara joked.

'It's no laughing matter.' Max was serious. 'Look what's happening in Germany with Hitler's National Socialists. They're vitriolic against the Left, openly anti-Semitic and gaining ground all the time.'

Clara saw her chance. 'I heard Frank Lewis was over there this summer.'

Max nodded. 'There was a trip organised by the WEA — youth-hostelling. It was Lillian's idea. Quite a few of them went.'

'Oh, so it was just a holiday?' Clara asked, feeling a flare of relief.

'It was for most of them. But Frank's stayed on.'

'Why?' Clara asked in dismay. Max shot her a look. 'It's just I didn't know,' she said hastily.

'Grown too grand to speak to the Lewises these days?'

'We had a falling out after Benny's arrest,' Clara admitted awkwardly. Max nodded as if he knew. 'Tell me about Frank,' she urged.

'He's decided to live with his Uncle Heinrich for a while.' Max sighed. 'He's a trade union leader and Frank feels he needs his support. It's a crucial time for democracy in Germany.'

'But why Frank?' Clara questioned. 'He's more English than German.'

Max gave an impatient sigh. 'It's not a matter of petty nationalism. Socialism is international. He's there to help his comrades, not because they're German but because they're fellow workers. And they need all the help they can get to fight off attacks from the Nazis.'

Clara felt heavy-hearted at the news. For all his passion on the subject, she did not see why Frank should get mixed up in German politics. They had enough problems here in Britain. Unemployment and bankruptcies were still on the rise. Why not stay and fight the injustice here? But Frank had made up his mind to live abroad.

'So Lillian didn't stay?' Clara forced herself to ask.

Max gave her his searching lawyer's look. 'No, but she's working a term's notice. She intends to join him again. I assume they'll marry out there . . .'

'Marry?' Clara's question came out as a croak.

'That's what Lillian says,' Max said. Clara glanced away from his shrewd eyes. She felt leaden at the news. But why be so surprised? she asked herself bleakly. The teacher was far more suited to him than she was. They both had a passionate belief in an international cause that Clara did not share. Her love for Frank had always been one-sided. He thought so little of her that he did not even think to say goodbye. It was time she grew up and stopped hankering after the impossible, Clara told herself harshly. She must put Frank from her mind once and for all.

She got up quickly to go in case Max saw the tears stinging her eyes. He put a gentle hand on her shoulder.

'Good luck with your work, comrade,' he said with an affectionate smile, 'and be careful what company you keep.'

She managed a laugh because she thought he was joking.

***

Clara threw herself into her work once more and allowed Vinnie to run her social life. They went to the theatre with the Blakes, dined out with the Templetons and Bell-Carrs, went dancing and to the premieres of new films. Clara's favourite was a sentimental musical, Goodnight Vienna, about a shopgirl courted by a wealthy man. Vinnie teased her that it was about the two of them and would break into Jack Buchanan songs from the film at the slightest opportunity. What he lacked in tunefulness he made up for in gusto.

It was after the romantic musical that Vinnie first kissed her on the lips. He drove them home via Jesmond Dene and parked under dark autumnal trees. He

117

reached across and pulled her towards him, tilting her face and brushing her mouth with a tickling kiss. His fingers stroked her face and neck. Clara's heart drummed hard as she leaned closer, searching for his lips again. Vinnie's fingers went into her hair and gripped the back of her head. He kissed her hard, opening his mouth, and she responded. They devoured each other with kisses, both hungry to explore the other. Clara put her hands round his face, feeling the smoothness of his jaw, running her fingers through his short hair, enjoying the scrape of his moustache on her skin.

'My God, Clara, I want you,' Vinnie murmured. He traced his fingers across her neck and began unbuttoning her blouse.

Clara pulled away, heart hammering, suddenly alarmed. This was how he would seduce her — and in a few weeks grow tired and move on to another. She was not going to be taken in by Jack Buchanan songs and sweet kisses.

'No,' she whispered. She could hear his laboured breathing.

'What's wrong?' he asked. 'I know you feel as strongly as I do.'

Clara pulled her jacket about her. 'I'm not used to this,' she said. 'We shouldn't have come here. Don't play with my affections, Vinnie.'

'I'm not playing,' Vinnie said sharply, 'I'm serious about you, Clara. I'm not after a quick affair.'

He sat back in his seat and let out a long breath, then started the engine. They drove back in silence; the atmosphere between them charged with uncertainty and suppressed passion.

After that, their goodnight kisses were brief and chaste, both pulling away before desire quickened. Clara found being with Vinnie exquisitely bitter-sweet. The less they touched, the greater her desire for him grew. Just the brush of his lips against her ear or the casual linking of fingers in the dark of the cinema set her pulse racing and her skin tingling. She began to need Vinnie's physical presence like a daily drug. No other man had made her feel like this. Benny's boyish kisses had been passionless. Even her love for Frank now seemed ridiculously romanticised. And what had it been founded on? No more than a young girl's calf-love. One that had not been returned.

Vinnie, on the other hand, made no secret of the fact that he desired her. He lavished her with presents and compliments. He insisted on buying her new clothes, jewellery and perfume if they were to meet up with their well-to-do friends. When Clara baulked at his generosity and tried to refuse, he seemed so hurt that she quickly gave in. He told her he was making good money at the boxing and his other businesses — the garage made enough now to employ Patience full time in the office — and it gave him pleasure to spend it on her.

'I love to see you dressed up to the nines, lass,' he said admiringly. 'You look better than any of the other women —.a real star. Don't you see the looks of envy I get from the other men?'

'Don't talk daft,' Clara laughed.

In November, for Vinnie's thirty-second birthday, Cissie organised a surprise party at the Sandford Rooms. She telephoned Clara at work and told her to alert as many of Vinnie's friends as possible. Clara had a slight pang of disappointment that the party was not to be at Hoxton Hall. Despite Cissie's many promises, they had never yet been invited to the country house. She suspected the brigadier vetoed the idea.

'Don't want that uppity little journalist, what!' she mimicked to Vinnie on one occasion.

'Give it time,' was all he would say.

She enlisted Dolly's help in contacting old family friends and the boxing fraternity and Ted Blake's for his Rotary friends. She insisted Patience must be there too. Her mother's excitement was infectious and Clara paid half a week's wages for a new dress for Patience in her favourite beige with a brown velvet collar. Clara asked Clarkie to help get Vinnie to the restaurant.

'What shall I say it's for?' he asked.

'A club lecture,' Clara suggested. Vinnie had recently become a member of the Thursday Club which met at the Sandford Rooms once a week for talks and dining. 'Say it's an extra meeting about Mosley's new British Fascists.'

There had been much talk about Mosley's latest political move at a recent dinner party at Madras House. The former Labour MP had formed another new party, the British Union of Fascists. The Bell-Carrs had seemed particularly excited by it. Clarkie winked at her conspiratorially. Clara knew he liked any excuse to drive Vinnie's gleaming green Austin Ten, bought that autumn. He arranged to pick up Clara, Patience and Dolly an hour beforehand.

When Vinnie arrived for the expected lecture, he was greeted by a roomful of raucous friends calling out 'Happy Birthday!' to the sound of hooters and popping balloons. For the first time in her life, Clara saw Vinnie quite lost for words as George Templeton led a toast in his honour and Cissie thrust a glass of champagne into his hand with a kiss.

'Great things are afoot in this country.' Cissie made an impromptu speech. 'There is a new thirst for change, for leadership. Strong men like Vinnie who care about the common people are the future. Here's to the British Union of Fascists!'

A few people raised their glasses, others looked bemused. Clara noticed the brigadier scowling at his wife. He obviously thought her intervention out of place.

Vinnie sensed the awkwardness and recovered his poise. 'To our most generous hosts, the Bell-Carrs!' he toasted them. Everyone followed. The lively chatter began once more.

'There's just one other thing I'd like to say,' Vinnie boomed out. 'Seeing as it's my birthday.' The noise petered out. He turned to Clara and pulled her forward, hugging her with his free arm. 'All of you know how much I dote on this lass.' There was a chorus of cheers. 'And there's only one birthday present I want this year. And that's for Clara to say she'll marry me.'

Clara's insides somersaulted as the guests gasped and called out encouragement. She stared at Vinnie. How could she refuse in front of all these people? She caught sight of her mother's face. It looked suspended in shock. Patience gave her a pleading look.

Clara felt giddy in the packed room under the glint of the chandeliers, the pungent cigar smoke and expensive perfume assaulting her senses. This was her future if she accepted Vinnie's proposal. She would never go hungry or lie awake sleepless fretting about debt again. They all waited. Her pulse drummed in excitement. Besides, she craved his sensuality, his maturity, his supreme self-confidence. She swallowed any lurking doubts about his single-mindedness or ruthlessness in business. That was just Vinnie's way. In the heat of that opulent room, Clara made the decision to abandon any last hankerings after Frank. She looked into Vinnie's brown eyes.

'Yes, I'll marry you.'

For a split second his eyebrows were raised in surprise. Then he was pulling her against his dinner jacket and kissing her roundly on the lips. Applause broke out around the room.

'Good lass,' he murmured.

Friends rushed to congratulate them and refill their glasses for more toasts. Patience fell on her daughter in a tearful embrace. 'I'm so happy!' she wept. She cried all over Vinnie too, wetting his starched shirt. He produced a handkerchief.

'Here, keep it,' he said, winking over at Clara.

Later, Cissie pushed them both on to the dance floor and they clung together, laughing at what they had done.

'Do you always get what you want for your birthday?' Clara joked.

'Always,' Vinnie answered, squeezing her closer.

The party went on till late. In the early morning, a yawning Clarkie dropped off Clara and Patience before taking Vinnie and Dolly home.

'You can count the days you'll live in this hole,' Vinnie told her, a little drunkenly. 'You'll all come to Larch Avenue.'

Patience burst into fresh tears. Jimmy was woken up and given the news. He whooped with excitement.

'I'm that proud of you.' He beamed at his sister. 'Me and Vinnie brothers-in-law! That's the end of all our troubles.'

'God willing,' Patience sighed.

Chapter 20

The wedding was set for January. Once marriage had been proposed, neither Clara nor Vinnie wished to delay.

'We'll go to Italy for our honeymoon,' Vinnie declared. 'Go and have tea with Mussolini in Rome, eh?'

Clara was thrilled with the idea. She had never thought to travel abroad. Vinnie was an increasing admirer of the Italian leader for his tackling of poverty and slum clearances through new public works.

'He's getting things done,' was Vinnie's opinion, 'while our government sits on its arse.'

Just before Christmas, Vinnie and Clara received an invitation to a house party at Hoxton Hall.

'Tea on Saturday afternoon,' Clara read out to Patience in excitement, 'dinner at seven-thirty followed by the Yuletide dance. The Templetons went last year. Willa says the dance is for all the estate workers and neighbours too. Then there's Communion at the parish church on Sunday and luncheon. Isn't that grand!'

Patience wanted to see the invitation for herself. 'So they're religious?' she asked with a raised eyebrow.

Clara shrugged.

Patience was blunt. 'So they won't approve of any corridor creeping on Saturday night.'

Clara went crimson. 'Mam! Vinnie's a gentleman, remember.'

Patience astonished her by saying, 'It's you I'm worrying about. Well, if you can't be good, be careful.'

'Nothing's going to happen before the wedding,' Clara insisted.

'The sooner you two are married the better,' her mother said with a knowing look.

Vinnie arranged for them to drive over to Hoxton Hall with the Blakes. It was a long winding journey south of the Tyne and west up through woods to the Durham fells. Clara sat in the back feeling slightly sick while Mabel talked endlessly about her sons' schooling and Ted discussed Mussolini and the railways with Vinnie.

She was thankful when they pulled up out of the damp mist into crisp wintry sunshine and the walled grounds of Hoxton Hall appeared. Stretching as far as the eye could see was moorland dotted with grazing sheep, and the occasional isolated farmstead. The Hall huddled behind its moss-covered walls, rooks screaming into the air out of the bare trees as Vinnie tooted the horn to announce their arrival.

The Hall was a solid red-brick mansion with faded green shutters at the windows, some of which were bricked up. The drive was choked with weeds and the lawn in front was more like a rough field, with ponies grazing on it. Clara had a momentary pang of disappointment that it did not resemble more closely a Hollywood depiction of a stately home.

They were greeted warmly by Cissie in a dingy wood-panelled hallway, its walls crowded with portraits and stags' heads. The stair carpet was threadbare but there were cheerful garlands of holly and ribbon adorning the banisters and rails.

A young boy, who turned out to be Cissie s eight-year-old son James, helped carry Clara's bag upstairs.

'You're in the pink room,' Cissie told her. 'I hope you'll be warm enough. There's no fire, but plenty of extra blankets in the wardrobe. Help yourself.'

The Blakes were in a room further down the corridor, while Vinnie was led away to the floor above by an arthritic footman. Clara's bedroom was arctic. It was plainly furnished with a washstand and chair, a high bed, a side table and a large wardrobe. The wallpaper was of faded pink flowers, as was the bedspread. She perched on the bed and it sagged in the middle. The small window looked out on to dilapidated sheds and stables. Clara was surprised by the shabbiness of Hoxton Hall. The slump had affected the Bell-Carrs too, it seemed.

Still, there was electric lighting and a bathroom at the end of the draughty corridor. It was more luxury than she had encountered for a long time. Clara forced herself to remove the winter coat that Vinnie had bought her — 'part of your trousseau, lass' — and headed down to the drawing room where a huge log fire blazed. An enormous Christmas tree filled the bay window, cheerily lit with candles.

'Come and sit by the fire.' Cissie beckoned her. 'You look frozen. Jane will pour you tea.'

A young girl in a long black uniform handed Clara tea in a china cup and a large wedge of cake on a matching plate. She sat beside Willa who was talking non-stop in her nervousness at finding herself next to her host Alastair. He was dressed in plus-twos and sturdy brogues that had left a trail of mud across the worn carpet. He grunted a couple of times at Willa's attempts to engage him in conversation then turned to talk politics with Ted Blake.

Clara tried to save her friend's embarrassment by asking after Robert.

'Oh, Baby's with Nanny for the night,' Willa said, eyes shining. 'We're going to have the most wonderful Christmas — he's so excited about Father Christmas this year.' Willa put a hand on Clara's lap. 'I can't wait for you and Vinnie to get started. Then Robert will have a new playmate.'

Clara laughed, not knowing what to say. Vinnie came over.

'Did I hear my name mentioned?'

The two women glanced at each other and burst into laughter.

'Yes,' Willa giggled, 'but we couldn't possibly tell you why.'

Clara smiled at him as he sat down next to her. 'Where's your room?' she asked quietly.

'With the bats in the belfry,' he joked.

'My room's freezing,' Clara whispered.

Vinnie gave her a look that made her insides melt. 'We'll have to do something about that.'

'Look at you two lovebirds.' Cissie came over. 'It's very sweet, but you can't keep Clara to yourself all weekend, Vinnie. You must allow her to meet our other guests.' She took Clara by the hand and introduced her around the room. One couple sitting in the corner, half hidden by the Christmas tree, looked familiar.

'Major and Mrs Lockwood,' Cissie announced. 'Dear friends of Alastair's. The major met my husband in a field hospital on the Western Front. Isn't that so, Major?'

'Major Lockwood!' Clara gasped. 'I knew I'd seen you both before. You used to go to those dances at the Cafe Cairo.'

'Indeed,' the major exclaimed. 'But I don't recall. . .'

'Oh yes, I do,' his wife interjected. 'Pretty young thing like you. You came with your friends — handsome dark-haired boy — couldn't dance.'

'Benny.' Clara laughed. 'That's right. His brother was in the band.'

'The violinist?' Mrs Lockwood asked. Clara nodded. 'He was awfully good. Is he still playing?'

'Probably,' Clara said, glancing in Vinnie's direction. She was aware of him watching her. 'He's in Germany now, I believe.'

'Whatever for?' cried the major.

Clara hesitated. She did not want to get embroiled in a political discussion and was not sure of the Lockwoods' feelings about Germans. 'I really don't know.' She smiled. 'I hope we'll get to chat more at dinner.' She retreated back across the room to Vinnie.

'Found someone you know?' he questioned, slipping a possessive arm round her waist.

'Not really; just met them the once,' she said lightly, smiling into his dark eyes. She experienced a sick surge of longing as his hand tightened on her hip. Then they were being ushered out of the sitting room to make ready for the evening.

Clara lay in a steamy stupor, luxuriating in the first hot deep bath she had had since leaving Tenter Terrace. The bathroom was icy, its tiles cold underfoot, but she was cocooned in warm water, thinking dreamy thoughts. Tonight, if Vinnie came to her room, she would let him make love to her, despite her assurances to her mother. She wanted him with the relentless nagging of toothache. Tonight she would show him how much she loved him.

Her skin was soft and wrinkled and the water tepid by the time she forced herself out of the bath. She thought with pleasure how soon she would be able to take as many baths as she wanted in Larch Avenue. Clara hurried back to her chilly bedroom and changed into a soft pink evening gown with a plunge back. She had deliberated long and hard about whether it was too risqué but Patience had urged her to buy it.

'Vinnie's a man of standing; you have to look the part too. All the society ladies are wearing them.'

Clara piled up her hair in loose coils on the top of her head to accentuate the slenderness of her neck and clipped on faux diamond earrings and a pendant that Vinnie had given her. She applied her make-up carefully in the long wardrobe mirror and was satisfied that she looked older and more sophisticated than her eighteen years. The look of admiration on Vinnie's face when they gathered in the drawing room for cocktails set her heart racing with expectation.

At dinner they had to gaze at each other from opposite sides of the vast dining table in the main hall. The only lighting was from huge silver candelabras and a deep open fire. On this special occasion, James was allowed to eat with the adults and sat next to Clara. He was shy and the woman on his other side talked exclusively to her neighbour about hunting and her dogs, so Clara made a point of paying the boy attention. He told her he was quite happy at school, though he missed his mother, and he wanted a bicycle for Christmas because horses made him nervous after he was thrown off one at six years old. His favourite films were with Charlie Chaplin and he would like to show her one in the library before she went home.

'That would be grand,' Clara grinned. 'Just you and me and a box of chocolates, eh?'

'I like you, Clara,' he said solemnly, 'even though you speak funny.'

She laughed and ruffled his hair. 'I like you too.'

Clara had never eaten so much food in one meal. There were five courses and she watched James carefully to see which cutlery he used. White wine was followed by red in a different crystal goblet. She began to lose count of how much she had drunk as the butler kept topping up her glass and Ted Blake, sitting to her right, patted her knee and encouraged her to indulge.

The conversation grew raucous, laughter echoing in the high-ceilinged room, and Clara felt bathed in a hazy contentment. After the pudding course of gooseberry and cinnamon pie, Alastair got to his feet.

'Like to propose a toast - on your feet!' he ordered.

Everyone stood up. Clara swayed and grabbed on to Ted to steady herself, giggling.

'To king and country!' Alastair growled, raising his glass high.

'To king and country!' the guests repeated.

'And to new beginnings!' Vinnie added. The words echoed down the table as people drank the toast.

Clara beamed at him happily, thinking he meant their forthcoming marriage. But when they sat down again, the men at once started to discuss Mosley's fascist party as the start of a new dawn. The brigadier's deep voice droned above the others.

'He's going to cleanse this decadent country — purify it! No more of this selfish individualism. We must have government based on muscular Christian principles — loyalty, unity and sacrifice. Fit in mind and body.'

'Not sure you'll get Christian principles from Mosley,' Mabel Blake tittered. 'I hear he's openly having an affair with that Mitford woman, Diana Guinness.'

Apart from a flicker of contempt, Alastair carried on as if she had not spoken. 'He's the man to take on the Red Front before it ruins the country and our Empire.'

'I agree,' said Ted Blake hastily, with a warning look at his wife. 'We need tariffs to protect our agriculture and industries. Free trade liberal policies have got us into a right mess with all these cheap imports.'

Vinnie joined in. 'Aye, Mosley says the Empire can be developed to give us new markets.'

'Precisely,' said Ted. 'But what does the Government propose? Start giving in to demands for dominion status from illiterate natives. They have to be stopped.'

'Quite so,' Alastair approved. 'Bunch of degenerates. And they would be nothing without those cosmopolitan financiers who bankroll foreign firms with no thought of loyalty to their own country. But then how can they have loyalty when they are aliens among us — leeches sucking us dry — intent only on advancing their own position.'

'Leeches?' Clara burst into sudden giggles. 'Sounds nasty, Ted.'

Alastair shot her a suspicious look. Ted laughed uncertainly. 'Yes, they are.'

Clara felt fuzzy-headed. Aliens and leeches? It all sounded so silly. 'Who are?' she asked in amusement.

Conversation around her died away as people turned to look. She must have spoken too loudly.

Ted faltered, 'Well, the plutocrats, the money-men—'

'The Jews,' Alastair said aggressively.

Despite being tipsy, Clara felt a stirring of unease. 'The Jews?' she slurred. 'The ones I know aren't rich.' She glanced around. People were beginning to stare. She struggled to master her thoughts. 'I mean, there's Max — he's a lawyer — but if folk can't pay he doesn't charge. Lives in two rooms — bit of a tip. And there's Mr Slater, but he's not rich either.' She looked across at Vinnie for help, aware that she was burbling. 'And Vinnie s had Jewish lads train at the boxing — not a penny to their name. Haven't you, Vinnie?'

Vinnie fixed her with a look which she could not fathom. He shrugged but said nothing.

'That's it, you see, Clara,' Ted said with an indulgent pat on her hand. 'They're either poor and a drain on our society, or extremely rich and robbing us blind. Leeches either way.'

Clara shook her head. 'Doesn't make sense — can't have it both ways, Teddy boy.'

She heard someone say, 'Tut-tut.'

'Listen, young woman,' Alastair barked, 'you may be too muddle-headed to understand the danger, but luckily there are some around this table who are not. The Jews and the Bolsheviks are intent on bringing our country down. Revolution is what they want; their views are spreading like a contagion across Europe!' His eyes bulged with indignation. 'They tried to betray our country during the Great War with their pacifism while we were sacrificing our lives at the Front. They were behind the General Strike and the depression in trade. They're at it now with so-called hunger marches, poisoning the minds of the unemployed, persuading them to give their allegiance to Red Russia. They've infiltrated every level of government and society.'

He paused to draw breath, his thin lips flecked with spittle. Some recklessness in Clara made her argue on. She spoke with slow deliberation to mask how drunk she felt.

'I remember — General Strike. Dad said — strikers were being loyal to the pitmen — and the pitmen were just trying to keep their jobs. How could it be to do with Red Russia or the Jews? It was a fight with the bosses.' She looked again at Vinnie for support. 'Vinnie, tell 'em! You ran a soup kitchen for the strikers at Craven Hall, didn't you, Vinnie? It was about supporting working people.'

Everyone turned to Vinnie. For a moment he looked uncomfortable, then gave a rueful smile. 'We were helping out the families, Clara, that's all. Whatever the rights and wrongs of the strike, you can't stand by and watch your neighbours suffer — the women and their bairns. I was taking care of them.'

There was a tense pause, then Ted announced, 'You're a fine man, Vinnie, just like your father Stan; he was a real gentleman.'

The brigadier glared at Clara as if this proved his point. 'That's because he was a true Englishman. The real patriots are the backbone of this country, whether aristocracy or common man. We have the same ties to the land — have done for centuries. The bourgeois cosmopolitans don't begin to understand what it's like to be a patriotic Englishman; they cannot be a part of it.'

Clara nudged James. 'Do you think your father includes us with our Irish blood?' she joked.

There were intakes of breath around the table and murmurs of, 'Disgrace — too much wine — no respect.'

Cissie stood up abruptly. 'Ladies, it's time we retired to the drawing room and let the men get on with their port. In an hour our people will be arriving for the dancing.'

'Mama,' James piped up, 'can I come with you and Clara?'

'Certainly not,' his father growled. 'You've stayed up long enough.' He wagged a finger at his wife. 'See that the boy is sent to bed.'

Crossing the gloomy hall, Clara felt dizzy in the sobering blast of cold air. By the time they reached the drawing room, she was already regretting her rash defiance of her host. She found him insufferably pompous and verging on the hysterical with his conspiracy theories, but she was aware that her words had not gone down well with the other guests either — especially her quip about being Irish. Vinnie had looked almost ashamed of her as she left the room.

125

She slumped into an armchair by the Christmas tree. The other women glanced at her warily and gathered round the fireplace to chat about their children and arrangements for Christmas. Clara closed her eyes. Her head spun.

'There's no need to put yourself into Coventry,' Cissie said with amusement.

Clara opened her eyes and struggled to sit up. 'I'm sorry. I've had too much wine. I didn't mean to be rude about you being——'

'You weren't,' Cissie interrupted. 'I rather enjoyed the look on Alastair's face. It's not often he's stumped for words. We can't let the men have all the say all the time, now can we?'

Clara's look was uncertain. 'So I haven't spoilt the evening?'

'Not at all,' Cissie assured her, patting her hand and perching on the chair arm. 'Here, this black coffee will sober you up.'

As Cissie lit a cigarette, Clara sipped at the hot bitter drink and eyed her hostess. She was slim and elegant in a black evening dress with silver straps, her hair neatly permed and a string of emeralds round her throat. Clara yearned to be as poised and sophisticated as her - and with a sweet-natured son who adored her as James did Cissie.

'James is canny,' she said.

'Yes, he's a dear thing.' Cissie smiled. 'Of course he'll have to toughen up a bit now he's at prep school.'

'Don't you miss him when he goes?'

'Dreadfully. But Alastair wanted him to go to his old school, of course.'

'Didn't you have a say?' Clara asked. 'He's just a bairn.'

Cissie gave her a sharp look through a gauze of smoke. 'I was in complete agreement. It's a terrific school — they do lots of sport and military training. The young men leave the senior school ready to serve anywhere in the Empire. And by golly, they'll be needed.' She held her cigarette away and leaned closer. 'You may look at my husband and see a man of strong convictions — maybe too strong in your opinion. But underneath all the bravado, he's had a very hard time of it. All the gentry have. Land values have fallen and so have the rents the tenants pay. And do you know why? Because of cheap imports of American grain and foodstuffs from everywhere else under the sun. It's ruined our agriculture. The only people who benefit are the speculators and big business. Maybe they're Jewish, maybe they're not.' She stubbed out her cigarette. 'All I know is that democracy has failed us. We need firm leadership and loyal followers if we are not to be overrun. A new world order, a reinvigorated Britain; that's what we shall have under Mosley. And James will be a part of it.'

Clara was taken aback by the sudden outburst. 'Sounds like you should stand for Parliament,' she teased.

Cissie smiled quickly. 'We women must certainly play our part.'

'And what's that?'

'Support our men — and nurture our children to be strong and patriotic. Love the Empire.'

Clara frowned. It all sounded too simplistic. She thought suddenly of the Lewises. They had loyalty to family in Germany, yet lived peaceably in England. Patriotism had seen their windows smashed. That's why Frank had taken up boxing.

'But isn't patriotism sometimes a dangerous thing?' she queried. 'It divides people against each other.' Cissie gave her a look of incomprehension. Clara ploughed on. 'Well, what about the natives of the Empire? Aren't they being patriotic by fighting for independence? Their patriotism is different from ours. So who is to say which one is right?'

For a moment, Cissie's hazel eyes regarded her coldly, her mouth tightening. Then suddenly she laughed. 'Goodness me, Vinnie's right. You never stop asking questions! Come on, girl, enough of politics. It's time we got the dance under way.'

Cissie pulled her to her feet, digging her nails into her bare arm, yet smiling as she did so. Clara was about to protest when Cissie let go and went to rally the other women.

The coach house at the back of the Hall had been cleared of farm implements, swept and decorated with garlands of ivy. Paraffin heaters stood in each corner giving off heady fumes. A stage had been erected for the three musicians: two fiddlers and a melodeon player. Storm lanterns hung from the rafters, bathing the room in a soft yellow glow. Soon it was filling up with new arrivals: labourers and their wives, tenants from nearby farms and their families. The house guests stood out in their evening finery and gathered at one end of the room, watching the country dancing. Clara sat with Willa.

'Don't worry about the brigadier,' Willa murmured, 'he ranted on like that last year. It's best not to say anything, though.'

Vinnie stood for a long time smoking cigars with Ted and George, deep in conversation. Eventually, he came over to claim Clara for a dance. She felt relief as he led her in a waltz, his hand warm on her bare back. But as soon as they began to spin round, she staggered dizzily. Vinnie held her closer, his look assessing.

'Keep off the booze in future,' he said with a smile, but his tone held a warning.

'I will,' Clara said, feeling a little queasy.

'You should listen a bit more, instead of saying the first thing that comes into your head,' he advised. 'Men like Alastair are not to be scoffed at, Clara.'

'Oh, Alastair is it?' she teased. 'First name terms.'

Annoyance crossed his face, then he gave a wry grin. 'You are a little worky-ticket, Clara Magee. The sooner you're married and brought into line, the better.'

She smirked. 'I go along with the married bit.'

Vinnie kissed her nose. 'We're going to have a grand future, me and you. I promise you that.'

As the night wore on, the house guests and the tenants began to mingle on the dance floor, exchanging partners in the fast-moving dances and chatting over the bowls of hot punch. Clara was asked to dance by several young men. She preferred to be up dancing than chattering with the house guests, some of whom were still giving her disapproving looks for her outburst at dinner. Only one man, a local vet who danced with her briefly in a progressive two-step, said, 'Well done for standing up to Bell-Carr. His politics are odious.'

'Why didn't you say anything?' Clara said with a reproachful smile.

'We all have to rub along together out here,' the man answered. 'Besides, it's only once a year — and he keeps a good cellar.' With a smile, the man passed her on.

Vinnie wanted to know who the man was.

'Didn't catch his name,' she said, shrugging.

After that, he allowed her to dance the large set dances with other men, but always claimed her in the slow intimate ones, stepping in if one of the local youths attempted to take her hand.

Eventually, the musicians played their last tune and the visitors thanked their hosts and made off into the frosty dark. Alastair invited the men into the library for a nightcap. The women said their goodnights and made for bed. Clara flopped on to hers in exhaustion. Someone had put a china 'pig' into the bed to take the chill off the sheets, but they were still damp with cold. She shivered. It was too cold to lie around on top. She got into her nightgown, put on a cardigan, woollen tights, gloves, and a scarf round her head, and threw on all the blankets she could find.

When she lay down, her head began to throb. Would Vinnie come to her? Her nose was freezing to the touch. She had never been this cold in Minto Street. Clara had a sudden image of an astonished Vinnie finding her lying bundled up like an old granny. A passion killer, Patience would call it. Clara began to giggle. She lay shaking under the covers, helpless with laughter. If anyone could hear they would think her quite mad, which only made her laugh the more.

Eventually, her laughter exhausted, Clara fell asleep. She awoke to the sound of knocking on her door and wondered where she was.

'Morning, miss.' Jane bustled in, switching on the light. 'Here's some hot water. Communion's in half an hour.' She slopped half a jug of steaming water into the basin on the washstand, drew back the curtains and left. It was still dark outside.

Clara lay back, head thumping and throat dry. Vinnie had not come to her after all. She did not know what to make of it. Was he being the gentleman or secretly angry with her for showing him up in front of the Bell-Carrs and their guests at dinner?

Washing and dressing in a warm woollen suit, Clara winced at bruising to her upper arm. She looked in the mirror and saw scratch marks; Cissie's nails. She tried to remember all that she had said the night before, worrying she had caused offence to her hosts. She recalled the brigadier getting enraged about Jews and calling her muddle-headed. And she had argued with Cissie about something to do with Empire. Clara went downstairs in trepidation.

But everyone was polite and welcoming as they gathered in the hallway for church. Clara whispered to Willa, 'Can't we have a cup of tea first?'

'Not before Communion,' Willa replied. 'Brigadier's very strict about that.'

Vinnie appeared and took her arm, giving her a peck on the cheek. 'Morning. How's the head?'

'All the better for seeing you.'

He gave her a satisfied look. 'Good lass. Remember, best behaviour from now on. No being sick over the vicar.'

Clara laughed under her breath. 'Promise not to.'

'And no more arguing with our hosts, all right?'

Clara slid him an amused look, but his face was serious. Something puzzled her, but she let it go. The next moment, the Bell-Carrs arrived and Alastair called for everyone to follow him outside. Cissie and James walked behind him and the guests trooped after them down the drive. St Oswald's stood in a clump of trees opposite Hoxton Hall gates. The incense in the small church made her nauseous and faint. To her horror, she had to dash from the church halfway through the service. Vinnie found her being sick into the frosty verge.

Silently, he handed her a clean starched handkerchief. Clara's look was contrite.

'Too much rich food last night,' she mumbled. 'I'm not used to it.'

He stood surveying her as if he was assessing one of his boxing protégés for match fitness.

'You look terrible,' he said. 'I'll take you home.'

She felt a wave of humiliation. 'I'm sorry. I've spoilt things, haven't I?'

'You're young,' Vinnie answered, 'and you'll learn.' He led her back to the hall to pack her bag.

Vinnie arranged for the Templetons to give the Blakes a lift back to Tyneside. He made excuses about needing to get back to sort out a business matter, but Clara was sure everyone knew it was her fault they were missing lunch. Alastair gave Vinnie a brief handshake and Clara a curt nod, but Cissie made a fuss of them.

'That's too bad; we've so enjoyed having you.' She kissed Clara's cheek warmly. 'James is quite smitten. You'll come again, won't you?'

'I'd love to,' Clara said weakly.

Vinnie gallantly kissed Cissie's hand. 'Thank you for a grand time.'

'A pleasure,' she smiled. 'Have a happy Christmas.'

On the drive home, Clara slept. She woke as they crossed the new Tyne Bridge into Newcastle. Vinnie put a hand on her knee.

'How's Sleeping Beauty?'

She clutched his hand, suddenly tearful. 'Oh, Vinnie, I've ruined things with the Bell-Carrs, haven't I? They won't come to the wedding.'

'It'll still be a canny wedding even if they don't.' He smiled. 'Alastair isn't God Almighty.'

Clara looked at him in surprise. She thought he was as much in awe of the brigadier as the rest of them.

'I love you,' she said on impulse. He squeezed her knee.

They drove towards Byfell. Just before they reached Minto Street she said shyly, 'You didn't come to warm me up last night. I - I hoped you might.'

Vinnie slid her a look but did not comment. Clara felt foolish. When he parked the car, he turned to face her and took her hand.

'You told me once not to mess with your affections — and I won't. I've got too much regard for you, lass. You're young and innocent and I love you for it. We're going to do this properly, Clara. I'll not lie in your bed till we're man and wife.'

Clara flushed at his blunt words, ashamed that she had spoken of her desire. He got out of the car and carried her bag to the door.

Brushing her cheek with a kiss he said, 'Sleep it off. I'll see you tomorrow. We'll go Christmas shopping; have tea at Carrick's.'

She watched him leave. Away from Hoxton Hall, Vinnie was back in control. It struck her that perhaps it suited him to leave early too. In Byfell, Vinnie was lord of the manor. He did not have to defer to the brigadier and his hysterical outbursts. Patience was right, Vinnie was a man of standing round here. As she traipsed upstairs, Clara marvelled that such a man had chosen her to be his wife.

Chapter 21

Clara and Vinnie were married at St Michael's in Byfell in the middle of January, 1933. Apart from invited guests, the church filled up with well-wishers — many of them young men who hung around the boxing hall. A car had been sent for Clara, Patience and Jimmy. When Clara stepped out on to the icy pavement, Max rushed out and thrust a bunch of snowdrops into her hands.

'Good luck, comrade.' He beamed and kissed her. She had wanted to invite him, but Vinnie had said no. He would not have a man at their wedding for whom she had scrubbed floors. The same went for the Lewises.

'They're my barbers, Clara,' he laughed, 'and your mam doesn't like them. It would be awkward. Anyway, you're not even friendly with them these days. We can't invite everyone.'

In the end, the wedding guests were largely friends of the Cravens, or members of their new social set, such as the Templetons and the Blakes. A sister of Dolly's came on the train from Doncaster. Clara's boss, Jellicoe, was invited and Jack Hopkins their bank manager. She was less pleased about the Laidlaws, whose sons had roughed up Jimmy for payment of her father's debts, but Vinnie told her bygones should be bygones and the Laidlaws were good punters at the boxing. Another surprise guest was Mr Simmons, the agent for their landlord at Tenter Terrace.

'How do you know him?' Clara had asked in dismay.

'He handles some business for me,' Vinnie said vaguely, 'an old family friend.'

To her relief, though, the Bell-Carrs declined to come. They were away that weekend at a shooting party, but sent a magnum of champagne and a copy of Mosley's new book, *The Greater Britain*.

'That looks light reading,' Clara joked.

'Aye, we'll take it on the train,' Vinnie said enthusiastically.

The idea of a honeymoon in Rome had been abandoned; too far in wintry conditions, Vinnie said, promising to take her there another time. He had booked a hotel in London instead. To Clara it was almost as exciting. She had never been to the capital.

Walking up the aisle on Jimmy's arm in a dress of white satin, a Juliet cap and a long veil, Clara dismissed any disappointment at the lack of guests on the bride's side and walked towards a smiling Vinnie. Patience was in tears, as she had been all morning.

'You look so bonny,' she had wept as they made ready. 'How I wish Harry was here to give you away.'

'Jimmy will do a grand job,' Clara had reassured her. Looking at her brother in his smart suit provided for by Vinnie, she felt very proud of him. At sixteen, and with much working out at the gym, he was as brawny as their father had been, his hair close cropped and with the hint of a moustache in mimicry of Vinnie's.

'You're doing the right thing,' Patience kept repeating. 'Vinnie'll look after you. All I've ever wanted is for you to be happy and have a good life.'

That morning, Clara puzzled at her mother's overwrought state. 'You're more nervous than I am, Mam,' she had teased. 'Of course I'm happy. We're all going to have a good life from now on.'

'Yes,' Patience had trembled, 'we are. Vinnie's the man.'

Clara had looked at her mother. 'How strange — I remember Dad saying that at Danny Watts's wedding when he got drunk. "Vinnie's the man".' She gave a wry smile. 'So stay off the sherry until it's all over.'

Patience's expression had crumpled as she burst into tears again.

'Mam, I'm only joking,' Clara said in astonishment. 'You can drink as much sherry as you want.'

Patience shook her head. 'It's not that,' she sobbed.

Clara held her. 'Then what?'

But her mother would not say. She hugged Clara fiercely in a way she had not done for years. In the end Jimmy had chivvied them downstairs.

'Hurry up. Mustn't keep the Cravens waiting.'

The service was over in a blur. On the way out, clinging on to Vinnie's arm, she glimpsed Marta and Reenie standing beyond the church railings. It gave her a shock to see them after all this time. They waved. Clara felt a fresh pang of guilt at their exclusion from her wedding. She smiled and waved back. She would go round and see them after the honeymoon, once she had settled into married life.

Married life! The thought made her sick with anticipation. They climbed into the back of Vinnie's car and Clarkie drove them to the Haldane Hotel in Jesmond for the reception. Vinnie had chosen it for its cosy intimacy. A coal fire roared in the dining room and forty of them sat down to a lunch of soup, roast pork and vegetables, then steamed pudding with custard. Dolly had chosen the menu with Clara, insisting that the guests would want warming food.

'We can't give them cold meats and trifle at this time of year.' Dolly had also decided where everyone must sit. 'Best leave it to me,' she told Clara, 'seeing as how I know them all.' It niggled Clara that Dolly had taken over most of the arrangements, but she could hardly argue as the Cravens were paying for it all.

Yet it was Dolly who had caused the only upset before the wedding by vetoing Vinnie's idea that all the Magees move into Larch Avenue.

'Don't know what he was thinking; there's simply not enough room.'

Clara was angry at this snub to her mother but Patience calmed her down.

'Don't make a fuss; Dolly's right and it isn't worth falling out over.' If Patience was hurt by Dolly's rebuff she did not show it, so Clara had let the matter go.

A pianist entertained them during the meal. Clara was delighted when he played all her favourite musical tunes. When he played *Goodnight Vienna* and Vinnie pulled her to her feet to dance, she almost wept with emotion. Everyone clapped as they watched them shuffle around the small open space beside the piano, holding each other close. Clara heard snatches of their comments.

'Don't they make a handsome couple! — very well suited — so pretty — mind you, he's a lot older — lucky girl — lucky man, more like — time he settled down — sad about the father — whole life ahead of them.'

Vinnie gave a short speech, thanking everyone for coming and saying how this was the happiest day of his life.

'I've watched this lass grow up into a beautiful young woman.' He smiled, a hand on Clara's shoulder. 'Years ago I knew she was the one for me — no other woman has come close. I'm only sorry my good friend Harry Magee isn't here to see us wed.'

Clara felt her eyes prickle and saw Patience clutch a handkerchief to her face. Vinnie squeezed her shoulder. 'But I'll let you into a secret. I once said to Harry "Harry, I'm going to marry your daughter one day. She's a beautiful English rose." And that tough war hero — you know what he did? — he was that overcome he couldn't speak — had tears streaming down his face when I called Clara that. Then he said, "Make her happy, lad, that's all a father wants." And that's what I intend to do.' Vinnie smiled down at her. 'So I think we have your father's blessing, lass.' He leaned down and kissed her tenderly.

'Hear, hear!' someone shouted and the guests began to clap.

Clara whispered tearfully, 'Why did you never tell me that before?'

'Saving it for the big day,' Vinnie smiled. 'And I wanted it to be your choice, us getting wed, not feeling you had to 'cos your dad had wanted it.'

'What a kind man you are.' Clara kissed him again.

Shortly afterwards, she went upstairs with Patience to change into her woollen suit for going away.

'Wasn't that strange what Vinnie said,' Clara gasped. 'Did Dad ever say anything to you?'

Patience shook her head as she straightened the wedding dress on the bed. Her make-up was streaked from so much crying. 'He was probably too drunk to remember.'

Clara eyed her mother, surprised by her brittle tone. 'Do you think Dad would have been pleased? He and Vinnie were good friends, weren't they?'

Patience took her time carefully packing the dress into a box. After a moment she said, 'Course they were. Your father was grateful to Vinnie — he helped him out.'

'Helped him out?'

Patience picked up Clara's hairbrush, unpinned her daughter's wedding cap and began tidying her hair. 'There were times your father needed Vinnie — things he couldn't handle himself. It's funny the way Vinnie looked up to your father when he was always the stronger character.' Again there was that note of bitterness in her mother's voice. 'Harry relied on Vinnie's knowing what to do.'

Clara had a sudden memory. 'Like when that tramp came bothering us? It was Vinnie you called round.'

In the mirror, Clara saw Patience go rigid, hairbrush suspended. Clara had a strong desire to tell her mother about the locket, tell her that she knew what the man had come about. She was a married woman now, old enough for her mother to confide in.

'Was that man blackmailing Dad?' she asked.

Patience began to fuss over her daughter's hair again. 'Whatever gives you that idea? No, no. He was just being a pest. Vinnie spoke to him and he never came back.'

Clara was disbelieving. 'Did Vinnie pay him off?'

Patience looked away. 'Maybe — I don't remember now. It's not important.' She picked off fluff from Clara's jacket. 'Let's take a look at you.' She spun her daughter round. 'You look a picture.' She kissed her forehead. 'The only thing that matters now is that you are happy with Vinnie.'

'I am.' Clara smiled, giving her mother a hug.

'Good,' Patience said. 'Just don't give him any cause for worry.'

'Why should I?' Clara asked, a little indignant.

'You're too quick to argue back; you mustn't upset him or his posh friends. And stay away from troublemakers like the Lewises. I saw them outside the church.'

Clara gave an impatient sigh. 'Yes, yes, and I'll brush my teeth and hair every day too.'

Patience laughed suddenly. 'Oh, pet, I'm going to miss you.'

'I'm only away for five days.'

'Yes, but you're Mrs Vincent Craven of Larch Avenue when you come back.'

Clara said impulsively, 'Once we can afford it we'll buy somewhere bigger and you and Jimmy can come and live with us too. Dolly won't be able to stop it.'

Patience's eyes swam with tears. 'I'd love that, but we must see what Vinnie says, mustn't we?'

Clara nodded. 'Vinnie's the man,' she quipped.

Twenty minutes later, Clara and Vinnie were being waved away from the hotel. Clarkie drove them to Newcastle Central Station where he carried their bags on to the London train.

'Look after things at the hall,' Vinnie told him, pressing a ten shilling note into his pocket. 'You're me right-hand man.'

'Have a canny trip.' Clarkie grinned and left.

They sat close together in the compartment, watching the city recede in a sudden flurry of sleet. Vinnie chatted to two men about boxing until they got out at Darlington. After that he produced the Bell-Carrs' gift from his case and began to read.

'I thought you were joking about bringing that,' Clara laughed.

'Thought I'd better read it before we go and see the man,' Vinnie said.

Clara gasped at him. 'We're going to see Oswald Mosley?'

'There's a meeting on Wednesday night; canny chance to hear him in the flesh, eh?'

Clara did not hide her dismay. 'I'd rather go to the theatre — a musical or something. It'll be our last night.'

Vinnie put an arm round her. 'We'll gan to the theatre as well, don't you worry. I've got it all planned.'

Much of the journey was in darkness and Clara dozed against his shoulder, unable to see out of the window. When they arrived in London, Vinnie commandeered a porter to take their cases to a waiting cab. Freezing fog swirled around them, obliterating any view.

'The Cavendish, Earl's Court,' he told the driver.

It was a small hotel in a terraced street run by a Mrs English.

'English by name, English by nature,' announced the jolly, red-faced landlady. The dining room was already closed and a group of young men sat smoking and playing cards in the sitting room.

'I can heat you up some soup,' said Mrs English. 'Mrs Craven looks frozen through. Go and sit by the fire.' She led them into the sitting room. 'Boys will pour you a couple of brandies.'

The men sprang to their feet at once and offered Clara the armchair nearest the fire. Large drinks were poured and Vinnie began to talk to them about sport. The brandy burned her throat, but left a warm sensation inside. She drank, her nervousness diminishing with each sip as warmth seeped into her cold limbs.

The men, five of them, had come from different parts of England to join Mosley's fascist party.

'We're part of the new self-defence force,' a man called Edwin from Manchester said proudly. 'The Blackshirts. We're stewards at his public meetings; make sure everything's run shipshape and no one tries to harm our leader.'

Paul, a young man about Clara's age, said with enthusiasm, 'Lodging 'ere till they find us proper barracks, then we can all be together.'

'We'll talk some more in the morning,' Vinnie said. 'But now me and the missus …' He winked and the men grinned, standing to attention as Clara got up and took her husband's arm. She noticed that Vinnie had hardly touched his brandy, whereas her glass was empty. Edwin and Paul insisted on carrying their

133

cases up to the first floor for them.

'Bathroom's at the end of the corridor,' Edwin said.

A coal fire warmed the room and the dark red velvet curtains had been drawn to make it cosy. There was a washbasin in the corner, a small wardrobe and chest of drawers, a reading lamp and table either side of the double bed. Mrs English had turned down the bedspread. Clara's heart lurched.

She unpinned her hat and threw her coat on the bed.

'Hang it up, lass,' Vinnie said. He was methodically unpacking his case and putting away clothes in drawers. Opening the wardrobe he took out a hanger and passed it over, then hung up his evening suit. He took off his jacket, waistcoat and tie, then unclipped his braces. He rolled these up with the tie and placed them neatly in the top drawer.

Clara watched in amazement. 'You would think you'd been in the army,' she teased.

He flashed her a look. Clara remembered too late that Vinnie was touchy about the subject. He had received his call-up papers the month the war ended. His father had forbidden him to join up any sooner saying it would be more than his mother could bear. Clara went to hang up her coat and placed the hat on the chest of drawers. She was going to have to be tidier than she had been with Patience.

'Did you know this place would be full of Mosley supporters?' she asked.

'Fair idea,' Vinnie answered. 'Ted Blake recommended it. Members of the BUF get a discount.'

'But we're not members.'

'Maybe we will be by the time we go home,' he winked. 'Now, you use the bathroom first,' he said, 'before you get undressed. Just in case any of the lads are about.'

Clara did as he said and went down the corridor. When she came out of the bathroom, he was hovering outside the bedroom keeping guard. He closed the door behind her and went off to the bathroom. She noticed her hat had gone from the top of the chest of drawers. She found it on a shelf in the wardrobe. Hastily, she unpacked, shoving clothes in the lower drawers, and pushed the case under the bed as Vinnie had done.

Clara was half out of her clothes when Vinnie came back in and locked the door. He smiled as he took off his trousers and shirt. His chest was covered in dark hair, his shoulders bulky. Clara stared. He helped himself to a cigarette from the bedside table, lit up and pulled back the covers. Then he lay watching her, humming softly and smoking.

'Hurry up, lass, it'll be time for breakfast shortly.' He grinned.

'Shall I turn the light out?' Clara asked, feeling a fresh jolt of nerves. The brandy was wearing off.

Vinnie switched on a side lamp and nodded. She felt better once the harsh overhead light was extinguished. The room fell into shadow, except for a pool of light round Vinnie on the bed. She turned her back and continued undressing, carefully placing each garment over the back of the chair. She heard him stub out his cigarette and stop humming. The next moment he was reaching across, touching her bare shoulders and kissing the back of her neck. It sent small shocks through her.

'There's nothing to worry about,' he murmured, nibbling her ear. 'We can take as long as you like.'

He began to unpin her hair, running his fingers through it, pulling it loose about her shoulders. All the time he spoke softly. 'I love you — I've wanted you for so long — let me love you, lass.'

He unzipped her corset, kissing his way down her back. His hands went round her, caressing, searching. Clara gasped in delight. She helped him shrug off her underclothes and climbed into the bed.

Naked, Vinnie threw back the covers and ran his hands over her body. 'You're perfect — I want to look at you. So pure,' he murmured, 'your skin — so pale.'

He climbed over her and kissed her hard on the mouth. Clara responded with urgency. He kissed his way down her neck, shoulders and breasts, nibbling and caressing. Clara grabbed his hair in her hands and dug her fingers into his back. Vinnie carried on exploring, kissing and probing until she could bear it no longer.

'I want you, Vinnie,' she gasped.

Finally, he made love to her. She moaned with pleasure. Never had she imagined such physical ecstasy. When it was over, he rolled off her with a long sigh of satisfaction. Clara found herself weeping. At once Vinnie was pulling her into his arms.

'What's wrong, lass? Did I hurt you?'

'No,' Clara whispered. 'I'm just that happy. I love you so much, Vinnie.'

He kissed her tenderly on the lips. 'Not half as much as I love you.'

They lay in each other's arms in contentment. As the fire died, Vinnie pulled the covers up round them. He reached to put out the light.

'No,' Clara said. 'I want to go to sleep looking at you.'

Vinnie smiled at her, stroking back her hair. 'Me too.'

She lay against him, fingering the hairs on his chest, wanting the flood of emotion she felt for him to go on for ever. Eventually, she fell asleep. A delivery van chugging in the street below woke her in the early morning.

Vinnie was sitting up in bed reading. 'Morning, Mrs Craven,' he smiled.

'What time is it?' She yawned.

'Five-thirty.'

'Couldn't you sleep?'

'I always wake early,' he admitted. 'Did you know you talk in your sleep?'

Clara blushed. 'What did I say?'

'Load of gibberish,' Vinnie chuckled, closing the book. He snuggled down beside her again.

'What have you planned for today?' Clara asked.

He ran a finger down her arm. 'Nothing,' he grinned. 'Sunday's a day of rest.'

'Good.' Clara smiled and pulled his head towards hers.

Chapter 22

To Clara, the days galloped by and their short honeymoon was over too soon. They took walks through the frozen parks, gazed at the opulent buildings and visited the sights. Outside Westminster Vinnie said contemptuously, 'All that power and what do our politicians do with it? Nowt!'

They took shelter from the bitter cold in Lyons tea rooms, eating well and listening to the orchestras. One night they went to a musical, *The Cat and the Fiddle*, the next to the pictures to see Greta Garbo in *Mata Hari*. On a third they went to a club where they danced until two. Vinnie's energy was boundless. After a packed day of sightseeing and an evening out, they would retreat to their cosy bedroom and make love. Clara would fall into exhausted sleep, always to find Vinnie awake and reading in the early morning.

On the final evening, they ate early at the hotel with the young men and went to hear Mosley speak. Clara thought how Reenie and her brothers would disapprove. She was a little uneasy too, but kept her scepticism to herself for Vinnie's sake.

The hall was full and heavily stewarded by bare-headed men dressed soberly in black. Clara noticed them on duty outside too. The drab interior had been decorated with striking black flags emblazoned with the fascist emblem, an axe and a bundle of sticks. They were early enough to get seats near the front. Clara was intrigued by a group of smartly dressed young women in black tops and grey skirts, sitting on the front row. A military band on stage played stirring music and the hall buzzed with excitement.

Suddenly the band struck up 'Rule Britannia' and people around them rose to their feet. A phalanx of young men in black uniform marched down the aisle. In their midst was a tall, handsome, mustachioed man in a smart suit. Applause rippled down the hall as he made his way on to the platform. Clara thought he looked bigger and more imposing in the flesh than in newspaper pictures. Even before he spoke, Oswald Mosley had a strong presence about him, exuding authority.

He smiled and held up his hands in greeting. His stewards and the eager young women on the front row raised their arms in a fascist salute. Clara thought them comical and tried not to laugh.

'Bit over the top,' she whispered to Vinnie. But he was still clapping and misheard.

'Aye, grand, isn't it?'

Imperiously, Mosley signalled for everyone to sit down. The music stopped and the audience took their seats. He stood at the podium surveying them until there was complete silence; then, with a disarming smile, welcomed them for turning out on such a wintry night.

He began by speaking about Britain's heroic past, its many heroes and patriots who had sacrificed so much to make the country great. What would they make of the present mess? Democracy was failing them, Mosley pronounced, and politicians were corrupt and selfish.

'They are only interested in lining their own pockets,' he declared, 'buying honours instead of earning them. Is that fair?' He stabbed the podium with his finger as he reeled off the failings of the coalition government: 'They care nothing for the plight of the people.' He grew angry. 'They have no pride in our country. But we do.' He began to pace the stage, gesticulating at the audience.

'Only Fascism cares. Only Fascism is rigorous enough to take on the great problems of the day — to stand up to the evils of Leninism, of divisive party politics, of self-interest—'

'Fascism is dictatorship!' a man shouted from a few rows behind Clara and Vinnie. 'You care nothing for the working classes — you're one of the privileged.' There were murmurs of disapproval.

'Sit down! — Shut up — Chuck the blighter out!'

Swiftly, stewards muscled forward along the row and grabbed the heckler, who continued to shout. Clara turned her head and craned for a better view.

'Just look at Italy and the Nazis in Germany — workers beaten up and worse —' He was manhandled out of the row and thumped. A group of five or six black-shirted men dragged him to the back door and bundled him outside. From the open door, Clara heard the sound of raised voices and chanting. The door slammed shut. The murmuring in the hall continued.

Mosley held up his hands for silence. 'That man is misguided. I cannot blame him, for the national press is full of misinformation about Fascism, and the great changes for the better in Italian society under Mussolini.' He shook his head in sorrow. 'If he had bothered to listen — had the courtesy to listen — he would have learned the truth.'

He told them of his visits to Italy and how Fascism had led that nation out of unemployment and slump, brought them together under a great Roman leader. 'Fascism is not anti-labour, it is against class conflict. It will harness patriotic labour to the national cause.' He came forward, eyes alight with passion. 'We in the BUF want everyone in this country to be enriched, not the leisured few. Under us, opportunity shall be open to all, but privilege to none. Under us, great position shall be given to those of talent and reward shall be accorded only to service. Under us, poverty will be abolished.'

There were murmurs of approval. Mosley's voice rose and fell hypnotically.

'We shall establish the corporate state, which will balance the needs of capital and labour for the benefit of both. There will be no profiteering. Workers will have a minimum wage. Their wives and families will be supported by a welfare system. The corporate state will allow modern science to flourish and have the power to tackle poverty once and for all. All men will have work. It is not only their right, but their lifeblood.'

Cheers of approval rippled round the hall.

'If that poor misguided man had stayed to listen,' Mosley thundered, 'I could have told him that we believe in destroying class barriers. They hamper progress. We want to release the energies of every citizen so they can be devoted to the service of the British nation. For we are a great nation! Thanks to the efforts and sacrifices of our forefathers, this country of ours has existed gloriously for centuries!'

There were louder cheers. His eyes blazed as his voice rose in a crescendo of passionate words. 'We need strong leadership and firm government — not futile debate and hand-wringing. We must be prepared for personal sacrifice to defend our country and our people, just as the Lost Generation did, spilling their precious blood on the foreign soil of Flanders' fields. We must be prepared to fight. Are you prepared to fight?'

A roar of assent went round the room. Vinnie shouting as loud as any.

'Citizens! We must be organised and disciplined like the great British legions of old. We must keep the flag flying forever high.' He threw his arms wide. 'We demand a free and greater Britain!'

The young women on the front row jumped to their feet, shouting, 'A free and greater Britain!' Others followed, clapping loudly. Soon everyone in the hall was giving their speaker a standing ovation. Music erupted again. Mosley stood saluting them, smiling in approval. Vinnie clapped and clapped. Clara was mesmerised. She too felt stirred by the passionate words. It made her want to rush out and start doing something for her country. It made her proud to be British. She revelled in the shared warmth of feeling in the people around her. On this icy January night, they all hungered for optimism and new beginnings. This is what Mosley was offering.

Clara thought of the Lewises and their endless discussions about putting the world to rights. They had been so negative about everything, full of warnings and gloomy predictions, whereas here in this hall everyone basked in the glow of Mosley's heroic future. He made them feel special. Clara could imagine Reenie mocking that it was just rhetoric. But Reenie was not there to experience it and Clara felt it was much more than that. This man had a vision of a better world. He made Fascism sound exciting yet reasonable; there were none of the hysterical conspiracy theories or derogatory remarks about Jews that she had found so distasteful in Bell-Carr. He had a plan for social reform that was every bit as bold as the Socialists'.

As Mosley strode from the hall with his entourage, Clara stood on tiptoe for a last glimpse. Vinnie put an arm about her.

'Haway, Mrs Craven,' he teased, 'you're supposed to have eyes only for me.'

'I do.' Clara kissed his cheek and grinned. 'But he is rather good-looking.'

As they filed out of the hall, they were met by a covering of snow and a barrage of shouting. Protesters who had stood outside in the freezing cold to heckle the fascists were determined to break through and confront them. A line of Blackshirts was attempting to push them back. Some ran after the armoured car taking Mosley away, thumping on its sides. Once he was gone, they turned back on the dispersing crowd. Stewards waded in and fighting erupted.

Clara froze, recoiling from the angry scene, but others jostled her forward, separating her from Vinnie. Then a volley of icy snowballs came hurtling over their heads and hit a man behind Clara.

'Damn Communists!' he shouted in anger and barged forward, knocking into Clara who slipped on the steps. The next moment she was tumbling down and grabbing at people to break her fall. Another woman fell with her and someone trod on her hand.

Clara yelled in pain. Someone beside her screamed. Stewards rushed forward to control the sudden panic of people rushing to get out of the way. She had to get on her feet or she would be crushed, but she was pinned to the ground by the force of bodies pressing from behind.

'Vinnie!' she cried out. A police whistle blew. There was screaming and shouting all around. Clara covered her head as legs clattered into her. Suddenly she felt herself being hauled to her feet.

'I've got you, miss!' It was Edwin from the hotel. She clung to him in relief as he steered her quickly to the side, barging through the crowd. Clara gulped for breath. Ahead, the police were rounding up a handful of protesters while the Blackshirts fell back.

Moments later, Vinnie found her and she fell into his arms.

'Clara, lass, are you hurt?'

'No, I'm fine,' she panted.

'Bloody animals, that's what they are!' he said in sudden fury.

'Let's just get away from here,' Clara pleaded.

With a protective arm about her, Vinnie led her down a side street away from the confrontation and hailed a cab. They sat in the back in silence, holding on to each other. Clara felt numbed by the unexpected violence after the high emotion of the meeting.

Back at the hotel, Mrs English fussed over her, bathing the cuts on her hand and sitting her in front of the fire with a mug of hot cocoa and a large glass of brandy.

'There's no need for it,' she said indignantly. 'They're just low types causing trouble. Probably put up to it by the Bolshies and their Jew money. Whatever happened to an Englishman's right to speak his mind?'

When the other men came trooping back, they sat around warming themselves and discussing the events of the evening late into the night. Clara was exhausted and longed for bed, but Vinnie was deep in debate, enjoying the companionship of the young men, fired up by Mosley's oratory and indignation at the anti-fascist yobbery. Clara said her goodnights and Vinnie promised to follow her upstairs.

She lay in bed, staring at the flickering light from the fire and the way it receded across the ceiling as the fire died. Soon, their idyllic few days alone would be over and she would have to adjust to life in Larch Avenue and sharing Vinnie with Dolly.

Sometime in the early hours, Vinnie came to bed and woke her with soft caresses.

'I'll never let that happen to you again, lass,' he murmured. 'I could kill those Bolshie troublemakers.'

'It'll take more than that to scare me,' Clara declared.

'That's my lass,' Vinnie said proudly and kissed her long and hard on the lips.

They made love with heightened intensity, their kisses urgent and possessive. Afterwards, they lay for a long time, wrapped in each other's arms.

'I'm going to join the BUF, Clara,' Vinnie told her. 'I want you to join too. Will you, lass? There's a Women's Section.'

Clara felt the strong beat of his heart under her cheek. Right at that moment, she would have done anything for him.

'Course I will,' she answered.

Vinnie squeezed her against his chest and kissed the top of her tousled hair. 'By heck, I'm proud of you, Mrs Craven. Together, there's nothing we can't achieve.'

Clara wished they could stay like that for ever.

Chapter 23

The spring months flew by as Clara adapted to her new role as Vinnie's wife. Her husband spent long hours at work, both at the boxing hall and taking care of his various business interests. From what Clara could gather, his consortium, Cooper Holdings, included Ted Blake and Mr Simmons. Vinnie told her he was also going into business with George Templeton.

From the start Clara had insisted that she carry on at the newspaper after marriage and was thankful that she had done so, for she would have gone mad sitting around Larch Avenue with too much time on her hands. Dolly disapproved.

'Don't know why you want to work when my Vinnie provides everything you want. I wish I'd had it so easy when I was young.'

'I work because otherwise I'd be bored.' Clara was blunt. 'Just as you do.'

Dolly flushed under her heavy make-up. 'I'm a widow. Vinnie and the boxing business are my whole world.' Her look was reproachful. 'Until you two give me grandbairns, that is.'

Clara ignored her mother-in-law's sly digs and got on with her full life. She was now Jellicoe's main feature writer, covering social events and interviews. After the London trip she wrote about the Mosley rally and did follow-up features on the new BUF branch in Newcastle and their Women's Section, run by Cissie Bell-Carr. There were a flurry of indignant letters at her articles, one from Reenie on behalf of the Women's Co-operative Movement. But others wanted to know how to join and Jellicoe was jubilant when their circulation went up.

'Populist, that's what we are,' he crowed, 'and no bad thing.'

Clara was pleased, though the angry letter from Reenie made her think twice about renewing contact with her former friend.

Socially, she and Vinnie were as busy as in their working lives. They dined out frequently with friends or entertained at home. While Clara attended talks and socials with the Women's Section, Vinnie went regularly to the Thursday Club at the Sandford Rooms for political meetings and dinners, finding it a fertile recruiting ground for the fledgling BUF. Vinnie was active in the Rotary Club; Clara went to Health and Beauty meetings with Willa. As the evenings lengthened, Vinnie taught Clara to drive.

'It's safer than you taking the tram,' he said, but Clara believed it was to keep upsides with the Bell-Carrs because Cissie could drive. He gave her the use of his old Albion.

On Sundays, they would fetch Patience and Jimmy for Sunday lunch. Clara was always glad to see her family, yet the meals could be awkward. She resented the way Dolly lorded it over her mother, constantly making reference to her menial clerical work at the garage and patronising Jimmy.

'You must be so proud of your lad, Patience,' Dolly declared, 'when you think what a tearaway he was. And now he's learning to be a mechanic. Vinnie's done wonders for him, don't you think?'

Clara marvelled at the way Patience kept her temper and agreed with whatever Dolly said. If she complained about it to Vinnie he just laughed it off.

'That's just Mam's way. Take it with a pinch of salt, lass.'

Dolly's overbearing attitude was the only complaint Clara had about her new life. She adored Vinnie and hated the hours they were apart. She loved the way he was always beside her when they were out together, never letting her out of his sight for a moment, holding hands, linking arms, squeezing her knee under the table.

On rare evenings when they had no social engagements, she was impatient for supper with Dolly to be over so they could go to bed. While the radio below played dance band music, they would make love as quietly as possible and whisper their undying love for each other.

As summer approached, a more frantic edge crept into their lovemaking. No matter how vigorous or regular the sex, Clara did not fall pregnant. A speaker came to the Women's Section extolling the virtues of motherhood. She was plump and motherly and spoke in a soft confiding voice.

'Our duty to our country is first and foremost as wives and mothers,' she beamed. 'It is our calling to promote the health and well-being of the next generation — those young Englishmen who are needed to serve in all corners of our great Empire. It is up to women like us — women of good racial stock — also to keep ourselves in good health so that we produce sons of manly physique and sound mind.'

She gave them a kindly smile. 'Ladies, we must guard against impurity - the mixing of races that leads to degeneracy and the weakening of our great British nation. For we are the cream of the human race; our dominance in the world proves it. So,' she gave a coy little chuckle, 'go home to your husbands and get to work.'

When Clara recounted this to Vinnie in bed that night, he laughed at her mimicry. 'Sounds good to me,' he teased. 'I want lots of bairns.'

Clara felt a stab of anxiety. 'What if we can't have them? You hear of some who don't. You will still love me, won't you?'

Vinnie pulled her to him. 'Stop worrying. We're going to have bairns and you're going to be the best of mams.' He kissed her roundly on the lips. 'Now, Mrs Craven, let's get to work.'

***

Clara grew closer to Cissie through their association with the Women's Section. Cissie appeared to hold no grudge over their argument at Hoxton Hall about patriotism and was delighted to have Clara join. Clara found the older woman fun to be with and refreshingly frank about her husband's shortcomings. Privately they poked fun at the more serious members of the group.

'They can sit and knit socks for the Blackshirts,' Cissie declared, 'and we'll toast them in champagne.'

After Clara confided her worry about not yet becoming pregnant, Cissie retorted, 'Forget about that "wives and mothers" claptrap. We all know who really hold the reins of power; women like us.' She offered Clara a cigarette from her gold case. 'We let our men think they are running the world, but they'd be nothing without us. They're the puppets and we pull the strings,' Cissie said with a cat-like smile.

Clara and Vinnie were invited out to Hoxton Hall on several occasions. Vinnie learned to shoot and Clara to ride. Cissie took her riding over the estate and Clara reminisced about her rambling trips with the YS where she had learned to love the countryside.

'My, you have come a long way from then,' Cissie observed. 'A long way in a short time. No wonder Vinnie's so proud of you.'

'Do you think so?' Clara laughed.

'I know so,' Cissie said. 'It's as plain as day how much Vinnie adores you.'

They kicked their horses into a canter and raced each other across the heathery moorland.

One time when James was back from boarding school, he spoke up at dinner when they were discussing Hitler's takeover in Germany.

'Mr Banks, my biology teacher, says Herr Hitler's doing a terrific job. Stopping the revolutionaries.'

Sir Alastair was disdainful. 'Still can't trust the Boche. Germany's a breeding ground for Bolsheviks and Jewish agitators.'

'I think we should give the Nazis the benefit of the doubt,' Cissie countered.

'Some German Rotarians are coming to visit soon,' Clara said. 'Isn't that right, Vinnie?' Vinnie nodded. 'Why don't you come along and meet them? Ask them what ordinary Germans think.'

'Ever the journalist,' Cissie laughed. 'That's a splendid idea. What do you say, Alastair?'

He scowled at Clara and blustered, 'You can go if you wish. I'll not sit down and eat with men who were butchering my friends last week.'

'Nearly twenty years ago!' Cissie remonstrated.

'Seems like last week,' Alastair muttered.

Later, on their journey home, Clara put her head on Vinnie's shoulder as he drove. 'Cissie's so lucky to have a big house like that,' she sighed. 'No wonder she has house parties every other weekend.'

'What are you saying, exactly?' Vinnie asked.

'Let's move somewhere bigger,' Clara urged, 'somewhere we can entertain properly. If we're going to put these German people up and give them good British hospitality, we need more space.'

'What's wrong with Larch Avenue?' Vinnie said defensively.

'Nothing at all.' Clara traced a finger down his arm. 'But you're an important businessman now — a leading light in the local BUF — you need a home that reflects your standing in the town.' Her fingers moved down to his thigh. 'And one day soon we'll need more space for all those sons and daughters we're going to have.'

Vinnie caught her hand. 'Careful, lass, or I'll have the car off the road.'

She nuzzled his cheek. 'Can we at least think about it?'

Vinnie gave a low laugh. 'And do you have somewhere in mind?'

Clara sat up. 'Well, there's a modern house in Gosforth up for sale — a bankruptcy so they're desperate to sell — practically giving it away. It's got four bedrooms and a huge garden and a Wurlitzer organ in the dining room. Imagine that!'

'How do you know all this?'

'Willa told me. I've only seen it from the outside. She wants us to live closer.'

'So, you've been hatching this plot with Mrs Templeton?' Vinnie cried. 'George could have warned me.'

'He doesn't know,' Clara smirked. 'So can we at least go and have a look?'

Vinnie kept his eyes ahead. 'We'll have to ask Mam. It's her home too.'

Clara hid her impatience. 'She'll love it. And we can ask Ella to come and cook for us too.'

'It's a canny drive from Byfell,' Vinnie pointed out.

'It's not that far,' Clara said, not wanting to admit that she increasingly craved to distance herself from the town. 'And it's just two tram rides for Ella.'

Vinnie raised her hand and kissed it. 'If it will make you happy then of course we'll go and look.'

Clara leaned up and nibbled his ear. 'I love you,' she whispered.

That night they went early to bed and made love till it was completely dark, Clara imagining them in the large house in Gosforth out of earshot of Dolly's radio, with only the sound of birdsong drifting in from the long tree-lined garden.

***

When Vinnie saw the grand house he needed little persuasion. A month later, at the end of June, they moved into The Cedars, in Gosforth. Dolly came grumbling about the distance from Craven Hall, but Clara did not give Larch Avenue a second glance. It had never felt like home, whereas The Cedars did and she set about its redecoration and furnishing with gusto. She enlisted Willa's tasteful help and by the time the Rotary visitors arrived in late July, the house was lavishly comfortable.

They had two couples to stay, businessmen from Hamburg and their wives, and enjoyed a packed week of sightseeing and social events. One of the couples was middle-aged and Clara wondered if the small, dapper husband had fought in the Great War or perhaps been on an opposing ship to her father's. But no one mentioned the bitter conflict.

The other couple was nearer Vinnie's age and full of fun. Herr Braun's English was accented but fairly fluent and he interpreted for the rest. He and Vinnie had long conversations about business and the possibility of setting up trade links.

On the final evening, Cissie came for dinner, along with the Blakes and the Templetons. The wine flowed and soon the topic of conversation that had been held in check all week came flooding out.

'What is it really like to live under Nazi rule?' Clara wanted to know. 'We read such conflicting reports. Are they really rounding up trade unionists and throwing them in prison? Even executing them?'

There was an intake of breath round the table and the elderly Germans asked what had been said. Vinnie was quick to apologise.

'Excuse my wife.' He smiled indulgently. 'She is a journalist and naturally nosy.'

Herr Braun waved away his concern. 'It is not a crime to be interested. You are intelligent people.' He turned to Clara and said, 'Hitler is bringing peace and prosperity out of chaos. It is what we all are wanting. This talk of executions, that is just the propaganda of the Left.'

Cissie nodded. 'I quite agree, Herr Braun. Hitler must be thanked for stopping the Communists in their tracks.'

'Their tracks?' Herr Braun repeated, puzzled.

She laughed. 'Stopping them from taking over your country.'

He smiled and nodded agreement.

'And the stories of arrests,' Clara persisted, 'they are propaganda too?'

'Where do you read such things, girl?' Ted Blake interjected.

'Clara reads the Manchester Guardian in the line of duty,' Cissie teased.

Ted snorted. 'That's for Reds and Pinks.'

'And financed by Jews,' his wife Mabel chipped in.

Vinnie turned to Frau Braun on his right and asked her about their travel plans. Dolly gestured across the table for Clara to serve out the pudding. But she would not be deflected.

'What about the Jews?' Clara challenged Herr Braun. 'Should they fear the Nazi takeover? Hitler makes no secret about his theories on racial purity. Yet what harm are they doing?'

She could see Vinnie tense in disapproval and avoided his look. Herr Braun twirled his glass before answering.

'I think it is different in your country, Frau Craven. You do not have the Jewish problem perhaps. But in Germany, they have — what you say? — the stranglehold on our economy — the banks, the business, the arts. They are different from us. We were in danger of being overrun by the lowest form of Jew — the Asiatic Jew from Russia and Poland. They infiltrate our society but their wish is to stir up revolution. Hitler is stopping that. He is putting the Germans first, that is all.'

There was a moment of silence round the table. Clara stared at this cultured man and wondered if she had heard him correctly. He spoke as calmly and dismissively as if they had been discussing a problem with dust mites.

'So Hitler's answer is to round them up and what? Drive them into the sea?'

'Clara!' Vinnie warned. 'Enough.'

Herr Braun laughed abruptly. 'Frau Craven, you have too much imagination, I think. Nobody is dying. Maybe a few have been arrested. But it is only for their own good. The — what you say? — dissidents — they are being re-educated to love the Fatherland and be useful citizens. Is that not a good thing? It is what your Mosley is saying, is it not?'

'Quite so,' Cissie said quickly. 'Patriotism is to be applauded. We can all agree on that.'

Herr Braun smiled at Clara. 'If you don't believe me, come and see for yourself. We would be honoured if you and Herr Craven came as our guests to Hamburg. Germany is a beautiful country.'

Clara glanced at Vinnie. He was giving her a thunderous glare.

'We'd love that, Herr Braun,' she answered, swiftly looking away.

After that, there was no more talk of politics. They ended up partying late into the night with Herr Braun playing the Wurlitzer and everyone singing raucously around him. When they went to bed, Vinnie chided her for her rudeness.

'You shouldn't have opened your gob like that,' he complained. 'Herr Braun's an important businessman — could be very useful to us.'

'I was only asking what we were all thinking,' Clara said defensively.

'It wasn't your place to,' Vinnie snapped. 'You think you know better than everyone else, but you don't — you're just a young lass.' He turned his back on her, muttering, 'Too much sherry; just like your mother.'

Clara was hurt by the attack but said nothing. Perhaps she had been too outspoken. She had not meant to upset their guests.

The next morning the Rotarians departed, urging them to visit Germany on a return trip, and Clara was relieved that no offence seemed to have been taken at her questions. But that evening, while Vinnie was kept late at a meeting, Dolly took her to task.

'You need to watch your tongue, young lady — causing my Vinnie embarrassment like that! And with that nice Mr Braun. Them Germans will think we English wives don't know how to behave.'

'Don't be daft.' Clara was impatient. 'Herr Braun didn't mind in the least. We were having a sensible political discussion, that's all.'

'Well, it's not for the likes of me and you to talk about such things. Leave it to the men. Women aren't made for politics.'

'Why have you joined the Women's Section then?' Clara challenged her.

'To support Vinnie and the other men of course,' Dolly replied. 'But that's as far as it should go.'

To Clara's relief, Vinnie did not refer to the matter again and was his usual charming self over the following days and weeks. August came and he took her away for a surprise weekend to Blackpool. They drove over and stayed in a grand hotel overlooking the front. The weather was too wet for the beach or the Ferris wheel but at night they danced at the Tower Ballroom and went to a show in the Winter Gardens. Clara revelled in having Vinnie all to herself, with no critical Dolly or demanding business associates monopolising his attention. He was funny and loving and they were as absorbed in each other as they had been on honeymoon.

With her husband in such good spirits, Clara raised the suggestion that Patience and Jimmy come to live with them. Clara missed her mother and wanted an ally against Dolly, but knew she had to be careful how she approached the subject.

'I hate to think of them still living in that terrible flat,' she said, snuggling into his hold after lovemaking. 'And we've plenty room now. Mam could have the smaller spare room and Jimmy could have the boxroom — he's tidy and doesn't need much space.'

Vinnie stroked her hair thoughtfully. 'Don't know what Mam would say about it.'

'My mam would be company for her — we're out that much of an evening,' Clara said reasonably. 'And Jimmy would be out more than in - she'd never notice him.'

Vinnie said nothing. 'Please,' Clara begged, 'at least think about it.'

He kissed the top of her head. 'I'll think about it.'

On the way back, they stopped at Carlisle where Vinnie made contact with a new branch of the BUF. They were organising a visit by a speaker from their headquarters in London.

'Black House are sending the *Blackshirt* editor, William Joyce. Heard he's a powerful young orator.'

Vinnie was eager to have Joyce come to Newcastle too and agreed to stay in touch. Once they returned home, he threw himself enthusiastically into organising local meetings, recruiting further members to their cause and planning a rally to welcome the firebrand Joyce. There was plenty of money coming from Mosley's headquarters to pay Vinnie's growing band of Blackshirts for stewarding duties.

To Clara's disappointment, nothing came of her suggestion for Patience and Jimmy to move in with them.

'Jimmy needs to live near the job,' Vinnie told her when she raised it again in September, 'and your mam does too. But I tell you what I'll do — pay their rent on a bigger flat in Byfell, away from the railway line. I've got just the place in mind — belongs to the consortium. The present tenants are bad payers and are on their last warning.'

Clara knew the compromise was all to do with Dolly's objection. She overheard her mother-in-law complain to Vinnie. 'Patience and Jimmy work for us — it would be awkward all living under one roof. I really can't see Patience wanting it any more than I do.'

Clara could not understand how Vinnie could be so tough in business and yet putty in his mother's hands. But she knew better than to object. She would bide her time until the day power tilted away from Dolly. Clara knew that once she gave Vinnie a child, her position of authority among the Cravens would increase. Within a fortnight, Patience and Jimmy were moving into a two-bedroomed flat in Glanton Terrace near Craven Hall. Patience was so grateful and enthusiastic about the larger accommodation that Clara accepted the

145

compromise without fuss.

During the following weeks, not only was Vinnie busy with the forthcoming visit of William Joyce, he was also involved in arranging a return visit to their Rotarian friends in Hamburg. The Blakes and the Templetons were going too.

'It'll be business as well as pleasure,' he told Clara, one autumnal day in October.

She was thrilled at the thought of going abroad with their friends and spent a happy afternoon off work round at Willa's, playing with Robert and planning their trip.

'George says we can take Baby too,' Willa said.

'I'm not a baby,' Robert shouted.

'Course you're not,' Clara agreed, 'you're a big boy called Robert.' She gave Willa an amused look and whispered, 'he's four years old. You really will have to stop calling him that.'

Robert began marching around the nursery swinging his arms. 'I want to be like Jimmy,' he cried.

Clara laughed. 'You look like a soldier to me.'

'Yes,' Robert said gleefully, 'like Jimmy.'

Clara looked at Willa in surprise. Her friend explained, 'Well, whenever Vinnie visits George here he's always got a couple of his men with him. Robert likes Jimmy best because he always slips him a sweetie. I suppose they look like soldiers in their black uniforms and short haircuts, don't they? Very smart, your brother.'

It had not occurred to Clara. But it was true that Jimmy and some of the other boxing lads were increasingly being called upon to act as bodyguard to Vinnie and, like Vinnie, they shaved the sides of their heads in military fashion. Recently, there had been a couple of scuffles outside Craven Hall after BUF meetings. 'Riff-raff and drunks,' Vinnie had dismissed the agitators.

But Patience told her they were greater in number and more menacing than Vinnie let on. Clara had worried about Jimmy, but her mother had shrugged. 'He's a big lad now and able to take care of himself; your Vinnie's taught him that.' Still, Clara liked to think Vinnie's Blackshirt strongmen were more for prestige than necessity, a sign of his status as chairman of the local BUF.

So far, the Templetons had not joined Mosley's party, despite Clara and Cissie's enthusiastic promotion of the Women's Section to Willa.

'George has never joined a political party in his life,' Willa said, 'and he doesn't think I should either.'

'Do you always do everything your husband wants?' Cissie had been mocking.

'I suppose I do,' Willa had replied sheepishly.

But Cissie was not going on the trip to Germany as she was away in Ireland visiting family and would not be back till the end of the month. While Robert stomped around the upstairs room, Willa gossiped. 'I think Cissie's not going because Alastair won't allow it. He's so anti-German. The trip to Ireland's just an excuse.'

Clara defended her friend. 'I'm sure Cissie would go if she could; she does what she likes as far as I can see. I miss her not being around. And there's this big meeting with Joyce next week and she's going to miss that as well. It's too bad.' Clara felt unexpectedly tearful. Willa hastily retracted.

'I didn't mean to upset you. I think Cissie's first class too. Are you all right?'

'Course I am,' Clara insisted, wondering what was wrong with her. 'Just a bit tired. I've been working late a lot recently.'

George arrived home and Clara left quickly. 'See you at the Sandford tomorrow night.'

The next day, Clara felt so ill she came back from work early. 'Must be something I ate at Willa's,' she told Vinnie as she lay in bed unable to move without feeling nauseous. 'I'm so sorry about dinner. And there's the meeting.' That evening, before eating at the Sandford Rooms, the Women's Section were to plan the catering for the meeting with Joyce.

'You mustn't worry about that,' Vinnie told her hastily. 'I'll cancel dinner.'

'But the meeting? Cissie's not there either,' Clara fretted.

'Mam can organise things for you. She knows more about catering than you do anyway,' he grunted. 'You take it easy, lass.'

Clara dragged herself into work the following day, ignoring Vinnie's and Dolly's protests that she did not look well enough. But she was sick again and Miss Holt sent her home, saying she would deal with Jellicoe. By Saturday, she was feeling no better. Vinnie cancelled a theatre trip and called out the doctor.

Dr Dixon examined Clara under a modesty blanket, asked a few questions and turned to speak to a hovering Vinnie.

'Your wife isn't ill, Mr Craven,' he declared. 'She's with child.'

Vinnie and Clara stared at him in disbelief.

'Clara's expecting?' Vinnie gasped. The doctor nodded as he crossed the room. 'She may feel sick for a few weeks, but it'll pass.'

Vinnie showed him out. Clara lay feeling light-headed, sick and joyful all at the same time. She was impatient for Vinnie to return. She heard him telling Dolly the news downstairs. Her mother-in-law shrieked with excitement and came rushing upstairs to throw her arms about Clara.

'That's the best news I've had in years! A baby on the way! My first grandbairn,' she crowed. 'And not before time.'

Clara looked pleadingly at Vinnie standing behind Dolly, hands on hips, face beaming.

'Mam, don't smother her,' he joked.

Eventually Dolly's gush of words stopped and she allowed Vinnie to sit on the bed. Clara held out her arms to him and he pulled her into a joyful embrace.

'I'm so proud of you,' he whispered, kissing her tenderly on the forehead.

She longed for Dolly to go so they could revel in the moment alone, but Vinnie's mother stood eyeing them.

'Best let Clara get some rest,' she decreed. 'We can't have her rushing around getting over-tired, now can we? You'll have to put your foot down, Vinnie. And have a word with Jellicoe; can't have her risking the baby's health with all those long hours at work.'

Clara gave Vinnie an impatient roll of the eyes, but he ignored the gesture.

'You're right, Mam.' He stood up. 'I'm going to wrap this lass in cotton wool till my son's born.'

Clara gave a weak laugh. But Vinnie's expression was quite serious. Dolly nodded in approval and they left the room together. Clara sank back, her eyes filling with sudden tears. The moment she had yearned for since their marriage had arrived but felt suddenly anti-climactic. She should be sharing it with Vinnie, laughing and planning their future as a family. Yet she felt sick and alone, listening to him retreat downstairs chatting happily to his mother. Disappointment flooded over her. She did not try to hold back the hot tears. At that moment, the person she longed for most was Patience.

Chapter 24

'You're not going and that's my last word on it,' Vinnie said calmly, crossing the bedroom in his black bathrobe.

'But I'm in the Women's Section — I've a right to go!' Clara argued. 'Everyone will be there to hear Joyce. Mabel Blake's going.'

'That's Ted's decision,' Vinnie answered, disrobing and reaching into his wardrobe for clean clothes. Clara watched his taut, muscled back in frustration. She was still feeling wretched with nausea and tiredness but was determined not to miss the rally for the London speaker. It was their biggest meeting yet.

'Well, this is my decision,' Clara said defiantly, 'and I want to go. I have to cover it for the paper; I promised Jellicoe.'

Vinnie turned from dressing, and eyed her as he buttoned up his dinner shirt.

'I would like nothing better than to have my bonny wife at my side for the meeting.' He winked. 'But you're not well. Jellicoe will understand. I'll get someone else to do a report for him.'

'And the supper afterwards?' Clara asked, feeling sick just at the thought of it.

'Mam will take your place.'

'I bet she will,' Clara muttered. 'She'll like nothing better than lording it around knowing I'm stuck here at home.'

Vinnie came over and sat on the bed. 'Don't be like that, lass. Mothers are the most important people on this earth. Never forget that. You're going to be one soon and then nothing else will matter — not the paper, not the Women's Section — none of it except bringing up our bairn.'

He kissed her tenderly on the lips. She knew there was nothing she could say to change his mind. Vinnie could be as stubborn as he was charming.

'Here, help me put in my cufflinks, lass,' he said, holding up his starched shirt cuffs.

As she did so, Clara said, 'So you won't mind me spending the evening at Mam's — seeing as mothers are that important?' Vinnie said nothing so she persisted. 'You can drop me off on the way to the hall. Clarkie can run me home.'

'Clarkie and all the lads will be busy tonight.' Vinnie said, standing up.

'All of them?' Clara queried. When Vinnie turned away and did not answer, she felt the stirrings of alarm. 'Is there going to be trouble?'

He shrugged. 'There's bound to be some who'll try to spoil it and stop free debate. But nothing to worry about. My lads will keep things orderly.'

'It won't be like the London rally, will it?' Clara asked anxiously. 'Tell me, Vinnie. Are you putting yourself in danger?'

He laughed off her concerns. 'Nothing I can't handle.' Then he was suddenly serious. 'But I don't want my pregnant wife there. I'll tell you what I'll do. I'll ring for Clarkie to drive Patience over here and keep you company. But you're not to try sneaking down to the meeting, do you understand?'

It was the first time Clara had seen her mother since discovering she was pregnant. They embraced tearfully, as Vinnie and Dolly left with Clarkie for the meeting. Mother and daughter spent the evening curled up on the deep sofa in front of the sitting-room fire, listening to Vinnie's collection of gramophone records. Clara sipped tea while her mother drank sherry.

'Ginger,' Patience declared, 'that's what you need to stop feeling sick. My mother used to swear by it. I'll make you some ginger biscuits.'

'You don't bake,' Clara teased.

'Buy you some then.' Patience smiled.

'You've never talked about my grandma,' Clara mused. 'Did she make you eat ginger when you were expecting me?'

Patience looked reflective. 'She died when I was twelve. That's why I went to live at the boarding house in Shields with my aunt. I had no other family. Couldn't get out of there fast enough. Luckily Harry came along — and you.' She took Clara's hand and squeezed it. 'Everything changed with you. I wanted you to have everything I'd never had — including a brother or sister. A happy family life.' Her expression darkened. 'But if life's taught me anything, it's that the best-laid plans never work out.'

Clara gripped her mother's hand. 'We had a happy family life. You and Dad gave us the best home we could have asked for when we were growing up.'

Patience's eyes swam with sudden tears. 'Do you really think that?'

'Yes, I do.'

Abruptly, Patience seized her in a fierce hug. 'Oh, lass, you have no idea how much that means to me - I've felt so guilty . . .' She broke down, sobbing into Clara's shoulder.

Clara held her close. 'You shouldn't,' she crooned. 'None of what happened was your fault.' She would not have her mother blaming herself for her father's infidelity or his weakness for gambling. 'And it's all in the past now — we don't have to talk about any of it ever again.'

Patience croaked, 'Thank you, pet. You're right. It's all in the past.'

They talked late into the evening, Patience regaling Clara with stories about her new neighbours and how impressed they were to hear that her daughter was married to Vinnie Craven and lived in a grand house in Gosforth. Clara talked enthusiastically about their social life and the Women's Section.

'Why don't you join, Mam? Then we can see more of each other. I'm so busy with work and all our other commitments, I don't have a spare minute to call round. You know I would if I could.'

'Don't feel guilty,' Patience reassured her. 'I'm that happy to see you doing so well and enjoying your life with Vinnie.'

'I do.' Clara was adamant. 'But I'd be happier still if you joined us in our new party. Vinnie's going to get things done for hundreds of people — thousands of men on the dole — not just our family.'

'That's grand,' Patience said, 'but politics isn't for me. I'm grateful to have the job at the garage. I keep my head down these days. All this marching around with flags and saluting isn't for me.'

'It's more than that,' Clara laughed. 'Mosley's going to change things for ordinary people — the ones in northern cities that the politicians in London have left to rot.'

'Stop!' Patience cried. 'I get enough speech-making from our Jimmy without you getting on your soap box. I'm going to make you more tea.'

By the time she came back, Clara was fast asleep on the sofa. Patience covered her daughter with a rug and went to doze in a chair.

They were both woken by a car in the driveway and raised voices as Vinnie, Dolly and two Blackshirts came clattering into the house. Patience sprang nervously to her feet while Clara roused herself from a deep sleep. As soon as her husband came into the room, she noticed blood spattered on his shirt front.

'Vinnie! What's happened?' she cried, sitting up. 'You're hurt.'

'It's nothing, lass,' he assured her, kissing her quickly on the head. 'There was more trouble at the hall than we'd bargained for.'

'It was a disgrace,' Dolly said, as Clarkie helped her into a seat. She looked very shaken. 'They didn't give the poor man a chance to speak.'

'We had to get him away in the end,' Vinnie said, going swiftly to pour himself a whisky from the decanter on the cocktail cabinet. That alarmed Clara even more, for he hardly ever drank.

'Didn't even have his supper,' Dolly said indignantly. 'None of us did.'

Clara looked at the carriage clock on the mantelpiece. 'But it's gone midnight. Where have you been?'

Dolly launched into a garbled tale. 'There was fighting in the hall as well as outside — the place is half wrecked — and then the police came. Vinnie's been down the station — and he took Jimmy to hospital—'

'Jimmy?' Patience cried. 'What's happened to him?'

'He got thumped,' Dolly began, but Vinnie held up his hand to silence her.

'Don't go upsetting Clara,' he ordered. He took a long swig from his glass and crossed the room to sit by his wife. 'Jimmy's in hospital,' he said quietly.

Patience gasped in horror. 'What's wrong?'

'He's all right,' Vinnie assured her. 'They think he's dislocated his shoulder. He'll be in overnight. Didn't want to stay in but the doctor insisted.'

'My poor bairn,' Patience cried. 'I want to see him.'

'I'll fetch him home tomorrow,' Vinnie promised. 'He's resting now and they wouldn't let you in at this hour. He said to tell you he's champion — knew you'd make a fuss.'

Clara gulped. 'How did it happen?'

Vinnie looked at her. 'He was defending the speaker — getting him to his car. Thugs set on him.'

Clarkie spoke up. 'Gave as good as he got, miss.'

'Thugs?' Clara echoed.

'Commies,' Vinnie said in disgust.

'Those Lewises were there in the hall,' Dolly said accusingly, 'stirring up trouble from the start. Even that lass Reenie; bold as brass, mouthing off.'

'Reenie!' Clara gasped.

Vinnie nodded. 'I let Benny and Reenie come in — for old times' sake — for Frank's sake, cos he was a friend of mine. And I thought it might make them see sense; you once told me Benny admired Mosley.' His voice turned hard. 'But they abused my trust and began heckling as soon as Joyce opened his mouth. That's the sort of people they are, Clara, ignorant and bigoted. They had no intention of listening to what we had to say. We chucked them out and then they caused a riot outside. I'll not let them near the hall again; my lads will see to that.'

Clara felt shame for her old friends. How could they have behaved like that? Benny maybe, but not Reenie. Their actions had put Jimmy in hospital. She reached out and touched Vinnie's arm. 'I'm so sorry.'

He smiled. 'You're not to worry. A few Bolshies aren't going to stop us. Now do you see why I didn't want you there?'

Clara nodded. She glanced at her mother. Patience was white-faced, subdued.

'Don't worry, Mam,' Clara said. 'Vinnie will take care of everything. He'll look after Jimmy.'

The next day, Jimmy was released from hospital and Vinnie sent Clarkie to collect him and bring him home. That evening, Clara badgered Vinnie to let her see her brother, so he dropped her off for a visit while he went to a Rotary meeting. She found Jimmy eating soup at the kitchen table, his left arm pinned in a sling, the radio playing. Patience hovered over her son, smoking.

150

The ground floor flat was homely. Clara realised guiltily that this was only the second time she had been there since they moved in over a month ago.

Jimmy shrugged off her sympathy. 'I'm all right. Don't fuss.'

'Does it hurt?' Clara asked, sitting opposite.

'Not much.'

'It does,' Patience contradicted, 'but he won't admit it.'

'And your lip's swollen.' Clara was worried.

Jimmy gave her a defiant look. 'I've had worse boxing. It's what you expect in this job.'

'But you're a mechanic, Jimmy,' Clara pointed out.

'I'm a Blackshirt; one of Vinnie's unit,' he told her proudly. 'We have to be prepared to fight. "Stand we fast to fight or die!" That's our motto.'

Clara exchanged glances with her mother. Patience looked tense, but said nothing.

'Vinnie said Benny and Reenie were there. Was it Benny who attacked you?' Clara asked.

'Might have been,' Jimmy said, unconcerned. 'There were that many of us scrapping outside, I didn't see the lad that knocked me down. I felled a couple mesel' first.' His eyes glinted with the memory. 'One of the London lads said next time I should keep a knife handy — cut their belts and braces so they can't fight back - too busy trying to keep their trousers up!'

Clara was aghast; her brother had enjoyed the fight. 'It's not a game, Jimmy,' she cried.

He gave her a hard look. 'You don't have to tell me that. Don't worry, I'm not ganin' to hospital again. Next time it'll be one of the enemy.'

Before Clara could remonstrate further, there was a knock at the front door.

'I'll go,' she said. 'It might be Clarkie come to fetch me.'

Clara opened the door and gasped in shock. Reenie stood there, holding a box of chocolates.

'Hello, Clara,' she said uncertainly.

'What are you doing here?' Clara demanded. 'Don't know how you can show your face.'

Reenie held her look. 'I heard at the hospital about Jimmy. Wanted to see if he was all right.'

'He is — but no thanks to you and that thug of a brother of yours.' Clara's anger spilled out.

Reenie's expression tightened. 'I'm sorry for what happened to your Jimmy — but they were giving as good as they got and more. We were there just to protest - they were spoiling for a fight.'

'I don't believe you.' Clara was blunt. 'I've seen the way the anti-fascists work — nails in snowballs. And your Benny's as violent as they come.'

'He's not a violent man,' Reenie replied. 'He'd only use his fists in self-defence. That's what Frank taught him. Not like Vinnie, who's training his lads for open warfare.'

'Don't speak about my husband like that.' Clara was furious. 'Vinnie's a good man who takes care of his lads. He's done more for the unemployed round here than anyone.'

'Maybe,' Reenie said, 'but he's getting himself mixed up with a bad lot - and so are you.'

'If you mean the BUF, I'm proud to be one of them,' Clara retorted. 'And if you really cared about the people round here you'd be supporting us too.'

Patience called from inside, 'Clara, who's at the door? If it's Clarkie, tell him to come in.'

'It's not,' Clara called back. 'I won't be a minute.' She turned back to Reenie and said in a low voice. 'I think you should go — Mam's upset enough as it is.'

'What's happened to you, Clara?' Reenie said in bewilderment.

'You should ask yourself the same question,' Clara hissed. 'I'm not the one starting fights and putting good lads in hospital.'

Reenie stepped towards her, blue eyes glittering with passion. For a split second they reminded Clara startlingly of Frank's.

'Do you know where Fascism leads?' Reenie demanded. 'Just look what's happening in Germany and see what it's doing to working people. Beating them to a pulp on the streets or rounding them up and putting them in concentration camps before executing them.'

Clara laughed in disbelief. 'Concentration camps! Don't be daft. I've spoken to Germans and there are no executions going on.'

'Then your German friends are lying,' Reenie snapped. 'There isn't one Socialist leader left in Germany who isn't dead or in prison or fled into hiding. The Nazis are allowing no opposition. They're terrorising the country. Hitler has promised to exterminate the Left. The prisons are so full of trade unionists they've had to open up these camps.'

Clara stood with her arms folded, fending off Reenie's sudden anger. 'And how do you know that's not just Bolshie propaganda?'

'I'll tell you why,' Reenie hissed at her. 'Because Frank's in one!'

Clara stared at her, nonplussed. 'Frank?' she repeated.

'Yes, Frank!' Reenie cried.

Clara's heart thudded in shock. She closed the door behind her and stepped into the dark street. 'Tell me,' she said tensely.

Reenie let out a long sigh. 'He was in Munich working for my uncle in the Boiler Makers' Union. One day they were both arrested at the union offices. The building was burned down. My aunt tried for days to find out what had happened to them. Eventually a friend used his contacts in the Nazi party. Both Frank and Uncle Heinrich are in a new camp; Dachau in Bavaria. It is run by a special unit, the SS, known as Blackshirts. They torture the prisoners and the prisoners are forced to make their own manacles and whips. They are allowed no visitors or letters.' Reenie gulped, her voice almost a whisper. 'My uncle was to be released, they said. He was found hanging in his cell on the day my aunt went to fetch him. Suicide, they said, but we don't believe it.'

Clara's heart drummed. After a long moment she said, 'I'm sorry for your family. But how can you know conditions were so bad if they can't even communicate? Isn't it just rumours? Maybe Frank isn't there at all.'

Reenie looked up sharply. 'How I wish that were true. A letter was smuggled out. It was written in the summer but only got here last week. A member of the YS brought it to Lillian.'

Clara's stomach churned. 'From Frank?'

Reenie nodded. 'It told of the terrible things that were happening. Frank wasn't asking anything for himself; he wanted us to tell what was going on under the Nazis' reign of terror.' Reenie looked at Clara, her eyes bright with tears. 'We don't know if Frank's still alive. We've written — Papa's even written to the Foreign Office — but we've heard nothing.'

Clara put her hand out to Reenie. 'I can't believe it,' she gasped. 'There must be something you can do for him. He's English. He shouldn't be there.'

Reenie shook her head. 'Frank was born in Germany and he's reverted to calling himself Leizmann. His English upbringing might even go against him

152

— not patriotic enough for the Fatherland.'

'Go to the papers,' Clara said in desperation.

'Lillian doesn't want us to make a fuss publicly, in case it puts Frank in greater danger.'

'Lillian's in England?' Clara frowned. 'I thought they were going to be married.'

'She never went back to Germany,' Reenie explained. 'Frank told her it was too dangerous.'

Clara felt helpless and confused at Reenie's sudden revelation. 'What can I do to help?'

Reenie's look was long and sorrowful. 'Nothing — except stop this obsession with the BUF.'

Clara's expression tightened. 'It's not an obsession. It's something Vinnie and I believe in.' She gazed at her old friend, wanting her to understand. 'If what you say about the Nazis is really true, then we're not like them; not at all.'

Reenie glanced away. 'We think you're on the same road — just not as far down it. That's why we have to break up your meetings. Benny and me — we do it for Frank.' She held out the chocolates. 'Here, give them to Jimmy and say we're sorry for his injuries.'

Silently, Clara accepted the box and watched her old friend walk quickly away.

***

Vinnie found Clara still arguing with her mother and Jimmy over the box of chocolates. Jimmy was for throwing them on the fire, Patience for letting Clara take them. Clara, badly shaken from Reenie's revelations, was shouting, 'It doesn't matter about the bloody chocolates, it matters about Frank!'

'I don't believe a word of it,' Jimmy replied. 'Load o' rubbish.'

'Hey, what's going on?' Vinnie demanded. 'Clara, sit down. You shouldn't be getting in such a state.' He threw Patience a look of reproach as he guided his wife into a chair. Then he watched Clara as she poured out the story once again, Clarkie and another Blackshirt standing behind him in the doorway.

'Sounds a bit hysterical to me,' he said evenly. 'Concentration camps, torture, smuggled letter! Who's to say it's not a fake?'

'Exactly,' Jimmy grunted.

'But what if it's true?' Clara cried. 'There must be some way of finding out what's happened to him.' She appealed to her husband. 'Maybe Herr Braun could find out for us?'

'He lives in Hamburg, lass,' Vinnie pointed out. 'Bavaria's the other end of Germany.'

'There must be somebody who can help,' Clara persisted. 'Frank's an Englishman; they can't just arrest him and lock him away.'

'He's German too,' Patience sniffed.

'And it depends what he's been up to,' Vinnie said. 'If he's been stirring it like the rest of his family, they may see him as dangerous — an agitator.'

'But you know Frank,' Clara exclaimed. 'He's not violent.'

Jimmy got up impatiently. 'Don't know why you're making such a fuss about him. It's not as if he's family.'

'You used to idolise him,' Clara reminded her brother.

'That's when I was a bairn.' Jimmy was dismissive.

Vinnie held up his hands. 'That's enough. I'll not have you falling out over this.' He put a hand on Clara's shoulder. 'I'll have a word with the German consul; he comes to the Thursday Club. Maybe he can make some enquiries.'

On the way back home, sitting in the back of the car, Clara said, 'Perhaps we can find out more when we go to Germany. Not just about Frank, but what's really happening over there — if these camps really exist.'

'Clara,' Vinnie took her hand, 'the Rotary trip is a cultural visit, not an excuse for you to write lurid articles for the *Tyne Times*. Reenie had no right to upset you with such tales. No doubt she's jealous of your success. You've left her behind socially and she doesn't like it.'

'She wants me to leave the BUF,' Clara admitted.

Vinnie was suddenly riled. 'I knew there'd be a reason behind all this. How dare she try to interfere in your life!'

'She didn't sway me in the least,' Clara said stoutly.

'Oh, but she did. She knew just how to play you — telling that sob story about Frank. She knows you've always had a soft spot for him.'

Clara reddened. 'Don't be daft.'

Vinnie leaned close. 'I know you, Clara. I know you better than anyone. It was obvious you had a girlish crush on the lad. That's why you're so upset now, isn't it?' Clara's mouth dried. 'See, you can't deny it.'

'Perhaps I did care for him,' Clara whispered, 'but that was before I fell in love with you.'

Vinnie pulled her close and kissed her. 'If I find out what's happened to Frank, will you promise me one thing?'

'What?'

'Not to see Reenie or her family again. She's a bad influence on you, lass — and I'll not have her upsetting you in your condition.'

Clara hesitated. She did not like to be told whom she could or could not meet. But she had little intention of renewing her friendship with Reenie anyway.

'The Lewises are in the past, as far as I'm concerned,' she answered.

'Good,' Vinnie said. 'Because if you did, I would take that as a mark of disloyalty to me and to the party.'

His hand resting on hers tightened in a firm grip. No more was said about the matter, but Clara had the feeling, as they sped away from Byfell, that she was severing some deep-rooted tie with her past that could never be repaired.

Chapter 25

Clara's initial fears over Frank's fate subsided when their enquiries through the German consul resulted in assurances that he was still alive and well and could be released at any time if he undertook not to plot against the German state.

'He is in a camp for the politically misguided,' the consul's letter explained. 'They are given light work to do and conditions are very good. They are encouraged to keep fit and there is even a swimming pool for their use. His family should have no fears about the lenient treatment shown to Herr Leizmann. He remains there for his own good.'

This was followed shortly after by a short handwritten note from Frank himself, in German. Below was an English translation from the consul. Clara's hands shook as she read it.

'. . . I am grateful for this chance to write to my family to tell them I am in good health and being well treated. I am learning much about National Socialism and the Fatherland. I am allowed to play my violin. Kindest regards, Frank Leizmann.'

Clara, relieved that he was alive and well, sent on the information to the Lewises. Vinnie had asked her not to go in person.

'I'll not have you getting upset again. You've done more than enough for that family,' he said firmly.

She received a polite letter back from Marta thanking her for her trouble, grateful for news of her son and saying she was welcome to call whenever she wanted. Clara was hurt that it was not Reenie who had bothered to write back. Perhaps she refused to believe that Frank was being well treated. Whatever the reason, her old friend was obviously ungrateful for the action she had taken on her behalf. It had caused tension between her and Vinnie and a reproachful lecture from Cissie when she had returned from Ireland.

'Goodness me, girl! Why are you getting het up about the treatment of a renegade Englishman — a Marxist? If he's in prison there must be a good reason. Vinnie's being very long-suffering about all this, if you ask me.'

Clara was almost glad when Vinnie announced that the Rotarian trip to Germany had been postponed until the spring when the weather would be better. She wanted to put the whole matter behind her. Far better to concentrate on what was happening in their own country. Frank had been foolhardy to go abroad and try to meddle in German politics. As Patience said, they did things differently in Germany and he should have known better. All he had to do was promise not to interfere again and he could come home. In the meantime, it appeared he was being fairly treated.

By Christmas Clara's nausea had worn off and they celebrated in their new home with turkey and plum pudding for Patience and Jimmy, and a party for their friends on Boxing Day. At the end of the year they were invited to the Bell-Carrs' for a New Year's house party and saw in the start of 1934 with champagne and games of charades.

There was an air of optimism among their set. There was a small but perceptible up-turn in the economy and Mosley's party was receiving more mainstream support, with the Daily Mail championing their cause. There was excited talk of Mosley himself coming to address them at a special rally during Race Week at the end of May.

'He wants a big platform and plenty of support,' Vinnie told them. 'It's a grand opportunity for the North to show our loyalty.'

Clara continued to work hard at the newspaper, ignoring Dolly's criticism that she was harming the baby and should be putting her feet up. But Vinnie backed his wife, saying she was doing an important job, using her position to advance their cause.

'It'll be different once the bairn comes,' he reassured his mother. 'She'll stop work then.'

Privately, Clara saw herself carrying on writing part-time for Jellicoe even after the baby was born. If they employed a nanny as Willa did, she could still cover some of the more interesting stories.

By February, Clara's pregnancy was showing and by March she was suddenly large-bellied and enjoying the feel of her baby kicking vigorously inside. Vinnie would lie in bed with his ear to her swollen belly and delight in any sudden movement. He was still making love to her before he went on the trip to Hamburg in April. Clara was tearful at his departure. It had been agreed that the pregnancy was too advanced for her to travel.

'I don't know how I'll manage without you for a fortnight,' she complained.

'Neither do I,' Vinnie agreed. 'But Mam's here to look after you.'

Clara ignored this. 'At least we've Mosley's visit and rally to look forward to next month.'

'And the birth of our baby in June,' Vinnie added. 'What a terrific summer we'll have!'

'Terrific?' Clara giggled. 'You're beginning to sound like Alastair.'

'You cheeky madam,' Vinnie laughed, tickling her until she begged him to stop. 'I shan't stop thinking about you and the bairn for one minute till I'm back.'

Clara knew the two weeks would drag without her husband's lively presence and the string of social engagements they were used to attending. Both the Blakes and the Templetons had gone to Germany too and she missed Willa's company and that of chattering Robert. Despite her advancing pregnancy Clara felt fit and full of energy. Jellicoe and Miss Holt kept asking when she would be giving up work, but Clara insisted on staying on.

'I'd go mad sitting around at home on my own. It's bad enough in the evenings, watching Dolly knit endless bootees.'

After four days, Clara packed a suitcase and announced to Dolly that she was going to stay at her mother's till Vinnie got back.

'It's a chance for me and Mam to spend some time together, and it's handier for work.'

Dolly protested. 'I don't know what Vinnie would have to say about this!'

'It's only for a few days and Mam'll take good care of me,' Clara said breezily.

Patience was delighted, Jimmy less so. 'Mrs Craven's making a fuss about it at the hall. Says Vinnie told her to keep an eye on you, but you wouldn't be told.'

'Well, you're one of his troops,' Clara smiled. 'You can look out for me instead.'

'Clara's got every right to come and see her mam,' Patience retorted. 'Vinnie's away having a good time, so why shouldn't we?'

Twice, Clara drove them to the Paramount in Newcastle, to see Mae West in *She Done Him Wrong* and Garbo in *Queen Christina*. They drove to the coast on Saturday afternoon and sat on the promenade eating ice cream.

'Just wait till the baby comes,' Patience said excitedly. 'We can bring her down here and push her along the prom this summer.'

Clara smiled. 'You think it's a she? Vinnie's convinced it's a boy. Says it's got a little boxer's fists.'

'I hope it is a lass,' Patience said.

'Why?'

'Cos Vinnie will dote on her the way he does on you.' Patience gave a small sigh. 'He'll be different with a lad — expect him to grow up hard, teach him to use his fists as soon as he can walk.'

Clara looked at her mother in surprise. 'I thought you would approve of that? You said Jimmy needed hardening up.'

Patience frowned. 'Jimmy's changing. Once he would only have fought to defend himself; now he seems to go looking for a fight. A lot of Vinnie's lads are like that; they egg each other on, see who can be the toughest.'

Clara said, 'That's not Vinnie's fault. Some of these lads come from bad homes; they were little criminals till Vinnie took them in hand. He's given them a chance when others have washed their hands.'

Patience still looked worried. 'Or maybe he picks them cos they like a fight. And I don't like all this black uniform business — makes them think they're a law unto themselves.'

Clara felt sudden annoyance. 'I can't believe you're saying these things about Vinnie. My husband teaches them discipline and loyalty. If they were doing anything illegal, the police would sharp step in.'

Patience gave a tight smile. 'I'm sorry. You're right. I'm just fussing over nothing.'

The next day, Clara went back to The Cedars, taking Patience and Jimmy with her for Sunday lunch. The meal with Dolly was strained as her mother-in-law made reproachful remarks.

'It's been so lonely in this big house — rattling around on my own like a pea in a drum. I wonder why you made Vinnie buy it if you didn't want to spend any time here. I was happier at Larch Avenue if truth be told, but I went along with it to keep the peace. And not a word from you all week. Anything could've happened to me; I could have fallen downstairs and lain all night and no one would've known . . .'

Clara went to lie down after lunch, her head pounding from Dolly's litany of complaints. When she got up for tea, Patience and Jimmy were gone.

'They've gone home,' Dolly told her. 'I rang Clarkie to come and fetch them.' Clara noticed the pleased look on the older woman's face. 'And I got Patience to pack up your things; Clarkie brought them back.'

'You had no right!' Clara protested.

'As Vinnie's mother, I've every right,' Dolly snapped. 'And don't think of sneaking off to Byfell. Your mam agrees with me — it's time you stopped at home where you belong. Can't have Vinnie coming back to find you gallivanting around town.'

Clara felt too drained to argue further. She retreated to her room and stayed there till morning. Dolly came up with an early cup of tea and fussed over her as if their disagreement had never taken place.

'I'm going to make sure you take good care of that grandbairn of mine,' she declared.

Two days later, Vinnie came home. Clara took the afternoon off work to go and meet the boat from Hamburg. Clarkie drove her down to the quayside and they sat for an age as wind and rain buffeted the car, waiting. The sailing was delayed by nearly two hours and Clara was chilled through by the time the ship docked.

157

Vinnie disembarked amid a crowd of Rotarians, laughing and chattering, while others looked pale and ill from the stormy crossing. He cried with delight on seeing Clara and rushed to embrace her. She felt exultant to be in his arms again.

'I've missed you so much!' she said, bursting into unexpected tears.

Vinnie laughed and kissed her. 'Funny way of showing it, lass.'

He steered her to the car and settled her in the back seat, Clarkie following with his baggage. Then he returned to say goodbye to his friends. Clara felt a stab of envy watching them laughing and shaking hands in farewell. They had all experienced a shared adventure, a camaraderie that she would never know. Willa waved to her as George led his wife and son quickly towards a waiting taxi. 'See you soon!' her friend mouthed and was gone.

Back at The Cedars, Vinnie bathed and changed and ate supper with Clara and Dolly. He was bursting with stories about his trip and how deeply impressed he was by German society. He had gifts from the Brauns and several films taken on his new Box Brownie camera to develop.

'I can't wait to show you what Germany looks like,' he enthused. 'The streets are that clean and the local parades are a sight to see; they're so patriotic with their bands and banners.'

When he finally paused for breath, Dolly lost no time in complaining about Clara's staying with Patience. Vinnie seemed taken aback. 'What did you do that for?'

'To spend time with Mam,' Clara defended herself.

'She could have come here.' Vinnie frowned. 'This is your home, lass. You don't go anywhere without my say-so.' Clara stared at him, on the verge of laughing, but he went on. 'And it's time you stopped work. I've let you go on too long. Herr Braun couldn't believe you were still working in your condition. You'd never see that in Germany. I tell you, Clara, it's been an eye-opener. Hitler praises women highly for what they can do for the Fatherland; Children, Church and Kitchen, that's their saying. Lasses over there are the backbone of a healthy society.'

'Good job I'm not German then,' Clara joked. 'Children I can manage, but we've never been churchgoers and I'm a danger in the kitchen.'

Annoyance flickered across Vinnie's face. 'Well, you'll have to learn, lass. Mam and Ella can give you lessons. Now that you're stopping work, you can do a bit of cooking and housekeeping in preparation for the bairn's coming.'

Clara looked at him in disbelief, but decided not to challenge him in front of Dolly. He was probably just trying to mollify his mother after her string of complaints. She would get round him later, when they were alone. Clara went early to bed, eager for Vinnie to join her. Ten minutes later, she heard the front door close and the car start up. She got to the window just in time to see Vinnie driving off.

Wrapped in her dressing gown, she padded downstairs and found Dolly listening to the radio and knitting.

'Where's he gone?' Clara demanded.

'Down to the hall,' Dolly said, needles clicking. 'Had some business to take care of.' She glanced up. 'It's grand having him back, isn't it?'

'Yes,' Clara agreed and retreated upstairs in disappointment. She determined to stay awake until he returned. But she fell asleep and had no idea what time in the early hours Vinnie finally came home.

Chapter 26

Clara spent the next two days in bed with a heavy cold and it was Vinnie who went to the *Tyne Times* offices and told Jellicoe she would not be returning. Her editor sent round a huge bouquet of flowers and a card signed by Miss Holt and Adam Paxton, wishing her well for the future. Clara's annoyance at Vinnie's high-handedness was tempered by his attentive concern.

'You must rest, lass, and get your strength up. Ella will make anything you want, you just have to ask. And I've asked Jimmy to run errands for you, so you don't have to go out for anything.'

Each evening, Vinnie would bring her a present: perfume, bath salts, a silk scarf. He brought up meals on a tray and sat with her, making sure that she ate everything up, before going back out. There was much to plan for Mosley's visit, as well as a series of lucrative fights at Craven Hall.

At the end of the week, when Clara was feeling better, she found her confinement frustrating. She wanted to be involved in the organisation of the summer rally, but Vinnie felt that the occasional trip to Willa's was enough exertion. By the middle of May, Clara was going mad with boredom. She missed her journalism most: the buzz of the office, meeting people as she gathered her stories and driving about the town. Her diary was a poor substitute; there was nothing to report in her long, languorous days. Never in her life had she had such time on her hands. She followed Ella around the kitchen, getting in the way, and made Jimmy play draughts with her until he complained it was not his job and refused to any more. She paced round the garden after Tom the gardener, badgering him to teach her what the plants were.

Finally her patience snapped. 'I'm not ill, Vinnie! I have to do something. Let me go to the Women's Section meetings. You must let me be a part of all the excitement. Women have their role to play in all this too, you know.'

Vinnie relented. 'Only if you agree to Clarkie's chauffeuring you around. It's not safe being out on your own. The Bolshies are stirring up a hornet's nest. Our success maddens them — they're out to spoil things for Mosley's visit.'

Clara leaped at the offer. 'I promise not to drive.' She put her arms about his neck and kissed him lingeringly. Desire flared inside, despite her heavy womb. Vinnie disengaged himself and gave her a chaste peck on the forehead. She swallowed her disappointment. They had not made love since his return from Germany. When Vinnie touched her at all, it was almost with reverence. 'You're carrying my child,' he told her. 'I'd do nothing to harm him or you.'

At the next meeting of the Women's Section, Cissie and Mabel gave Clara a warm welcome. 'Thought Vinnie had put you in purdah,' Cissie teased.

'As good as,' Clara grinned. 'I can't tell you how glad I am to be with you all again.'

Cissie stood back from hugging her. 'Goodness me, I felt the baby kick. Not long now, girl. We don't want you giving birth at the rally.'

'It's a good six weeks away, Dr Dixon reckons,' Clara answered.

After the second meeting, with only a week to go before Race Week and the big rally planned for the Town Moor, Clara asked Clarkie to drop by the *Tyne Times* offices.

'Just want to thank Jellicoe for the flowers he sent,' she told him. 'Never had the chance to say goodbye.'

As soon as she entered her old office, Clara felt a wave of regret that she was no longer working there. Adam was busy getting an article finished; Miss Holt was on the telephone and waved in surprise. Clara knocked and went in to see her editor. She was touched by his obvious delight at seeing her. He cleared a chair for her to sit on and she bombarded him with questions about what had been happening in her absence.

Eventually they were interrupted by Miss Holt's knocking and entering. 'Sorry, Clara, but your driver Mr Clark wants to know how much longer you'll be.'

'Tell him two minutes,' Clara said, rising reluctantly. The secretary went out. 'Let me cover the rally for you,' she pleaded. 'You know I'm your best contact for this.'

Jellicoe snorted. 'Look at you. You're in no state to be covering stories.'

'Just this once,' she urged. 'I bet I could get an interview with Mosley.'

'Does Vinnie know about this?' he asked cautiously.

'Vinnie supports my work for the Women's Section,' Clara was evasive, 'and this will be from the women's point of view. He'll be more than happy at the publicity.'

Clara left triumphant with the commission from Jellicoe. Clarkie commented, 'You took a long time over a bunch of flowers.'

'It was a big bunch of flowers.' Clara smiled, already planning how she was going to cover the forthcoming events. Mosley was not due to come until the end of a week of marches and meetings, culminating in his triumphal appearance before thousands of Tynesiders at a massive rally on the Town Moor.

There had already been disturbances at a BUF parade in Gateshead where anti-fascists had turned up to heckle and fight. The Newcastle meeting was to be on an altogether bigger scale. Vinnie was frantically busy with preparations. Jimmy boasted to Clara that he was to be part of the guard at the meeting.

At the last moment, when she thought it too late for Vinnie to protest, Clara told him that she would be attending with the Women's Section.

'Cissie will look after me,' she assured him.

Vinnie stared at her as if she were mad. 'You're not going.' He was adamant. 'Mam's taken the day off work to be here with you.'

'She doesn't need to,' Clara protested. 'Vinnie! This is the most exciting thing to happen to our branch; you can't be so cruel as to stop me being a part of it.'

Vinnie looked at her in exasperation as he dressed in his new black uniform. 'I don't want you there,' he said distractedly. 'It's too risky in your condition. You'll stay here and keep out of harm's way.'

Clara bit back a retort. He could not stop her. It was already arranged that she would meet Cissie at Willa's and they would all go together. Willa was showing greater interest in joining the section since the trip to Germany and Clara was sure the rally would be the spur that she needed. The women would show that they were as brave and loyal as the men.

Once Vinnie had left, Clara told Dolly she was going for an afternoon rest. She changed into a dark grey smock and black jacket with the BUF badge and listened out for her mother-in-law. The radio was playing in the sitting room. She slipped out of the house. It was only when she started up the engine of the Albion that Dolly came rushing to the window, banging on the glass and shouting. Clara drove off. She felt exultant at having escaped and was still in a state of feverish excitement when she arrived at Madras House in Jesmond.

Cissie was suspicious. 'I thought Vinnie would be dropping you off. He does know about our arrangement to go together?'

Clara glanced away. 'Of course he does. I told him you would look after me.'

'Clara?' Cissie eyed her.

Clara was defiant. 'He doesn't want me to go, but I'm one of the Women's Section and I've just as much right to be there as he has.'

Cissie threw back her head with laughter. 'You naughty girl.'

Willa was shocked. 'You shouldn't go against what your husband says. It is going to be safe, isn't it?'

'Of course it is,' Cissie said dismissively. 'The Blackshirts will protect us.'

Even before they got near the meeting hall, they could see throngs of people hostile to the march gathering in the surrounding streets. There were hundreds of them ranged under banners: Socialists, Communists, the Women's Cooperative Guild, and trade unions. Mounted police were positioned on street corners. Clara had her first sharp pang of doubt. She clutched at Cissie's hand.

'I had no idea there'd be this much opposition,' she gulped.

'Hold your head up, girl,' Cissie ordered.

She took both Clara and Willa by the arm and walked them briskly up the street to join the procession. As they turned the corner, Clara was gladdened to see rank upon rank of Blackshirts and BUF supporters — students, ex-servicemen with medals, the well-dressed middle class and down-at-heel men in frayed suits — all assembling behind fascist banners and Union flags. But what made her heart jolt with fright was the seething mass of protesters beyond the cordon of police. They had come in their thousands, not hundreds. They bayed like dogs, drowning out the noise of the BUF bands.

Her legs buckled and she clutched her belly, heart racing. Cissie gripped her.

'Perhaps Vinnie was right. You feeling up to this, girl?' she asked.

Clara nodded.

Willa said in a frightened voice, 'I think it's safer to go on than turn back now. Let's just get into the hall.'

Together they marched forward, holding their heads up, ignoring the jeers. The men in front began to boom out a Blackshirt song:

'Mosley, Leader of Thousands! Hope of our manhood, we proudly hail thee!
Raise we this song of allegiance, for we are sworn and shall not fail thee!'

It gave Clara courage. Blackshirts surrounded the hall entrance and guarded the approach. Just as they reached the door, she heard someone shout out her name. She turned to see a man trying to push his way through the fascist guard.

'Clara!' he bellowed. 'Traitor! You should be ashamed of yourself!'

Clara faltered. A moment later, he was grabbed and hurled back into the crowd. But she had glimpsed enough of his dark hair and angry face to recognise him.

'Benny,' she gasped, feeling winded. Cissie held her up.

'You know that man?' she said in distaste.

'He was a friend once,' she panted.

'That could be useful to Vinnie,' Cissie murmured. '"Know thine enemy."'

The next minute they were inside, joining the ranks of saluting supporters.

Dressed in her thick clothing, Clara found it unbearably hot in the crowded airless hall. She was thankful to sit down, but even then found it hard to catch her breath. She sat with her eyes closed as the band struck up the National Anthem and Vinnie marched in with the other local leaders and climbed the steps to the platform. She did not have the energy to take notes.

At once, hecklers began to spring up among the audience and disrupt the speeches. The Blackshirt stewards were swift to root them out and eject them from the hall, but the atmosphere was ill-tempered, always simmering and threatening to get out of hand. Every time the outside door opened, they could hear shouting and chanting in the street. Clara was astounded at how organised was the opposition against them. Why were they so unpopular?

After half an hour, Vinnie declared the meeting over and it descended into chaos as people scrambled for the door. Clara watched Vinnie leave the stage, grim-faced. She wanted to rush to him but dared not show herself. Better if he never knew she had been there. He might blame Cissie or Willa and that would not be fair. He joined the procession as it was jostled out of the hall.

Willa began to shake and sob. 'I'm not going back out there! I just can't!'

'Don't be so weak-kneed,' Cissie said impatiently. 'Clara's not scared and she can't run half as fast in her condition. Come on, we'll face it together.'

Clara had a sudden thought. 'The back entrance might be quieter,' she said. 'It's only a street away from headquarters. We can take refuge there till all this dies down. Just listen to the noise out there.'

Cissie was scathing. 'I'm not going to scurry out the back like a frightened mouse. This is the time to show what we fascist women are made of.'

'Look at the state Willa's in,' Clara pleaded. 'And I'm not feeling grand either.'

Cissie sighed impatiently. 'I'll go after Vinnie. He'll have to be told. You stay here.'

She disappeared into the crush of people. They waited, Clara imagining what Vinnie would have to say on finding her there. She thought she would faint. Cissie did not come back.

'I must have air,' Clara panted.

'Let's try the back door,' Willa said, shaking.

They pushed against the flow of people down towards the stage and through a door that led into a dingy passage. Others followed them. Minutes later, they were out of the back door and into the glare of the hot narrow lane. Clara was momentarily dazzled. She gulped at the fresh air.

'There's no one here,' Willa gasped, clutching her.

Squinting, Clara saw that the back street was almost empty and could not believe their luck. The back entrance was hidden by dustbins and an old advertising hoarding.

'Let's make a dash for it,' Willa urged, pulling her by the arm.

Just then, a surge of people ran out of the hall behind them, clattering into the bins. Protesters at the top of the back lane turned and spotted them.

'Stop the fascist bastards!' they yelled, and gave chase.

'Run!' Clara shouted, grabbing a screaming Willa and pulling her along.

Fear made her move more quickly than she could have imagined. Holding each other's hand they fled together down the lane, clattering across the cobbles in their high heels. Willa's hat flew off.

'Leave it!' Clara ordered as the crowd gained on them.

A group of the men who had escaped from the back entrance turned and faced their pursuers. Clara felt sick fear at the sound of fists slamming into flesh as the two sides met. But it gave the women the extra valuable seconds to flee into the next street and batter on the door of the BUF offices.

A Blackshirt looked out and quickly bustled them inside, slamming the door shut behind them. Clara collapsed into a chair, shaking and feeling sick. Moments later, noise erupted right outside as violence spread into the street. A brick came hurtling through the window and glass splintered at their feet.

Willa screamed.

'Quick, get upstairs,' a clerk ordered.

He guided Willa. Clara followed, breathless and weak-legged, hauling herself up behind them to an upstairs committee room where a young secretary and an elderly volunteer were taking refuge.

'Major Lockwood!' Clara panted.

'Dear girl,' he greeted her, 'what on earth—'

Before he could finish, there was more splintering of glass and shouting below. Clara wondered wildly if their attackers had broken in. The clerk rushed to the window.

Willa cried hysterically, 'I should never have come — I want George — I wish I'd never come — they're going to kill us!'

Clara pushed her into a chair next to the terrified secretary and went to look too.

'We're surrounded,' the clerk muttered tensely.

There was chaos. Within minutes the lane had filled with men. They charged with sticks and banner poles, missiles flying over their heads; they screamed and cursed as they punched each other and fell to the ground. It was hard to tell which side was which, each attacking with equal ferocity. Clara watched in horror as one man lay helpless in the dust while three others kicked him until he stopped moving. She wanted to vomit. She covered her mouth, swallowing down bile.

'My God, they're killing that man! We have to help him.'

'He's a Bolshie,' the young man replied in distaste.

Clara stared at him in disbelief. 'Does it matter?'

He gave her a hard look. 'Yes, it does. They started all this.' He turned abruptly and strode to the door.

'Don't leave us!' Willa wailed.

Clara went to her quickly. 'It's all right, we're safe in here. Cissie will guess where we've gone and tell Vinnie — he'll rescue us. You mustn't worry.'

But Clara did not believe her own words. She had seen the hatred on the faces of the fighting crowds. If they broke in. . .

'Barricade the door after me,' the clerk ordered. She watched him disappear and felt fear rise up and choke her.

Chapter 27

Clara forced herself to act. She began dragging a heavy table in front of the door. Major Lockwood came swiftly to help.

'You shouldn't be doing this in your condition,' he rebuked her. 'Please sit down with the ladies.'

A sharp pain stabbed at her insides. Clara clutched her stomach, stifling a cry.

'What's wrong?' Willa asked anxiously.

'Nothing,' Clara gasped.

'Is it the baby?' Willa fretted.

Clara did not answer as she retreated to a chair, heart racing, brow perspiring. She felt hot, clammy and unwell.

'Mary, fetch Mrs Craven a glass of water,' Major Lockwood commanded. The secretary hurried into the adjoining kitchen.

Clara's distress seemed to shake Willa out of her paralysis. She helped Clara out of her jacket and loosened her blouse. Mary came back with a cup of lukewarm water.

'Thank you,' Clara whispered.

The major came over and sat with them, telling them how he had tried to attend the meeting but had been turned back by the police for his own safety.

'Where are the police now?' Willa demanded tearfully.

'They can't cope,' the major replied. 'We must rely on our own troops for protection, like that brave young man downstairs.'

Clara wondered where Jimmy was at that moment; it filled her with anxiety to think what might be happening to him. Was Vinnie safe? And what had become of Cissie?

A few minutes later, they were startled by the sound of boots clattering on the stairs and people pushing against the door. The major jumped up to defend them.

'Let us in!' someone shouted, hammering on the door. 'Lads are injured. We're Blackshirts.'

The major went to pull back the table. In came two men dragging a third between them. His face was streaming with blood, his jacket torn. Behind stumbled two more, one holding a limp arm, the other with gashes to his temple and cheek. The first two laid the semi-conscious man on the floor and rushed back out.

Willa began to moan, 'I think I'm going to be sick,' and dashed into the kitchen.

Clara got up unsteadily and went to help. She asked Mary to fetch a bowl of water and any towels she could lay her hands on, while she stooped and spoke to the man.

'Can you hear me?' The man stared at her with glazed eyes and did not respond. She put a finger to his bloodied neck and found a pulse. 'You're going to be all right. You're safe now. We'll get you cleaned up.'

Mary came back with water and an armful of tea towels and they washed the blood from his face. There was a deep cut on his forehead. Clara ripped up one of the towels and bandaged the man's head to stem the bleeding. Mary fed him sips of water. The major gave swigs of whisky to the other injured men while Clara bathed their cuts too. The man with the dangling arm cried out in pain when she touched it.

'It might be broken,' she said gently. 'Give him another nip of whisky, Major.'

Taking her jacket, she cradled it round his arm and tied it round his neck in a sling. Reenie had once practised putting slings and bandages on her during her training. Clara thought fleetingly of her old friend. Was she out demonstrating on the streets like Benny or nursing the injured like Clara?

The man on the floor was pale and sweating. She sat with him, holding his hand and murmuring encouragement. This is madness! she thought. We're fighting our own people; it's civil war.

There was no let-up in the running street battles below. They raged on all afternoon and the wounded and bleeding were hauled into the besieged building. Clara and the others did what they could to help. The stench of sweat and blood in the stifling upstairs room was overpowering, but when they opened the window for air, missiles were hurled in through the gap. They pulled the shutters closed and turned on the lights.

It was like a scene from a field hospital and Clara kept busy to stem the horror that threatened to overwhelm her. They soon ran out of towels for bandages and used the men's shirts instead. Even Willa overcame her terror to help nurse the casualties. A young medical student who came in with a leg injury did what he could to assist them. All the time, Clara tried to ignore the increasing pains that gripped her insides and left her breathless.

She could not believe the anarchy outside or that they had been left by the police to fend for themselves. There would be a lull in the fighting and someone would venture downstairs to see if it was safe to leave, only to find the enemy had regrouped and were ready to attack again.

As evening came and the fighting outside subsided once more, Clara realised how parched and thirsty she was. Walking into the kitchen, she was overcome by a sudden acute pain. She collapsed on the floor and passed out.

Coming to, she found herself lying on the kitchen floor, Willa, Mary and the major staring at her in consternation. Her skirt and knickers were drenched. Pain gripped her like a vice.

'Willa!' she cried out in fear. 'What's happening to me?'

Willa seized her hand. 'Oh, Clara! Your waters have broken; I think the baby's coming.'

Mary looked on in bewilderment. 'You can't have it here, miss.'

Willa turned to the major. 'Major Lockwood, do something! You have to get us out of here. Clara might lose her baby.'

Galvanised, he headed out of the kitchen and ordered the young medic in to help.

'I don't know the first thing about babies,' the student protested.

'You soon will,' the major snapped. 'Just sit with her. I'll see if we can negotiate our way out.'

He disappeared. The wait seemed interminable; Clara lay in agony, feeling the baby pressing down heavily inside. She was terrified of losing it. Half an hour or more passed before the major returned with two Blackshirts. Clara sobbed with relief. Major Lockwood leaned down and gingerly patted her shoulder in reassurance.

'They're calling a truce to let you and the other women out. They're bringing in an ambulance.'

It seemed an age before word came through that the ambulance had arrived. By that time Clara was writhing in agony. The men helped her to her feet. She nearly fainted again from the pain and her legs buckled. They carried her between them, Willa and Mary following.

She was only vaguely aware of reaching the street outside and being carried to the end and into an ambulance. There was noise about her, staring faces, and then she was in the vehicle with Willa holding her hand. She wanted to tell one of the Blackshirts to get a message to Vinnie, but did not have the strength to speak. She closed her eyes as the van jostled forward, the stabbing pains now unrelenting. An orderly placed a damp cloth on her sweating brow and told her to hold on.

But she could not. Ten agonising minutes later, Clara felt a huge force tear through her and knew her baby was coming. She tried to sit up as she yelled in pain and terror. Her baby was born as the ambulance swung in through the gates of the maternity hospital.

'Let me see!' Clara panted, struggling to move. She saw a tiny, red slippery creature in the orderly's hands. It spluttered as if it were choking. The man looked uncertain what to do.

'Clear its mouth so it can breathe!' Willa cried.

He held on to the baby until the ambulance came to a halt. Clara was stretchered into the hospital, calling out in distress for her baby.

She remembered nothing after that, until later she came round in a high-ceilinged ward and it was dark. She could hear the querulous cries of babies in the distance. Clara was too weak to move. She felt as if she were floating above the room and not a part of anything below — the pain and feverishness seemed to belong to someone else. She tried to float out of the room to search for her baby, but could not find the door.

She had no idea how long she remained in her semi-conscious state; it could have been hours or days. She was half aware of doctors and nurses coming and going, staring down at her, taking her temperature, administering injections.

One morning she finally awoke feeling clear-headed yet painfully weak. Early morning light was streaming in at the window and she wondered where she was. Gradually, she realised she was on her own in a small side ward. Her first thought was for her baby. Where was it? What was it? Was her baby alive? Then she had a flood of longing for Vinnie. How desperately she wanted him to be there with her now, his vibrant presence assuring her that everything was all right. Did he even know where she was yet? Was he unharmed from yesterday's conflict? Or was it longer ago than yesterday?

The nightmarish scenes of running battles and the terrible fetid room full of the wounded came back in a vivid rush. What had become of their glorious movement that it could descend so quickly into thuggery and violence? Both sides had seemed as bad as the other in their brutality. Clara turned her face into the pillow and wept. Yet even as relief came with her tears, she berated herself for her weakness. Crying would not help her discover what had happened to her baby.

A nurse came in as she was trying to struggle out of bed.

'Get back in at once,' the nurse ordered. 'Goodness me, it's good to see you in the land of the living. I'm Nurse Brown. Can you manage something to eat?'

'My baby,' Clara croaked. 'I want my baby.'

'Baby Craven is under observation,' the nurse said.

'What for?'

Nurse Brown came to her bedside and took her hand. 'You both had a rough time of it during the delivery.' She was direct. 'She's very immature and weak.'

'She?'

'Yes, you have a girl. Did you not know?' she asked in surprise.

Clara shook her head. The nurse patted her hand. 'Perhaps that's little wonder; you've been in a fever these past three days. Don't worry, we're doing what we can to save her.'

Clara felt hot tears well up once more. 'Save her? She's not going to die, is she?'

'I didn't say that.' The nurse went to leave the room. 'You try to rest.'

'My husband,' Clara called after her, 'does he know—'

'He's been here every day, but you've been too ill for visitors. Mr Craven will be allowed in at the visiting hour today,' she promised as she left.

Clara lay in a sweat of anxiety. Her daughter was lying somewhere in the same hospital, her life slipping away and Clara not there to comfort her. By the time a doctor came to see her, she was half mad with worry and dark thoughts.

'The baby is doing better by the hour,' he said, trying to calm her, 'but she's still in a poorly state.'

'Can I go and see her?' Clara pleaded.

'Tomorrow perhaps. I'm afraid you're too weak at the moment,' he said with a pitying look. 'Your blood pressure has been dangerously high — it's lucky that both you and your baby are alive. It's very important that you rest.'

Clara's agony of mind was only relieved when, later, Vinnie appeared at the door. Clara burst into tears at the sight of him holding an enormous bouquet of flowers. He plonked them on the bed and rushed to take her in his arms.

'Oh, lass! I've been that worried about you.'

'Vinnie,' she sobbed, 'I'm so sorry.'

'What you sorry about?' he exclaimed.

'I should never have gone to the rally. I'm sorry for not listening to you. It was terrible what happened. I can't bear to think about it. But Willa was scared and I thought we could escape out the back. Then they chased us and all those lads fighting — I thought it would never end — and the blood — oh, God, Vinnie, I'll never be able to forget—'

'Stop it,' Vinnie said firmly. 'You mustn't upset yourself any more. They're nowt but a pack of animals — trying to terrorise women. I hope you see that now — what we're up against?' He kissed her forehead. 'All that matters is that you're safe and the bairn's been born alive.'

Clara gasped, 'Vinnie, have you see our daughter?' He nodded. 'Tell me what she's like.'

'The littlest nipper I've ever seen,' he said wryly.

'Who does she look like?' Clara asked eagerly.

He shrugged. 'No one. But one day she'll be as bonny as her mam.'

A sob caught in Clara's throat. 'I want to see her. Why can't I see her?'

'All in good time. The doctors know best.'

'Where is she?'

'In a special ward,' Vinnie said, standing up.

Clara looked at him in dismay. 'Are you going already?'

'There's a lot to do,' he answered. 'Mosley's due in Newcastle the day after tomorrow.'

Clara felt light-headed. In her anxiety over the baby, she had forgotten all about their leader's visit. She realised she knew nothing of what had happened to the others after the siege at headquarters.

'What about Willa? Is she all right?' Clara reached out to stop him going. 'And Major Lockwood was there too.'

'They're canny,' Vinnie assured her. 'After you went in the ambulance, the police moved in to round up the riff-raff.'

'And Cissie? She went to find you—'

'She did, but not in time to rescue you and Willa. And before you ask,

167

Jimmy's fine too — proved himself a man that day.' His eyes shone with pride. 'I told Jimmy he could bring your mam in to see you tomorrow.'

'Thank you, Vinnie.' She smiled weakly. 'Do you forgive me for going?'

He paused before answering. 'I'm not best pleased you disobeyed me — and Mam's still ranting on about the way you gave her the slip. But Major Lockwood said you were a real little Florence Nightingale. You showed great bravery and for that I'm proud.' His face clouded suddenly. 'But it could so easily have ended badly for you and the bairn,' he added sternly. 'You must never do anything like that again.'

He leaned down and kissed her swiftly on the head, then he was striding to the door and waving goodbye.

'Vinnie!' she called out. 'Wait. What are we going to call the baby?'

Without hesitation he announced, 'We'll call her Sarah — after my grandmother and aunt.' With a brief smile he was gone.

***

The following day, Patience came with Jimmy. Clara had a tearful reunion with her mother. They clung together while Jimmy stood awkwardly at the end of the bed.

'What were you thinking of, going on that rally?' Patience scolded. 'I've told Jimmy he should have kept an eye on you instead of marching around like Mussolini.'

'Vinnie gives me orders, not you,' Jimmy muttered.

'Then he's as much to blame for all this as anyone.' Patience was blunt.

'No he's not,' Clara defended him. 'He didn't want me to go. It's all my fault. I only went 'cos I wanted to cover it for the paper — couldn't resist a good scoop.'

Patience clucked in disapproval.

'Where is Vinnie?' Clara asked.

Patience and Jimmy glanced at each other. 'He's sorting things out for tomorrow — something to do with Mosley's visit,' Patience said evasively.

'The police are trying to stop him coming,' Jimmy added.

'Mosley?' Clara said. 'But they can't do that.'

Jimmy shrugged. 'Vinnie's letting off steam about it, I can tell you.'

Patience quickly diverted the conversation. 'I've seen my granddaughter.' She smiled. 'Only through the window — they wouldn't let us on the ward. But she's a little dazzler.'

Clara gave a trembling smile. 'I just want to see her, Mam. It's as if I don't really have a bairn.'

She was too embarrassed to say in front of her brother that her whole body cried out for her baby. Her breasts were aching and hard, swollen with milk. Her arms longed to hold her. Too soon it was time for her mother to go.

'I'll come in at the weekend,' Patience promised. 'You just get your strength back.'

After they had gone Clara was overwhelmed with loneliness. When Nurse Brown next appeared she badgered her to take her to see Sarah.

'You could wheel me in a chair,' she insisted. 'Please! Just for a look.'

The nurse went off to consult and returned with the young doctor who had spoken to Clara the previous day. He agreed that she could go for a few minutes. It took a huge effort for Clara to move from the bed to the chair, so feeble were her legs, but she set off in triumph for the baby ward. She passed a large ward full of the insistent cries of the newborn and glimpsed rows of tiny cots in a sunlit room.

Two corridors away, she was wheeled into a smaller room. Heat hit her as soon as they entered. Beyond a glass screen she could see that three of the six cots were occupied by tiny babies swaddled tightly and wearing knitted hats. One of them bleated softly.

The matron pointed to the far one. 'There she is, Mrs Craven. You can't go any closer in case of infection.' Immediately, Clara detected hostility in the woman's voice and wondered why.

Clara pressed her face against the glass, her heart stopping at the sight of her daughter's minute crinkled face under her woollen cap. She had an unhealthy yellowish hue and lay so still that Clara feared she was dead.

'She's not moving,' she said in agitation, putting out a hand on the glass. 'Is she breathing?'

'Yes,' said Matron. 'Now you mustn't fuss.'

'I should be feeding her,' Clara said in frustration. 'Why can't she be brought to me? I'm full of milk.'

'She's far too small and weak to latch on yet,' the matron explained. 'We're feeding her with a pipette. You'll just have to be patient; not something your lot are used to,' she muttered.

Clara ignored the baffling jibe. She longed to stroke her daughter's cheek. What a strange creature she looked, like a wizened old man. Then Clara felt disloyal for having such a thought. A minute later the matron was ordering her to be returned to her room. She sank back into bed completely exhausted from the effort.

'What's that woman got against me?' she asked Nurse Brown.

'You're a bit notorious,' she answered dryly. 'Everyone knows you were involved in the battle of Clayton Street — it was in all the papers. Matron MacCarthy's a member of the Labour Party. Doesn't approve of you.'

Clara fretted. 'She won't take it out on my daughter, will she?'

Nurse Brown gave her an offended look. 'We're all dedicated to our work here whatever our beliefs,' she snapped.

'I'm sorry,' Clara said quickly, 'I didn't mean—'

'No? Well, think before you speak, my father used to say,' she said reprovingly and marched from the room.

The following day, Clara expected no visitors because of Mosley's arrival. She imagined the great rally taking place on the Town Moor and how Vinnie would be in his element. So it was to her great surprise that Vinnie turned up that evening with Dolly.

At once she noticed his angry mood. He gave her a perfunctory kiss and stood back.

'Police stopped Mosley coming,' he said bitterly, 'said they couldn't guarantee his safety. Had to cancel the rally.' He glared at her as if it was somehow her fault. 'After all that bother in Clayton Street.'

'Oh, Vinnie, that's terrible,' Clara sympathised.

Dolly chipped in. 'They made a real song and dance about you going into labour after all the fighting.'

'Aye,' Vinnie agreed, 'chief copper kept using that as an excuse. As if it was all our fault and not the bloody Reds!'

'Well, it was six of one and half a dozen of the other,' Clara commented.

Vinnie gave her a sharp look. 'Whose side are you on?'

'Don't be like that,' Clara said in dismay. 'You shouldn't need to ask.'

'No I shouldn't. But you weren't just there to support the Women's Section like you said, were you, Clara?' he accused her. 'Jimmy tells me you went cos

169

you wanted a story for your precious newspaper.'

Clara flushed. How dare Jimmy! Yet she could not deny it.

Dolly gave her an indignant look. 'Jellicoe sent flowers to the house — the cheek of it! Vinnie sent them straight back. You were supposed to have stopped working weeks ago.'

Vinnie's voice rose. 'And Cissie's not best pleased either. She thinks you used her — got her to take you under false pretences. Then you didn't even stick with her like you were supposed to — if you had none of this would've happened.'

Clara was shocked by his vehemence. 'Well Cissie's changed her tune — she was all for me going.'

Dolly joined in. 'To think you put the bairn in danger just on a selfish whim and to please that Jellicoe. What were you thinking of ?'

'I was thinking of publicity for the movement here in Newcastle,' Clara said defensively.

'Aye, you got them publicity all right — the wrong sort,' Vinnie snapped. 'And now the rally's off.'

'You can't blame me for that,' she protested. 'It was the violence. I wasn't the one kicking lads to a pulp on the streets. I thought Blackshirts were supposed to be disciplined?'

'They are,' Vinnie barked. 'But it was no Sunday school outing, Clara. Luckily for you and that daft Willa, our lads weren't shy in using their fists to defend you.'

Clara was shaken. She had never seen her husband so furious and it was all directed at her. Dolly was perched on the edge of a chair full of disapproval. She had not even asked how Clara or the baby was. Clara swallowed down tears of indignation. A nurse put her head round the door.

'Is anything the matter?' she asked.

Vinnie changed in an instant. 'No, thank you, Nurse,' he smiled.

The woman hesitated, and then disappeared, closing the door. Clara and Vinnie looked at each other, chastened. Clara was the first to relent.

'I'm sorry about Mosley not coming, Vinnie. I know how much it meant to you.'

Vinnie sighed. 'I can't deny it's a setback, but we'll not let our enemies have the last word. We'll organise something else.'

'Is Cissie very cross with me?' Clara asked uncomfortably.

'You know Cissie,' he grunted, 'speaks her mind. Says you're selfish for putting your newspaper story before loyalty to the party.'

Clara felt hurt. 'Has this spoilt things between us and the Bell-Carrs?' she asked.

Vinnie's look was rueful. 'I doubt it. I told her you were young and naive, but not disloyal. She's not the kind to hold a grudge.'

Dolly grew impatient, insisting she wanted to see her new granddaughter. She led Vinnie away. The next time Vinnie came to visit he was more his old self and Clara put down his angry behaviour to the disappointment of the failed rally. The newspapers were full of how the anti-fascists had disrupted the event and been victorious over the local BUF. Clara was shocked to see Benny Lewis described as one of the former's leaders and quoted as saying it was a great triumph for the Left and for democracy. But Vinnie was bullish.

'Our numbers have gone up since the battle of Clayton Street — they're joining in droves. And you know why? Cos of the Red menace. Decent people don't want them terrorising our streets. We're the only ones standing up to them.'

By the next week, Clara was recovering and her energy returning. Vinnie

170

wanted her home. She was impatient to go home too, yet did not want to leave Sarah behind. The baby was not thriving. She had put on no weight and seemed uninterested in feeding. The hospital, however, said there was nothing Clara could do and sent her home. It was a tearful wife that Vinnie came to fetch. Once home, she was engulfed in a feeling of anti-climax. She should have been a new mother revelling in the job of nursing her baby, yet she had nothing to do except fret.

She lived for the brief hour each day when Vinnie drove her to the hospital to see their daughter. Whenever Clara saw her, the baby lay listless and quiet. She hardly ever cried. It was Dolly who suggested they should have Sarah baptised.

'Just in case the worst happens,' she said bluntly.

The hospital chaplain conducted the simple ceremony, with just Clara and Vinnie in attendance. Clara held her daughter for the first time and felt a flood of emotion for the helpless, trusting infant in her arms. She could not bear the thought that this might be her one and only time — that it was possible Sarah might not survive — and wanted to hold on to her for ever. Vinnie stood close, his jaw tight and his eyes shining with tears. The service was over in minutes but Matron MacCarthy took pity on Clara and let her hold on to her baby until Vinnie coaxed her to hand her back.

'I can't bear it, Vinnie,' Clara wept into her husband's shoulder.

'She's a Craven — a little fighter,' Vinnie said savagely. 'She's not ganin' to die.'

Chapter 28

Each time they visited and found Sarah still alive seemed a small miracle. After witnessing Clara's distress at the baptism, Matron allowed her to hold Sarah and feed drips of milk from the pipette into her tiny rosebud mouth. Tears streamed down her face as she watched her baby splutter and struggle to drink the milk.

Vinnie found these visits trying and grew angry in his frustration at not being able to do anything for his daughter. It was almost a relief when he went off to London for a huge BUF rally at Olympia, taking Jimmy and five others of his troop. Clara paid scant attention to the uproar in the press when the massive meeting descended into violence. She was too consumed with worry over her daughter.

At home, Dolly fretted that the party, and therefore Vinnie's standing locally, had been damaged by the ruthlessness of Mosley's Blackshirts at the London rally, but Vinnie came back buoyed up by the experience.

'The press made it out to be worse than it was,' he assured them both. 'And no one's going to push us around at our own meetings. We're fighting for freedom of speech.'

Clara felt detached from it all and wondered how Vinnie could find it so important when their daughter struggled daily for survival. Gradually, Clara noticed a difference. Each day, Sarah appeared to grow a little stronger, a little more interested in feeding. She was beginning to win her battle to hold on to life. Finally, by the end of June, even Dolly was remarking on her granddaughter's progress; she was putting on weight and becoming more responsive. Her eyes could now focus and she made small grunting noises whenever someone came near. In the middle of July, the hospital agreed to let her home.

Clara carried Sarah out of the hospital, clutching her close, terrified of dropping her. The matron had given Clara strict instructions on regular feeds, and that the baby should be kept calm and not handled too much. Vinnie drove them back to The Cedars, Clara urging him to drive more slowly.

Dolly took charge the minute they got there, ordering Ella to heat up a bottle of milk so she could feed her. Clara's milk had dried up, so she could not retreat upstairs to feed Sarah herself. She hovered over Dolly, itching to hold her daughter again. Vinnie poured himself a large whisky and proposed a toast. 'To all my favourite lasses; Mam, Clara and bonny Sarah!'

That night Sarah slept beside their bed, snuffling and grizzling. Clara got up to warm a small bottle of milk in the early hours. The baby took ages to drink the milk and then she brought half of it back up again, all over Clara. Sarah wailed and woke Vinnie. Too soon it was time to feed her again. After three nights of this, Vinnie told her Sarah would have to sleep in her own room.

'We've done it all out for her and she might settle better.'

Clara spent the next night listening out for Sarah's cries. She woke with a start in the middle of the night and was alarmed by the silence. Rushing to Sarah's room she peered into the cot. She was lying as still as stone. Clara prodded her hard. Sarah let out a querulous cry and Clara clutched the cot side in relief.

In the daytime, Clara was left alone for long hours while Vinnie and Dolly went off to Craven Hall. She was grateful for the company of the uncomplaining Ella, who helped her heat up milk and wash nappies between her other chores. Vinnie came back one day to find Clara sitting in the garden with Ella, laughing and drinking homemade lemonade, while Sarah slept in the large hooded pram.

'Ella, I don't pay you to sit around gossiping with me wife,' he said. Ella jumped up, apologising. Clara thought he was teasing.

'Finish your drink.' She smiled at Vinnie. 'It's the first time we've got Sarah to sleep all day. Ella's got a way with her.'

Later, Vinnie told Clara off. 'I'll not have Ella interfering. She's not a nanny — she's the cook. You're Sarah's mam — it's your job to care for our daughter and no one else's.'

Clara gawped at him. 'She just helped settle the bairn to sleep. It's hard work, Vinnie,' she protested. 'She takes ages to feed — and she's always being sick.' Suddenly she was in tears.

He softened at once. 'Haway, lass, I didn't mean to upset you.' He put his arms round her and kissed the top of her head. 'You'll get used to it — all mams do. It's natural for women, isn't it?'

Clara smothered a retort that it did not seem natural to her. It was the most fraught week of her life. She felt totally responsible for this tiny, demanding creature — saw the daily care that Sarah would need stretching ahead for an eternity. Yet she had never felt more inadequate. Clara sniffed. She would just have to get on with it, as Dolly kept telling her when she complained of lack of sleep.

Soon she would get into a routine and find time for seeing her friends again. Willa had sent a card congratulating her on Sarah's birth, but had not called to see her. Neither had Cissie. She would organise an 'at home' for her friends. But it was Dolly who pre-empted Clara's idea by announcing they would have a belated christening party for the baby.

To Clara's dismay, it grew into a huge event, with large numbers of business friends and new neighbours being invited. Jellicoe and her former colleagues were pointedly left off the list, despite her plea that they be included. Vinnie had his men parking cars and serving out drinks. Patience and Jimmy were there, along with the Blakes, the Templetons and the Lockwoods. Clara, kept busy upstairs coping with Sarah, heard the party getting under way. When the Bell-Carrs made a belated entrance, Vinnie came rushing in to the nursery where Clara was changing Sarah after another unsatisfactory feed.

'Bring her down,' he said impatiently. 'Everyone's waiting.'

'You take her,' Clara said, holding the baby out to him. 'I just want to put on some lipstick.'

'You look fine as you are.' Vinnie frowned. 'You don't need make-up.'

Clara stalked past him, thrusting Sarah into his arms. 'I may feel like a wet dishcloth, but I'll not look like one in front of all those people.'

Exhausted, she sat at her dressing table and peered with dissatisfaction at her image. She looked pale and tired, her eyes dark-ringed and her hair lank. She brushed it back and pinned it up, rubbed rouge into her cheeks and put on crimson lipstick. At least she was able to get into last year's summer dresses; weight had fallen off her during these past weeks of worrying over Sarah. Her mother told her she was too thin. As she descended, she could hear the noisy hubbub of chattering guests.

'Clara!' Cissie cried, waving her over. 'You look wonderful, girl.' She embraced her as if there had been no cooling of relations since the May rally.

Others followed Cissie's lead and kissed Clara in greeting. Willa looked tearful.

'How are you? I've so wanted to come and see you, but George . . .' She was whispering, glancing round. 'He took the whole thing rather badly. Not that any of it was your fault. But he's not so keen on all this fascist business since that awful affair.'

Clara squeezed her arm. 'But we are still friends?' she asked anxiously.

'Of course,' Willa assured her, quickly disengaging as her husband appeared at her side.

Clara looked about for Sarah. Dolly was fussing over her granddaughter more than usual, carrying her around and showing her off as the guests drank cocktails. Clara took a glass of champagne from a tray Jimmy was offering around and drank quickly. She felt immediately light-headed and began talking garrulously about the baby to anyone who would listen.

Soon, Sarah began to grizzle and then wail. Dolly joggled her. 'There, there, what a fuss.' Sarah went puce and screamed all the harder. People began to stare. Dolly pushed her way towards Clara. 'Here, you take her. She must need feeding.'

'It's not time; she fed an hour ago,' Clara answered. But her mother-in-law plonked the baby into her arms.

'She needs her mother,' she declared.

Everyone was watching. Vinnie grinned as if he expected her to instantly calm the squalling infant. Sarah's high-pitched wailing jarred her frayed nerves. She felt resentment surge towards the overbearing Dolly, towards Vinnie and his demandingly high standards, even towards her difficult baby. Tears of frustration stung her eyes. She clenched her jaw, refusing to succumb to the desire to weep.

It was Patience who came to her rescue. 'We'll take her upstairs,' she said, plucking the bawling baby from Clara's tense grip. 'Plenty of time for parties when she's older,' she joked.

When they got upstairs, Clara burst into tears. 'I don't know what to do with her, Mam! I can't feed her properly. I can't get her to stop crying. I don't get a wink of sleep!'

Patience paced the room calming the baby. 'At least you've got Dolly to help.'

Clara exclaimed, 'She doesn't lift a finger! Neither does Vinnie, for all he says he's so proud of her.'

'Men are different.'

'Maybes, but he won't let Ella give me a hand either — says it's all my job. Well, if I'd known how hard it was, I would never have bothered in the first place.'

'You don't mean that.'

'I do!' Clara railed. 'I don't think I even like the bairn. I worry over her all the time — but that's not the same as love, is it?' She threw herself on the bed and covered her face. 'I'm hateful! How could I say such a thing?'

Patience came over and sat beside her. Sarah, exhausted from crying, had abruptly fallen asleep sucking on her grandmother's little finger. Patience laid the baby on the bed and turned to Clara. 'All new mothers feel like this at times,' she said gently, stroking Clara's hair.

Clara looked up. 'Were you like this with me?'

Patience stared off into the distance. 'Yes,' she admitted. 'I took a little while to get used to you. But once I did — I loved you more than anything in the whole wide world — even Harry.'

Clara leaned up and threw her arms about her mother's neck. 'Help me, Mam,' she sobbed, 'help me to love Sarah.'

174

Patience kissed her wet cheek and disengaged her hold. 'Are things all right between you and Vinnie?' she asked.

Clara glanced away and shrugged. 'Canny enough,' she answered.

She wanted to ask her mother if it was normal for a husband and wife not to make love for weeks after giving birth. In fact, she and Vinnie had not had sexual relations since his spring visit to Germany. Although Clara was constantly tired, she longed for intimacy with Vinnie. She wanted things to be as good between them as they had been before she fell pregnant. Yet Vinnie still treated her as if she were recovering from some illness and could not be touched.

'Things will get back to normal soon enough,' Patience assured her, as if she guessed her daughter's fears.

A strange noise from behind made them both turn round together. Sarah was coughing, her eyes staring ahead. Suddenly her body went rigid and she began to jerk.

'What's wrong with her, Mam?' Clara cried, seizing her daughter. Sarah's face went red, and her eyes rolled upwards. She shook violently in Clara's hands, choking and spluttering. 'Mam, do something!' Clara screamed.

Patience snatched the baby from Clara and dashed for the door. She ran downstairs shouting for help, Clara following in a frenzy of panic. It took a few moments for Patience's urgent shouting to be noticed over the merry chatter and laughter of the party. Vinnie came rushing over, demanding to know what was wrong.

'She's having a fit,' Patience gasped. 'Get her to hospital!'

Vinnie commandeered Clarkie to drive them and the two women sat in the back, Patience clutching Sarah, who was still having convulsions in her arms. Vinnie sat in the front barking directions at Clarkie and shouting at him to speed up.

Halfway there, Sarah went limp. Clara screamed, 'Vinnie! I think she's stopped breathing!'

When they pulled up outside the hospital, someone at the party had had the presence of mind to ring ahead and a nurse was awaiting their arrival. Patience ran, holding the baby out. 'Help us! I don't think she's—'

The nurse grabbed Sarah and hurried inside. They ran after her, but she disappeared down the corridor and through swing doors. Another nurse ushered them into a small waiting room. Clara went to Vinnie and they hugged in distress.

'If she dies, I'll never forgive myself,' Clara sobbed.

Vinnie gripped her tightly to him. 'She's not going to die! She's a Craven; she won't give up that easy.'

They sat numbly in the waiting room, the minutes dragging.

'It's taking too long,' Clara fretted. 'Why won't they tell us what's happening?'

Vinnie paced in and out, trying to get information from passing staff.

'Doctor will come and speak to you as soon as he can,' one said sympathetically.

Patience smoked a cigarette. Clara sat shaking, feeling sick with shock.

Finally, a doctor came and found them. His smile made Clara's heart leap.

'Is she alive?' Vinnie demanded.

The doctor nodded. 'She had stopped breathing — you did well to come so quickly. Another few minutes. . .'

Vinnie let out a groan of relief. Clara held his hand tightly. 'Can we see her now?'

The doctor gave them a direct look. 'Before you do, I need to ask a few questions.'

Clara's heart lurched. Patience's face mirrored her anxiety.

'What?' Vinnie asked impatiently. 'We want to take her home.'

'Your daughter was born prematurely?' They nodded in agreement. 'How has she been since you've had her at home?'

Vinnie said at once, 'She's been like any new bairn — sleeps, eats and cries.'

Clara swallowed. 'No, she hasn't,' she contradicted. 'She doesn't eat properly.'

'Does she respond to your voice? Your movements?' the doctor asked.

Clara hesitated. It had not struck her before, but she saw now that Sarah seemed to show no particular signs of recognition when she came near. She shook her head. Vinnie withdrew his hand.

'What do you mean?' he cried. 'You're her mam — of course she knows you.'

'It makes no difference who picks her up,' Clara told the doctor. 'She doesn't seem to respond any differently.'

The doctor persisted. 'And you had a difficult birth?'

'Yes,' Clara whispered, avoiding Vinnie's look. 'They told me I had very high blood pressure.'

The doctor nodded. 'I'm afraid it's had an effect on your baby.'

Vinnie said angrily, 'What are you saying? What sort of effect?'

'We think your baby suffered brain damage at birth,' he answered with a pitying look. 'The seizure is a symptom. It may happen again.'

'Brain damage?' Clara whispered in distress.

Vinnie looked appalled. 'You calling my bairn mentally retarded?'

Clara flinched at the disgust in his voice.

'It's too early to say,' the doctor answered. 'But she may not develop like a normal child.'

Vinnie stood up and stabbed the air savagely with his finger. 'My lass isn't backward — she's as normal as they come. What the hell do you know?'

'I'm sorry, Mr Craven—'

'Come on, Clara,' Vinnie ordered, striding to the door. 'We're taking our lass home now.'

Clara hurried after him, still in shock, with Patience following.

Chapter 29

Vinnie refused to believe the doctor's diagnosis and forbade Clara or Patience to mention a word of it to Dolly or anyone else. But Sarah took further fits and had to be hospitalised twice more. The nursing staff showed Clara what to do at the onset of a seizure to ensure the baby did not swallow her tongue. By the autumn Clara was worn down with worry and exhaustion from the constant vigilance. Vinnie, who was out long hours, did not understand how jaded she felt. He expected her to resume her former role of supporting him at social events and had begun lovemaking again. To Clara's concern, she had lost the appetite for either. As Vinnie's passion rekindled, hers was petering out.

At her mother's insistence, she attempted to regain some social life and took Sarah with her to visit Patience, Willa and Mabel. But she knew that rumours about her daughter's problems had spread among their friends and they never fussed over Sarah the way they would over a healthy baby.

Clara saw the way they looked warily at her daughter and never volunteered to pick her up for a cuddle. Sarah lay passively in her carrycot, dribbling and staring ahead, unresponsive to the sounds about her, or else started a high-pitched screaming that only Clara could pacify. When Clara picked her up, her head lolled as if it were too heavy for her skinny body. She showed no signs of sitting up on her own.

Her friends began to make excuses that they were busy when she rang to invite them over for lunch. She took Sarah to a meeting of the Women's Section, but the baby did not settle and screamed until she was puce-faced.

Cissie made it quite plain that this was unacceptable. 'Better to leave the baby at home with Ella next time,' she told Clara firmly. 'We really can't have such interruptions and we're not a crèche.'

But Clara was too anxious to let Sarah out of her sight. She gave up going to the women's meetings instead.

'It's not as if they do anything,' she confided in Patience. 'They bicker about who should lay on tea for the men's meetings. Not that the men even care — most of them think the women are just meddling in their business. Last week George Templeton had a blazing row with Cissie in front of everyone about whether our section should be allowed to speak at meetings. He said only unnatural women got mixed up in politics. Cissie nearly punched him. And Vinnie was fuming. It's taken him months to get George back to meetings since the May rally. He still won't let Willa join.'

'Sounds to me like you're best out of it,' Patience commented, joggling Sarah in her lap.

'So then Vinnie and Cissie had a spat,' Clara went on, 'and Cissie showed him up in front of the others. Said women were the backbone of the movement — our symbol of purity — and he'd better start appreciating us or else.'

'He wouldn't like that,' Patience snorted.

'No,' Clara said ruefully. 'I got the backlash, of course. Vinnie said he didn't want me going to the Women's Section meetings if all they were going to do was cause trouble in the local branch. And to be honest, I don't have the energy.'

'You've enough to cope with at the minute,' Patience said. She lifted Sarah up and kissed her, pulling silly faces. 'Isn't that right?' she said to the baby. 'Mammy's got her hands full with you. Look, she's smiling, Clara. That was definitely a smile.'

Clara went quickly to look, but to her Sarah looked the same as always. She felt a flood of warmth towards her mother. She was the only one who treated her daughter with love. Dolly always made excuses not to be left minding her.

'It's so long since I handled a bairn,' she would say. 'I wouldn't know what to do if she had one of her turns.'

Even Vinnie shrank from picking her up these days. Clara had never seen him so short-tempered as after the public row with Cissie. He fretted that the local party was fragmenting into rival cliques. The most recent meetings had not been well attended and he blamed this directly on the well-organised and vocal anti-fascists who disrupted them at every opportunity. In Byfell they were led by the Lewises.

'Those damn friends of yours,' Vinnie fumed, after a meeting at Craven Hall had been broken up by the police because of fighting outside. 'They need teaching a lesson.'

'I'm not friends with them anymore,' Clara protested. 'Quite the opposite. It's Benny Lewis caused all that trouble in May. We know he was one of the ringleaders. If it hadn't got so nasty I would never have been stuck in that place and Sarah would never have been—' She broke off, tears flooding her throat at the terrifying memory.

It would haunt her for ever, that terrible day. She tortured herself daily with the question, what if. . . ? It was easier to shift the blame on to the men of violence like Benny, who had forced her to take refuge for her life in Clayton Street, than to dwell on her own responsibility for Sarah's traumatic birth. Yet deep down, she was plagued with guilt about it and knew that it ate at Vinnie's heart too.

Every day she prayed that by some miracle Sarah would develop normally and prove the doctors wrong.

Vinnie gave her a long, considering look, but said nothing more. A week later, he told her he was taking the Bell-Carrs out to dinner after a boxing match at Craven Hall, as a peace offering to Cissie.

'I want you to be there,' Vinnie said, 'and looking your best.'

Clara felt tired just thinking of the effort it would take. 'But what about Sarah?'

'Mam can hold the fort,' he answered. 'Or ask Ella to stay and watch her.'

'Ella's got her own family and she doesn't like staying late.' Clara made excuses. 'I can't leave Sarah for that long. Could we not invite them here for dinner?'

'No.' Vinnie turned on her in exasperation. 'Why can't you think of anyone else but the bairn? I need you too, Clara! You should be at my side supporting me. Is that too much to ask?'

Clara was taken aback. 'One minute you're telling me that being a mother to Sarah is the most important thing in the world — now you're saying I have to be a social butterfly. Which is it, Vinnie?'

'Both,' he snapped. 'Cissie pulls it off, so you can too.'

Clara was stung. 'Cissie has a household of servants,' she retorted, 'and her son's at boarding school.'

Just then, Sarah began to wail in the adjoining room. Clara stalked out to see to her. As she was pacifying the baby, rocking her on her shoulder, which Sarah seemed to like best, Vinnie came to the nursery door. They eyed each other frostily.

'This is really important to me,' he said, his voice quietly determined. 'We need

Alastair's backing if the party is to survive locally. He has the right connections — the influence we need. He's a credible figurehead.'

Clara regarded him. 'Seems to me it's Cissie's feathers you've ruffled, not the brigadier's.'

'That's why I need you there to help me,' Vinnie replied. 'We can't afford to get on the wrong side of Cissie.' He gave a sudden disarming smile. 'And she's always had a soft spot for you.'

'She's hardly spoken to me since Sarah was born.' Clara was unconvinced. 'Still in a huff over the May rally.'

Vinnie shook his head. 'Cissie admires you cos you speak your mind — and you don't lick the boots of your social betters. She hates snobbery more than anything. That's why we can both win her round. Please, Clara, do this for me.'

Clara's resistance crumbled at his appeal. He was right: she was in danger of becoming a recluse at The Cedars, totally absorbed in Sarah's needs. She had to regain a life beyond the nursery.

'I'll ask Mam to come and stop over,' she suggested.

The dinner was such a success that it ended with Cissie's inviting them for a weekend to Hoxton Hall. Vinnie was cock-a-hoop. But as the time approached, Clara began to fret about Sarah. The baby sensed when she was in strange surroundings and became distressed easily. She would be a real handful at draughty, musty-smelling Hoxton Hall. Then Vinnie came back from work and told her that they would not be taking Sarah.

'I've asked Patience to have her for the weekend,' he announced. 'She's more than happy.'

Clara was aghast at leaving her daughter for so long. 'But what if something happens to her?'

'It won't.' Vinnie was adamant. 'She hasn't had a fit in two months — and your mam's a natural with bairns. Look at the way you and Jimmy turned out.' He grabbed her round the waist and kissed her with more enthusiasm than he had done in months. 'Just think of it,' he said, grinning, 'a whole weekend away with no worries —just the two of us.'

'And the Bell-Carrs and all their other house guests,' Clara said dryly. But despite her fear of leaving Sarah, she felt a flare of excitement. They had not been to Hoxton Hall since before her pregnancy and it would be a chance for her to relax, even to reignite her lost passion for her husband.

The weekend was bitterly cold and a mist hung over the treetops and shrouded the moors around the Hall, so shooting and riding were called off. They ventured out on a short walk, and then hurried back for afternoon tea. Cissie organised her guests into parlour games in the drawing room beside a blazing log fire. At six o'clock they retired upstairs to bathe and get ready for dinner.

'It's going well, don't you think?' Vinnie said eagerly, half undressed. 'We're back in favour. And this must be one of the main bedrooms, with a coal fire.'

Clara was wrapped in a faded silk dressing gown provided for guests, ready for a bath. She was trying to imagine what would be happening at her mother's house. Was Sarah feeding all right without her? Had Patience tried some mashed carrots as she had suggested? What if she was having one of her screaming fits and the neighbours complained?

'Come here, Mrs Craven,' Vinnie said, spinning her round and pulling her towards him. 'What you looking so glum about?'

'I was just thinking—' She stopped herself. 'Nothing.'

Vinnie kissed her hard on the mouth. 'Good. Just think about the two of us,' he murmured, covering her face and neck with kisses. He untied the sash of her dressing gown and slipped it off her shoulders. He looked her over in the firelight, running his hands over her breasts and belly.

'You're too thin,' he said. 'You should start eating more.'

Clara felt exposed and tried to shrug back into the dressing gown. Vinnie stopped her.

'I still want you, lass,' he insisted. 'I'll always want you.' He pulled her down on to the hearth rug and began kissing her urgently. Clara glanced anxiously towards the door.

'What if someone comes in?'

'What if they do?' Vinnie laughed. 'We're man and wife — we've every right.'

He swiftly discarded the rest of his clothes and straddled her. He loomed above, muscular and roused.

'Not so quickly,' Clara whispered, pressing her hands to his torso.

'I can't wait,' Vinnie hissed, kissing her impatiently and grasping her hair.

Moments later he was entering her. Clara gasped in pain as he writhed on top, shuddering with pleasure. Then it was over and he was drawing back.

'Oh, lass, that was grand,' he groaned, rolling off. He lay regaining his breath, a hand resting possessively on her thigh.

Clara said nothing, shocked by the speed at which he had relieved his arousal. She could feel a burn mark on her lower back from where he had pinned her to the rug. She was sore inside. She felt indignant. There had been none of the gentle, erotic foreplay on which Vinnie prided himself and which used to make her desire him to distraction. But this was quite the opposite. It was almost as if he were angry with her for something.

The next minute, he was standing up. 'Haway, go and have your bath,' he ordered. 'We mustn't be late for dinner.'

Clara scrambled up, pulled on the dressing gown and hurried from the bedroom. In the steamy, chilly bathroom she sat hunched in the bath and scrubbed herself vigorously. The savage lovemaking left her feeling unclean; she wanted to wash it away. By the time she returned to the bedroom, she had convinced herself that there was nothing malicious in Vinnie's action. He was exuberant about the weekend, over-excited, and it had made him too hasty in their intercourse.

The rest of the evening passed pleasantly enough and Vinnie hovered near her attentively, as if he was loath to let her out of his sight or earshot. After dinner, the men retired to the billiard room to smoke cigars and talk politics. Clara went to bed, longing for a night of uninterrupted sleep. She was woken by the sound of the telephone ringing and jerked awake in alarm. Something must have happened to Sarah! Vinnie had not yet come to bed. Clara rushed out on to the landing and peered over the banisters. Below she could hear the rumble of a man's voice. The short conversation ended. There was the click of the receiver being replaced and a man crossed the hallway below. It was Vinnie.

She hissed his name. He looked up, startled.

'What's wrong?' she called down.

Swiftly Vinnie mounted the stairs. 'What you doing wandering around in your nightie?' he said in amusement.

'Has something happened to Sarah?' Clara asked in agitation.

'No, course not,' Vinnie assured her.

'Then who was ringing you?' she asked in confusion.

'Jimmy,' he said at once. 'I asked him to ring — let me know that everything was canny at your mam's with our Sarah. And she's grand — sleeping like a top.'

Clara looked at him in amazement. 'You asked Jimmy to do that? Why didn't you tell me?'

Vinnie smiled fondly. 'I didn't want you fretting all evening waiting for the telephone call, did I?'

She felt a rush of gratitude towards him. Sometimes he amazed her with his care and concern for her. Now he had shown that he really did care for Sarah too. 'Thanks Vinnie.' She smiled, kissing his cheek. 'That was very thoughtful.'

He looked her over. 'Think I'll come to bed now, an' all.'

'What about the billiards?' Clara reminded him.

'I've just let Alastair win,' he grinned. 'They'll not miss me.'

He followed her back to the bedroom. Warming up under the bedclothes, Vinnie made love to Clara again, this time more languorously. Afterwards, Clara lay encircled in his arms listening to his regular breathing. She had misjudged him. He was still the loving, passionate Vinnie with whom she had fallen in love. The sleep of exhaustion overcame her.

***

It was late on Sunday evening when they returned to Tyneside and, although they had arranged with Patience to collect Sarah in the morning, Clara wanted to go straight round to her mother's. Vinnie persuaded her against it.

'No point waking the bairn and having to settle her twice,' he reasoned.

Once home, Clara slept badly and clock-watched through the night. Unable to sleep, she got up before dawn and drove herself down to Glanton Terrace. It was the first time she had driven since having the baby and she was nervous. Gripping the steering wheel, she crawled down Byfell High Street and turned down Tenter Terrace. Passing her old home, she peered at it in the dark.

Clara did a double take and stalled the car. The Lewises' shop front was gone. The large window was boarded over, the red and white barber's sign broken. When had they closed? And where had they gone? Fancy neither Vinnie nor Patience mentioning it. A delivery van hooted behind and Clara drove on.

She found Patience feeding Sarah an early morning bottle, and rushed to embrace them both.

'What are you doing here so soon?' Patience said in a fluster. 'Does Vinnie know?'

'No, but I'll be back before he needs to leave for work.' Clara smiled, plucking Sarah from her mother's hold and giving her a hug. Sarah jerked in her arms. Clara buried her nose in the baby's neck, breathing in her soft, milky smell. 'How's she been?'

'Champion,' Patience replied. 'But I can see why you get so tired. She doesn't sleep much, does she?'

'That's not what Jimmy said,' Clara laughed dryly. 'Sleeping like a top, he told Vinnie. Still, it was nice of our Jimmy to ring and let us know she was fine.'

'Did he?' Patience frowned. She stretched and got up. Crossing the room to the fire, she lit a cigarette in its embers. 'He never said.' She inhaled deeply. She seemed tense.

'Well he did — Saturday night — late on,' Clara said. 'Must have gone down the street to telephone.'

Patience blew out smoke and did not answer. She stared into the dark street.

181

'What's wrong, Mam?' Clara asked, rocking Sarah on her shoulder.

Her mother hesitated. 'Did you speak to Jimmy?'

'No,' Clara admitted, 'but Vinnie did. I heard him.'

Patience turned, her look anxious. 'Jimmy wasn't here on Saturday night.'

Chapter 30

Clara was unnerved by her mother's look. 'If Jimmy wasn't here on Saturday night, where was he?'

'He slept at Clarkie's,' Patience said tensely, 'or so he said.'

Clara was baffled. 'But the phone call — was he just making it up about Sarah?'

Patience turned and faced her. 'Or Vinnie was.'

'Why should he do that?' Clara was disbelieving.

Patience stubbed out her cigarette, her look haggard. 'There was trouble on Saturday night, big trouble. The Lewises' hairdresser's was smashed up. Benny was badly beaten.'

Clara's legs buckled in shock. She sat down, aghast. 'How badly?' she whispered.

Patience said tightly, 'Whoever did it put him in hospital. Police came round early Sunday morning looking for Jimmy.'

Clara exclaimed, 'Not our Jimmy! They can't think . . . ?'

Patience went on in a bleak voice, 'Took him down the police station and questioned him for hours — and Clarkie and half a dozen others. They let them go, but said they had to stay around Byfell till they'd finished their inquiries.'

'Where's Jimmy? In his room?' Clara demanded, standing again. 'I'll have it out with him.'

'He's not here,' Patience said. 'We had a row about it — I told him if he had anything to do with the attack or knew anyone who had, he must tell the police.'

'What did he say?'

'I thought he would deny it, but he gave me such a mouthful.' Patience trembled. 'Said, why was I sticking up for scum like Benny Lewis — specially after what happened to you? Clara, I think Jimmy was mixed up in it.'

'Oh, Mam!' Clara gasped. 'Our Jimmy wouldn't harm the Lewises.'

Patience's look was harrowed. 'I know I've said some bad things about that family — about Benny — but that doesn't mean it's right to attack them. I feel ashamed to think my lad could have done such a thing.'

'We don't know that, Mam,' Clara insisted. 'I'll get Vinnie to talk to him.'

Patience said dully, 'No doubt they'll want to question Vinnie too.'

Clara stared at her. 'Vinnie? Whatever for? He wasn't even in town.'

Patience gave her a pitying look. 'Cos he's in charge of those lads, that's why. He might not have been there, but he gives them their orders. You know our Jimmy would walk through fire for that husband of yours.'

Clara was shocked by her mother's bitter tone. She had never talked about Vinnie like that before.

'Vinnie's no thug!' Clara protested. 'It's no secret that he doesn't like the Lewises, but he fights them fair and square at political meetings. He would never order their shop to be smashed up, let alone Benny beaten up. Never!'

Sarah began a sudden wailing at Clara's agitation.

'Here, give her to me,' Patience said. Taking her from Clara's trembling hold, she laid her on the floor and grabbed a homemade toy — a string laced with silver cigarette paper and bottle tops. She swung it over Sarah's squalling red face.

Swiftly, the baby calmed down, mesmerised by the swinging string glinting in the lamplight.

Clara kneeled down beside her mother, asking awkwardly, 'You don't really think Jimmy had anything to do with such a thing?'

Patience sighed. 'I don't know any more. He's that secretive about where he goes and what he does. I'm the last person he'd tell.'

Clara persisted. 'But Vinnie? I can't believe you'd even suspect him of something so horrible.'

'Then why did Jimmy ring him at Hoxton Hall?' Patience challenged her. 'It was nothing to do with Sarah.'

Clara frowned. 'If Jimmy thought he was in trouble, he'd turn to Vinnie first, wouldn't he? Vinnie just told me it was about Sarah to stop me worrying over Jimmy.' She grew defiant in Vinnie's defence. 'He's a good man — you've said so yourself a dozen times.'

'I know,' Patience said. 'And he is good — to his own kind.'

'What's that supposed to mean?' Clara asked accusingly.

Patience met Clara's angry look. 'Vinnie has a hard streak too — ruthless even.'

Clara went crimson. She jumped up. 'I'm not staying to hear my husband insulted,' she said fiercely. When she reached for Sarah, Patience caught her hand.

'Don't be angry with me,' she pleaded.

Clara snatched her hand away, glaring. 'Then tell me why you think Vinnie's capable of such a thing.'

Patience's voice shook. 'He once did us a favour — got rid of someone who was pestering your father. Harry was frightened — we both were. He asked Vinnie to get him to go away — because he knew that was the sort of thing Vinnie could arrange.'

Clara's heart went cold. 'What do you mean, arrange?'

Patience swallowed. 'Vinnie has contacts -— men who hang around on the fringes of the boxing hall ready to do anything for a bit pay. Your father asked him to pay the man off — not to harm him — just give him some money and frighten him off a bit. Harry gave Vinnie money to do it.'

Clara asked in bewilderment. 'Why didn't Dad just give the man the money himself?'

Patience stared into her lap. 'Cos he knew this man would not be bought off easily — he would need a bit of extra persuasion — the kind Vinnie could give. I encouraged him to go to Vinnie. That man—'

'It was the foreigner, wasn't it?' Clara said in sudden realisation. 'You're — talking about that tramp.' Patience nodded slowly. Clara gulped. 'So — what happened to him?'

Her mother's chin trembled. 'I don't know. But we never saw him again — not once.'

'He must have taken the money and gone, the way you wanted,' Clara exclaimed.

'That's what I kept telling your father,' Patience said tearfully, 'but he wouldn't let it rest. Kept badgering Vinnie to tell him. In the end Vinnie said he'd never hear from the man again; he'd seen to it, good and proper.'

'What are you saying?' Clara demanded. 'That Vinnie's a murderer?'

Patience met her look.

'My God!' Clara gasped. 'You are, aren't you?'

Her mother shook her head. 'I didn't believe it, but your father was full of guilt; it tore him apart. That's when the drinking and gambling really started. Harry was trying to forget, but he never could . . .'

'You could though,' Clara said in a tight, accusing voice.

184

Silent tears ran down her mother's cheeks. 'As far as I was concerned, Vinnie had done us a favour. That man was threatening my husband, my family. I'd have done anything to protect them; anything short of murder. I still couldn't imagine Vinnie being capable of such a thing. But with this attack on Benny Lewis, it's brought it all back.'

Clara was stunned. She refused to believe her husband could organise such violence. Yet a worm of doubt wriggled in her mind. He had been furious about Benny's recent successes in disrupting his organisation. He had talked of teaching the Lewises a lesson. Fear clutched her insides. She had stoked up his fury, reminding him of Benny's part in the May street fighting.

'Dear God,' she whispered, 'I encouraged him to blame Benny for Sarah's premature birth. If Vinnie's behind this, I'm guilty too.'

Patience seized her hand again. 'No you're not! None of this has anything to do with you. Vinnie and Jimmy are getting in too deep in this fascist business — too ready to use their fists.'

Clara pulled away. 'And I'm a part of it too,' she said bitterly. 'I've glorified the BUF in newspaper articles and marched as proudly as any of them. Now you tell me that my husband's been a thug all along. Why did you not tell me any of this before?' she said angrily. 'Why wait till I was married? You encouraged me to marry him!'

Patience brusquely wiped her tears. 'And for good reason. Vinnie was offering security and luxury beyond anything I could ever offer. Can you imagine how terrible it is to lose your husband, your livelihood, and see your children suffer because of it? These are dark days. Vinnie was offering a hand out of the nightmare — for all of us. And he loves you like no other. Whatever he may or may not have done to that foreigner, I know he would never hurt you or Sarah in a million years.'

Clara glared at her mother in disbelief. 'And that makes it all right?'

'No,' Patience was defensive, 'but I'll always put my bairns first whatever. You're a mother now; I bet there isn't anything you wouldn't do for Sarah.'

Clara snatched her baby from the floor. Sarah cried out, startled. 'Then why tell me your nasty suspicions about Vinnie?' Clara said hotly. 'Cos that's all they are. You don't know what happened to that foreigner and you don't know about Benny.'

She plonked the wailing Sarah into her carrycot and swiftly gathered up her things. Why had she listened to her mother's wild accusations? Patience hated to admit that Harry had lost all his money through his own weakness for drink and gambling, so she had to blame it on someone else.

'I'm sorry. You're right,' Patience said, pacing after her. 'Please don't be angry. I should never have said—'

'Thank you for looking after Sarah,' Clara said curtly. 'I have to get back home.'

'Please don't tell Vinnie what I said about him.'

Clara's look was impatient. 'I'm not likely to, am I?'

'Let me carry the baby,' her mother said, trying to make amends. Clara bundled everything into the car and left without another word. Dawn appeared like a red gash downriver as she drove past the Lewises' forlorn shop front. She did not want to look but could not stop herself. Small shards of broken glass still glinted in the early morning light like scattered diamonds. Upstairs, the curtains were drawn against the world.

Clara felt a stab of pity as she thought of Marta and Oscar hiding behind them, worrying over Benny. How was Reenie coping? What news did they have

185

of Frank? Clara flushed with guilt that she did not know, had actively stayed away from them and hardened her heart towards her old friends. What sort of selfish person had she become?

Abruptly, she parked the car and knocked on the Lewises' front door. Nobody answered. She tried again.

There was only silence. Clara turned in frustration. Of course the family would be wary of any callers. They were all the more vulnerable without Benny there to defend them. She turned back to the car where Sarah lay still crying. As she did so, a curtain flicked back at the bay window above. She glanced up and it dropped back at once. Shame flooded her. They would not want to see her. She was Vinnie's wife, one of the fascist elite of Byfell and therefore their enemy. Clara hurried to the car.

'Clara,' a voice called quietly behind her. She turned to see Marta peering out from the half-closed front door. 'Come, come.' She beckoned her back.

Clara's heart lifted. 'I have the baby with me . . .'

'*Ja*! I hear her,' Marta said. 'Bring her up.'

Clara was hit by a mix of emotions as she entered her old flat. It was still painted in her mother's beloved browns and beiges, yet it was not her home. There were books everywhere — the remnants of Frank's bookstall perhaps — and it smelled different, of Marta's German cooking and Oscar's pipe smoke.

Oscar was sitting in his vest at a table in the window, unshaven and haggard. Clara was shocked by how much he had aged. He stood up politely.

'Look, Oscar, it is Clara and the baby. *Das ist gut, ja?*' Marta pushed Clara forward into the room and took the wailing Sarah from her. 'What a noise, little one,' she fussed, rocking her vigorously. 'Are you hungry? I'm sure you are hungry. Clara, do you have milk for the little angel?'

Clara fished in her bag and handed over the half-drunk bottle. 'She can be difficult,' she apologised.

'She's a baby,' Marta exclaimed, as if this was reason enough. Taking the bottle, she started to feed Sarah in her arms. The baby's crying turned to snuffles and gulps. 'See, she is happy now,' Marta said, looking pleased. 'Sit down, Clara. Oscar will pour you some tea.'

Clara stared in amazement as Oscar did as he was told while Marta smiled and cooed over Sarah. 'She is beautiful, *ja?*'

Suddenly, Clara was blinded by tears. No one, not even her mother, had ever called Sarah beautiful. How could a baby who squinted and gaped, took fits and screamed till she went purple be anything but ugly? Yet, watching her lying contentedly in Marta's arms, sucking and raising a starfish hand, Clara saw the beauty that Marta saw. Sarah broke off drinking and Clara tensed in expectation of her howling. Abruptly, Sarah's mouth opened in a lopsided smile. Marta responded with an answering one.

'You are playing with me!' she laughed.

A sob welled up inside Clara. 'I'm so sorry!' she cried. 'I can't believe what's happened to your shop — to Benny. It's wicked. I know we don't see eye to eye on many things, but not this—'

Oscar saw her distress and guided her into a chair. Marta clucked. 'It is very bad.'

'Is Benny going to be all right?'

'We hope,' Oscar said with a fatalistic shrug.

Clara twisted her hands together. 'Do — do you know who did this to him?'

She saw the couple exchange a wary glance. Marta said, 'We were in bed asleep. There is loud noise in the street — glass breaking. Oscar looks out.'

'It was dark,' Oscar said. 'They had scarves tied across their faces — four or five of them. Benny went down to stop them—'

'We shout at him not to,' Marta added in distress, 'but he is not listening.'

They both fell silent, then Oscar continued, 'By the time I got down, Benny is lying in his own blood and the men are gone. So quickly,' Oscar said hoarsely.

'Reenie, she stop the blood,' Marta said, tears in her voice. 'My poor boy!'

Clara went to her and hugged her, Sarah jammed between them. 'Let me help you,' she pleaded. 'I have money saved from my job — Vinnie doesn't know about it. Perhaps Benny needs special care?'

Marta shook her head. 'No, Clara, we cannot take your money.' She handed Sarah back. 'But we will take your prayers.'

'Prayers!' Oscar said in disgust. Clara turned to him, surprised by his unusually bitter tone. His look was angry. 'All we want is to find the men who did this to my son.'

Clara's insides lurched. Please God, may Jimmy not be one of them. 'Is Reenie here?' she asked tensely.

'She is at the hospital watching her brother,' Marta answered quietly.

Clara made for the door. 'You must let me know if there is anything I can do. I'm sorry I've stayed away. Whatever my differences with Benny and Reenie — I've always been grateful for your kindness — both of you.'

Marta nodded and followed her; Oscar watched her go, his look wary. Downstairs, Clara forced herself to ask, 'Have you heard from Frank?'

Marta gave a small sigh and shook her head. 'The consul he say Frank is to be — what you say? — repatriated. But nothing. No word, no news.'

Clara leaned forward and gave Marta a swift kiss on the cheek, then hurried from the forlorn place. When she got home, Vinnie was dressed for work and frantic with worry.

'Why didn't you wake me? I would have fetched Sarah. You shouldn't be driving.'

'Why not?' Clara asked. 'I'm perfectly fit now.'

'Why did you take so long?' he asked, suspicious.

'Don't you even want to say hello to your daughter?' Clara handed him the carrycot.

He carried it inside and put it on the hall table. 'I'm going to be late for work.'

Clara blurted out, 'The Lewises have been attacked. Did you know about it?'

Vinnie was startled. 'Attacked?' he repeated.

'Their shop's smashed up and Benny's in hospital,' Clara said, heart hammering. 'Tell me you had nothing to do with it.'

He stared at her. 'Me? How could I have had anything to do with it?'

'Mam says Jimmy and the lads have been questioned; there must be a reason the police picked on them,' Clara persisted.

Vinnie ran a hand over his lacquered hair. 'Aye, picking on them. That's typical they'd try to point the finger of blame on my lads.'

'So it's not true?' Clara held his look.

'Course not.' Vinnie was indignant.

'Why did Jimmy ring you on Saturday night, then? It wasn't about Sarah; Mam says he wasn't there.'

Vinnie looked annoyed. 'Is Patience trying to stir it up between us? Is that what this is about?'

Clara trembled. 'It's nothing to do with Mam. I just want to know if you're behind the attack.'

Vinnie stepped close, his eyes blazing. 'I'll not have my wife questioning me like a criminal,' he hissed. 'I'm sorry for the Lewises but Benny's had it coming for a long time. I'm surprised you're so concerned for him after what he did to you and the bairn. You should be worrying about your brother and his comrades being falsely accused. That's the only thing that bothers me!'

He pushed past her, grabbed his hat off the stand and strode out of the house. Clara was left shaking and more confused than ever. Immediately, Dolly appeared from the kitchen. Clara knew she had been listening to their argument.

'What you go and upset him for?' she reproached Clara. 'My Vinnie's given you more than you could ever have dreamed of; the least he can expect is a little more loyalty.'

Clara was about to tell her to mind her own business when Sarah started to cry. Nerves jangling, she picked her out of the cot and fled upstairs.

Chapter 31

A tension hung over The Cedars all week, as the impact of the attack on the Lewises reverberated around them all. Somehow Vinnie got to hear that Clara had gone to see Marta and Oscar. He came home furious and ordered her into the sitting room, slamming the door behind them.

'How do you think that looks?' he accused her. He gave her no time to reply. 'It looks like we're guilty or some'at, that's what!'

'No it doesn't.' Clara was shocked by his vehemence. 'I just wanted to see that they were all right.'

'You wanted to see Benny, didn't you?' he said, full of suspicion. 'Do you still care for him?'

'Don't be daft,' Clara replied. 'He was in hospital, remember?'

'It looks disloyal,' Vinnie railed. 'My own wife sneaking around in the early morning fraternising with the enemy.'

Clara was dumbfounded. 'The enemy?' she cried. 'Marta and Oscar don't deserve any of this. They're canny people. You should've seen the way Marta handled Sarah — like she was a normal bairn.'

'You had no right to take my daughter in there,' Vinnie snapped.

'You had someone watching the place, didn't you?' Clara retorted.

'People talk,' Vinnie said coldly. 'There's nothing goes on in Byfell I don't know about. Just remember that.'

But Clara would not let it go. The doubt about her husband was gnawing at her all the time. 'Then tell me, Vinnie,' she challenged him, 'if you know everything, who did attack the Lewises? Tell me to my face you had nothing to do with it.'

He grabbed her by the arms and shook her hard. 'I had nothing to do with it! Why do you doubt your own husband?'

Clara gritted her teeth, suppressing her fear. 'Because of what you did for me dad. You killed a man for him!'

Vinnie looked thunderous. 'What are you talking about? I've never killed a man!'

'Arranged it then,' Clara cried. 'Mam said you arranged to get rid of him — the foreigner — six years back.'

Vinnie looked at her with incomprehension. Then suddenly his expression changed. 'Brodsky?'

'I don't know his name,' Clara gasped.

Vinnie barked with laughter and let go. 'I didn't get rid of Brodsky,' he snorted, 'at least not in the way your mam said.'

Clara rubbed her arms. 'In what way then?'

Vinnie's look was still cold. 'I shouldn't have to explain any of this to you — it was an arrangement with Harry. But just to satisfy your journalist's nosiness, I didn't have Brodsky done away with.'

'Then what became of him?' Clara demanded.

'I employed him.' Vinnie looked pleased at Clara's surprise. 'He was a clock-maker — mended watches. He was useful. I sent him round country houses mending their grandfather clocks — until he disappeared.'

'Disappeared?' Clara echoed.

'He was unreliable so I sacked him,' Vinnie said with disdain. 'But that doesn't surprise me — he was a Jew and Russian — the worst sort. I strongly suspect he was a Communist spy. If he turned up again I'd send him packing or have him arrested.'

'Why should my father be so afraid of a Russian clock-maker?' she said, puzzled.

'Probably after him for a load of money he couldn't pay.' Vinnie was dismissive. 'Brodsky was a money-grabbing little Jew.'

Clara flinched at his tone; he had never spoken like that about Jews before. Vinnie misinterpreted it for doubt.

'Believe me, I did Harry a favour as a friend. Patience should show more gratitude.'

'But she said that was the cause of Dad's drinking and gambling,' Clara croaked, 'thinking you'd done something terrible to the foreigner.'

Vinnie grew angry again. 'That's a load of rubbish! Harry just had a weakness for drink. He never asked me about Brodsky, else I could have told him, couldn't I? Now don't ever ask me about my business dealings again.'

Clara bit her tongue. She was shaken by their argument. Vinnie took her silence as a sign of acceptance.

'Listen, lass,' he said, his tone suddenly conciliatory, 'let's not fall out over ancient history. I'm just asking you to stay away from the Lewises. I'm worried for my lads — and for you. I don't want them Bolshies taking advantage of your kind heart.'

Clara let it drop. She was relieved her mother's suspicions about Vinnie were unfounded, yet his hardness over the matter disturbed her. She felt a nagging unease that there was more to the Brodsky affair than either Vinnie or Patience was letting on, but she could not see what. Vinnie had made it plain he would talk no further about it — or about the Lewises.

Clara found herself marooned at the house, starved of information while Vinnie spent long hours at work. He had the Albion taken away, saying it was needed elsewhere. Clarkie, she was told, was far too busy to run her around. She rang her mother at the garage, but all she could gather from the snatched conversation was that Benny was out of hospital. She rang the Lewises' shop but there was no answer. The operator said the line was dead.

Jimmy moved in. Clara suspected it was to keep her brother out of the way until the fuss died down, but Vinnie said otherwise.

'It's to protect you and Sarah,' he told her. 'In case some Bolshies take it into their heads to have a go at us.'

'But you said the BUF had nothing to do with it,' Clara challenged him.

'We didn't,' he said tersely, 'but that doesn't mean some hotheads won't think we had and try a tit-for-tat. They're itching to have a go at us.'

Jimmy slept downstairs in the dining room next to the front door. He was tight-lipped about the whole affair, except to inadvertently let slip that he had never rung Hoxton Hall.

'What's the number of the Bell-Carrs' place?' she asked him. 'I want to ring Cissie.'

He shrugged. 'How should I know?'

'You rang us there that Saturday night,' she reminded him.

'I never—' He stopped abruptly.

'Why should Vinnie say you rang if you didn't?' Clara asked.

Jimmy flushed in annoyance. 'That's Vinnie's business,' he mumbled.

Her brother spent a large amount of time in the kitchen drinking cups of tea with Ella or listening to the radio with Dolly, who made a show of spoiling him while criticising Clara as if she was not there.

'You'd think your sister would be content with all this,' Dolly needled, with a sweeping gesture of the room, 'but no, our Clara is always hankering after something else. It was her idea to come and live here in the first place, Jimmy. Now she spends all her time trying to go back to Byfell. Some people are never satisfied.'

The weather was bad, but Clara made a point of pushing Sarah out in the large pram to escape the claustrophobic atmosphere. Irritatingly, Jimmy would follow her. He never offered to push the pram or chat, just kept two paces behind like a shadow she could not shake off.

At the end of the week, while Dolly was snoozing and Jimmy was in the kitchen, Clara quietly telephoned her old newspaper. She spoke to Jellicoe. He sounded cautious.

'Things are pretty tense around the town,' he said. 'The Lewises are keeping their heads down, not speaking to the press. Benny's been seen out on crutches, but not even he wants to talk. I think it's shaken them badly.'

'Are they open for business?' Clara whispered.

'After a fashion,' Jellicoe confirmed. 'Their Labour friends have rallied round and cleared up the mess, but the window's still boarded over. It'll remain to be seen how much it's damaged their business.'

'And there's no word about who was responsible?' Clara asked nervously.

'None. They've covered their tracks well, and no one's talking — not one witness has come forward. Amazing, isn't it?'

'The police must have their suspicions,' Clara pressed him.

'They're keeping an open mind,' Jellicoe said sardonically.

'And you?'

He paused. 'Off the record?'

'Yes,' Clara said.

'I assumed the BUF were behind it — or a renegade group from their ranks. It's possible Vinnie knew nothing about it. Now there's a counter-rumour going about that left-wing extremists did it, to provoke a revenge attack on the BUF. But maybe your husband's behind that one. All I'm certain of is that no one trusts anyone else — and everyone's watching their backs.'

Clara glanced nervously at the kitchen door. 'Will you do something for me?' she asked quickly. 'Arrange for a glazier to replace their shop window. I'll pay you back — I've got money of my own.' There was silence at the other end. 'Please, Mr Jellicoe.'

'Does Vinnie know about this?' he asked.

'He doesn't need to know,' Clara said hastily. 'It's just between you and me.'

'Guilt money?' Jellicoe was blunt.

Clara winced. 'They were good friends of mine once, that's the only reason.' She heard movement in the kitchen. 'I have to go. Please say you'll do it.'

'Very well.'

'And let me know if you hear any more about the Lewises.' The kitchen door opened and Jimmy came out. Clara said clearly, 'And a quarter pound of salami, my husband's favourite. No, that's all, thank you. Goodbye.'

She heard Jellicoe chuckle on the other end, 'Goodbye, Clara — and good luck.'

Two weeks on, Vinnie seemed more relaxed. The police investigation had found nothing to link the attack to the BUF, except the accusations of the anti-fascists. He came home with a copy of the *Tyne Times*.

'Anonymous donor paid for their window to be fixed.' He showed Dolly. 'Waste of money, mind.'

191

'Why?' Clara asked, her heart skipping a beat. She had slipped out and posted the money to Jellicoe the previous week.

He eyed her. 'Cos they're moving.'

'Good riddance,' Dolly declared, 'after all the trouble they've caused.'

'Where too?' Clara tried to keep the tremor out of her voice.

Vinnie shrugged. 'Rumour has it Max Sobel has found them somewhere. Probably all for the best; they were struggling to pay their rent on Tenter Terrace.'

'How do you know?' Clara asked in surprise.

'Questions, questions!' Dolly interrupted. 'Do you ever stop? Put your feet up, Vinnie, and Clara will fetch you a whisky.'

Vinnie handed Clara the newspaper and sat down. 'I bet the landlord's happy with the arrangement,' Vinnie commented, 'getting his window replaced for free and the Lewis family out.'

Clara dropped the newspaper on the table and walked to the door.

'Where you going?' Dolly called after her.

'To see to Sarah,' Clara answered without a backward glance.

***

It was nearly Christmas before Clara discovered what had become of the Lewises. She ran into Max in Newcastle, as she came out of the Laing Art Gallery with Willa. They had gone there for an exhibition while Ella looked after Sarah for a brief afternoon. Their husbands were now working in closer partnership, though neither wife knew the details.

'Clara!' Max cried. 'You look well.'

Clara smiled and introduced him to Willa. After a few stilted pleasantries, she dared to ask, 'How are the Lewises?'

His look was guarded. 'They're surviving. Oscar has a small shop in Sandyford.'

'Is that where they're living?'

Max nodded.

'And Benny?' Clara asked awkwardly.

'He's just off his crutches,' Max said, 'but the mental scars will take longer to heal. He keeps to himself these days.' His voice took on an edge. 'While the brutes who put him in hospital walk freely on our streets. Makes you proud to belong here, doesn't it?'

Clara said a swift goodbye, uncomfortable at the encounter.

'I didn't like his attitude,' Willa complained. 'Made it sound as if we were responsible.'

Clara said nothing. She wanted to forget the whole matter. She had convinced herself that Vinnie was not involved. Jimmy might have known more than he let on, but the police had found no evidence that he had taken part in the attack, so who was she to judge her own brother?

Jimmy continued to live at The Cedars. Dolly liked to have him around to fetch and carry for her and he was learning to drive, so when Vinnie presented Clara with a second-hand Morris Minor for Christmas, Jimmy became her unofficial chauffeur.

'Why can't Mam come and live with us too?' Clara suggested to Vinnie, thinking how Patience would be an ally in the household.

'She's handy for the garage where she is,' he pointed out, 'and I pay her rent so she's well looked after. She'd only annoy Jimmy with all her fussing. Things are grand the way they are.'

Patience was allowed to come and stay for Christmas and Clara enjoyed having her help with the baby. But the respite from Sarah's demands was short-lived. When 1935 arrived her husband was as involved in his business activities and the party as ever, and Clara was soon coping on her own again.

Vinnie travelled all over the north, speaking at branch meetings to drum up new recruits. Party membership had slumped after the violent rallies of the previous year and Vinnie agreed with those who thought they should be copying the successes of the National Socialists in Germany. The economy under Hitler was reviving, the Left were being obliterated and all classes were uniting in a new sense of national pride. He was exultant when asked to join the newly formed Anglo-German Fellowship, along with George Templeton.

'It's very prestigious,' Vinnie said proudly. 'Only the most important businessmen are invited.'

He and George went to frequent dinners and film shows extolling Nazi Germany and were encouraged to forge stronger links with their counterparts across the North Sea. As a result, Clara and Vinnie were once again invited round to the Templetons' on a regular basis. Clara saw a lot more of Willa through the spring and early summer, and increasingly left Sarah with Ella. Vinnie no longer seemed to mind.

She organised a party on Sarah's first birthday with balloons and cake. Willa brought Robert, and Cissie and Mabel came, but it was obvious to all that Sarah was not developing. She sat propped up on cushions, dribbling and grunting. She was making no attempt to crawl, let alone signs of wanting to walk.

Robert stared at her. 'Can't she say anything?'

'Not yet,' Clara said, embarrassed.

'She stinks,' Robert said in disgust, pinching his nose and running around in a circle. 'Poo-eee!'

Vinnie came back to find Clara in tears. 'I'm sorry I missed it, lass. I had this meeting—'

'It was a disaster!' Clara cut him short. 'Even Robert made fun of her, poor little mite.'

Vinnie calmed her. 'She'll do things in her own time. All bairns develop differently.'

Clara knew that neither of them really believed that, but they went on pretending.

Vinnie grew increasingly impatient if Sarah's routine impinged on dinner or their social life. As Patience bluntly told her, 'He wants you at his side when it suits him and at home when it doesn't.'

Whenever they were invited to the Bell-Carrs', Sarah would be left with Patience. It was at Hoxton Hall that Clara learned of a trip being organised to attend the Nuremberg Rally in Germany at the end of August. Cissie was highly excited because Alastair had agreed to go with her.

'It would be such fun if Clara and you would come too,' Cissie said to Vinnie over dinner.

'I couldn't leave Sarah for that long,' Clara said at once.

'Of course you could,' Vinnie contradicted. 'Your mother could cope.'

'I'm sure the holiday would do you good,' Cissie encouraged her. 'It would only be for a week or so.'

But Clara knew it was too much to ask of Patience, who was exhausted after a weekend of looking after her granddaughter, let alone longer. The older Sarah grew, the more difficult she became for others to handle, even Patience. Only

Clara seemed able to understand what her daughter wanted.

'I'm sorry, I can't.' Clara was adamant. 'You go if you want, Vinnie.'

She was openly relieved when Vinnie reluctantly refused to go without her. 'Why don't we take Sarah away for a holiday instead?' she suggested. 'We could rent a cottage — give her some country air.'

'What's wrong with the air in Gosforth?' Vinnie looked at her as if she were mad. 'I haven't time for holidays.'

'You were prepared to go to Germany,' Clara pointed out.

'That was business,' Vinnie was sharp, 'and you put the spanner in the works.'

'I'm not stopping you going,' Clara said.

'I wanted to go with me wife at me side,' he replied, 'like Alastair and Ted. But if you think Sarah's needs are more important then that's that.'

The Bell-Carrs and Blakes returned from Nuremberg bursting to tell the Cravens about the four-day extravaganza.

'The parades!' Cissie exclaimed. 'You've never seen anything like it. So many smart young men in uniform from all over the country.'

'They housed them in hundreds of tents,' Mabel added. 'And the speeches were given under this huge golden eagle.'

'Not that we could understand a word,' Ted chuckled.

'No, but the atmosphere,' Cissie marvelled. 'It was like an electric shock when Hitler appeared. Wasn't it, Alastair?' Her husband grunted in agreement.

'Tell them about the Blood Banner,' Mabel urged.

'Oh, yes,' Cissie said breathlessly. 'Hitler had this piece of blood-soaked banner — something to do with his failed coup in the Twenties. He used it to bless all the other banners and there were hundreds of them. Then he took the salute of thousands of men.'

'And the Hitler Youth,' Ted added, 'all so eager and proud. Wish there was something like that for our boys.'

'And for James,' Cissie agreed. 'It's so good for the young to have plenty of physical exercise and discipline. Don't you agree?'

Clara glanced at Vinnie and saw the embarrassed look on his face. She knew he longed for a son and they had been trying for another child all year. Cissie waved an apologetic hand.

'How thoughtless of me,' she cried. 'But it's not your fault that Sarah's the way she is.'

'No,' Mabel said with a pitying look. 'And you're bound to have other children.'

'Course in Germany,' Cissie continued, 'they put unfortunate children like that into institutions where they can be properly looked after.'

Clara flushed. 'We have no intention of doing that. Sarah is just a bit slow, but she'll catch up.' She looked at Vinnie to back her up, but he said nothing.

Afterwards, Clara was furious. 'How dare they talk about Sarah like that, as if she's subnormal? Why didn't you say anything?'

Vinnie gave her a bleak look. 'Perhaps they're right.'

'No they're not! I'd never agree to have Sarah locked away.' Clara was indignant. 'And I don't believe you would either. She's still a baby; lots of them don't walk at her age.'

Vinnie turned on her aggressively. 'It's not just that she can't walk; she can't do anything by herself. Not eat, not babble like a baby — she doesn't even smile.'

'She does,' Clara protested. 'She smiles at me.'

'Believe that if you want.' He was dismissive. 'I'm just saying I think we should get a doctor's opinion. You're wearing yourself out looking after her.'

'That's my choice.' Clara was stubborn.

'Not just yours,' Vinnie said coldly. 'Mine too.'

After that, Clara was more wary of going to stay at Hoxton Hall. Their friends continued to harp on about their German trip and the way things were done there. They would discuss Nordic beauty and the merits of being an Aryan race. Clara, late for afternoon tea, caught them in mid-conversation about eugenics and what to do with the unfit in society. They broke off when she entered and she suspected they had been talking about Sarah. They grew increasingly anti-Jewish and approved the new Nuremberg Laws outlawing Jews in Germany.

'Course we asked our hosts about the Jewish question,' Cissie declared, 'and they said the Jews in Germany are only one per cent of the population. Hitler was looking after the other ninety-nine for a change.'

'Quite right too,' Ted agreed. 'You can't say anything against them without getting into trouble.'

'I've been saying for years they've got far too much influence in this country too,' Alastair complained, 'but did anyone listen?'

After a lot to drink, Alastair would end up giving a toast. 'England for the English!'

'And Jews out!' Cissie would add.

To Clara's dismay Vinnie joined in with enthusiasm. But she was fearful of tackling him about it when they were alone, because he always returned from these visits dissatisfied about her behaviour or arguing about Sarah's future.

'You wear too much lipstick,' he said critically. 'Cissie doesn't anymore.'

'She doesn't need to,' Clara replied. 'She's beautiful.'

'Neither do you,' Vinnie said. 'You've got perfect pale skin — you've got Nordic beauty.'

'How can I have?' Clara joked. 'I'm Geordie with a bit Irish. They do talk a lot of nonsense sometimes when they've had a few too many cocktails.'

'Don't speak about our friends like that.' Vinnie was offended.

'Anyway, I like wearing lipstick,' Clara persisted.

'Well, I don't want you to,' Vinnie announced. 'It makes you look cheap.'

Eventually his criticism wore her down and Clara stopped wearing make-up. They had heated arguments about Sarah too. Vinnie grew increasingly convinced that they should put her in an institution.

'Somewhere canny in the countryside,' Vinnie suggested, 'like Gilead. She'd be better off there among her own kind.'

Clara shuddered. 'We're her own kind,' she protested.

'With people who know how to treat her right,' Vinnie persisted.

***

1936 came and the talk was all about the death of King George and the succession of Edward VIII.

'Just what the movement needs,' Alastair declared excitedly, 'a young king in touch with the people to reinvigorate the monarchy and rule from the top.'

'And such a handsome, dashing one too,' Cissie said with a coquettish smile. 'Aryan good looks.'

Vinnie's convictions became more entrenched as the BUF modelled itself more and more on the Nazis. They changed their name to the British Union of Fascists and National Socialists, adopted a new banner with a Nazi-like flash in a circle and added military caps and jackboots to their uniform.

195

At dinner parties, their friends defended Germany's occupation of the French Rhineland, as they had defended Italy's invasion of Abyssinia the previous autumn.

'As long as they're not threatening our interests, let them get on with it,' was Alastair's opinion.

Vinnie got involved with George and Ted in the Mind Britain's Business campaign and had Jimmy and his troop out daubing the slogan on railway bridges and pavements.

'The Germans can't be blamed for going into the Rhineland.' Alastair was bullish. 'It's a desperate measure to avert a revolution.'

None of their friends had any sympathy for the French who had elected a socialist government.

'France is weak,' Cissie said with disdain. 'They're always allowing strikes. Germany have a right to defend themselves from such chaos.'

'Shows what can happen when you let in the Bolshies,' Vinnie agreed.

'And now it's happening in Spain.' Cissie was indignant. 'We should be thankful that Germany and Italy are there as a counterbalance on the Continent.'

Clara sat mutely through these conversations. Her interest in the movement was on the wane. She watched them in animated discussions, but felt nothing of their enthusiasm. Their dismissive attitudes towards anyone but themselves — Abyssinians, Rhinelanders, French, Jews, Socialists, Spanish or Liberals — made her increasingly uncomfortable. Yet they took more notice than she did of what was going on abroad and had visited Germany, so who was she to contradict them? Perhaps the Jews and the Communists really were a threat to their whole way of life; Vinnie certainly thought so.

Vinnie no longer talked about improving the lot of the working class, but of business being allowed to flourish under a benign dictator. Clara did not argue; it all seemed too removed from her everyday concerns. These revolved around Sarah. At two years old, her daughter was still not walking or showing any signs of talking. Clara still had to spoon-feed her. That summer, Vinnie insisted that they take Sarah to a specialist that Cissie had recommended. The doctor confirmed that the girl was not only mentally handicapped, but paralysed from the waist down. She would always be incontinent and never able to walk.

'This child will never lead a productive life,' he told Clara brutally. 'She will always be a burden.'

Stunned by the stark prognosis, Clara began to think the unthinkable. It might be best if Sarah was cared for in a children's hospital after all. The child was now almost too heavy for her to carry around. What would happen when she grew older and too big to be pushed in a pram? She would need a wheelchair. How would they get her upstairs? How would Clara bath her or cope with her incontinence?

What Clara could not admit to Vinnie was her overwhelming sense of inadequacy as a mother. She would for ever blame herself for Sarah's traumatic birth, but what plagued her more were her bouts of resentment towards the child. She did not love Sarah enough — not the way a mother should. At times her frustration with her daughter came close to hatred. When Sarah was having a tantrum or being impossible to feed, Clara would slam down the spoon.

'You ungrateful lass!' she cried on one such occasion. 'You're nothing but trouble. I wish I'd never had you. And I don't care what I say — you don't understand a ruddy word anyway!'

She left Sarah screaming in the dining room and grabbed one of Dolly's cigarettes. Jimmy found her in the garden in tears, trying to smoke.

'Vinnie's right,' he said. 'You shouldn't have to put up with this.'

'I didn't mean what I said,' Clara wept. 'I do love her, you know.'

Jimmy was unusually forthright. 'Don't let the bairn come between the two of you. You're blind if you can't see what's ganin' on.'

'What do you mean?' Clara sniffed.

Jimmy looked on edge. 'Just do what Vinnie wants. Don't throw everything away because of that bairn. Or you'll spoil it for all of us.'

Clara was baffled by her brother's words but he would say no more.

While she and Vinnie wrangled over what to do, Clara discovered she was pregnant again. Vinnie was overjoyed, and became instantly more attentive. Clara too was relieved, yet she dared not hope too much.

'What if something goes wrong again?' she fretted to her husband.

'Nothing will,' he declared. 'I'm not going to let you out of my sight — or Jimmy's. You're to rest up and be a lady of leisure.'

'What about Sarah?' Clara said. 'Perhaps now's the time for Mam to come and stay — help out a bit.'

Vinnie held her in his arms, his words resolute. 'No, Clara. Now is the time to put Sarah in a new home. I'll not have you endangering your health or the baby's. I've arranged for us to go and have a look at Gilead.'

Clara burst into tears. But they were tears of guilt, for deep down she felt a surge of relief. She had a proper excuse to put her daughter into the care of professional nurses. She must not jeopardise the life of her unborn baby.

On a sunny day in July, they drove up the Tyne valley and entered the wooded grounds of the large brick-built hospital. Clara thought of the disabled veteran Bob Grayson, whom she had met years ago at Willa's fundraiser, and wondered if he was still there. Against all expectation, she found the setting beautiful. Some of the patients were sitting out in wheelchairs under the trees. The superintendent showed them the chapel and the theatre.

'They have entertainment?' Clara asked in astonishment.

'Oh, yes, it's part of their therapy,' he told them. 'And there's a swimming pool for hydraulic therapy. We treat the body as well as the mind.'

They were taken on to one of the wards. It was spartan and smelled of incontinence but appeared spotlessly clean. Clara's nerves jarred at the sound of screaming from one end of the ward. A large youth was being rebuked by a nurse. Vinnie saw her agitation and curtailed their visit.

'My wife isn't very well,' he explained. 'But I'm more than impressed by the place. We'd like our Sarah to come here.'

After that, the idea of Sarah being admitted to Gilead was accepted by everyone and Clara could not summon any resistance. She convinced herself that her daughter would be well looked after and might improve with expert carers. Vinnie promised her he would drive her up there once a fortnight for a visit and they would take Sarah out for the day. Clara warmed to this idea; it was something they could do together — something they had never done with Sarah up until now. Things would be better. When they saw her, Sarah would have the undivided attention of both parents — even if she was unaware of it. And by next spring there would be another baby to take her place in the empty nursery.

A week later, they went back to Gilead with their daughter. Clara steeled herself for the moment of separation. They were shown on to the locked ward and taken to the cot allocated for Sarah. It was by a tall window and sunlight spilled across the floor and the bars of the cot.

'Would you like me to take her?' the nurse asked.

Clara clung on. 'She has to have her food mashed or stewed else she chokes.

197

Stewed apple's her favourite. And she doesn't like being left alone for too long. You will pick her up, won't you? She likes a cuddle — but not too tight. And she can't sleep in the dark; she needs a light on. She makes a lot of noise, but it's not always crying, it's as if she's trying to sing — but she hates loud noises — shouting or banging . . .'

'Clara, hand her over,' Vinnie said firmly. The nurse smiled and held out her arms.

'No, I want to put her in her cot myself,' Clara said. Holding Sarah, she turned towards Vinnie. 'Say goodbye to your dad, little pet.' She waited for him to kiss his daughter or say something, but Vinnie just stood there embarrassed, staring beyond them to the high window and the world outside. Sarah struggled restlessly in her arms, grunting softly.

Heart hammering, Clara kissed her daughter's soft forehead and smoothed back her dark hair. 'Goodbye, little one,' she whispered tearfully and laid her down on the starched sheet. Sarah jerked her arms wildly, her grunting becoming more urgent. Somehow she knew she was being left behind. Clara leaned over and held her hand.

'She'll be fine,' the nurse said encouragingly. 'Best not to make a fuss.'

Vinnie took Clara by the arm and pulled her away. 'We'll be back here the week after next,' he reminded her. 'It'll be no time at all.'

Clara let go. Sarah strained round, her brown eyes fixed on her mother. Vinnie guided her firmly up the ward. Clara was shaking, swallowing down sobs. Sarah began flailing her arms about, hit the bars and started to wail. Clara halted and looked round. Vinnie stopped her rushing back to Sarah's cot.

'You're making this ten times worse,' he hissed. 'Just leave her to settle in. She'll be champion the minute we've gone.'

As he hauled Clara away, the sound of her daughter's screaming cut through her like a blade. She knew Sarah would not stop crying. Without her to pick her up, she would carry on till she was scarlet in the face and completely exhausted. An orderly unlocked the door, ushered them through and locked it behind them. The howling grew fainter. Swiftly Vinnie marched her out of the building and into the blustery outdoors.

Gulping for air, Clara rushed over to the nearest tree, bent over and heaved up her breakfast. Vinnie stood over her in concern, his customary handkerchief at the ready. He rubbed her back.

'Haway, lass, you mustn't upset yourself. Is it the baby making you sick?'

She took his handkerchief and held it to her mouth, unable to answer.

They drove back to town in silence. As they neared Newcastle, Vinnie began to whistle 'Smoke Gets in your Eyes'. Clara burst into tears. Quickly he put a hand on her knee.

'You'll feel better for a cry,' he soothed her. 'We've done the right thing, Clara. It may not feel like it right this minute, but it will do soon.' He squeezed her knee. 'Just me and you again,' he smiled. 'Be like old times.' Then he rested his hand gently on her stomach. 'Until the nipper comes along.'

Chapter 32

Clara tried to be positive about what they had done. It was for Sarah's benefit. She would be surrounded by professionals who would know how best to help her, and Clara herself, freed from the worry that her own care was inadequate, would be able to love her unreservedly — like a proper mother, she thought. It would also help mend her frayed marriage. Between the suspicion and tension following the attack on the Lewises and their rows over Sarah, her relationship with Vinnie had come under increasing strain. She longed to recapture their loving intimacy.

When he was away from the house, he rang several times a day to speak to her, to make sure she was all right.

'Don't want you fretting on your own,' he said.

'I'm not on my own,' she reminded him, 'I've got your mother and the Shadow.' This was her nickname for Jimmy.

'Good,' Vinnie chuckled. 'I'll be back as soon as I can.'

But she was often in bed by the time he returned and he would protest that she had not waited to dine with him. She dared not tell him that her days were achingly long and empty without their daughter to look after. Going to bed was an attempt to shorten their tedium.

'Sorry, I was tired,' Clara said, although she lay awake half the night, listening out for Sarah's crying. Sometimes she heard a noise that was so like the child's wailing that she sprang from bed and rushed into the darkened nursery, only to find it was the call of a neighbouring cat prowling across the roof. Staring at the empty cot in the moonlight made her wince with pain. Only the thought of the new baby kept at bay her feelings of loss over Sarah. Placing her hands on her belly, which had yet to swell, Clara murmured encouragement to her unborn.

'Please be all right. Please be everything Vinnie wants.'

When she returned to bed, Vinnie would sleepily throw a protective arm about her. But as she snuggled into his hold, he would stop her exploring hand. He had imposed the same rule of abstinence as in the latter stages of her pregnancy with Sarah. There would be no lovemaking until after the baby was safely born.

The days dragged until the Saturday when Vinnie had promised to take her up to Gilead.

'I'm sorry, lass, but this promoter's coming up from London specially and I have to gan into town,' he told her two days before.

'Vinnie, you promised!' she cried in disbelief.

'We can gan up next week — half day Wednesday,' he promised.

'I can't wait till then!' Clara protested.

'The lass isn't ganin' to be any the wiser,' he said shortly.

'But I am,' Clara said, 'and I want to see her on Saturday. If you can't take me, I'll drive up there myself.'

'No you won't.' Vinnie was firm. 'Not in your condition.'

'Please, Vinnie. You said we could visit every fortnight. Let Jimmy take me.'

Vinnie relented. 'All right, but only if Jimmy does all the driving — and you don't go over-tiring yourself or getting in a state.'

Clara got Jimmy up early on the Saturday morning, as excited as if she was on a Sunday school trip, and packed a picnic. Her brother grumbled at the early start but seemed quite amenable to the idea of a jaunt into the countryside and the chance to give the car a good run out. However, he baulked at her suggestion that he should go into the hospital with her, so he waited outside while she went through the lengthy process of signing in and being escorted to the ward. Sarah could be taken out for two hours around the grounds.

'She must be back for dinner time at twelve,' the matron told her.

'But I've brought a picnic,' Clara explained.

Matron shook her head. 'It's important she sticks to her regime, otherwise she becomes distressed.'

Clara bristled at the way the woman spoke about her daughter as if she knew her better than she did, but bit her tongue for fear of being prevented from seeing Sarah.

Her daughter lay in the cot, exactly as she had left her. Clara's heart squeezed with longing. Sarah was gazing at the sunlight peeping in at the high window, making her usual snuffling noises. Clara leaned over her. Sarah jerked round. Her eyes were unfocused for a moment, then something in them changed; a spark of recognition? Sarah's upper body began to writhe and her mouth opened to let out a high-pitched squeal.

Clara laughed. 'Yes, it's Mammy!' She reached down and seized the small girl, swinging her out of the cot. Sarah threw her arms about and grunted in delight. Clara kissed her fiercely and hugged her so tightly, Sarah began to scream.

'Mrs Craven,' the matron chided, 'you mustn't disturb the other children.'

Clara apologised and hurried out after the orderly, unable to keep her own sobbing quiet. She and Jimmy pushed Sarah around in a hospital pram, her brother hauling the pram up the steeper pathways between the thick rhododendron bushes. It was spitting with rain, but they stopped under a sheltering willow tree, spread out a rug and laid Sarah between them. Bashfully, Jimmy tickled his niece under the chin and she let out a shriek. He recoiled. Clara was quick to reassure him. 'Don't be shy of her — she likes that.'

'Does she?' he asked dubiously.

'Honest.' Clara laughed.

Jimmy tickled her again and Sarah let out a noise like steam in a kettle. He laughed. 'She's a funny 'un.'

Clara inspected her daughter. She seemed healthy enough, even if her hospital clothes felt a bit hard and starched. She propped Sarah up between her knees and fed her some stewed apple she had brought for their picnic.

'Don't tell Matron, eh, bonny lass? Or we'll both be in trouble.'

Jimmy watched her. 'Why do you bother speaking to her when she can't understand a word?'

Clara kissed the top of Sarah's head. 'Maybe not the words but she understands the meaning behind them.' He looked puzzled. 'From the sound of my voice, she knows I'm speaking to her — and she knows I love her. That's what matters, isn't it?'

Jimmy shrugged. 'Suppose so.'

A nurse met them at the entrance to Sarah's block. 'Matron doesn't want you taking her back to the ward,' she said with a look of apology.

Clara kissed her daughter a swift goodbye and hurried away, knowing that to look back would only prolong the agony. She cried quietly for most of the drive home. She was grateful that Jimmy did not whistle or try to coax her out of her sadness with false promises that she would soon feel better, as Vinnie had.

She was supposed to be meeting Vinnie at the Sandford Rooms for dinner that evening, but she told Dolly to ring him and say she was unwell and went straight to bed. She lay listening to the sound of children playing in a neighbouring garden, clutching a clump of dark hair that she had snipped from Sarah's head that morning. If she pressed it to her nose she could capture a faint smell of her daughter.

Vinnie was cross with her for missing the dinner with their friends, but when she said she was feeling sick with the baby, he was quickly mollified.

The next week dragged, worse than the one before, Clara knowing there would be no visit to Gilead at the end of it. She knew the emptiness would not last once their second baby was born, but that day stretched a long six months away. She would go mad if all she had in her life was those brief precious hours with Sarah, once a fortnight.

'Go and visit Willa or Mabel,' Vinnie suggested when she complained of having nothing to do.

'I can't do that every day,' Clara said restlessly, 'and they've got their boys to look after.'

'And so will you soon.' Vinnie grinned.

'Not soon enough,' Clara answered. 'Why don't we go to the pictures? We used to go two or three times a week. Just you and me, Vinnie? Sneak off work and go to the matinee.'

'I'd like nothing better,' he said, 'but I haven't got the time. Get Jimmy to take you, lass.'

Finally, frustrated at her idleness, Clara confronted her husband.

'I want to go back to work, Vinnie. At least for a couple of months.'

'Work?' he said sharply.' For Jellicoe?'

'Just part time,' Clara bargained, 'the odd feature — keep my hand in.'

He gave her a stormy look. 'No, never! You're not working for him again. I can't believe you're even asking after what happened with Sarah.'

'That wasn't his fault,' Clara insisted. 'I badgered him to let me cover the rally.'

'It makes no difference. You're not going back to that paper — or any paper for that matter. Your job is being my wife.'

Clara was filled with frustration. 'Then let me work for you! Anything; I could help Mam with the paperwork at the garage, or down at the hall.'

He shook his head in incomprehension. 'I've slaved for years to give you all you've ever wanted — this house, a car, dinners out, posh friends. What you want to gan working for? That's what working-class lasses have to do. You've left all that behind; *we*'ve left it behind. How do you think it would look, you ganin' to work for me like a common clerk, like I can't afford to keep you properly?'

'Cissie works for the Women's Section,' Clara retorted, 'and no one calls her a common clerk.'

'That's different,' Vinnie said. 'She's doing political work, supporting her husband. She doesn't do the menial jobs; she raises funds from her rich friends.' He eyed her. 'If you must do something, why don't you do charity work like Willa and Cissie? That would look good among our supporters — raising money for veterans or something.' He nodded in approval at his idea. 'I'll have a word with George about it.'

Clara turned from him in disappointment. She did not want to attend endless luncheons or hold 'at homes' with the same small group of people they always met. The more she thought about her old life as a reporter, the more she hankered to be out and about, meeting new people and hearing their stories. But Vinnie would never allow it.

She resigned herself to joining in Willa's charity work. August came and the next visit to Gilead. This time Vinnie came with her, but vetoed any idea of a leisurely walk and a picnic in the grounds. Clara had barely an hour with her daughter, sitting with her on a bench outside the children's block while Vinnie paced up and down, pulling out his pocket watch on its gold chain every five minutes.

She determined that next time she would take Jimmy again. Vinnie showed not the slightest interest in Sarah and Clara hid her resentment with difficulty.

A few days later, Vinnie came home grinning with news.

'I've got something that'll cheer you up,' he said. 'No more being bored for my wife.'

'What?' Clara asked, intrigued.

'We're going to go to Germany with the British Legion! The Bell-Carrs are organising it and they've asked us to come too. How about that?'

'When?' Clara gasped.

'End of August,' Vinnie announced. 'We'll visit the Brauns in Hamburg so I can do a bit of business. Then a few days touring afterwards with the Bell-Carrs.'

'How long for?' Clara asked.

'Fortnight.' Vinnie beamed. 'Always said I'd take you abroad one day, didn't I? Well now's your chance.'

Clara's first thought was that she would miss one of her visits to Gilead. But she tried not to show her reluctance. The Clara of old would have seized the chance to travel. Why was she so unsure?

'It sounds grand,' she said cautiously, 'but I'm not sure I should be travelling while I'm expecting.'

'I'll take good care of you,' Vinnie assured her. 'Nothing too strenuous. Cissie will look after you when I've got trade meetings. I hate the thought of going away and leaving you at home. I want you with me, Clara.'

Clara was encouraged by his tender words. Perhaps this would be just the time they needed to bring them closer together again.

'Do we have to travel with the Bell-Carrs?' she asked. 'It would be so nice just to be the two of us together.'

Vinnie looked at her in astonishment. 'It's thanks to them we're going,' he told her. 'We wouldn't be invited without them.'

Clara determined to throw herself into the holiday with as much enthusiasm as possible. She enlisted Willa's help in a shopping trip, Vinnie insisting she must have new clothes for the visit. Clara confided in her friend that she was pregnant again. Willa was delighted.

'Oh, I'm thrilled! It makes up for—' She broke off, blushing. 'Well, you know what I mean.' She squeezed her arm. 'It's wonderful news. I bet Vinnie's over the moon.'

'Yes, he is,' Clara admitted.

Jimmy collected them both with the shopping and took Clara home. She was upstairs laying out her new clothes to show Vinnie later when it happened without warning. She felt sudden stomach gripes and rushed to the bathroom. To her horror she was bleeding. She stayed there for several stunned minutes. What did this mean? Was she losing the baby?

'Please don't let me lose the bairn!'

She cried out to Dolly for help. Her mother-in-law sent Jimmy for Dr Dixon and ordered Clara to bed. She lay there, trying not to move, willing the nightmare to vanish. After examining her, the doctor said, 'I'm sorry, but you're probably going to miscarry. All you can do is wait and see. If the bleeding gets much worse, call me again.'

By the time Vinnie came home, Clara was bleeding continuously.

'Why did no one tell me earlier!' he shouted.

'Because there's nothing you can do about it,' Dolly said with a pitying look.

The doctor rang for an ambulance. 'Given your wife's earlier complications, it's best if this is handled in hospital.'

'What will they do?' Vinnie demanded. 'Can they save the bairn?'

Dr Dixon shook his head. 'This is for your wife's safety.'

Clara watched them all mutely: Vinnie's angry face, Dolly's tight-lipped frown, the doctor's resigned expression. Only Jimmy, hovering in the doorway, was looking at her with sorrow.

Later, lying alone in the hospital bed in the early hours, Clara let her tears come. The weight of failure was suffocating. It was then that she realised how much she had relied upon this baby to fill the void in her life; a void created by Sarah's absence, by Vinnie's preoccupation with work and his own political advancement, by her enforced idleness. She had yearned for this baby as the key to making her life vibrant and fulfilling once more.

Early the next morning she was taken away to the operating theatre and put into merciful oblivion. When she awoke, she was back on the ward and told it was all over. She should go home and recuperate for a few days. It was Jimmy who came and collected her. Vinnie was at work. Patience came to see her and sat holding her hand while Clara wept.

'You'll try again,' her mother tried to console her.

'I wanted *that* baby!' Clara cried angrily. 'I don't want some far-off, try-again baby.'

'I'm sorry.'

'Oh, Mam,' Clara said in despair. 'How can I bear the emptiness?'

Patience stayed with her until Jimmy was sent up by Dolly. 'Mrs Craven says you should gan now — doesn't want you here when Vinnie gets home.'

Patience said bitterly, 'No, it wouldn't do to have the staff fraternising with his missus.'

Jimmy looked uncomfortable. 'I'll run you home.'

When Vinnie arrived back, Clara heard him go into the sitting room first and talk to Dolly. She longed for him to come up and put his arms about her. She ached for physical comfort and for him to tell her that he felt as bereft as she did. It was ten minutes before he appeared, his breath smelling of whisky.

'You all right, lass?' he asked, his look uncertain.

She nodded, waiting for him to embrace her, but he turned and began changing out of his suit. He went into the bathroom and she heard him running a bath. The door closed. She waited. When he returned, a towel wrapped round his waist, she asked, 'You're not going out again, are you?'

'BUF meeting,' he answered. 'Lots to sort out before we gan to Germany next week.'

She looked at him in disbelief. 'Vinnie, you're not still thinking of going?'

'It won't be a late one,' he said, buttoning up his black tunic, 'I promise.'

'I meant the trip to Germany,' Clara croaked.

He turned and stared at her. 'Course we're still ganin' to Germany. Why ever not?'

Clara was too stunned by his insensitivity to reply.

'Doctor said there was no reason why you shouldn't travel, long as you take it steady. It'll be just what you need after this. We'll put it behind us, Clara, try again.'

She turned her face from him, shuddering at those trite words, try again. Dressed immaculately, his hair oiled, Vinnie leaned over and kissed her forehead.

'That's right, lass, you get a good rest. Get your energy back.' He stood back. 'Tell you what; I'll gan in the spare room tonight so as not to disturb you when I get in.'

Then he was marching out of the room, his leather boots squeaking. Clara lay in the large bed listening to him chattering to his mother. The front door closed and she heard the car engine rev as her husband drove off to town. She pulled the bedcovers over her head and wept in desolation.

Chapter 33

Vinnie never mentioned the miscarriage again. Clara hardly saw him all that following week. She sat at the bottom of the garden in a deck chair, staring at the trees, sheltering under an umbrella if it rained. Dolly could not persuade her to come in. Only Vinnie, ordering her inside after dark, registered through the fog of her unhappiness.

Clara had no appetite and ate little. Vinnie appeared to eat out most days, but she did not ask where or with whom. She was just thankful he did not make her go along too, for she dreaded having to make social conversation with their friends as if nothing had happened.

As far as she knew, only Willa had been told of her pregnancy. Dolly had cautioned them not to tell anyone until it was more advanced. Now Vinnie acted as if it had never been. Willa had sent a small note, expressing regret that she was 'indisposed' and hoping to see her after the holiday. So that was how Vinnie was explaining her absence to their social circle: she was mildly ill.

Two days before the boat sailed for Hamburg, Clara faced up to him.

'I'm not going with you,' she told him quietly.

'Don't be daft. Of course you are,' he replied.

'I don't feel up to it. I'll only spoil it for you and the Bell-Carrs.'

'But the doctor said it would do you good—'

'The doctor isn't me,' Clara said firmly. 'I know he's well meaning, but only I know what I'm fit for — and it's not gallivanting around Germany.'

Vinnie grew angry, but his shouts of accusation that she was being selfish and he needed her there with him made her withdraw further into her bleak, isolated world.

'I can't face all those people,' she tried to explain.

'Course you can. I've spent a fortune on new clothes so you can look the part,' Vinnie complained.

'Is that all you want, Vinnie?' Clara accused him wearily. 'The blonde, blue-eyed Nordic wife to hang on your arm and impress your business partners?'

He stormed up to her and for a fearful moment Clara thought he would strike her. But he clenched his fists and hissed, 'Stay then and stew in your own misery! But don't whine about it afterwards — and don't say I never gave you the chance to gan abroad and see a bit of the world. That's your trouble, Clara, you're too bloody narrow-minded. I thought you shared my vision, saw beyond Byfell. But now I'm not so sure. You've lost your spark,' he said in contempt. 'I hope for both our sakes you find it again quick.'

He left her reeling from the savagery of his words. He hardly spoke to her again before he left. On the day of departure, Clarkie came to carry his luggage and take him to the quayside.

Vinnie kissed her briefly on the cheek. 'Behave yourself while I'm away,' he said brusquely. 'I've told Jimmy and Clarkie to keep an eye on you — and Mam, of course. You're not to gan anywhere without them knowing, do you hear? And no running off to your mam's like last time; I want you here where you can be looked after.'

Clara bit back a caustic reply that she was his wife not his prisoner. She would do as she pleased, but there was no point in antagonising him at the last minute.

She forced herself to say, 'Have a canny trip.'

For the first couple of days after Vinnie had gone, Clara continued as before, content just to sit in the garden, a book unread on her lap, ignoring Dolly's reproachful comments.

'Better pull yourself together by the time my Vinnie gets back. You're not the only lass that's ever miscarried, you know. Never took you as the sort to go to pieces. I warned him you'd lead him a merry dance. You should have gone with him.'

Finally Clara lost patience. 'No, you should have gone with him, Mrs Craven. You've still got him tied to your apron strings.'

'The cheek of it!' Dolly exclaimed. 'Wait till I tell my Vinnie.'

Clara felt a small flicker of triumph as her mother-in-law stalked off and left her alone. She leaned back in the mild sunshine, realising she could fritter away the whole day like this if she pleased. There would be no Vinnie ringing up every hour to check on what she was doing and no need to dress for dinner and await his return. She did not have to get up to make his breakfast or lay out his clothes, did not have to search for things to say to him about her empty days. She did not have to do anything to please Vinnie for a whole two weeks. The thought was liberating, like a shaft of sunlight breaking through the black cloud of depression that weighed her down.

The next day, Clara rang her mother at the garage. 'I'm coming to stop with you till Vinnie gets back. I can't bear it here with Dolly's catty comments and everyone watching me.'

'No, pet,' Patience whispered. 'I'm sorry, but you can't.'

'Mam? Just for a few days then — till my next visit to Gilead. We could go together.'

'Sorry. I can't explain over the telephone,' she said in agitation.

'Something's happened,' Clara said suspiciously. 'Has Vinnie had words with you?'

There was silence, then Patience said, 'Yes.'

Clara felt suddenly tearful. 'I need you, Mam. What does it matter what Vinnie says?'

'Clara,' Patience said urgently, 'Vinnie told me I'll lose my job if I take you in.'

Clara was flabbergasted. 'Why would he say such a thing?'

'Said he wouldn't be made a fool of behind his back. What sort of man couldn't control his own wife? that's what he said.'

Clara began to shake. Patience promised she would come and see her as soon as possible, then quickly rang off. The words rang in her head; *control his own wife*. That's exactly what Vinnie was doing, controlling her and every aspect of her life. Even when he was not there, he still dictated her movements: whom she saw, where she went, what she did. What a fool she was to think she could do as she pleased even with her husband out of the country. Clara went and sat outside.

When had the restrictions begun? After Sarah was born or further back? During the first pregnancy, perhaps. Clara thought back to their marriage, their courtship. Even before that, Vinnie had had a say in her life and the life of her family. He had always been there offering help — a job, a loan, a lift in his car — his generosity making them feel somehow beholden. He had taken over the organising of her father's funeral; he had taken care of Brodsky. Even at Danny Watts's wedding all those years ago, Vinnie had contrived that she and Reenie should attend.

That was the way he operated, drawing people in and making them dependent on him and his largesse. But it was not just her. He controlled everyone: her family, his boxers, his business partners, his Blackshirts, his mother. In a strange way, even Alastair and Cissie, who thought everyone obeyed their commands,

206

were manipulated by Vinnie's charm and forcefulness into doing what he wanted. Two years ago, Alastair would rather have died than set foot on German soil.

Yet there was one man who had defied Vinnie, refused to take his money or make use of his contacts. Frank Lewis. Idealistic, optimistic Frank, whom his family suspected was dead. How could they bear the uncertainty? The Lewises had stood out against Vinnie's controlling grip, but had paid the price. Whether he was the instigator of their being hounded from Byfell, she might never know. But she felt a deep shame when she thought of them. She had willingly turned her back on her old friends, eager to follow the heady fascist dream. She had allowed herself to be seduced by its promise of self-glorification and power; had wanted it not just for Vinnie but for herself. Clara stared back at The Cedars. She was like a bird in a gilded cage of her own making. She realised she was frightened of Vinnie and his power over her, but what frightened her more was the person she had become. She made up her mind there and then that she must flex her wings before it was too late.

On the pretext of going to visit Willa, Clara got Jimmy to drop her in Jesmond at a time she knew Willa would be out shopping. As she went to ring the doorbell, she waved Jimmy away. Once he had driven off, Clara walked swiftly down Willa's street and headed for Sandyford, a ten-minute walk away. It was easy to recognise the Lewises' hairdresser's by the anti-fascist poster in the window and another one asking for donations towards the Republican cause in the newly erupted Spanish Civil War. Clara smiled at this outward sign that their campaigning spirit had not been quashed.

She stood on the opposite pavement, summoning up the courage to go in. Half obscured by the posters, she thought she saw Oscar's bald head at the window.

'Looks like you could do with a perm and set.' A voice startled her from behind. She whipped round to see Reenie standing eyeing her; blonde head cocked quizzically, a parcel of groceries in her arms.

Clara gulped. 'I need more than that,' she murmured. 'But you look grand, Reenie.'

'What are you doing here?' Reenie asked suspiciously. 'Are you on your own?'

Clara felt tears flood her throat. She nodded, unable to speak.

Reenie stepped forward. 'You all right? You look terrible.'

Clara stood shaking uncontrollably, trying to speak. 'R-Reenie — I'm so s-sorry . . .' She let out a sob from deep inside and started to cry.

Quickly Reenie shifted her parcel into one arm and put the other round her old friend. 'Haway, Clara,' she said gently, 'come inside.'

Reenie guided her across the street and into the shop. Oscar looked up from shaving a customer, his mouth dropping open in surprise. Marta was washing a woman's hair at the sink on the other side of the divide. She broke off in mid-sentence.

'Clara!'

'We're going upstairs,' Reenie said at once, steering Clara straight through the back of the shop. 'Clara needs a sit-down.'

She pushed Clara into the small sitting room-cum-kitchen at the top of the stairs. It was full of familiar furniture, reminiscent of the Lewises' old home in Drummond Street. Reenie dumped down the groceries, poured Clara a glass of water and told her to sit down. They sat in silence for several minutes while Clara, head bowed, wept quietly.

Eventually, her tears subsided and she looked up. Reenie was watching her,

her look guarded.

'Do you want to tell me what's happened?' she asked.

'I don't know where to begin,' Clara whispered.

'I've got plenty time,' Reenie assured her. 'I'm off duty.'

Clara swallowed. Hesitantly, she began to tell her old friend all her troubles. Soon the words were tumbling out about her guilt over Sarah, her friends' rejection of her disabled daughter and Sarah's admission to a children's hospital. She told Reenie of Vinnie's growing attraction to extreme right-wing politics, his increasing intolerance and the way he controlled her life. Finally, she spoke of her miscarriage. The pain was still so raw that her voice broke.

Reenie took her hand and held it in hers. 'I'm sorry, Clara,' she said softly. 'I had no idea.'

Clutching Reenie's hand tightly, Clara said in a voice that trembled, 'I came here to say sorry, not the other way round. I feel that bad about what's happened to you and your family — feel responsible. I've been a bad friend. Can you ever forgive me?'

Reenie put her arms about Clara and hugged her in reply. 'I don't blame you; I blame Vinnie Craven for turning your head. Everyone could see you were head over heels in love with him — except our Benny.'

Clara hugged her back. 'Poor Benny! How is he?'

Reenie drew away and sighed. 'He's throwing himself into this aid relief for Spain; he has to have something to get angry about. Doesn't work much in the shop any more — too busy fundraising or organising hunger marches. It's like he's trying to make up for—' Reenie broke off and shook her head.

'For what?'

'For not being Frank,' Reenie said, her expression unutterably sad.

Clara's heart squeezed. 'Is there still no news of him?'

Reenie shook her head. 'We all think he's dead,' she whispered, 'except for Mam. She will never believe it. But those camps; we've heard terrible stories.' She shuddered.

Clara put out her hand. 'Perhaps they're not as bad as all that. I've heard they're better than some prisons—' She stopped at the sight of Reenie's angry frown.

'Don't be so naive,' Reenie snapped.

'Sorry.' Clara flushed. She no longer knew what to believe.

They eyed each other warily. Perhaps the gulf between them was too wide after all; the attempt to bridge it too late. Then Reenie surprised her.

'If you really want to know what's going on in Germany, come along to our meeting on Friday night. City Hall. The MP Ellen Wilkinson's speaking.'

Clara hesitated. 'I'm not sure I can . . .'

Reenie's look was challenging. 'You really are afraid of Vinnie, aren't you? Even when he's hundreds of miles away.'

Clara was stung. 'I'm not!'

'Then come along. I'll meet you outside at seven o'clock.'

Clara agreed, wondering what she was going to tell Dolly and Jimmy. Soon after that, she left. On the way out, she promised a waving Marta that she would come back soon for a proper visit. Outside, she clasped Reenie's hands in hers.

'Thank you for listening.' She smiled tremulously. 'I haven't been able to tell all that to anyone — not even Mam.'

Reenie smiled back briefly. 'I'm glad I could help.'

'Can we be friends again?' Clara asked bashfully.

Reenie eyed her. 'That's up to you, Clara. You know Vinnie will try to stop it.'

Clara felt a lurch of fear at the thought and knew Reenie was right. 'I'll come on Friday,' she promised, determined to be brave.

'Friday then.' Reenie nodded and waved her away.

When Jimmy picked up Clara outside the Jesmond tea room to which she was supposed to have taken Willa, she told her brother straight away. 'I'm going with Willa to a concert on Friday night. We might have supper afterwards, so it'll be late. I'll drive myself so you don't have to wait up.'

'I don't mind,' Jimmy answered. 'That's my job.'

Clara said, 'Well, I'd like to drive myself sometimes. If I don't, I'll forget how to do it. What's the point of Vinnie giving me a car if I never get to drive it?'

Jimmy looked uncomfortable. 'Vinnie said I had to drive you everywhere. Those were his orders.'

'He doesn't need to know,' Clara said with a look of appeal.

Jimmy glanced at her in shock. 'I'm not ganin' to lie to him for you,' he muttered.

'Don't then,' Clara said shortly. 'But while he's not here, I'll not be dictated to by my kid brother. I shall drive myself into town on Friday night, and that's that.'

They drove the rest of the way home in stony silence.

Clara looked forward with nervous excitement to the Friday meeting. Dolly surveyed her critically when she was on the point of leaving.

'You haven't made much of an effort to dress up for a night out with the Templetons,' she remarked. 'Don't know what Vinnie would say.'

'He'd say, have a canny evening,' Clara answered and went into the kitchen to find Jimmy. Reluctantly he handed over the car keys. Clara left feeling light-headed with the small triumph.

Arriving outside the City Hall, she peered anxiously among the crowd for Reenie.

'There she is!' a voice cried. 'Clara, over here!'

Clara turned to see Reenie and Benny beckoning her through the open doors. Benny looked thinner-faced, his hair severely cropped. He smiled a little warily.

'Reenie didn't think you'd come,' he said. 'It's very brave of you.'

'Not really,' Clara said breathlessly, her heart banging with nerves. 'How are you, Benny?'

'Still alive,' he said with a twisted smile. 'And you?'

She nodded. 'I'm sorry—'

'Don't be,' he interrupted.

'Come on, both of you,' Reenie said, pushing forward impatiently, 'let's get a good seat.'

Clara and Benny exchanged looks. 'Still bossing us around,' Clara said.

'Just like old times,' Benny agreed. They moved forward together. 'You're not wearing your fascist uniform under that coat, are you?' he teased.

Clara blushed but quipped back, 'No, just a badge or two.'

Benny chuckled. 'Remember, no heckling or saluting, or you'll get us thrown out.'

'Have you ever been to a meeting where you haven't been thrown out?' Clara asked dryly.

'Not one of your husband's,' Benny grunted.

Reenie broke in, 'That's enough. You can argue afterwards.'

Laughing, Benny linked an arm with both of them and pushed them towards the stalls.

Clara had expected to be bored by the meeting; her only reason for going had been to please Reenie and rekindle their lost friendship. But she was captivated by the oratory of 'Red' Ellen Wilkinson who spoke stirringly about a planned hunger march from Jarrow to London that she intended to lead. Clara thought how Vinnie would pour scorn on such attempts to sway the politicians in London, but she was struck by the woman's courage and optimism. Red Ellen believed in the power of ordinary people.

The MP went on to talk about the plight of the Spanish people, fighting for their elected government against Franco's fascist coup. Clara noticed how Benny shouted out vociferously in agreement. Then Ellen introduced a German refugee on to the stage. His suit hung off his skeletal frame, his face was pinched and grey.

The audience went quiet as the man spoke haltingly but with dignity about the persecution of left-wingers like himself, and now Jews, under the Nazis. He had been tortured for printing leaflets critical of Hitler's hooligans and taken to Dachau. Clara felt Reenie and Benny flinch at the mention of the concentration camp.

'We are beaten daily,' he said dispassionately. 'They are putting the sacks over our heads to muffle the cries.' He held up his wrists. 'We work ten hours every day. We are making our own manacles for in the cells and we make the whips that they beat us with. That is our work.'

He went on to describe further terrible punishments, made all the more shocking by his quiet delivery of the routine and casual cruelties. The prisoners were put on half-rations and tortured with burning cigarettes, their feet lacerated with wet towels. Well-known Communists were beaten to death. When he opened his shirt to show them the welts and burn marks that scarred his body, the audience gasped in shock.

He touched his head. 'But the worst torture is in the mind. They say we can write letters, but they do not send them. They do not give us letters from our families. They say no one writes to us because we are traitors to the Fatherland and our families hate us. We must become Nazis like them. We do not know what to think any more. Some men, they go mad. What is there to live for? They hang themselves.'

Clara reached for Reenie's hand and held it. This man could have been Frank. It was unbearable to think of him suffering in this way. She gulped back her own tears as Reenie's hand squeezed hers for comfort. The refugee told how he had escaped by creeping under a delivery van while the driver was bartering cigarettes with a guard and clinging on to the underside while he drove out of the camp.

They gave the refugee a standing ovation when he left the stage. Afterwards, Benny pushed his way through to speak to him, Reenie following. Had he come across their brother, Frank Leizmann? Clara could hardly keep from weeping when the man shook his head sadly and said he had not met anyone of that name. Subdued, they left the hall.

Clara tried to lift their spirits. 'Just because he never knew Frank doesn't mean that he's. . .' She hesitated.

'Dead?' Reenie finished for her, her eyes glittering with pain. 'Why can no one bring themselves to say it?'

'Because it's too terrible,' Clara whispered.

Benny looked at her, his dark eyes haunted. 'Now do you believe what's going on in Germany? Or is this all Red propaganda like your husband says?'

Clara winced, but held his look. 'I have to believe it,' she answered quietly.

210

'I've seen the marks on that man's body.'

They stood mutely, locked in their own thoughts, as the crowds around them ebbed away into the night. Clara said suddenly, 'I don't want to go straight home.'

They went round the corner to a cafe run by Italians that stayed open late serving hot drinks and ice cream, and ordered a pot of tea. The place was full and the atmosphere jovial. To Clara's alarm, Lillian was there with a group of friends and they squeezed on to their table. Lillian's look was hostile. 'Surprised to see you here, Mrs Craven.' She almost spat out the name.

Reenie quickly avoided embarrassment by introducing Clara to the others as a former member of the YS rambling group. Benny fell immediately to talking about the meeting, Reenie telling Lillian how they had asked the refugee about Frank.

Lillian reached across the table and touched Reenie's arm. 'We have to accept that Frank's gone. We'll go mad otherwise.'

Clara asked, 'How can you be sure? Isn't there the slightest possibility he's alive?'

Lillian's eyes narrowed as she answered in a bitter tone, 'Frank and I were going to be married. He was to follow me back here once he'd helped his uncle. But his uncle was murdered and Frank arrested. If Frank had ever been released, he would have come home to me. Apart from that one letter he was forced to write from the camp, we've heard nothing.' She looked at Clara with dislike. 'Probably drawing attention to Frank like that was the worst possible thing,' she accused her. 'The Nazis had to silence him.'

It had never occurred to Clara that her actions might have put Frank in further danger. She was too guilt-ridden to speak.

After an awkward pause, Benny swiftly turned the conversation to Spain. Clara sat back and listened. It seemed a lifetime since she had been in such a place, sipping strong tea and listening to Reenie and Benny putting the world to rights. Despite Lillian's animosity, she was glad to be there rather than at home. It was so refreshing to hear them debating; to see the women as animated as the men and the men listening to what they had to say. How trivial the conversation of her new friends was in contrast. They could talk endlessly about school uniforms, unreliable servants or the price of decorating their homes. Even the Women's Section, which was confined to squabbles over catering for the men in the BUF, was now moribund.

It was with reluctance that Clara walked back to her car, offering Reenie and Benny a lift home to prolong her time with them. Benny was impressed she could drive.

'But do you still walk anywhere or take the tram?' Reenie asked.

'No, our Clara's too grand for that,' Benny teased.

'I'm not allowed—' Clara stopped herself, blushing at her meek words.

Reenie got out of the car. 'While the cat's away, the mice can play,' she said. 'I've got Sunday off. Why don't you come hiking with us?'

Clara stared in alarm. How could she manage to escape for a whole Sunday? Yet she yearned to walk in the countryside with them.

'I'm not very fit these days,' she said cautiously.

'We can take it steady,' Benny encouraged her. 'Or you can drive your car and we'll walk alongside — talk to you through the window.'

Clara snorted with sudden laughter. 'I'd like to come. Let me pick you up.'

Reenie smiled. 'Eight o'clock. Come for breakfast and let Mam fill you with pancakes.'

Clara drove home, singing to herself. She caught her breath at the sound. She had not sung a note since Sarah went away. She carried on, sobbing and singing at the top of her voice, feeling more alive than she had done in months.

Chapter 34

By the end of Vinnie's first week away, Clara was in open defiance of Dolly and Jimmy. Dolly had her followed. 'You lied to your own brother about visiting the Templetons. You've been seeing them German riff-raff,' she said in disgust. 'It's got to stop.'

After Clara disappeared all day to walk with the Lewises, Dolly ordered Jimmy to confiscate the car keys.

'He'll not drive you up to Gilead on Saturday if you don't toe the line,' she threatened.

But Clara had had the best day for an age, walking along the river at Hexham, and she had promised Reenie and Benny she would do it again soon. They had made her laugh and talk more in those few hours than she had in the past year with Vinnie.

'There's no harm in it,' she told her mother-in-law, 'and you can't stop me.'

'We'll see about that,' Dolly said.

Clara continued to visit the Lewises, taking the tram into town on her own. Dolly retaliated by refusing to give Clara any of the allowance Vinnie had left for his mother to dole out to Clara when she needed it. Patience was hauled up to Gosforth to have words with her daughter.

'Please, Clara, just do as they ask. I couldn't cope if we had to go back to the way we lived before. If Vinnie threw you out—'

'Don't be daft,' Clara cried, 'he's never going to do that. He prides himself on our model marriage,' she said in self-mockery. 'It's good for his image. All he needs is the blond, blue-eyed children.'

'You mustn't speak like that.' Patience was shocked at her bitter tone. 'I thought you were happy with Vinnie.'

Clara glanced away. She could not explain how this brief separation had made her see things quite differently.

'Don't do anything rash,' Patience fretted. 'He'll take it out on us somehow. I'll lose my job, or Jimmy'll get the sack.'

Clara looked at her mother more closely. When had she grown so thin and drawn-faced? She heard the fear in her mother's voice and recognised it. Vinnie might as well have been there in the room with them; even the thought of him cowed them both. Clara went and held her mother.

'I'll look after you, I promise.'

It was only when Clarkie was summoned to talk to her that Clara realised the trouble she was in. Dressed in Blackshirt uniform, Vinnie s right-hand man ushered her into the sitting room as if he owned the place and told the others to leave.

'Sit down, Mrs Craven,' he smiled. When she continued to stand, he settled himself into Vinnie's armchair by the marble fireplace. He got straight to the point.

'Don't want the boss to hear of you fraternising with the enemy, do you, Mrs Craven? He'd be right upset. And you'd hate something to happen to the Lewises because of it, wouldn't you?'

Clara was shocked. 'Like what? Their shop smashed up and Benny put in hospital again?'

'Now that's just being hysterical,' he said, as if speaking to a child. 'Vinnie would never allow some'at like that, would he?'

Clara glared at Clarkie as he lolled in his boss's chair, quite at ease. He was mocking her and trying to scare her with threats against the Lewises. It made her almost certain he must have had something to do with the original attack. The thought sickened her.

'Get out of Vinnie's chair,' she told him. 'I'll not be bullied by the likes of you.'

'Temper, temper,' he goaded, getting up slowly and sauntering towards her. He swept her with a predatory look, the sort she used to see in Vinnie's eyes. 'Remember you weren't always so high and mighty. Harry Magee was a drunk and a laughing stock. If you hadn't been so bonny — and willing,' he mocked, 'you Magees would be in the poorhouse.'

Clara gasped in shock. She raised her hand to slap his insolent face, but Clarkie caught it and gripped her hard.

'Don't think you're any better than me,' he hissed. 'We all have our price, Mrs Craven. You gave Vinnie what he wanted, just like we all do — if we know which side our bread's buttered. But cross him, and you could be back in the gutter the morra.'

Clara struggled to release his iron grip. 'How dare you! We were never in the gutter!'

Clarkie smiled to see her riled. 'You don't know how close you were, Mrs Craven,' he sneered.

'What do you mean by that?' she demanded.

'Vinnie's like God over us. We do what he asks and he looks after us. Your job is to be a good wife and give him bairns. My job is to protect him — even from his nearest and dearest, if I think they're harming him. And I'll gan to any lengths to do it.'

He released her hand and walked out of the room. She stood rubbing the red finger marks on her wrist, gulping for breath. Clarkie was a ruthless bully and he frightened her. But it was Vinnie who gave the orders. Clarkie would never have spoken to her so brutally if he had not been sure that Vinnie would back him up. The thought made her blood run cold. She dreaded her husband's return.

Badly shaken, Clara sought out Jimmy. 'Run me into town. I'm supposed to be meeting Reenie today. I need to explain that I can't go round to hers anymore.'

Reluctantly he agreed. 'This is the last time, mind.'

When she explained to her friend in the cafe, Reenie laughed in disbelief. 'Don't be so dramatic.'

'I'm serious. I'm being watched all the time.' She glanced around nervously. 'One of Vinnie's bully boys has threatened me about seeing your family. I don't want to bring trouble to your door again.'

Reenie grabbed her arm. 'What sort of people are you mixed up with, Clara?' she cried. 'You can't let them rule your life like this.'

'It's not just a matter of my life,' Clara said unhappily, 'it's Mam and Jimmy too. I'm scared. I have to be more careful. We can still meet up in town now and again.'

Reenie shook her head in bewilderment. 'How did it ever come to this? You of all people, Clara. You used to stand up to anyone.'

Clara's head sagged. 'It's been different ever since having Sarah,' she admitted painfully. 'I lost all my confidence. I should have taken care of her, but I wasn't up to it. It pulled the rug from under my feet good and proper. I haven't got the fight to take on Vinnie.'

Reenie sighed and gave her a hug. 'I wish I could help more.'

'You have.' Clara smiled. 'Just knowing you're my friend again means that much. I don't feel so alone anymore.'

'Oh, Clara, I've missed our being friends! I wish you and Benny could've . . .'

Clara glanced away. Reenie said more briskly, 'You need something to take your mind off your troubles, something you can really care about. Why don't you start writing again?'

Clara returned her look. 'I did think about it, but Vinnie wouldn't let me.'

Reenie let out an impatient breath. 'I'm sick of hearing you say that; you're like a stuck gramophone record! Write something and send it to Jellicoe.'

Before they parted, both agreed they would meet at the Italian cafe once a week on a Saturday morning when Clara went into town to have her hair done. If Reenie was working she would leave a message there.

Clara had a sleepless night, turning over Reenie's words. In the early hours she got up, went to her dressing table and pulled out her old diary for 1934. She had stopped writing it after Sarah's birth and she tore out some empty pages. She began to write about the meeting at the City Hall, describing the moving testament of the German refugee. The words came pouring out as if the article was writing itself. Tired at last, Clara shoved it in a drawer and went to bed.

When she awoke, Clara's first thought was to tear up the article and throw it on the fire. But having reread it, she decided to write it up neatly, addressed it to Jellicoe and pushed it into her pocket.

'I'm going for a walk round the block,' she told Jimmy. 'You can follow me like a spy if you want.'

He flushed. 'If you're more than half an hour, I'm coming looking for you,' he said and skulked back into the kitchen.

Clara posted the letter in the pillar box two streets away before her nerve failed. She had asked Jellicoe not to use her name, but even so was shaken with nerves at the thought of Vinnie finding out.

Three days before Vinnie's return, Dolly walked into her bedroom waving a letter.

'What you been sending that editor?' she demanded.

Clara's heart thumped. 'You've been opening my mail!' She dashed forward and snatched the letter.

Dolly sneered. 'He doesn't want it, anyway.'

Clara read the stark letter of rejection. There was no personal message. It could have come from a complete stranger. She felt a wave of disappointment.

'Not surprised,' Dolly said. 'My Vinnie's told him he's not to give you any work.'

Clara's jaw dropped open. 'He can't tell Jellicoe what to do.'

Dolly snorted, 'Course he can. Why do you think that man gave you a job in the first place? Only 'cos my Vinnie asked him to — said he'd pay well for advertising the boxing if he took you on full time. Don't you remember getting a pay rise for doing nothing?'

Clara's head reeled. 'I don't believe you,' she gasped.

Dolly laughed. 'Do you really think a proper newspaper would have taken on a lass like you without any training if Vinnie hadn't given them a back-hander? More fool you,' she said and walked out.

***

The day before Vinnie came home, Jimmy drove Clara and Patience up to Gilead to see Sarah. It was raining, so they sat with her in the chapel, Sarah's shrieks echoing around the vaulted ceiling. Patience made attempts to chatter, but soon lapsed into silence. On the way back to the ward, they passed the imposing stone-built swimming baths.

'Let's have a nose in,' Patience suggested.

But the doors were locked. On returning to the children's wing, Clara asked the matron about the hydrotherapy Sarah had been promised.

'The Board can't afford it,' she said. 'The pool was built before the Great War — money was no object then. We do our best for the inmates,' she said stiffly, 'within our limited means.'

'Of course you do,' Clara said quickly, not meaning to criticise. But she left feeling more depressed than before. She hated the way Sarah had been referred to as an inmate, as if she were imprisoned. But then, that's what it amounted to. Her daughter was hidden away behind locked doors. Clara sat in the back of the Austin, holding her mother's hand. Her life was as proscribed as Sarah's was. She tried to stem the panic that welled up inside at the thought of Vinnie's return. Her brief taste of freedom was over.

Chapter 35

At first Vinnie would not believe that Clara had been seeing the Lewises again. But Dolly was quick to ruin his homecoming with tales of Clara's misdeeds.

'Bare-faced lies she told us. You'll have to have words with her,' Dolly nagged. 'She wouldn't be stopped.'

Vinnie s retribution was swift. Jimmy was banished back to Patience's for allowing Clara to drive the car and demoted to car minding outside Craven Hall.

'If you need to gan out anywhere, Clarkie will drive you,' Vinnie commanded.

'Not him!' Clara protested.

'It's for your own protection,' Vinnie told her. 'We've had death threats at the BUF and you've shown you can't be trusted on your own.' There was a new contempt in his voice that really frightened Clara.

He demanded to know the contents of the article she had sent to Jellicoe. Clara, thinking he would find out anyway, told him the truth. Vinnie went white with fury.

'Not only did you go to a Bolshie meeting, but you tried to get it in the papers!' he fumed. 'Are you trying to ruin me, you stupid little bitch?'

Clara recoiled. He had never sworn at her before. She wanted to tell him about the German refugee but knew he was beyond listening.

Vinnie stood over her. 'From now on, you do as I say. I'll not have my wife making a fool of me.' His look was hard, calculating. 'Don't make me regret weddin' you, Clara.'

After that, Vinnie treated her with a coldness of which she had not thought him capable. He punished her by withdrawing his affection, moving into the spare bedroom and only coming to her bed twice a week. He would make love to her mechanically and leave swiftly afterwards, telling her that he wanted her pregnant again by Christmas. He no longer took her out to dinner with him and went to the Bell-Carrs' house parties on his own.

'They don't want you there,' he told her callously, 'not since it got out about you ganin' to meetings with the anti-fascists. You're an embarrassment.'

'Why are you being so unkind to me?' Clara asked in bewilderment. 'Don't you love me anymore?'

'I'm teaching you a lesson for being disloyal to me,' Vinnie said brutally.

'And how long must I go on being punished for daring to speak to old friends?' Clara demanded.

'Till you can prove yourself a dutiful wife,' Vinnie replied, 'and give me a healthy son.'

Clara lay awake late, listening out for him coming home and breathing more easily when she heard him go into his room and stay there for the night. Sometimes he never came home at all and she wondered where he went. Once, she dared question him.

'I slept at the hall,' he snapped, 'not that it's any business of yours.'

'I'm your wife,' Clara protested. 'Of course it's my business.'

He scrutinised her with hard dark eyes. 'Then do your job and give me a bairn.'

'You've got one,' Clara answered.

He looked contemptuous. 'That thing lying up at Gilead's not a bairn. I want a normal one. Give me a son, Clara, and things can go back to how they

217

were before between the pair of us.'

At that moment Clara hated her husband. Things could never go back to how they were. How had she ever loved him with such a passion? It must have been infatuation not love, for now that it was gone she felt empty and numb to any feeling.

It was painfully obvious that he had fallen out of love with her too and seemed to get pleasure only out of controlling her. Those two weeks of separation had changed Vinnie as much as they had her. She suspected he was seeing other women, reverting to his habits of old.

Vinnie never resorted to physical violence to make her do as he wanted. He did not have to, for she lived in fear of him. He resumed the frequent telephone calls he made from work to check up on her movements and she dreaded his return in the late afternoon when she would have to account for every minute of the day. On Wednesdays, Clarkie would drive her to Willa's for lunch and on Fridays to the library so she could change her books. She was allowed to see Patience and Jimmy at Glanton Terrace on Sunday afternoons, but they were no longer invited up to The Cedars.

Yet Jimmy would not allow his mother and sister to say anything disloyal about Vinnie.

'You've brought this trouble on yourself,' he told Clara resentfully. 'Why did you have to gan stirring things up?'

'I just wanted a bit of my life back,' Clara tried to explain.

Jimmy looked at her in bewilderment. 'But you've got everything! Half the lasses round here would swap places with you tomorra.'

'And me with them,' Clara muttered.

Clara lived for the fortnightly visits to Gilead and the brief half-hour on a Saturday morning when she left the hairdresser's early to meet Reenie in the cafe. It was Reenie who encouraged her to think of small rebellions: throw away her fascist badges and write anonymous letters to the *Tyne Times* in support of anti-fascists in Spain and Germany. Clara slipped these letters to Reenie who passed them on to Jellicoe.

'He wanted to publish your article,' Reenie told her, 'but he's too afraid of Vinnie's thugs.'

Sometimes Benny would be there to meet her too. Clara was always torn between delight at seeing him and fear that one of Vinnie's men would catch them together.

One day, just before Christmas, Benny came alone. He reached across the table and took her hand eagerly in his. Embarrassed, Clara pulled away.

'Why do you stay with that man when he makes you so unhappy?' Benny said angrily.

'I don't have any choice,' Clara replied.

'Yes you do,' Benny insisted. 'I could take care of you.'

Clara laughed bitterly. 'Do you think Vinnie's just going to stand by and see me go to you?'

'Would you if you could?' Benny challenged her.

Clara sighed. 'Don't ask me, Benny, when there's no point.'

'But what if we didn't stay here?' Benny said excitedly. 'What if we went far away?'

Clara shook her head in bafflement. 'What are you talking about?'

He leaned across the table, his eyes full of fervour. 'I'm going to Spain — with the International Brigade, to fight the fascists.'

Clara looked at him in concern. 'Oh, Benny!'

'Something has to be done,' he answered impatiently. 'Our government stands by watching while a democracy is butchered. That bombing of Madrid last month when hundreds were killed — they were mostly women and children. I'm going to help. Come with me, Clara.'

She looked at him in disbelief. 'Go away with you? I - I couldn't. . .'

'Why not?' he demanded. 'You've nothing to keep you here.'

Her head reeled at the possibility. She said nervously, 'I have Sarah.'

'For two hours every fortnight, if you're lucky,' Benny pointed out. 'I can't sit back any longer seeing that man make your life a misery.'

Clara stared at him. He was offering a lifeline, a reckless adventure. How typical of Benny. If she got up now and went with him, she would never have to return to The Cedars and Vinnie's cruel control. But her courage failed her.

'I can't just run away,' she said quietly. 'I would only have to face him again sooner or later — and he would make things ten times worse for our families here.'

Benny gave her a stormy look. 'If I was Frank you'd come with me, wouldn't you?'

'Frank?' Clara flinched. 'Why do you say that?'

'Because you loved him,' Benny said. 'You always loved him better than me, didn't you? I saw it even if Frank and Reenie didn't.'

Clara's heart thumped hard. She could not deny it. Benny gave her a look of desperation.

'No one misses Frank more than I do — but Frank's dead. You don't love Vinnie anymore. But I still love you, Clara, and I know I could make you happy. Come away with me,' he urged. 'Don't we deserve some happiness?'

Clara said bitterly, 'I've got what I deserve — and that's a life with Vinnie.'

Benny looked at her in frustration. 'After all that man has done to my family, you're still prepared to stay with him?'

'It was never proved Vinnie was behind the attack on your shop,' Clara said, tired of the old arguments.

'He would have had us out of there one way or another,' Benny said angrily. 'He was the landlord, after all.'

Clara gaped at him. 'The landlord of Tenter Terrace?'

'Aye. Didn't you know?' Benny looked sceptical.

'No, of course not.'

'Part of a consortium; Cooper Holdings.'

Clara's insides clenched. 'But why would he smash up his own premises? Surely that shows Vinnie had nothing to do with it?'

Benny gave her a pitying look. 'Your husband would go to any lengths to punish us for standing out against him and his glorious crusade for Fascism — even if it meant a loss of rent for a few weeks. Especially when he blamed us for you getting caught in that battle in Clayton Street. He threatened me that I had it coming.'

Clara felt fresh pain at the memory. 'I saw you there outside the hall,' she accused him. 'I can't blame Vinnie for being angry over that.'

Benny exclaimed, 'Clara, do you have any idea how your husband operates? He deliberately incited the anti-fascists to meet the BUF head on that day. He sent round his bully boys with loudhailers to provoke us the week before. Vinnie knew there would be trouble, because he made sure there would be!'

'No!' Clara gasped.

'Yes, Clara! It's a well-known fascist tactic to stir up a bit of interest — make us out to be the attackers and them like soldiers defending their leaders. I bet your

219

membership went up after those street battles — brought in lads on the dole with nowt else to do.'

Clara shuddered at the thought of Vinnie's having orchestrated the whole confrontation.

'You would have turned up to defy them no matter what,' she pointed out.

'Aye, but it might not have got out of hand.'

Clara's eyes smarted. 'It wasn't Vinnie's fault that I got stuck at Clayton Street, whatever else he did.'

'We tried to call a cease-fire several times that afternoon, but the fascists wouldn't have it.'

'You were there in Clayton Street?' Clara cried.

Benny nodded. 'When we heard there was a lass gone into labour, it was my lads called the ambulance and forced a way through so they could carry you out. I didn't know then that it was you, else, by heck, I would have carried you myself!'

'Oh, Benny,' Clara said unhappily, 'what a terrible, terrible mess.'

He reached out and held her hand again. They sat for several minutes saying nothing. Then she pulled back with a sigh.

Benny said, 'You're not coming with me, are you?'

Clara shook her head. He glanced away, his face tense with disappointment.

'But you've shown me one thing,' she said gently, 'I have to fight my own battles. No one else can do that for me.' She stood up. 'I have to go. When will you leave?'

'Soon as I can,' Benny said, his voice tight.

'Please be careful,' Clara urged. Leaning briefly towards him she brushed his cheek with a kiss. 'Maybe when you come back, things will be different.'

With a defeated expression, he watched her go. Clara hurried out, wondering if she had thrown away her one chance of escape. But how could she leave Sarah and Patience and Jimmy to the mercy of the Cravens? Somehow, she had to find another way out of the imprisoning fear and dependence in which they were all held captive.

Chapter 36

1937

When Vinnie came to Clara's room, late on a spring evening, she told him.
'I'm pregnant again.'
He stopped his undressing and stared at her. 'Pregnant? Are you sure?'
'Quite sure. I'm feeling sick just like I did with Sarah.'
Vinnie's expression softened. 'That's grand news!' He came and sat on the bed. 'Have you seen Dr Dixon?'
'I don't need to,' Clara said. 'I know the signs.'
'Still, he should come and check you're all right.' Vinnie was firm.
Clara clapped her hand over her mouth and groaned. She sprang out of bed and dashed for the washbasin in the corner. She retched loudly into the basin and opened the tap. Splashing her face, she turned. Vinnie was already pulling on his trousers.
'I'll not bother you tonight,' he said. As she returned to bed, he caught her by the arm. 'I'm really pleased.' Pulling her to him, he placed his hand over her stomach and caressed it. Clara tried not to tense. Vinnie kissed her forehead. 'This is going to be a good year for us,' he said. He tilted her chin and kissed her full on the mouth for the first time in months. Clara froze.
When he pulled away, she saw the desire flicker in his eyes. He ran his hands over her body. 'Perhaps I'll stay a little longer,' he murmured.
'I'm sorry,' Clara croaked, 'but I'm feeling too sick.'
He scrutinised her. 'You do look a bit pale,' he conceded. 'You must get plenty rest.'
She nodded and he left her. Clara rushed to the basin and spat into it. She ran the water and dowsed her face, rubbing at her lips till they were sore. The very thought of him kissing her like that made her nauseous now. Listening, she heard Vinnie go back downstairs and out of the house. The car started up and he drove off. She sank back on the bed in relief. If she managed the situation well, there would be no more twice-weekly visits from Vinnie to her bed for months to come.
At breakfast, a few days later, Clara asked Vinnie for advice.
'I'm helping Willa with a spring bazaar for the veterans' charity,' she said as she buttered his toast for him, 'and we need publicity. Willa wants me to write something for the papers, but—'
'But what?' Vinnie asked, slurping tea.
'Well, I had to tell her you don't want me writing anymore,' Clara said with an apologetic look.
'I never said that,' Vinnie blustered. 'Just don't want you writing about things you don't understand.'
Clara paused. 'So you don't mind if I send something to the local paper?'
'If it's in a good cause,' he relented, 'then yes you can.'
Dolly flicked Clara a disapproving look. 'Which local paper? Not the *Tyne Times*, I hope.'
'Well, they do have the biggest circulation north of the river,' Clara pointed out, 'and Willa says George agrees. What do you think, Vinnie?'

'George approves, does he?' Vinnie queried. Clara nodded.

'But that Jellicoe!' Dolly said in disgust.

'My wife asked my permission not yours,' Vinnie snapped at his mother, 'and the answer's yes.'

Clara hid her glee. 'Perhaps Clarkie could run me over there tomorrow?'

Vinnie looked uncertain. 'Just get him to drop it off for you.'

Clara gave a disappointed look. 'It's always best to discuss coverage of an event in person. I might be able to persuade them to do a front-page piece — it's the twenty-first anniversary of the Somme coming up this summer.'

'Hark at her,' Dolly said bad-temperedly, 'blowing her own trumpet.'

Clara ignored her. 'I could take Willa with me,' she suggested.

Vinnie stood up. 'Aye, that's a good idea. I'll tell Clarkie to make himself useful.'

When he had gone, Dolly rounded on her. 'Vinnie may have gone all soft on you 'cos of the baby, but I know you're up to no good. What is it?'

Clara gave her an innocent look. 'I'm just trying to be a good wife to Vinnie,' she answered. 'Isn't that what you want?' She retreated upstairs to write her article, unable to keep the grin off her face.

Clara lost no time in organising the visit to the Tyne Times, picking up Willa on the way. Her friend was full of excitement, never before having been inside a newspaper office. Clara dispatched Clarkie at the door, telling him to pick them up in an hour. She introduced Willa to Jellicoe, who gave them tea in his office. After they had chatted politely about the charity for a few minutes, Clara suggested Miss Holt show Willa around the printing works. Left alone with Jellicoe, she came straight to the point.

'I want to start freelancing again. Will you help me?'

He was cautious. 'If you have your husband's agreement.'

Clara was impatient. 'I wouldn't be here if Vinnie hadn't agreed to it.'

'For this charity piece, yes,' Jellicoe eyed her. 'But he'll not want you making a habit of it. And I can't imagine you just want to cover fetes and tombolas anyway.'

'I'll cover anything just to get started again — fetes, tombolas, missing cats. I need to work, Mr Jellicoe,' Clara said urgently.

'And I need to know I'll not have some Blackshirt biff-boy breaking my windows,' he replied.

'We all have to take a bit of risk in life,' Clara challenged him, 'stand up to the bullies.'

Jellicoe snorted. 'That's rich coming from a fascist.'

Clara flushed. 'I'm not any longer.' She glanced round nervously at the door. 'I despise what they stand for.'

'You're still married to one,' he said. 'If we were in Germany, your husband and his friends would have Miss Holt out of a job and destitute by now just for being Jewish.'

'Miss Holt's Jewish?' Clara asked in surprise. Jellicoe nodded.

'Then for her sake, have the courage to face up to them before it happens here,' Clara urged. 'I've seen how Fascism infects people like a cancer — its hatred of Jews and foreigners, of handicapped children. I've seen it change Vinnie and it almost ruined me. Help me to fight it. Give me work!'

Jellicoe looked at her, baffled. 'You know I won't take anything too political — and it defeats me how your husband's even allowed you to come here. He made it quite clear to me a couple of years ago that I was never to let you write for this paper again. Why has he changed his mind?'

222

Clara hesitated. 'Because I'm pregnant and that makes Vinnie happy.'

Jellicoe let out a breath. 'I see. Congratulations.'

'No you don't see,' Clara said quietly. 'If you won't publish my articles then I'll find someone who will. I need independence and a source of income that does not rely on my husband.'

He frowned as he answered, 'You're playing a dangerous game, Clara.'

'I know.' She held his look. 'So will you help?'

Reluctantly, Jellicoe nodded in agreement.

***

Clara was amazed at how Vinnie's attitude to her changed over the following weeks as she visibly gained weight. He stood up for her in the face of Dolly's carping.

'She's eating us out of house and home,' Dolly complained.

'She's eating for two; must be a lad with an appetite like that,' he said proudly. 'Don't you gan upsetting her with your sharp tongue. If you can't manage the housekeeping, Clara will.'

Not only did Vinnie give Clara control of the weekly shopping, but he allowed her out of the house more to pursue her charity work as long as Clarkie drove her about. He even permitted her to cover social events and interviews for the *Tyne Times* as long as her articles showed the Cravens and their associates as generous benefactors. She once more accompanied him to dinners and boxing matches. She blended into the background but listened attentively to private conversations. What Vinnie did not know about were the articles she wrote anonymously, detailing the infighting between the local and national BUF and criticising their support for Franco's fascists in Spain.

Through Reenie, Clara made contact with Max Sobel and fed him articles for more radical journals. With Vinnie's restrictions on her movements relaxed to some degree, she was able to meet up with Reenie more often. The friendship was like a lifeline. At every meeting, Clara would ask for news of Benny, but Reenie could tell her little.

'What did you say to him before he went?' Reenie once asked.

'He wanted me to go with him,' Clara admitted with embarrassment. 'I said I couldn't.'

Reenie sighed, 'Daft lad. Of course you couldn't. It's just. . .'

'What?' Clara asked, sensing that something troubled her friend.

Reenie looked sad. 'He said something about wanting to prove to you he was as brave as Frank. But why would he want to do that?'

Clara glanced away guiltily. 'I don't know,' she murmured.

Sometimes the friends would meet at the cinema. Both would watch Pathe News before the main film with breath held, eager to find out the latest from Spain. Clara siphoned off housekeeping money each week, donating it to Max and Reenie's emergency relief fund for Spanish civilians. The news was increasingly worrying for the Republican cause, as Franco made gains in the south. So in mid-April Reenie was overjoyed to receive a letter from Benny. He was alive and well. He could not say where he was, except they were moving northwards.

Then, at the end of April, shocking news broke. An aerial bombardment had reduced a government-held town, Guernica, to burning ruins. It was market day and the town was full. Eye-witnesses, including the Dean of Canterbury, saw airmen machine gun down fleeing children, women working in the surrounding fields, even flocks of sheep. Hospitals and homes were reduced to rubble; the roads were choked with refugees. Word was soon spreading that German bombers and pilots were used in the attack.

Clara was desperate to talk to Reenie and Max about the massacre, but she and Vinnie were both invited to the Bell-Carrs' for the first time since her fall from grace. She found the visit intolerable. Alastair was almost gleeful at the carnage.

'It's Basque country anyhow.' He was dismissive. 'They're peasants — little better than savages.'

Clara wanted to ask which part of Spain belonged to the Basques, but did not want to draw attention to herself.

'I think the whole thing's Red propaganda,' Vinnie declared. 'They've bombed their own people so they can blame it on the Germans. They're trying to provoke non-aligned countries like ours into interfering. Shows how desperate they're getting.'

Clara watched him sipping Alastair's whisky in his Blackshirt uniform. She wanted to shout at him that of course the Nazi regime was involved. A German battleship had been used to bombard Malaga in February which led to the fall of the town into Franco's hands. It was common knowledge among the Left that both Germany and Italy were supplying Franco with arms and troops. Now this bombing of civilians had plunged the bitter civil war into a new depth of barbarity.

With barely suppressed rage, Clara forced herself to sit in silence and listen to the callous comments of the Bell-Carrs and their protégés.

Cissie startled her from her thoughts. 'Clara, are you feeling unwell?'

Clara blushed. 'A little.'

Vinnie rose in concern, but Cissie put out a restraining hand. 'Don't fuss. I'll take Clara for a breath of air.'

Outside the drawing room, Clara said, 'I'd rather go and lie down.'

But Cissie gripped her arm and pulled her to the front door. 'No, no, fresh air will do you the power of good. We girls need to talk.'

Clara's insides clenched. Had Cissie somehow found out about her journalism, or had she been spotted meeting Reenie or Max? Cissie led her down the steps on to the cinder drive. Clumps of dying daffodils swayed in a stiff breeze.

'Vinnie's told me your wonderful news,' Cissie began. 'You must take extra care of yourself this time — it would be more than he could bear if you gave him another subnormal child.'

Clara flinched, but Cissie continued oblivious. 'You know, in Germany, they sterilise women who produce mental defectives. It's one way of keeping the race strong.'

Clara stopped and tried to disengage her arm. 'I'm feeling faint; I want to go back.'

Cissie held on. 'Darling girl,' she cried, 'I didn't mean to upset you. I just wanted to give you a friendly piece of advice; one friend to another.'

'I am taking good care of myself.' Clara forced a smile. 'You shouldn't worry on my behalf.'

'No, darling, I worry for Vinnie. He needs your understanding at a time like this,' Cissie said. 'It's difficult for a man when his wife's with child.'

'In what way?' Clara asked, baffled.

'Men have needs,' Cissie explained, 'especially the more vigorous and manly. We women have to accept that while we are the sacred vessels of their unborn children, our men must have an outlet for their — urges, shall we say.'

Clara gawped at her, speechless. She was telling her to turn a blind eye to

224

Vinnie's philandering. How dare she!

'It doesn't mean that Vinnie doesn't love you.' Cissie smiled pityingly. 'He does — despite the disappointment you've been to him at times. But you do understand that the price of being married to such an important man is to accept your role as an obedient wife without complaint?'

'That's a matter for me and Vinnie,' Clara said stiffly.

'I'm afraid not,' Cissie replied. 'It's a matter for all of us — for the whole Movement.'

'What on earth are you saying?' Clara demanded.

Cissie patted her arm. 'It's of utmost importance that you stay together as man and wife. Leaders like Alastair and Vinnie must be seen to be standing for the values of sound marriage and family life. People in the Movement look up to them as their ideal. We women know that everything is not always plain sailing in a marriage, but we must strive to show a united front to the outside world. There are those who would try to show us in a bad light. We mustn't give them any cause to do so.'

Clara stared in disbelief. This outrageous woman was telling her to overlook Vinnie's unfaithfulness while preserving their sham of a marriage — and all for the good of the BUF!

Shaking, Clara said, 'You have a strange view of marriage, Cissie. Are you going to tell me who is having an affair with my husband?'

'Goodness, girl!' Cissie cried. 'I said nothing about an affair. No, you've missed my point entirely. I'm just asking you to be understanding. Vinnie is important to our great Cause. It wouldn't do for any silly little marital spats to be aired in public. You do understand, don't you?'

'Perfectly,' Clara said, tense with revulsion. She could not wait to get away from Cissie. Quickly, she made feeling sick an excuse to escape upstairs.

***

As luck would have it, Vinnie was away on business for three days the following week. Clara went to the Italian cafe and left a note for Reenie to meet her on Friday morning, knowing her friend was on nightshift. But when Clara returned at the end of the week, there was no Reenie. It was too risky to visit the Lewises' shop in person, for Vinnie was quite capable of having it watched. Worried, she went round to Max's office and prayed Clarkie was not following her.

As soon as she saw his expression, Clara knew something was terribly wrong. He stood up at once and came to her.

'Clara—'

'What's happened?' she gasped, clutching her stomach. 'Is it Reenie?'

Max shook his head. 'They've had news from Spain. It's Benny.' He reached out and took hold of her hands. 'He was caught up in last week's raid — outside Bilbao. I'm sorry, Clara. He's dead.'

Chapter 37

With Benny's death, Clara found a new courage. She was rocked with guilt that she had made no attempt to persuade him to stay, or that she had not gone with him. She should have been more honest with him years ago and told him that she could never love him as she had loved Frank. Had she filled him with false hope?

While his family grieved, Clara knew that Benny had gone to try to prove himself as deserving of her love as Frank. Even though she was married to another, the headstrong Benny had gone to war partly to win her love and admiration. Clara was burdened with the belief that she had never been worthy of such devotion.

Yet, even as she was riven with guilt, Clara was in awe of the quiet dignity and stoicism of Oscar and Marta at the loss of another son. Defying Vinnie, she went round to see them and was humbled by their kindness in the face of such pain. Behind the drawn blinds of the upstairs flat they served her tea and talked with sadness and pride about their second son, emotional yet laughing as they reminisced over family stories.

'How can they be so brave?' Clara said tearfully to Reenie as she left.

'Because they are proud of what Benny did, however much they miss him,' Reenie answered.

Clara swallowed tears. 'But it's such a waste! Benny was so full of life . . .'

Reenie said, 'Not a waste. Benny knew the dangers. He believed passionately in what he was doing. He would have felt a lesser man if he hadn't gone.'

Clara hung her head. 'But I feel so responsible for his going.'

Reenie touched her shoulder. 'Clara, maybe he wanted to impress you but he would have gone anyway. Benny always put his words into action — he was never one to stir things up then expect others to do the dangerous work.'

Clara felt a jolt. 'Like Vinnie, you mean?'

'Benny had ten times the courage of him,' Reenie said with fierce pride.

Clara looked at her friend in desolation. 'I feel so useless. Is there anything I can do for your family?'

Reenie studied her. 'Do something that would have made Benny proud,' she answered.

Clara spent a long time pondering Reenie's words. She wrote an obituary of Benny for one of Max's journals, but it did not seem nearly enough to assuage her feelings of remorse and helplessness. She continued to visit the Lewises openly and when Vinnie tried to bully her not to, she faced up to him.

'Haven't they been through enough? What harm is there if I visit?'

'Loyalty to me, that's what.' Vinnie grew angry.

Clara stood her ground. 'They're ordinary hard-working people with hardly two pennies to rub together. Why are you so afraid of them?'

'Afraid?' Vinnie blustered. 'No one frightens me! Least of all those foreign Bolshies.'

'Then leave them alone,' Clara said. 'And if you want me to produce a healthy son in five months' time, then you'll not go upsetting me either.'

Vinnie did not know how to answer her, and marched out of the room in a temper. But from then on, he turned a blind eye to Clara's visits to the Lewises.

It was shortly afterwards that the opportunity came for Clara to act on Reenie's challenge to do something in Benny's memory. In midsummer, while visiting Oscar and Marta, she learned of a trainload of Spanish refugee children, made homeless by the war, coming to Tyneside.

'We are having one of them here,' Marta told her. 'Poor little lambs — they have nothing, no home, no parents.'

Clara was struck again by the Lewises' fortitude. Where others would have crumbled under the strain of losing two sons, here they were offering a home to some stranger's son or daughter. They had precious little to spare, too.

She found out from Reenie that Max was involved in the billeting of the dozen or so children, and went to see him.

'I want to offer a home to one of the Spanish children,' she told him.

Max laughed out loud. 'The Cravens taking in an alien refugee — and probably a Communist one at that? I've heard it all now.'

'I'm serious, Max,' Clara said impatiently. 'We've plenty room.'

'And Vinnie?' he asked.

'Vinnie won't complain. We're offering a temporary home to an orphaned child. It's not a matter of politics.'

He smiled. 'I admire your guts, but why are you doing this?'

'For Benny,' Clara said quietly, 'but that's between you and me. There's only one thing I ask — make sure it's a boy we're given.'

'Why?' Max asked.

'I have my reasons,' Clara said.

Max shrugged. 'I'll see what I can do.'

Clara went with Reenie to greet the new arrivals at a church hall in Newcastle. She was trembling with nerves at what she was doing, for neither Vinnie nor Dolly knew of the plan. Max introduced her to a bewildered, dark-haired boy clutching the hand of an older girl.

'This is Paolo. He's eight years old. And Terese. We think they're cousins. She'll be staying with Reenie.'

Clara smiled at the boy, who stared at her fearfully as she tried to reassure him about the house he was going to and the room he would sleep in.

'I'm afraid he doesn't speak English,' Max said. He taught Clara a couple of phrases of welcome.

After twenty minutes of chatter among the group and a general agreement to let all the children meet up there once a week, Clara took Paolo by the hand and led him out. He said something in an urgent voice to Terese, but she reassured him and waved him on.

'I'll bring him to see her on Saturday,' Clara told Reenie.

Clarkie was waiting outside and gawped in astonishment when she opened the car door and coaxed the boy inside.

'Who's this?' he asked suspiciously.

'Paolo from Spain,' Clara said. 'Take us home, please.'

Dolly was equally dumbfounded when Clara brought the boy in and showed him around the house and garden. He looked anxiously up at the sky, then took Clara's hand and went quickly back inside. Clara took him into the kitchen; Dolly followed, stuttering with questions.

'I'll eat in the kitchen with Paolo tonight,' she told her mother-in-law. 'We're both very tired. The boy's had a long train journey.'

She served them up the fish pie that Ella had left in the oven and poured him a glass of milk. Dolly glared at the boy.

'You can't stay here! What will Vinnie say?'

'He doesn't understand you,' Clara answered, 'so it's no good shouting at him. Unless you speak Spanish.'

'Spanish?' Dolly fulminated. 'Spanish!' She stalked from the room.

Clara had Paolo bathed and in bed in Sarah's old room before Vinnie returned late from a meeting at the Thursday Club. She chattered gently to the boy and sang him songs as she stroked his dark head on the fresh pillow.

'My daughter never grew big enough to use this bed,' she murmured to him. 'It's good to see a child tucked in here. I hope you'll be happy with us, Paolo. At least you're safe. Benny would have wanted me to do this; he went to Spain to give freedom to children like you. Now he's dead and I miss him very much. But I'll do everything I can to give you the love that's been taken away from you, I promise. And you'll see Terese soon.'

'Terese?' the boy repeated, his eyes dark with anxiety.

She smiled and nodded. 'Soon.' She made a sleeping gesture with her head and hands. 'Paolo sleep, Terese sleep. See each other in two days.' She held up two fingers.

She left the door open and indicated her own room across the corridor. 'Sleep tight,' she said softly.

Downstairs she was ready to confront Vinnie. When he came in, she had a whisky poured and told him enthusiastically about the boy upstairs, before Dolly could get a word in edgeways.

'Your mother thinks I'm being foolish,' she said with a hurt expression. 'But it's an act of mercy for a poor orphaned boy. I knew you'd be keen to help. It's what you've done for lads like him round Byfell, isn't it?'

Vinnie looked at her in confusion, and gulped back the whisky. 'But a Spanish lad?' he questioned. 'A refugee, you say? From which side?'

Clara shook her head. 'Impossible to say. He doesn't speak a word of English — not yet. But Vinnie, a lad of eight doesn't take sides. All we know is that his parents are dead and he's got nowhere to live.'

Vinnie sighed in disbelief. 'Why didn't you consult me first?'

'I only just heard.'

'From who?' he asked suspiciously.

'Through my charity contacts,' Clara said vaguely. 'A relief organisation — non-political.'

Vinnie shook his head. 'He can't stay here. We can't bring up some foreign child!'

'That's exactly what I said,' Dolly agreed in satisfaction.

Clara quelled her panic. She could not bear to see Paolo uprooted again so soon.

'Come and see him,' she urged. 'He's a canny little lad.'

'He's a scrawny little ragamuffin,' Dolly said with distaste.

Reluctantly, Vinnie followed her upstairs, leaving Dolly huffing with disapproval. Thankfully Paolo was sleeping, his face empty of its strained look, his thumb half in his mouth. Clara's heart squeezed in pity. She longed to keep the boy. This was not just for Benny, she realised, but for Paolo. She had so much love to give him and wanted to protect him from the world. Vinnie stood looking from the door.

'This is going to be the bairn's room,' he growled.

'Paolo won't be here for ever,' Clara whispered. 'Let him stay until the baby's due.'

He looked from the boy to her in indecision. She sensed he was weakening and played to his vanity.

'You'd be so good with him,' she pleaded, 'the father figure he needs. And it will be practice for me in being a good mother to a boy — for when the baby

228

comes.'

She held her breath, waiting.

Finally he grunted, 'I suppose I could teach him a few things — turn him into a civilised little Englishman. Just till the bairn comes.'

Clara felt a surge of triumph. She forced herself to smile at him and say, 'Thank you, Vinnie. You're a good man.'

Chapter 38

To Clara's surprise, Patience took to Paolo immediately.

'Reminds me of our Jimmy at that age,' she said smiling, ruffling the boy's spiky black hair, when Clara brought him down to Byfell for Sunday tea.

Paolo dodged away, scowling, and grabbed Clara's hand, which only made Patience snort with laughter.

'See that look? Just like Jimmy.'

Jimmy also showed the boy some attention. Paolo crept up to study him as he polished his boots and badges and Jimmy let him finish off buffing them with a yellow duster.

'Like this,' Jimmy said, spitting on the toecaps. Solemnly, Paolo spat in imitation. When Jimmy praised him, he gave a shy smile, understanding the tone rather than the words.

'You can bring him down here any time,' Patience said, 'specially if you're getting tired and need to rest. I see your ankles are swelling up in the heat. You need to take care.'

Clara blushed, helping herself to yet another slice of her mother's coffee cake — the only thing she ever baked — and brushing off her concern.

'I'm fine — never felt better.'

At home, it was more difficult. Vinnie soon tired of trying to instruct the boy, frustrated at Paolo's nervous incomprehension. He took to shouting at him in English.

'I think he's only ten pennies in the shilling, that one,' he said dismissively. 'And he's soft as clarts. You just have to look at him and he bursts into tears.'

'He's had a frightening time of it,' Clara said defensively.

'So you say.' Dolly was disbelieving. 'How do we know he's an orphan? Bet his family sent him over here to scrounge off us English 'cos we're that generous-hearted. Next thing you know, there'll be a whole family of peasants on our doorstep.'

Clara struggled to keep her temper. She found it increasingly difficult to stay in the same room as Dolly or Vinnie. Dolly refused to allow Paolo to eat with them in the dining room, insisting he took his meals with Ella in the kitchen. At every opportunity Clara took him out for walks and picnics in the park or to visit Terese at the Lewises'. There he became animated, chattering to his cousin and happy to play in the street with other children. Clara loved to see him laugh and noticed how Marta brightened when the boy was around.

Terese was taking English lessons from a friend of Max's and was soon interpreting for Paolo.

'Is he happy?' Clara kept asking anxiously.

'Happy yes,' Terese assured her, 'with you and with house. But not soldier and grandmother. Too much shouting.'

'Soldier?'

'Man in black,' Terese said. 'Senor Craven, yes?'

Clara felt dashed. 'He must not worry about them,' she told Terese. 'I'll look after him.'

Gradually, she began to gain Paolo's trust. The boy was quick to understand her words, though spoke little. Clara would doodle pictures and words on a drawing pad to communicate with him. One day, she found a picture he had drawn of a huge aeroplane covering the page and a house on fire beneath its wings. In the corner, a stick figure stood watching, the only human in the drawing. Beside him was an animal, perhaps a dog.

Clara went to find Paolo in the garden where he was helping Ella pick pea pods. She beckoned the boy to her, holding out the picture. Paolo hesitated. Clara hurried towards him, eyes smarting with tears.

'This is you? This is Paolo?' She pointed at the stick figure. The boy nodded, his face crumpling. Clara held her arms wide and Paolo rushed into them. She hugged him fiercely. He sobbed and clung on to her.

'I'm so sorry,' she whispered, choking with emotion. 'My poor, poor bairn.'

It was from Terese that she learned how Paolo had witnessed his house and family being destroyed by a bomber flying back from a raid. He was playing by the river, the only one of his family to ignore his mother's call for the evening meal.

After that discovery, Clara took Paolo to choose a puppy and they returned with a West Highland terrier called Dougie. Dolly was horrified, but boy and dog became inseparable. Paolo, ignoring Dolly's command that Dougie sleep in the garden shed, sneaked out after bedtime and carried him into his room at night. The boy began to smile and laugh more readily, and it warmed Clara's heart.

When Paolo had been with them for two months, he asked to go with her to Gilead. Clara had left him with Patience on previous visits, trying to explain about Sarah, but he had grown agitated when she was away so long.

'Why don't you take him with you?' her mother had suggested.

'He might be frightened of such a place.' Clara was unsure.

'I doubt it — not after what he's been through,' Patience said.

Vinnie wanted nothing to do with the trip. 'You'll give the lad nightmares,' he said unkindly, 'putting him with all the loonies.'

Clara was full of apprehension, but Paolo was excited about going in the car and Clara had managed to persuade Clarkie to let Jimmy drive them up there. Dougie came too and yapped in the back at the occasional passing car, while Paolo chattered away to him in a mix of languages.

Jimmy stayed outside with the boy and the dog while Clara went to fetch Sarah. Her daughter kicked and squealed to see her.

'She's moving her legs much better,' Clara said eagerly to the matron.

'The swimming baths have been opened up. We take her into the shallow end for hydrotherapy,' Matron said proudly. 'She loves the water.'

Taking her out in her chair, Clara introduced Sarah to Paolo. He looked at her curiously and said hello.

'She can't talk back to you,' Clara tried to explain.

Paolo pulled a face at the small girl. Clara felt a pang of shame, but Sarah gave a screech of delight and tried to grab at him. Paolo repeated the gesture with more exaggeration and clowned around in front of her. Sarah laughed and threw up her hands, banging them on the sides of the chair. Clara smiled in relief as she pushed the chair forward and Paolo ran along beside it, making animal noises and trying to tickle the giggling Sarah. Jimmy followed, whistling, with Dougie on his lead.

They picnicked under the trees and Clara was amazed at Paolo's patience with her daughter. He spent ages entertaining her on the rug, playfully imitating her noises while Sarah rolled around, watching his every move. Eventually, he grew bored and rushed off with Dougie into the trees. Sarah wailed with disappointment.

'He's coming back,' Clara reassured her, propping her up between her legs so she could watch Paolo running and tussling with the dog.

When she took Sarah back to the ward, Clara felt a wave of longing even more acute than usual. She left her daughter trying to pull herself up on the bars of her cot, her dark bewildered eyes watching her go. Only Paolo's grinning face, waiting for her in the car, eased her unhappiness at leaving Sarah.

'Thank you, Paolo.' She hugged him and kissed the top of his head. 'You're a kind lad.'

He gave her a quizzical look, but burrowed under her arm on the journey back as if he sensed her sadness over Sarah.

***

As summer wore on, Clara wished that these long days full of activity with Paolo could go on indefinitely. She took him with her when covering stories for the local papers and found that many people were put at ease by the presence of the bashful handsome boy. But she knew that the happy time was running out. Vinnie only tolerated the situation because of her pregnant state and he was coming under increasing pressure from their friends, especially the Bell-Carrs, to hand Paolo back.

Alastair and Cissie were aghast at the presence of the Spanish boy in their midst. Clara had thought that James Bell-Carr could be a playmate for Paolo at Hoxton Hall, but Cissie would not hear of it.

'I'll not have him stay with us, Clara, it's quite out of the question,' she pronounced over the telephone. 'I don't know what Vinnie's thinking of, taking in an enemy alien.'

'Enemy? Don't be so dramatic! We're not at war with Spain,' Clara dared to retort. 'He's a small boy without a home.'

'You're giving succour to a little Bolshevik,' Cissie said querulously. 'I forbid you to—'

'If Paolo can't come to Hoxton Hall, then I won't either,' Clara interrupted and put down the receiver. She stood shaking for several minutes at her defiance of the powerful Cissie, but soon felt better for it. Cissie was as much a bully as Alastair or Vinnie and she was tired of doing her bidding.

Vinnie went alone to the Bell-Carrs' and returned full of renewed indignation. All that week he harangued Clara about Paolo and on Friday it came to a head.

'The boy has to go,' he ordered, swigging back his third whisky. 'Alastair is determined to have the alien children repatriated. We've given them homes for long enough. Now they should go back where they belong.'

Clara stemmed her panic. 'Send them where? Paolo's home was destroyed in the bombing. There's civil war — it's far too dangerous.'

'Franco has all but won,' Vinnie said dismissively, 'and Spain will have stability again. Alastair says the refugees have nothing to fear.'

'How would he know?' Clara cried. 'He hasn't lost his home and family. Paolo will end up in some orphanage or on the street — or worse. To force him back when we can give him a home is cruel — unthinkable.'

Vinnie gave her a hard look. 'We agreed he would go before the baby's born. I want him out by next week. You can hand him back to whatever charity dragged him here in the first place.'

'And if I refuse?' Clara challenged him.

A flicker of uncertainty crossed his face, and then he was bullish again. 'I'll throw the lad out myself and you'll go back to stopping in the house all day.'

Clara felt sickened by his words, yet that glimpse of doubt on Vinnie's face gave her courage. Vinnie was not God, as Clarkie had said. She would not become his prisoner again and she could no longer keep up the pretence of the past months. It was time to act.

On Saturday, Clara filled a large handbag with jewellery, silver pill boxes and housekeeping money. Despite the warm weather, she wore her fur coat and nagged Paolo to wear a jacket and cap. Pretending to go to the hairdresser's, Clara went straight to Patience for help.

'I won't let Vinnie throw the lad out. Can I bring him here, Mam?'

Patience stared in consternation. Paolo was playing in the back yard with Dougie, aware that something was wrong. He kept dashing back in to make sure Clara was still there. Jimmy sat at the table darning a sock, looking warily between the women.

'I doubt Vinnie would allow me to take him,' Patience said worriedly. 'He pays the rent on this house remember; he can hoy us out whenever he pleases.'

'What if I paid the rent from now on?' Clara asked. 'If I came here too. Started working full time again.' They stared at each other. Jimmy stopped his darning.

'Are you talking about leaving Vinnie?' Patience asked nervously.

'Yes,' Clara said firmly.

Patience let out a shuddering sigh. 'You know you can't. You're carrying his baby; he'd never let you go. And how could I keep you both? Vinnie would sharp give me the sack — maybe Jimmy too.'

'Not me!' Jimmy was indignant. 'I know where me loyalty lies.'

'Perhaps the Lewises could take Paolo,' Patience said in desperation. 'With the baby coming you'll have your hands full anyway—'

'I'm not pregnant!' Clara blurted out.

Patience gawped at her in bewilderment. 'But—'

'I made it up,' Clara confessed. Jimmy was open-mouthed.

'Whatever for?' Patience gasped.

Clara reddened. 'To stop Vinnie bothering me in bed.' Jimmy looked away in embarrassment. Clara ploughed on, thankful to be telling someone. 'I knew if I pretended I was carrying his child he would treat me better — loosen his grip. I've been writing again — not just silly bits and pieces on Willa's charities and church fetes but interviews and things about the BUF for the socialist press.'

'You've done what?' Jimmy scowled.

Clara answered, 'You can tell Vinnie if you like, I don't care anymore.' She got up restlessly and looked out of the window. Paolo was throwing a stick for Dougie to catch.

'Once I'd started the lie I couldn't stop,' she went on, 'so I made sure I ate twice as much to make myself fat. That's all I am, Mam, fat. When the chance came along to take Paolo, I knew I had to keep up the pretence. He's the best thing that's happened to me since Sarah—' Clara broke off. She turned and faced her mother. 'I'm not giving him up,' she said stoutly.

'Heavens above!' Patience cried, covering her face. 'Vinnie will kill you for this! For lying to him about the baby.'

Clara went to her mother and took her by her skinny arms. 'I've been living a worse lie for years! Thinking I was in love with that man — believing all that poison he preaches about Reds and Jews — lapping up all the luxury while half of Byfell goes hungry for food and work. My God, what sort of lass was I? Greedy and selfish, that's what!' She clutched her mother; she felt bony and fragile. 'Well it stops now. I'm not going back to Vinnie. I'll find somewhere for me and Paolo to live. Reenie will help me if you won't.'

Patience let out a sob. Clara let go and turned away. 'I'm sorry if I've spoilt

233

everything for you and Jimmy,' she said with regret, 'but I can't live Vinnie's way any longer. He might be pleased to be rid of me,' she added bleakly. 'I think he's carrying on with other women anyway.'

At once, she felt her mother's hand on her shoulder. 'Oh, Clara, my poor pet! Why didn't you tell me things were that bad with Vinnie?'

'He is carrying on.' Jimmy suddenly spoke up. They turned to see him standing up, clenching his fists in agitation. 'I've wanted to tell you, Clara, but it wasn't me business.'

'Who with?' Clara asked, her stomach leaden. 'One of his music hall acts?'

'Mrs Bell-Carr,' Jimmy muttered.

Clara was stunned. 'Cissie?' she cried in astonishment. 'He wouldn't be that daft!'

'There've been rumours among the Blackshirts.' Jimmy blushed. 'Clarkie told me to keep me trap shut.'

'Since when?' Clara gulped.

'The trip to Germany last year,' Jimmy said, 'though Clarkie thinks it's longer.'

'What a stupid, stupid man!' Clara said angrily. 'And I've been just as daft for not seeing what was under my nose. That woman practically told me to my face.'

Clara sank on to a chair, shaking. She felt revulsion at the thought of Vinnie and Cissie's greedy infidelity. Had Vinnie tricked her all along? Perhaps he had never loved her, just groomed her from girlhood as a suitable wife who would be naive enough to do his bidding. He and Cissie might have been lovers for years, for all she knew. Together they were a dangerous, ruthless pair. She shuddered.

'I'm sorry,' Jimmy mumbled, seeing the state his sister was in. 'I shouldn't have told you.'

Clara looked up. 'No, it's not your fault. I'm glad you did. It makes it easier to stand up to him. I hate him now more than ever.'

'No, you mustn't hate him,' Jimmy cried in agitation. 'It's that Bell-Carr woman; she led him on. She's to blame. Vinnie's still our leader and we have to do as he says.'

Patience and Clara looked at him appalled. His mother said, 'How can you say that after the way he's treated your sister?'

'She's lied to him!' Jimmy pointed savagely at Clara. 'And she's betrayed the Movement. She's brought this on herself. I'm not ganin' to run away like a coward. Vinnie's like a father to me. I'd choose him over you any day!'

He kicked away his chair and stormed from the room. The women stood frozen in shock as they listened to him clatter out of the house and slam the front door. Clara saw the look of pain on her mother's face and reached out to her. Their arms went round each other in a fierce hug.

'He doesn't mean it, Mam,' Clara comforted her.

'Oh, but he does.' Patience stifled a sob. Holding Clara's face tenderly between her hands, she whispered in a trembling voice, 'I'll help you — of course I will. You mean the world to me. If I can protect you from Vinnie, I will.'

234

Chapter 39

Leaving Patience to pack up a suitcase of possessions, Clara went quickly to the Italian cafe to meet Reenie. Her friend offered at once to take them in but Clara said no.

'It's the first place he'll come looking. I don't want your parents suffering any more on my account.'

Within an hour, Max Sobel had come to her aid and let Clara move into his flat, insisting he would stay with a friend until she found her own place. She was aware it could only be a temporary solution and that she would be safer leaving Byfell altogether. For all her brave words, she knew that Vinnie would not let her go without a fight. She wrote a letter to him explaining that she had never been pregnant, was not going back and wanted nothing more from him. If he tried to come after her she would make public his long-standing affair with Cissie and ruin both their reputations. She paid two girls playing hopscotch in Glanton Terrace to deliver it to Craven Hall, then left swiftly with Patience and Paolo before Jimmy reappeared.

On Monday, Patience did not turn up for her job at the garage and stayed indoors at Max's flat with Paolo while Clara went to work. She hid the handbag full of jewellery and pawned the fur coat that Vinnie had given her to pay for food. When Jellicoe discovered that she had walked out on Vinnie, he nearly sacked her.

'He won't touch you,' Clara promised. 'I've something on him that he'll never want made public.'

Yet she waited in trepidation for Vinnie to waylay her in town or find out where she was hiding and confront her. Three days later, she came home to find the door to the flat kicked in and a scene of destruction. Crockery was smashed and Max's books lay scattered and torn across the sitting-room floor. Dougie was whining beyond the bedroom door. In a panic, she rushed in to find Patience cuddling a frightened Paolo. Clara was filled with shame and fury that she had allowed the boy to be terrorised again.

'Vinnie?' Clara demanded. 'Did you see him?'

Patience shook her head. 'We were out walking Dougie — only gone ten minutes. They're watching the place.'

'Jimmy must have worked out we'd come here and told the others,' Clara said bitterly. 'Vinnie's brainwashed him. We can't stay in Byfell. This'll just keep happening.'

Before they had time to clear up the mess in Max's sitting room, there was a commotion at the door. Clarkie appeared, shoving Jimmy ahead of him. Jimmy staggered and fell at Clara's feet, his left eye cut and swollen from a beating. Patience screamed and rushed to her son.

'What have you done to him?' she cried.

Jimmy groaned as Clara and her mother lifted him to his feet and into a chair.

'That's what happens to those who don't obey me,' Vinnie said, strolling in behind. 'Young Jimmy didn't want to tell me where you were. It was that noisy mongrel gave you away.' He kicked out viciously at Dougie.

Clara looked at him with loathing. 'Get out of here!'

Vinnie laughed harshly. 'Don't tell me what to do.' He stepped forward menacingly. 'I've had enough of your awkwardness.'

'Shall I give her a slap or two?' Clarkie asked, grinning.

'Oh, Clara will do as she's told without that,' Vinnie answered, 'won't you, Mrs Craven?'

Clara's heart thumped in fear. 'I'm never going back to you, whatever you do to me. Our marriage is over, Vinnie.'

Vinnie's expression darkened. 'You'll come back cos I say so,' he threatened, 'and stop this silly rebellion. You can't survive without me — look at this place! You and your pathetic family are nothing without me. You've always needed me! If you come back without any more fuss, I might just forgive you — and take your half-wit brother back into my troop.'

Patience was holding a damp cloth to Jimmy's face. 'Clara's right, you're nothing but a bully,' she hissed. 'I'll not let her go back to you.'

He looked at her in disdain. 'And how are you going to do that? You're nothing but a daft weak woman who's sponged off me for years. Don't know what Magee ever saw in you. No wonder he took to drink.'

As he turned from her, he caught sight of Paolo standing rigid in the bedroom doorway. Quick as lightning, he crossed the room and grabbed the boy. Paolo wailed in terror.

'Leave him alone!' Clara shouted, reaching out for the petrified child. Clarkie pushed her aside and she stumbled against the table.

'If you don't come back with me like a good wife,' Vinnie bellowed, 'Clarkie will give the lad a good kicking.'

Clara pulled herself up, smothering a sob. She would rather die than let him hurt the boy. There was nothing for it but to do as Vinnie demanded.

'All right,' she gasped, 'I'll come. Just promise me you won't hurt the lad or my family.'

'That's better.' Vinnie smiled coldly and let the boy go. Paolo fled to Clara and threw his arms round her waist, shaking. She held him close. 'Now, say goodbye to the little peasant and come with me,' Vinnie ordered.

'No!' Patience spoke up. 'I'm putting a stop to this evil once and for all.'

Vinnie barged past her as if she had not spoken. She caught his arm.

'You listen to me, Vinnie Craven! You'll not want a wife like Clara when I tell you what I know,' she cried. He shook her off but she pursued him. 'If the newspapers get hold of this story, you're finished in the BUF. And I don't mean some grubby little affair with Cissie Bell-Carr.'

He stopped and whipped round. 'What are you talking about?'

For an instant, Patience glanced across at Clara. Her expression was full of regret. Then she faced Vinnie. 'Clara is Jewish!'

There was a moment of silence, of incomprehension, as they all stared at Patience.

'Harry's not her father,' Patience said, trembling, 'Leon Brodsky is; the man we paid you to get rid of. What was it you called him; a money-grabbing little Jew? It wasn't money he was after — he never cared about that — it was Clara.'

'Mam?' Clara gasped, her heart pounding in shock. 'You can't mean—'

Patience looked at her with deep sorrow. 'I'm sorry, pet. I'm not your mam either.'

'Not my mam?' Clara echoed, quite at a loss.

'Your mother was a Russian lass.' Patience spoke in a strained voice. 'The Brodskys were Communist Jews staying at my aunt's boarding house — they'd escaped from Russia and were half starved. Leah died giving birth to you. Your father tried to keep you, but the war broke out and he was rounded up and sent back to Russia to fight.' She swallowed and went on. 'Harry and I were betrothed. We told Brodsky we'd take care of you till he could come back. But none of us thought he would — him being Jewish and a radical one at that. Brodsky said himself that returning to Russia was like a death sentence. It was the biggest shock of our lives when he turned up all those years later — like a ghost from our past. We thought he was long dead.'

'You're a lying bitch!' Vinnie shouted. 'I don't believe a word of it. You're just desperate to turn me against Clara so you can keep her to yourself.'

'It's Clara I've lied to,' Patience cried. 'Do you think I'd willingly tell my lass all this when I've spent a lifetime keeping it buried? I've carried it around like a stone in my heart since the day she was born. I loved her from the minute I held her,' Patience said with vehemence, 'but that's not the reason we took her. It was much more selfish. I wanted Harry to marry me quick and get me out of that common boarding house — and he saw it as a way of avoiding joining up.'

'Joining up?' Vinnie frowned.

Patience goaded Vinnie with her words. 'Yes, Harry Magee, the man you praised as a war hero — he never was one. We knew as a married man with a bairn, he could avoid conscription for longer. Harry said conscription would come in sooner rather than later; there were that many lads been killed in Flanders or sunk at sea. Well, he didn't want to be one of them. So you see, Vinnie, we took a Jewish baby off a penniless Russian clock-mender and his dead Communist wife to save my Harry from going to war.'

Clara struggled for breath, her mind reeling. She found it as hard to believe as Vinnie did. Clarkie and Jimmy were staring at her as if she had two heads. Vinnie would not look at her.

'Prove it,' he hissed. 'Prove to me my wife is nothing but a foreign Jewess — daughter of penniless riff-raff. She doesn't look it to me.'

'Does she look like me or Harry?' Patience demanded wildly. 'Look at her! She's got her mother's fair hair and slanting eyes.'

Suddenly Clara gasped as if winded. 'The locket? The woman in the locket!'

She rushed into the bedroom and returned with the handbag full of jewellery, hastily spilling the contents on to the table. Grabbing the cheap locket she opened it out and thrust it at her mother. Patience stifled a cry.

'Where did you get that?'

'It was in the lining of Dad's coat — Mr Slater returned it to me when we pawned his clothes. Is this. . . ?'

'Yes,' Patience whispered. 'It's your mother.'

Vinnie snatched it out of her hand. 'Let me see!' He stared at the photograph in the locket and then at Clara.

'Can't you see how alike they are?' Patience railed at him.

Vinnie let out a savage oath and flung the locket across the room. It hit the wall and dropped from sight behind Max's desk.

'You're a wicked bitch!' he raged at Patience. 'You've deceived me all these years — lived off my generosity like a leech. You tricked me into marrying that lass.' He stabbed a finger at Clara. 'My perfect English rose!' He spat out the words.

Clara was stung by his vitriol. She rounded on him. 'No one tricked you but yourself. You and your delusions of grandeur! You think you can mould everyone to how you want them — charm or bully them till they submit — but you can't. We're real flesh and blood people, Vinnie, not pawns in your selfish little games.'

His look was full of loathing. 'I'll not be preached at by a common little Jew. I don't know you anymore. You're an impostor. You and that conniving woman — you both disgust me!'

'Then go,' Clara ordered, 'and leave us alone!' She squared up to him. 'And I'll tell you this for nothing — you stay away from us or you'll be sorry. If any of your thugs threaten me or my family again, I won't just go to the police; I'll go to the papers. You and the story of your shameful marriage will be headline news. Imagine what Mosley would have to say,' she taunted, 'one of his most trusted lieutenants married to the daughter of Jewish Bolsheviks!'

Vinnie looked thunderous, but Clara held his look. She saw the tell-tale flicker of fear as he glanced away. Then he swung round and marched to the door, nodding at Clarkie to follow.

'The lot of you can gan to hell!' he blazed. 'I'll divorce you, Clara, cut you off without a penny — and I'll make sure none of you Magees get work round here again.'

As he went, Clara heard him snap at Clarkie, 'Breathe a word of this and you're out on the street.'

Clara slumped into a chair, her legs shaking with shock. She could hardly take in what had happened. Where had she got the strength to stand up to Vinnie and threaten him like that? She looked at Jimmy's stricken face, then at her mother's. Except Patience was not her mother. It was as if the world had shifted beneath her and nothing was solid any more.

Patience looked at her with remorse. 'I'm sorry I ever had to tell you — but I knew Vinnie would never let you be.'

Clara gulped, feeling the first tears sting her eyes. Were they tears of anger at Patience or relief at being free of Vinnie?

Patience came closer but did not dare touch her. 'I may not be your natural mother,' she said, 'but I've always loved you like my own — always. I couldn't bear the thought of losing you to Brodsky — and neither could Harry.'

Just then, Paolo crept round the chair and silently climbed on to Clara's knee. Clara felt tears flood her throat as she put her arms round him. She had only known this boy for a matter of months, yet she loved him deeply. Patience had loved her with such a passion that she had gone to extreme lengths not to lose her to Brodsky.

'Please don't hate me,' Patience whispered.

Clara put out a hand and Patience seized it. 'How could I hate you?' Clara said hoarsely. 'You're still my mam. I wouldn't have gone with Brodsky even if I'd known. You and Dad were my parents — and Jimmy's my brother,' she added with a tearful glance at him. 'Brodsky must have seen that for himself.'

Patience sobbed in relief, pressing Clara's hand between hers. 'Poor Leon,' she cried, 'we should never have treated him so badly. And now it's too late to make amends.'

Clara hesitated, stroking Paolo's head in thought. 'Maybe not,' she murmured. 'Remember Vinnie said he never got rid of him; had him mending clocks instead. Perhaps we can still find him.'

Chapter 40

By autumn they had moved to an upstairs flat in the same street as the Lewises' in Sandyford. Paolo was delighted to be near Terese and they both went to the same school where he picked up English fast. More amazingly, Patience put aside a lifetime's prejudice against Germans and made friends with Marta, helping out in the shop in return for free wash and sets and midday meals. 'I suppose I was jealous,' she confessed to Clara, 'because you always felt so at home among them.' At Christmas, she persuaded Marta to sell decorations, ribbons and small toys to her customers. She talked everyone who came into the salon to buy some gift and the profit was spent on presents for the Spanish children.

'In the spring you can sell cotton gloves and chiffon scarves; maybe brooches and earrings,' Patience enthused.

'Your mama,' Marta said to Clara in admiration, 'she is top businessman, *ja*?'

Clara smiled in agreement. The Lewises knew of Clara's parentage — Reenie had been trying to help her trace Leon — but to the outside world they carried on as before. Clara was getting plenty of work from Jellicoe and from Max, and was sending off articles to the national newspapers in the hope of being published more widely. She drove herself relentlessly, for it stopped her having to think too deeply about who she was.

She still struggled to accept the story of her birth parents. She did not feel the least bit Russian or Jewish. What should she feel like? The heroines of romantic novels, orphaned and brought up by strangers, always knew they were somehow different; a square peg in a round hole. But Clara had no such feelings. She was a Tyneside lass with a fierce and loving loyalty to the parents who had brought her up. She had no feelings at all for the woman in the photograph. Only on restless nights, when she could not sleep, did she take out the locket and gaze at Leah and wonder what this unknown mother had been like.

As for Leon, she remembered him with alarm as the dishevelled man who had stalked her when she was fourteen years old. In truth, she was reluctant to meet him; frightened that she would find him dislikeable. So her attempts to trace him were half-hearted and she kept telling Reenie she was too busy with work to have time to spare on a wild goose chase.

Jimmy was Clara's one real worry. Against all their pleadings, he had returned to Vinnie, begging to be taken back, unable to bear the humiliation of being punished by his own comrades and losing their tight-knit friendship.

'I'm worth nowt without them,' he told Clara when she tried to stop him. 'The BUF's me life.'

'They're finished,' Clara protested. 'No one takes them seriously anymore.'

'That's not true,' Jimmy said stubbornly. 'Plenty support us and they'll come back in their thousands once they see us taking power. Just like Hitler.'

'It'll never happen,' Clara insisted, 'not while the trade unions and the Left are strong. Don't let Vinnie rule your life again.'

'Don't tell me what to do,' Jimmy glared. 'You're not me real sister. You're foreign filth.'

He had left before Christmas and never contacted her or Patience since.

'He's lost to us,' Patience mourned. 'My own flesh and blood. Who would have thought we would grow so far apart?'

'He's still young and naive,' Clara reasoned. 'One day our Jimmy will see things differently.'

Vinnie was true to his word. In early 1938, divorce papers came through, citing adultery with Max Sobel and giving details of her living at his flat. Clara wanted to contest this, but Max told her he was happy to be cited if it freed her from Vinnie for ever. She followed her estranged husband's movements from afar; the boxing hall was doing well as was his business with Templeton selling machine tools to Germany. Yet there was mounting unease in Britain about the Nazis as Hitler took supreme command and marched into Austria in early March, annexing the neighbouring country for Germany. There was talk of rearmament once more and a national register for war service was prepared. Perhaps Vinnie's business was not so secure.

On a personal front, he grew quite brazen about being seen out with Cissie at the theatre, the boxing or the Sandford Rooms. Clara wondered if Alastair condoned the affair or was too far removed in his feudal world of Hoxton Hall to notice. Vinnie seemed to thrive on taking risks, as if to prove he was invincible. He organised a Blackshirt march through Byfell at Easter which ended in mayhem, with dozens of people injured including three policemen. Vinnie was quoted in the *Tyne Times* as blaming the police for not giving them protection. Jimmy escaped with a broken nose.

Covering the story, Clara came face to face again with the BUF's vicious messages of hatred and intolerance. Reporting from the sidelines, she shuddered in shame to think she had once worn the black uniform and marched under their fascist flags. She unburdened her self-disgust to Reenie.

'How can I make up for being a part of all that?' she fretted. 'I was going along with some terrible things — hatred of the very people I'm supposed to belong to ...'

Reenie squeezed her arm. 'Say it,' she encouraged her. 'Say you are Jewish.'

Clara shook her head, her eyes smarting with tears.

Reenie said gently, 'You have to find your father. You're never going to have peace of mind until you do. Only he can answer all your questions.'

'I don't have any questions for him,' Clara was defensive.

'You're a journalist,' Reenie retorted, 'you're bursting with questions. But you're avoiding them by doing nothing but work.'

Clara gave her a haunted look. 'But what if he's dead and I'm too late? Or gone abroad?'

'He came back for you, didn't he?' Reenie said. 'I don't think he would have left unless he had to.'

Another thought struck Clara and made her blanch. 'But if he did stay around, he would have known about me marrying Vinnie — being mixed up with the BUF.' She covered her face in horror. 'He'd hate me for it. He might want nothing to do with me.'

'It would give you the chance to explain,' Reenie urged. 'I'll help you. Don't lose your courage now, Clara.'

With Max's help they trawled through parish records and old newspapers for deaths, census records for the living, lists of clock-makers and jewellers for whom Leon might be working. They trudged round boarding houses and asked at the synagogue, but no one knew of him.

'What if he changed his name after Vinnie sent him packing?' Reenie pondered one day.

Clara sighed at the hopelessness of the task. 'Maybe he just doesn't want to be

240

found.'

Max turned to Patience, offering her a cigarette. 'Is there anything else about Brodsky you can recall from the boarding house? Any interests — relations — friends?'

She frowned in concentration, then shook her head. 'It's so long ago — and I didn't really know them, my aunt kept me that busy.'

'Just a thought,' Max shrugged.

As he left, Patience said suddenly, 'He had a nice singing voice.' Max stopped and looked at her. 'I remember him singing while he was shaving — it carried all over the house.'

One spring evening, while Clara, Patience and Paolo were sharing a meal with the Lewises, Max appeared in a state of excitement. He waved a leaflet at them.

'What is this?' Marta cried. 'Another of your meetings that Reenie and Clara must attend, Max?'

'No, no,' he said urgently, making straight for Clara. 'It's for a concert in Blyth; a Communist fundraiser to bring refugees over from Austria.'

'*Das ist gut*', Oscar said in approval. 'We can advertise it in the shop.'

'Too late for that, I'm afraid — it's tonight,' Max said sheepishly. 'Someone brought it in days ago, but it must have got hidden under a pile of papers.'

'Why am I not surprised?' Clara teased.

Max held her look. His blue eyes shone with excitement behind their spectacles.

'What is it?' she asked, heart thudding.

'The male voice choir performing — it lists their names,' Max said. 'One of the tenors.' He thrust the leaflet at her, pointing. 'Mr L. Brodsky.'

Her mouth dropped open. Max nodded frantically. Reenie jumped up to look.

'Oh, Clara!' she gasped. 'You have to go.'

Clara looked at Patience in fright. She nodded in encouragement.

'Come on,' cried Max, 'I'll drive you there!'

***

Reenie went with them, driving up the Northumberland coast to the busy port of Blyth. It was over forty minutes, with Max getting lost twice, before they found the hall. The concert was nearly halfway through. They squeezed in at the back of the packed rows. A colliery band was playing on stage. Two men got up and insisted Clara and Reenie took their seats.

Clara's heart raced and her palms sweated. What on earth was she going to say to this man if she managed to speak to him? Try as she might, she could not think of him as her own flesh and blood. Harry Magee was the man she saw when she thought of her father. This man could never take his place.

Just before the choir came on, Reenie reached out and pressed her hand in hers. The men filed on, most dressed sombrely in suits, one or two of the younger ones in shirtsleeves and waistcoats. Clara scanned the rows but could not pick out Brodsky. The man she had seen nearly ten years ago had been shabbily clothed, unshaven and emaciated. These men looked vigorous and smartly turned out.

They began by singing rousing north country songs, then a medley of more popular ones. Clara let herself be carried away by the music. It was an age since she had enjoyed such an outing and she had forgotten how uplifting music could

241

be. She promised herself she would save up and take Paolo and Terese to a musical show or film soon.

'Which one do you think he is?' Reenie whispered. Clara was jolted back to their reason for being there.

'I don't know,' she said, feeling foolish.

Just then, the conductor announced that two singers would perform a folk song in their native language, Russian. The men stepped forward and Clara knew at once that the smaller, leaner one was Brodsky. His hair was turning grey, but the jutting jaw and large dark-ringed eyes were the same. When he broke into strong, rhythmic singing, Clara caught her breath at the sound. His voice reverberated around the hall, belying his stooped, fragile frame. It rose and fell like the rushing of the mighty river of which he sang, while the bass singer sounded like the rumble of a deep waterfall. It made the hairs on the back of her neck stand on end.

At the finish, the audience clapped enthusiastically and Brodsky's face briefly lit up in a smile. Clara felt a kick of recognition. She found it hard to breathe. How could she know that smile? She glanced at Reenie. Her friend's eyes were glittering with tears. Clara looked away quickly for fear her own emotion might overwhelm her.

When it was all over, Max touched her shoulder. 'I'll enquire round the back if you like.' Clara nodded.

Reenie stayed with her while the audience filed out, chucking extra money for the refugees into buckets as they went. She was amazed by the generosity of men dressed in threadbare jackets, their families in hand-me-downs. They handed over what they could not afford — what she and Vinnie had thought nothing of spending at the cinema on a dull afternoon.

The hall emptied and they waited. Max finally reappeared.

'There's a room behind the stage,' he said with a kind smile. 'Your father's waiting for you.'

Clara felt a jerk of panic and grabbed Reenie's hand. 'You'll come with me?'

'No,' Max said, 'it's best if you see him alone. He's quite overwhelmed.' He led Clara backstage and gently pushed her towards a door left half ajar. He nodded for her to go in. 'Reenie and I will be outside waiting. Take as long as you need.'

On trembling legs, Clara entered the room and closed the door behind her. It appeared to be a meeting room. Brodsky stood behind a table, clasping his hands in front of him. They stood staring at each other, speechless.

'Your singing,' Clara managed at last, 'it was beautiful.' With alarm, she saw his eyes fill up with tears. 'I didn't mean to upset you by coming here,' she said hastily. 'This was Max's idea.'

He shook his head. She saw his throat constricting as if he was trying to swallow down his words. Was he angry at being found? She felt an urge to explain.

'I've only recently discovered about you — about my natural mother. Mam — Patience — had to tell me in the end — to save me from someone who dominated me.'

'Your husband?' he said abruptly, his voice deep and croaky.

Clara flinched. 'You know who he is?'

'Vinnie Craven.' Leon nodded. 'I worked for him. He is a cruel man. He take away my job because I am Jewish, and told me to go far away. If not he will kill me.'

Clara stepped towards him. 'But you didn't. Why did you stay?'

242

Leon gazed at her with his fierce blue-grey eyes. 'To be near you,' he said.

Clara felt her throat flood with tears.

Leon went on, 'I could see I was too late to take you back — Patience and Harry they had brought you up well — made you happy. But I could not turn my back on you again. I followed you from a distance. I have a scrapbook of newspaper cuttings — your wedding, your articles, your baby daughter.'

Clara's heart squeezed. 'You must have been so ashamed of what I became,' she whispered, head drooping.

Leon said quietly, 'I was sad you marry that man, but I think maybe you do not know what he is like. But then I see you marching with the fascists — I read what you write against people like me — then I nearly go away for ever. I think my daughter is lost to me.'

'I was,' Clara admitted painfully, 'I was lost in a dark place.'

'That is when I come to Blyth,' Leon went on. 'I looked for a boat to work my passage back to the Soviet Union. Then I hear you have baby daughter and I think how I left you as baby — and I think of my Leah—' He broke off. 'I get job as school caretaker. If I cannot be a father to my own child, I can be a father to others.'

Clara gasped and looked up at him. 'That is how I feel about Paolo — my Spanish boy.'

Leon looked at her quizzically.

'He's a refugee — I took him in a year ago. It's the reason I left Vinnie, 'cos he was trying to send Paolo away. And I couldn't bear the thought,' Clara said, fighting back tears, 'not after losing Sarah.'

'Sarah?' Leon asked in shock. 'Your daughter is dead?'

'No, but I did a terrible thing.' Clara caught a sob in her throat. 'I gave her away — put her in an institution. She cannot speak or walk. Vinnie says she's a mental defective. There's not one day I haven't felt guilty about it.'

She looked pleadingly at Leon. He stepped swiftly round the table and came to her. There was a moment of hesitation and then their hands went out to each other.

'My poor Clara!' he cried as he enfolded her in his wiry arms.

Clara clung to him, surprised at how comforting it was. He smelt of cheap soap and mothballs. But it was the kindness of his touch and the compassion in his eyes that soothed her aching heart.

'I've done so many wrong things as Vinnie's wife,' she confessed, 'but I can't just blame him. For a time I wanted those things too — material things, social standing, power over others.'

Leon drew back a fraction. With his warm hands on her shoulders, he gazed at her troubled face.

'What is it you want now, Clara?' he asked gently.

Tears welled in her eyes as the truth suddenly struck her. 'I have what I want,' she managed. 'Patience and Paolo living with me — my work and my old friends back — to be free of Vinnie. And,' she swallowed, 'I've found you. I want to get to know my father better.'

His eyes brimmed with tears. He cried out something in Russian and hugged her to him. Together they clutched each other and wept.

When he could speak again, Leon said huskily, 'Your mother and I — we escaped from Tsarist regime to England to start new life. We are not looking for the moon. Leah, she say all we want is a handful of stars — a little bit of luck. She say you will be that first star.'

Clara looked at him pityingly. 'But you've had nothing but bad luck.'

'No,' Leon said with a tender smile, 'your mama was right. Tonight, I am given this gift — the brightest of the stars. You, Clara, have come back to me.'

Chapter 41

It was the start of regular contact with Leon. Each week, Clara would travel to Blyth to see her father, or he would get the train to Newcastle to visit her. Bit by bit, she learned of his former life as an idealistic revolutionary in Russia with a passion for singing, who had turned his back on his Orthodox upbringing and eloped with fellow student Leah Aronavitch. They were going to change the world and put an end to persecution. He had his father's trade as clock-mender to fall back on when, escaping a pogrom in 1913, they reached the safety of Tyneside.

Forced back to Russia in 1914, Leon was imprisoned and harshly treated. Saved by the Revolution but with his health further weakened, he tried to make a new life in the Soviet Union. Yet the thought of never seeing Clara again, or knowing what had become of her, brought him back to England.

Each visit to Clara's, Leon enjoyed the company of Reenie and her parents more and more. Oscar delighted in debating politics with a fellow comrade. Clara had never seen Reenie's quiet father so animated. Paolo loved Leon, who showed him how to play chess and whistle with his fingers and told him stories at bedtime. He was soon calling him Grandpa.

Patience found it the hardest to adjust to Leon's reappearance. Clara knew her mother still felt deeply guilty over denying Leon his daughter back, yet also resented the way Clara delighted in his company.

'It's not a matter of loving either one or the other,' Clara tried to explain. 'I'll always be closest to you, Mam. How could it be otherwise?'

In the end, it was Leon's own compassionate nature and quiet stubbornness to endure that won Patience over. She realised that he made Clara happy and was so different from Harry as to make comparisons futile.

In May, Clara asked Leon if he would go with her to Gilead. It would be Sarah's fourth birthday. Max drove them out there with Paolo and Patience. Marta had baked a birthday cake and Patience had made a family of rag dolls.

It rained, so they wheeled Sarah into one of the glasshouses and spread out the birthday tea. Over the noise of the drumming rain, Paolo entertained the excited girl with whistling and Clara's conjuring trick with a penny. He and Patience drew pictures in a pad and coloured them in, showing them to Sarah. Leon sang while Clara cuddled and talked to her daughter.

Towards the end of the visit, Sarah began to jerk and scream. Clara looked at her in consternation. 'Perhaps it's time we took her back.'

Paolo scrutinised the girl, then picked up the drawing pad. He drew a series of pictures, the way Clara had done when first trying to teach him English. A cake, a person, a bed, a car, a bird, a cup.

Sarah jerked urgently. Paolo held the pad close and Clara took hold of the girl's hand. 'Which one, pet?'

She guided Sarah's finger across the page. At cup, Sarah gave a high-pitched scream. Clara exchanged looks with Patience.

'She's thirsty,' Paolo said at once, dropping the pad and grabbing Sarah's beaker. He held the straw to her lips and she sucked hard. Afterwards, she gave a squeal of triumph and threw back her head in a gurgle of laughter.

Clara looked at Paolo in awe. 'She understands.'

'Why-aye!' Paolo grinned. 'Course she does. She's not daft.'

Clara gulped back tears. She grabbed Paolo into a hug with Sarah and kissed them both. 'You clever lad,' she cried. 'And you clever little lass!'

On the way home, Leon broke the subdued silence. The matron had been disbelieving about Sarah's ability to recognise pictures.

'Why don't you bring her home with you?' he suggested. 'For good.'

'How could we possibly cope with her?' Clara said miserably. 'I'm at work till all hours and Mam's helping Marta. She's enough on her plate looking after Paolo.'

'I could look after Sarah,' Leon said with quiet determination.

Clara looked at him, startled. 'You? But you'd have to give up your caretaking job, which you love—'

'And we'd need a bigger flat — a ground-floor one for a wheelchair,' Patience pointed out. 'How could we afford that?'

'I could mend clocks again,' Leon said stoutly. 'Sarah would learn so much quicker being with her family. I could give her exercises like the nurses do.'

'I know you're trying to be kind,' Patience said a little dismissively, 'but you're not trained to look after a handicapped child.'

He looked at their dubious faces. 'I will learn,' he said simply. 'She is my granddaughter.'

A couple of weeks passed with nothing more said, but the idea grew in Clara's mind until she could think of nothing else. She talked it over with Reenie.

'I'd be happy to help Leon with Sarah when I can,' her friend offered. 'Between us all, I'm sure we could manage.'

Clara gave her a grateful hug. 'I don't know what I'd do without you Lewises.' She smiled.

But Patience was still cautious. 'It's not Leon coming to live here that bothers me — it's what Vinnie will have to say about you taking Sarah.'

'What's Vinnie got to do with it?' Clara was impatient.

'He's still the girl's father,' Patience answered. 'He signed her over to the hospital. Won't he have to give his permission for her to be let out?'

Vinnie had had so little to do with Sarah that it had not occurred to Clara that he could stop her taking back their daughter. It would be just the sort of thing he would do to prove he still had control over her life. Clara fretted over what to do. In the end, she thought there was nothing for it but to go to Vinnie and plead for Sarah's release.

Then, as she was plucking up courage to go and confront him, she got an urgent telephone call at the *Tyne Times*.

Miss Holt told Clara, 'The line was bad, but the gentleman was very agitated. Foreign sounding. Mr Brodsky. Gave an address in Blyth — asked you to go there at once. I said I couldn't promise.'

'Is he all right?' Clara asked in alarm.

The secretary held out the piece of paper on which she had taken down the address. 'Didn't sound it. Is he a friend of yours?'

Clara dropped everything and rushed to the station. An hour later she was in Blyth searching for the hall near the docks where, in March, she had first heard Leon sing. When she got there, it was full of frantic activity. A soup kitchen had been set up and was doling out food to rows of people. Elsewhere, fresh clothes and blankets were being handed out.

Clara stopped one of the helpers. 'What's going on?'

'New arrivals from Austria. Mostly Jews,' the woman told her. 'Escaped with nothing but the clothes they're standing up in. Some of the stories make your hair stand on end.' She looked Clara up and down. 'You a journalist or

246

something?'

'Yes, I am,' Clara said hastily. 'I need to speak to Leon Brodsky. Where can I find him?'

'Oh, Leon's gone off to the hospital,' she replied. 'Poor man collapsed—'

Clara turned and dashed from the hall. She begged a lift from a passing grocery van which dropped her at the hospital gates. Sprinting into the building she asked breathlessly for help.

'My father,' she panted, 'he's been brought in. Mr Brodsky. I must see him.' Clara was filled with a sudden terror of Leon's dying before she could see him again. She had known him for such a short time. Now all her dreams were collapsing about her as panic set in.

'There's no Brodsky.' The woman shook her head.

'There must be!'

Suddenly a voice called from along the corridor. 'Clara!' She spun round to see Leon making towards her. Clara dashed to meet him.

'Papa!' she cried, flinging out her arms. 'I thought you were dying. A woman at the hall said you'd collapsed.'

He seized her, exultant at hearing the endearment. It was the first time Clara had called him that. 'I'm fine, I'm fine,' he assured her.

'Then what is this all about?' Clara asked, pulling away in bewilderment.

He took her hands. 'I bring in one of the refugees. He is very very weak. A bit — how you say? — delirious.' Leon's eyes were bright with emotion. 'But the extraordinary thing — he keep saying your name.'

'My name?' Clara was baffled. 'How could he possibly—'

'No one knows who he is,' Leon said, steering Clara back along the corridor. 'He's not Austrian — possibly German.'

'I did meet Germans from Hamburg once.' Clara searched her memory. 'They stayed with us — Vinnie did business with them.'

Leon glanced at her. 'I don't think this is Hamburg businessman. I'd say prisoner.'

He led Clara into a side room where a man was lying in bed. He was skeletal, his cheeks hollow and his eyes sunken into their sockets. His sparse hair was shorn back to his scalp and the arm that lay across the white sheet was emaciated, the long slim fingers huge and knuckled in comparison. She stared.

'Do you know him?' Leon asked urgently.

Clara shook her head. The man looked more dead than alive. Even in the depth of the slump around Byfell, she had never seen anyone this dangerously malnourished. Then the refugee turned his head on the pillow and opened his eyes. He took a moment to focus, then fixed them on Clara. She gasped in shock at their blue intensity, and stepped towards the bed, peering closer. She touched his hand tentatively. A flicker of a smile showed on the man's translucent lips.

She took his hand gently between hers and lifted it to her cheek. 'Is it really you?' she whispered in wonder.

He struggled to speak. 'C-lara,' he croaked.

Tears flooded her vision. He had come back from the dead. She kissed his hand and let out a sob of joy.

Leon touched her shoulder. 'Clara, you know this man?'

'Yes,' she said. She leaned closer to the man in the bed and softly touched his cheek. 'Oh, Frank!'

Chapter 42

Frank was too weak to tell them anything for days. For the first week, Clara stayed with Leon and visited him daily, taking it in turns with Reenie to be with him. Gradually, he grew strong enough to be wheeled out in a chair in the summer sunshine. Oscar and Marta came with home cooking to tempt back his appetite, marvelling at the miracle that had brought one of their beloved sons back to them. They got word to Lillian, who came rushing to see him, quite overwhelmed by his being alive. It was she more than any of them who managed to draw out Frank's painful story of imprisonment and near execution.

His talent for playing the violin had kept him alive: he was made to entertain the camp staff. He escaped during a thunderstorm that caused a power cut and plunged the camp into chaos. It was thanks to a Lutheran priest, who hid him for several months, that he eventually got across the border into Austria. Penniless and broken in health, Frank thought he would die when the Nazis occupied Austria. But he was rescued by a Jewish family who took him under their wing and got him away on a train to Belgium and then the boat to Blyth.

After Lillian appeared, Clara went back home. Before going, she spoke to Leon about asking Vinnie for Sarah's release.

'Are you still willing to come and live with us?' she asked.

'Of course.' Leon was adamant. 'Why not?'

'I can see how much you are needed here with the refugees at the moment.'

'My family comes first.' Leon smiled. 'And you, Clara? You are still certain that is what you want? Perhaps your life will now take a different road.'

'What does that mean?' Clara asked uncomfortably.

'You care very much for Frank, I think.'

Clara reddened. 'I care for all Reenie's family.'

'But with Frank it is something more,' Leon persisted. 'You are in love with him.'

Clara looked at her father in amazement. Was it so very obvious? There was no use pretending to Leon. She knew she could tell him anything in confidence. 'I've always loved him,' she admitted. 'But Frank was engaged to Lillian. She has a greater claim on his love than I have.'

Leon was reflective. 'Maybe. But it was your name he kept repeating when his mind was confused, not Lillian's.'

It was another week before Clara mustered the courage to seek out Vinnie at Craven Hall. She went with heart pounding, remembering all the times she had gone there as an excited girl and later as Vinnie's wife. Now their divorce was proceeding and she was a figure of hate at the boxing hall.

To her relief, the place seemed almost deserted and there was no sign of Clarkie or his henchmen. The first person she ran into was Jimmy. She had not seen her brother all year and it threw him into a state of agitation.

'What you doing here? You shouldn't have come. I'll not speak to you.'

'I'm looking for Vinnie,' Clara cut in. 'How are you, Jimmy?'

He gave her a strange look. 'He's not here.'

'Will he be back soon?' Clara asked. 'I can wait.'

'No,' Jimmy said in alarm, 'you can't. He won't be in today.'

'When then?'

Jimmy glanced around nervously. 'He's not coming in much. Better see him at

The Cedars.'

'I'm never going back there.' Clara was adamant. It suddenly struck her how quiet everything was. There was no bustle of people in and out of the training hall, no gang of boys hanging around the entrance or minding the cars. 'Where're Clarkie and the others?'

Jimmy's lip curled. 'Nicked off,' he said sourly, just 'cos the money from HQ has dried up. Clarkie and them were just a bunch of scroungers. The BUF's not about money.'

Clara sighed in frustration. Turning to go, she caught sight of Vinnie's car through the side window. She swung round.

'You're lying, Jimmy,' she accused him. 'His car's parked round the side. Is he in his office?'

'You can't gan in,' Jimmy said at once, trying to block her way. She barged past.

'This is about Sarah,' she told him. 'I want nothing else from him.'

Through the swing doors, Clara hurried to Vinnie's office and went in without knocking, Jimmy close behind her. The stale smell hit her at once. The room was a mess of half-eaten meals, dirty clothes and bedding strewn over the sofa. Empty whisky bottles lined the desk. A pall of cigar smoke hung over everything. Clara put her hand over her mouth to stop herself gagging.

'It's a pigsty,' she cried. Surely it was not Vinnie camped out here?

Abruptly a figure lurched up from a chair by the fire. Vinnie, hair awry and clothes dishevelled, squinted at them. He looked ill, his once handsome face bloated and pasty.

'What y' want?' he slurred.

Clara stared at him in incredulity.

'I said no visitors!'

'I tried to stop her,' Jimmy said.

'I'm not stopping long.' Clara found her voice.

Vinnie gave a harsh bark of laughter as recognition dawned. 'It's me wife, the Bolshie Jewess! Come crawling back, eh? Think I'd have you back in me bed?'

Clara struggled to mask her disgust. 'Vinnie, I want only one thing from you; to agree to have Sarah released from hospital. I want to take care of her. I shan't ask you for money to keep her, just to sign her over to me.'

He frowned at her, swaying on his feet. 'You want what? She's nowt but a vegetable.'

Clara tensed. 'That's not true. She understands more than we ever imagined. I want a second chance to care for her — to love her.'

Vinnie sneered. 'Should've been strangled at birth. Not my daughter. Unnatural. I blame you. Inferior, foreign stock. Polluting our race. Isn't that right, Jimmy? He hates you and that lying mother of his. Wants nowt to do with you.'

'Leave Jimmy out of this.' Clara lost patience. 'I'll come back when you're sober.'

'Don't turn your back on me!' Vinnie growled. 'Show me respect, damn you!'

'Respect?' Clara cried. 'Look at the way you're living in this place. Is this what you've come to, Vinnie; seducing women on a dirty sofa? Can't imagine Cissie stooping this low.'

Jimmy let out a gasp. Clara glanced round and saw the look of warning on her brother's face. But it was too late.

'Cissie?' Vinnie shouted, staggering forward. 'That stuck-up Irish whore! Nicked off back to Ireland with Alastair bloody Bell-Carr! Says England's ganin' to the dogs. Think they're better than everyone else. Think I care? Don't need 'em.'

'So she's gone?' Clara said without relish.

'Told her to go,' Vinnie snarled. 'Alastair found out about us. Tried to kick me out the party. Bloody cheek! Think the BUF's their private plaything. They used me,' he said. Suddenly, his face crumpled with self-pity. 'Clara, I knew you'd come back. You're the only one who understands me.' He swayed in front of her, holding out his arms. 'I forgive you.'

Clara said, 'I haven't come back, Vinnie. I only wanted to talk to you about Sarah.'

At once, Vinnie's mood turned ugly again. 'You can't have her,' he scowled, 'not unless you come back to me.'

She stared at him. She was beyond hating him. She felt nothing but contempt. 'Never, Vinnie,' she said with vehemence.

'Then your bairn can rot in the loony bin till it dies,' Vinnie said savagely. 'I'll sign nothing!'

Clara turned in despair, not wanting him to see how much he hurt her. He lurched forward and grabbed her. 'I haven't finished! You're to blame for all this. You ruined it all. I gave you everything — we could have been great. I was meant to be a leader like Mosley. You made a fool out of me!'

She shoved him off. 'You're pathetic. I can't believe I've spent so long being afraid of you.'

'Go to hell!' Vinnie roared.

She retreated to the door, glancing at Jimmy as she went. He had the look of a bewildered boy, the brother of old who would come to her for comfort. Briefly she put out a hand and touched him. He tensed.

She mouthed, 'I love you, Jimmy,' then pushed through the door and left.

Vinnie's ranting and foul-mouthed swearing pursued her down the corridor. She fled outside, gulping in the salty river air as if it could cleanse her of the rancid hatred that permeated Craven Hall.

Spirits dashed from her futile visit, she wondered where Clarkie and Vinnie's other bodyguards had gone. Was it a case of the rats deserting the sinking ship? Only her brother, blindly loyal, would probably remain with Vinnie no matter how low he sank. However misguided Jimmy's loyalty, she had to admire him for that. But as she made her way uphill, she felt crushed by bitter disappointment that her plans to reclaim Sarah had come to nothing.

***

A week later, Frank came home to his parents in Sandyford. It took him an age to climb up and down the stairs from the flat to the shop, but he did it with quiet determination. Paolo observed this new addition to the Lewis household with curiosity. He was incredulous that this gaunt frail man had been a boxer and a violin player. Clara told the boy how Frank had played with a professional band at tea dances and cinema halls. It gave her the idea to write an article about Frank's experiences in Germany and his miraculous escape as a warning against Fascism. Jellicoe put it on the front page of the *Tyne Times* where it provoked a flurry of letters to the editor, mostly in support. Jellicoe showed Clara a vitriolic response from Vinnie that was too abusive to publish.

'I thought Frank used to be one of his boxers?' the editor said in surprise. 'I had no idea he hated him so much.'

'Vinnie hates the world these days,' Clara replied, tearing up the letter and throwing it in the bin.

From a telephone call to Willa she had learned of the showdown at party headquarters that had ended in Vinnie's humiliation. Vinnie had expected Cissie to leave her husband for him, but Cissie had denied the whole affair and turned Alastair against her lover. 'George says Vinnie's unstable and not the sort of business partner he wants,' Willa had said. 'He's dissolving their partnership.'

Clara had investigated further. The policeman Hobson, now a sergeant, told her that Clarkie and two other ringleaders from Vinnie's troop had disappeared, rumour had it to Dublin. Clara speculated that they had gone to work for the Bell-Carrs, seeing Vinnie as a spent force. 'Can't say I'm sorry,' Hobson had grunted. 'There's less bother around the town since they left.'

A fortnight later, Clara spotted an advertisement that was about to go in the newspaper for a second-hand violin. She begged Jellicoe for an advance of a week's wages and promptly bought it.

She and Paolo took it round to the Lewises' one warm July evening and presented it to Frank. Lillian, who was helping Marta wash up, observed them suspiciously across the room. Frank sat with the violin a long time, just looking at it, touching it with shaking fingers.

'It's very kind of you,' he said awkwardly.

'Play a tune,' Paolo said impatiently, 'please! Mam says you're a canny player.'

Frank's expression was harrowed. 'I can't — I don't remember how.'

Lillian crossed the room and took the violin. 'Isn't this a little bit insensitive?' she said accusingly, putting a protective hand on Frank's shoulder. 'Frank hasn't played since prison — it's too painful a reminder. He never wants to play again.'

Clara flushed. 'I'm so sorry. I didn't—'

'Think?' Lillian cut in. 'No, that was always your problem, Clara.'

Paolo looked between the adults in confusion. Quickly, Clara put out a hand to him. 'Frank needs to rest,' she told the boy. 'We'll come back another day.'

She went, too embarrassed to look at Frank, berating herself for her foolish gesture. It would be better if she stayed away for a while. She was allowing herself to care too much about Frank again. Even seeing him in this diminished state, robbed of his youthful energy and verve, haunted by the horrors of his captivity, Clara still loved him. It was not the quick-fire, obsessive love she had felt for Vinnie, that had flared and died with equal speed. Neither was it the fondness that she had experienced with Benny. Just one glance from Frank's vivid blue eyes made Clara's heart ache with longing. Every fibre of him was dear to her, every smile like a shaft of sunlight on her face. He was traumatised by his ordeal, yet beneath she was sure he was still the brave, kind, idealistic, quietly passionate man she had fallen in love with all those years ago.

The summer holidays were about to start and Lillian would be around even more; she could not bear to watch the teacher fussing over Frank or the way he looked at Lillian, following her every movement. Perhaps she could take a couple of days off and treat Paolo and Terese to a holiday in Blyth with Leon. Clara immersed herself in work, smothering disappointment at failing to release Sarah and her rekindled love for Frank.

The next time Leon came to stay, Clara made the suggestion about the holiday. Her father was keen. 'We take day trip over to Morpeth or go to beach,' he enthused. After tea, he decided to drop in on his friend Oscar. 'You come to see Frank?' he asked on his way out.

Clara shook her head. Patience shrugged at Leon as if to say something had happened but she did not know what. Paolo disappeared into the lane to play. Shortly afterwards he came rushing back in, eyes wide in alarm.

'Police!' the boy cried. 'They're asking for you, Mam.'

Clara got up from writing at the kitchen table and put her arms round Paolo. Her first fear was for the boy. It was still possible he might be taken from her and sent back to Spain. Sergeant Hobson knocked at the open door and entered, a constable following.

Seeing Clara rigid with fright, Patience smiled and ushered him in. 'Sergeant, there's a cup still in the pot. Have a seat. What can we do for you?'

He stayed standing, looking at them gravely. 'I'm afraid we've come with bad news.' He glanced around the room. 'Your son Jimmy . . . ?'

'What's happened to him?' Patience gasped, her hands flying to her face. Clara moved towards her.

'We don't know,' Sergeant Hobson said. 'We're looking for him. Is he here?'

'No,' Patience said in bewilderment. 'We haven't seen him for months.'

Clara spoke up. 'I saw him a couple of weeks ago — down at Craven Hall. Tell us what's happened.'

The policeman seemed momentarily lost for words. 'Mrs Craven, I'm sorry to report there's been an incident. Your husband's been found in the river. Mr Craven's dead.'

Clara looked at him, stunned. 'Vinnie's dead?'

Hobson nodded. Patience gestured for him to sit down. 'Tell us, please.'

'No one had seen him for days.' The sergeant sighed heavily. 'His mother reported him missing. But he was in the habit of staying over at the boxing hall so she wasn't concerned at first. She said Jimmy was keeping an eye on him.'

Clara reached for a chair and sat down too. Paolo clutched on to her. 'Yes,' Clara whispered. 'Jimmy was with him when I went down there.'

'Can I ask you what it was you discussed with Mr Craven?' Hobson asked.

'Our daughter,' Clara answered. 'I wanted our daughter back.'

The sergeant said, 'Dolly Craven thinks your visit had something to do with it. Said her son was very upset the last time she saw him — and he was going on about that article you'd written about Frank Lewis.'

Patience came to the defence. 'My son-in-law was drunk and abusive to Clara when she went to see him. It was he who was doing the upsetting.'

Clara put out a hand to quieten her mother. 'Do — do you think Vinnie took his own life?'

'We don't know. There was no note left or sign that he intended to do so.' He paused. 'That's why it's important we speak to Jimmy. We believe he's the last person who saw your husband alive. There's a witness saw two men arguing down on the dockside a few nights ago. They fit the description of Mr Craven and your Jimmy.'

Patience looked at him in horror. 'You're not saying Jimmy had anything to do with his death?'

Hobson gave her a pitying look. 'We're keeping an open mind. That's why it's very important we speak to him, Mrs Magee. Please tell us at once if he turns up.' He stood up to go.

Clara voiced her fear. 'But what if Jimmy went in the river too?'

He frowned. 'It's a possibility, but we don't think that's what happened. Jimmy's belongings have gone from Craven Hall — all except his Blackshirt uniform.'

Clara exchanged glances with Patience. A flicker of hope lit inside her that Jimmy was safe.

Hobson nodded at them as he left. 'I'm sorry for your loss, Mrs Craven,' he mumbled uncomfortably.

For a long moment after the police had left, there was silence between the women. Paolo broke it. 'What the police mean, Mam?' he asked. 'What you lost?'

Clara encircled him with her arms and pressed him to her in relief. 'Nothing, pet. You mustn't worry.'

Patience put her hand on Paolo's head and looked at Clara. 'You're free,' she murmured. 'You're free of him at last.'

***

Word soon spread about Vinnie's untimely death. Patience fretted that Dolly might take it out on Clara and cause trouble, but they soon heard through Ella that she was selling up — the house and the boxing hall — and moving to her sister's in Doncaster. 'Mrs Craven can't bear any of it without Vinnie,' reported Ella. Patience discussed Vinnie's death with Leon out of Clara's hearing. 'The police mentioned her article about Frank — how Vinnie was upset by it. Perhaps he thought it the final straw.'

Leon was puzzled. 'The final straw?'

'The thing that made Vinnie see that Clara was never going to go back to him,' Patience explained. 'Vinnie was always jealous of Clara's friendship with the Lewises. I'm afraid I helped encourage him,' she sighed. 'I still feel guilty for burning a sympathy card from the Lewises on the first anniversary of Harry's death. Clara was upset to think they didn't care enough to send one. At least I've told her the truth about it now. I pushed her towards Vinnie instead. I used to think the Lewises weren't good enough for her. How wrong I was.'

Leon said gently, 'We all have things we wish we had done differently. You did what you thought right for Clara.'

'Thank you,' Patience whispered gratefully.

Leon sighed, his face perplexed. 'But why is Clara keeping away from the Lewises now? Marta is upset.'

'I think it's finding Lillian round there every time she goes,' Patience said. 'She's full of herself, that one; and Clara can't bear the way she's so bossy to Paolo.'

Leon's frown cleared. 'Ah, Lillian. Yes, now I understand.'

'Leon,' Patience said worriedly, 'what's happened to Jimmy? Do you think we'll ever hear from him again?'

Leon put a hand on hers. 'I think Jimmy look after himself.' He smiled in encouragement. 'He is son of brave lady.'

***

On the day of Vinnie's funeral, Clara took the day off work. But instead of attending, she and Reenie took Paolo and Terese on the train to Whitley Bay. She had asked tentatively if Frank would like to come too, but Reenie told her that Lillian had other plans for them.

While the children played on the beach and paddled in the sea, the friends leaned against the promenade wall and reminisced about the time they had gone there with Benny and danced to Frank's band at the Cafe Cairo. But Clara refused to be emotional about the past. She had to look to the future and the plans she had with her family.

'Leon's moving down to be with us in August,' Clara said. 'I hope by September we'll have found a bigger flat — and then we'll fetch Sarah home.'

'Leon is an amazing man,' Reenie said in admiration. 'My parents count him as their closest friend — it's as if they've known each other all their lives.'

Clara smiled. 'I know what they mean. I'm so lucky to have found him again.'

'And then there's Frank,' Reenie went on.

'What about him?' Clara asked, feeling herself redden as she glanced away at the children.

'Leon's done marvels with him,' Reenie said. 'He's the only one Frank feels comfortable with talking about his experiences in Germany. Everyone else just wants him to get back to his old life and forget about it. But Leon knows what it's like to be imprisoned; what it does to the mind as well as the body.'

'That's good,' Clara murmured. 'I didn't know that's what they talked about.'

'No, well, you've been neglecting us these past weeks,' Reenie chided, with a playful nudge. 'Too busy forging your career.'

'That's not fair,' Clara protested.

'I'm teasing,' Reenie reassured her. 'But you must come up soon and hear Frank play.'

'Play?' Clara stared at her. 'Not the violin?'

Reenie laughed. 'Yes, the violin. Leon's got him playing again.'

Clara felt sudden tears sting her eyes and looked away quickly. That's grand,' she gulped, 'really grand!'

***

That evening, Reenie offered to take Paolo for the night. 'It's been a strange day for you. You have a bit of peace with Patience,' she suggested.

Clara accepted gratefully. The day had tired her out and she was feeling reflective about Vinnie. On a whim, she looked out her old diaries from her days in Tenter Terrace and began to read through them. Perhaps in them would lie the clue as to why she had fallen under Vinnie's spell.

While Patience smoked, and mended a pair of Paolo's shorts, Clara became absorbed in reading about her past. The young Clara who had written these pages was thirsting for experience, frustrated by the confined world of Magee's gift shop. She was inquisitive and observant, yet trusting and naive; at times level-headed, at others romantic and fanciful. It was little surprise that a bright, inexperienced girl with a passion for life would have been attracted by what Vinnie had to offer. Yet, as she re-read her immature thoughts, Clara found it hard to imagine she had ever yearned for such things.

She stared at the diaries in her lap. There was one consistent thread; her friendship with the Lewises and her deepening love for Frank. She blushed again at her girlish crush, but the emotions she had felt then were still as strong.

'What's that?' Patience asked, interrupting her thoughts.

Clara looked up, startled. 'I'm just reading—'

'No, that sound.' Patience put down her mending and cocked an ear. 'Listen.'

Clara sat still. At first she thought it was a wireless playing in a neighbouring flat. The evening was warm and still and the windows were thrown open. But the music wavered, not quite perfect, and grew louder by the minute. Someone was playing a violin outside their door. Clara and Patience exchanged looks of incredulity.

Leaping up, Clara scattered the diaries as she raced to look out of the window. Standing in the street below was Frank, his fair hair still short and spiky, bent over his instrument. She stared in wonderment, catching her breath. He was playing one of her favourite dance tunes from the Cafe Cairo.

'Well, go and let the lad in,' Patience remonstrated.

Clara clattered downstairs, heart pounding as if she were sixteen again. She flung open the door. Frank finished the piece, his face in the twilight suffused with its former intensity and passion. Someone across the street clapped from an open window. Frank stood clutching the violin, grinning bashfully, his chest heaving at the exertion.

'Thank you,' Clara murmured. 'That was beautiful.'

They carried on gazing at each other. Words seemed inadequate after the emotion of the music. What did it mean?

'W-would you . . . like to come in?' Clara asked, her voice shaking with nervousness.

'Clara,' he spoke her name urgently, 'I have to talk to you — I have to tell you now.'

'What?' Clara felt sudden alarm. 'Is it about Lillian?'

He stepped towards her. 'Lillian?'

Clara gulped. 'Are you and Lillian going to marry?'

His perplexed look dissolved. 'Clara, it's you I love, not Lillian!' he blurted out.

'Me?' she gasped.

'Yes,' he insisted, 'always. I went to Germany partly to get away from seeing you with Vinnie. It was too much to bear. Even when I came back and found you had left him, I still thought as long as Vinnie was alive he would have the power to make you go back to him.'

Clara stepped towards him, light-headed from the revelation. 'And I thought you and Lillian . . .' she whispered.

'I told her today that there was never any possibility of my marrying her. That it was you I loved and always would.' He reached out and touched her face. 'The thought of you kept me alive in that death camp — kept me fighting to live — to escape.' His voice deepened with emotion. 'I didn't think you could love me — not the way I am now — a broken man. But Leon gave me the courage to tell you. He said you loved me too. Is it possible?'

Clara's eyes stung with tears. She clutched at his hand. 'Yes, it is. Since Reenie first brought me into your family, I've loved you, Frank. How could you not see it?'

'You always seemed too bright a star for me to grasp,' Frank murmured.

Clara laughed softly, 'You were the one out of reach.'

'Not now,' Frank said, bending close to kiss her.

As Clara felt the first touch of his lips on hers, she gave silent thanks for her brave, compassionate father who had brought them together at last. Their arms went round each other in a tender embrace. Frank kissed her with a sweet urgency, as if he could make up for the wasted years. She held on to him, never wanting to let go.

'Are you bringing that lad inside or not?' Patience cried from the top of the stair.

They broke apart, laughing. 'Coming, Mam!' Clara called.

Frank took her hand and squeezed it. 'Do you think she'll have an old Bolshie for a son-in-law?'

Clara's heart soared at his words. 'Play her a few more tunes like the last one, and she's bound to say yes.'

Together, they mounted the stairs.

***

On the day that Clara and Frank were to be married, a postcard arrived for Patience and Clara.

'It's from our Jimmy!' Patience exclaimed, her hands shaking.

Clara rushed to read it too. It had been sent from western Canada. He had joined a merchant ship and was sailing the Pacific.

'I'm a canny seaman,' it read. 'I like to think me dad would be proud. The thing I did, I did it for you, Clara, so you could have your Sarah back. It's what you deserve. Gan canny. Yours, Jimmy.'

'What did he do?' Clara puzzled over the words. Then, as realisation dawned, the two women stared at each other. Clara gasped. 'Is he saying he pushed Vinnie in the—'

Quickly Patience put a finger to Clara's lips. 'Don't say it. We don't know what happened.'

Clara watched her mother take the postcard, kiss it, then tear it up and throw it on the fire. Patience put out her arms to Clara and held her. There was a squeal from behind.

They turned to see Sarah kicking in her wheelchair, flinging her arms wide in excitement. Clara's eyes stung with tears of pride at the sight of Sarah in her blue satin bridesmaid's dress, and she laughed, rushing to her daughter. 'You can have a hug too.' She held her tight. 'What a special day this is, my bonny!'

***

If you have enjoyed A HANDFUL OF STARS, you might like to read another of The Tyneside Sagas: THE TEA PLANTER'S DAUGHTER

1904 INDIA: Clarissa Belhaven and her younger sister Olive find their carefree life on their father's tea plantation threatened by his drinking and debts. Wesley Robson, a brash young rival businessman, offers to help save the plantation in exchange for beautiful Clarrie's hand in marriage, but her father flatly refuses. And when Mr Belhaven dies suddenly, his daughters are forced to return to their cousin in Tyneside and work long hours in his pub.

In Newcastle, Clarrie is shocked by the dire poverty she witnesses, and dreams of opening her own tea room, which could be a safe haven for local women. To provide a living for herself and Olive, Clarrie escapes her dictatorial aunt and takes a job as housekeeper for kindly lawyer Herbert Stock. But Herbert's vindictive son Bertie, jealous of Clarrie's popularity, is determined to bring about her downfall. Then Wesley Robson comes back into Clarrie's life, bringing with him a shocking revelation ...

Set in the fascinating world of the Edwardian tea trade, THE TEA PLANTER'S DAUGHTER is a deeply involving and moving story with a wonderfully warm-hearted heroine.

Reviews:

'Irresistible'
Sunderland Echo

'A wonderfully moving, deeply emotional tale'
Daily Record

'Trotter uses her experiences and imagination to bring strength and depth to her novels. Another thought-provoking book'
Lancashire Evening Post

'Another action-packed, emotionally charged page-turner'
Newcastle Journal

'A moving saga set against the backdrop of the thriving tea trade in turn-of-the-century Tyneside'
Peterborough Evening Telegraph

'A gripping and heartrending novel... An unforgettable novel of courage, suffering and enduring love'
Bolton Evening News

Read a bonus chapter from THE TEA PLANTER'S DAUGHTER

CHAPTER 1

Assam, India, 1904

'Gerr out!' bellowed Jock Belhaven from his study. 'And take that stinkin' food away!'

'But sahib, you must eat—'

There was a splintering crash of china hitting the teak door frame.

'Try to poison me, would yer?' Jock ranted drunkenly.'Gerr out or I'll shoot you, by heck I will!'

In the next room Clarissa and Olive exchanged looks of alarm; they could hear every word through the thin bungalow walls. Olive, round-eyed with fear, dropped the bow of her violin at the sound of their father smashing more plates. Clarrie sprang up from her seat by the fire.

'Don't worry, I'll calm him.' She forced a smile at her petrified younger sister and dashed for the door, nearly colliding with Kamal, their Bengali khansama, retreating hastily from her father's study, his bearded face in shock. A stream of foul abuse pursued him.

'Sahib is not well,' he said, quickly closing the door. 'He is snapping like a tiger.'

Clarrie put a hand on the old man's arm. Kamal had served her father since his army days, long before she was born, and knew the raging drunk beyond the door was a pathetic shadow of a once vigorous, warm-hearted man.

'He must have been to the village to buy liquor,' she whispered. 'He said he was going fishing.'

Kamal gave a regretful shake of his head. 'I'm sorry, Miss Clarissa.'

'It's not your fault,' she said hastily. They listened unhappily to the sound of Jock swearing as he threw things around the room.

'Your father is not to blame,' Kamal said. 'It is the ague. Whenever it is attacking him, he drinks to stop the pain. He will be right as rain in a few days.'

Clarrie was touched by the man's loyalty, but they both knew it was not just bouts of fever that bedevilled her father. His drinking had grown steadily worse since the terrible earthquake in which her mother had died — crushed by a toppling tree as she lay in bed, pregnant with their third child. Now Jock was banned from buying alcohol at the officers' mess in Shillong and treated warily at the tea planters' club at Tezpur on the rare occasions they travelled upcountry for a gymkhana or race meeting. No longer able to afford cases of whisky from Calcutta, he was dependent on cheap firewater from Khassia villagers or bowls of opium to numb his despair.

'Go and make some tea,' Clarrie suggested, 'and sit with Olive. She doesn't like to be on her own. I'll deal with Father.'

With a reassuring smile at Kamal, she took a deep breath and knocked firmly on the study door. Her father shouted back in a jumble of English and Bengali. Bravely, Clarrie opened the door a crack.

'Babu,' she called, using the affectionate name from her childhood, 'it's me, Clarrie. Can I come in?'

'Gan t' hell!' he snarled.

Clarrie pushed the door open and slipped inside. 'I've come to say goodnight, Babu,' she persisted. 'I wondered if you would like some tea before bed?'

In the yellow glow of the oil lamp she could see him swaying amid the wreckage like a survivor from a storm. Mildewed books torn from their shelves and shards of blue and white china — her mother's beloved willow pattern — were scattered across the wooden floor amid a splattered mess of rice and dhal. A fried fish lay stranded at his feet. The room stank of strong liquor and sweat, although the air was chilly.

Trying to hide her shock, Clarrie moved into the room, stepping over the mess without comment. To draw attention to it now would only madden him. In the morning her father would be full of remorse. He watched her suspiciously but his protests subsided.

'Come and sit by the fire, Babu,' she coaxed. 'I'll get it going again. You look tired. Did you catch any fish today? Ama says her sons caught some big mahseer in Um Shirpi yesterday. Perhaps you should try there tomorrow. I'll ride out and take a look, shall I?'

'No! Shouldn't be out on yer own,' he slurred. 'Leopards. . .'

'I'm always careful.'

'And those men.' He spat out the word.

'What men?' She steered him towards a threadbare armchair.

'Recruiters — sniffing around here — bloody Robsons,' he growled.

'Wesley Robson?' Clarrie asked, startled. 'From the Oxford Estates?'

'Aye,' Jock cried, growing agitated again. 'Trying to steal me workers!'

No wonder her father was in such a state. Some large tea estates like the Oxford were ruthless in their quest for new labour to work their vast gardens. She had met Wesley Robson at a polo match in Tezpur last year; one of those brash young men newly out from England, good-looking and arrogant, thinking they knew more about India after three months than those who had lived here all their lives. Her father had taken against him at once, because he was one of the Robsons of Tyneside, a powerful family who had risen from being tenant farmers like the Belhavens, making their money in boilers and now investing in tea. Everything they touched seemed to spawn riches. The Robsons and the Belhavens had had a falling out years ago over something to do with farming equipment.

'Have you seen Mr Robson?' Clarrie asked in dismay.

'Camping over by Um Shirpi,' Jock snorted.

'Maybe it's just a fishing expedition,' she suggested, trying to soothe him. 'If he was recruiting for the tea gardens, he'd be round the villages dishing out money and opium as if he owned the place.'

'He's trying to ruin me.' Jock would not be mollified. 'Old man Robson was the same — put me grandfather out of business. Never forgive 'im. Now they're in India — my India. They're out to get me—'

'Don't upset yourself,' Clarrie said, guiding him quickly into the chair. 'Nobody's going to put us out of business. Tea prices are bound to go up again soon.'

He sat watching her, hunched and gaunt-faced, while she blew gently on the dying embers of the fire and added sticks. As it came alive again with a crackle, the room filled with the sweet scent of sandalwood. She gave her father a cautious glance. His chin was slumped on his chest, his hooded eyes drowsy. His face was emaciated, the skin as creased as old leather and his head almost bald. But for his European clothes, he looked more like a Hindu ascetic than a soldier turned tea-planter.

She sat back on her haunches, feeding the fire. In her mind's eye she could hear her mother's silvery voice gently chiding her: 'Don't squat like a common villager — sit like a lady, Clarissa!' It was sometimes hard to conjure up her mother's face these days; her cautious smile and watchful brown eyes, her dark hair pulled into tight coils at the nape of her neck. There was a photograph on her father's desk of them all taking afternoon tea on the veranda; baby Olive on her father's knee and an impatient five-year-old Clarissa pulling away from her mother's hand, her face blurred, bored with keeping still for the photographer. Yet her mother had remained composed, a slender, beautiful pre-Raphaelite figure with a wistful half-smile.

Ama, their old nurse, told her that she grew more like her mother the older she got. She had inherited Jane Cooper's dark complexion and large brown eyes, while Olive had the pale red hair and fairer skin of the Belhavens. The two sisters looked nothing like each other, and only Clarrie's appearance betrayed the Indian ancestry of their mixed-race mother. Sheltered from society as they were, growing up at Belgooree, she nevertheless knew that they were marked out in British circles as mildly shocking. Many men took Indian mistresses, but her father had broken ranks by marrying and settling down with one. Jane Cooper, daughter of a British clerk and an Assamese silk worker, had been abandoned at the Catholic orphanage and trained as a teacher at the mission school in Shillong.

As if that were not offence enough, Jock caused further embarrassment by expecting his daughters to be welcomed into Anglo-Indian society as if they were pure English roses. And to cap it all, this jumped-up soldier from the wilds of Northumberland thought he knew how to grow tea.

Oh, Clarrie had heard the hurtful comments at church and clubhouse, and felt the disapproval of the women from the cantonment in Shillong who stopped their conversations when she entered the shops of the bazaar. Olive hated these shopping trips, but Clarrie refused to let small-minded people upset her. She had more right to live here than any of them and she loved her home among the Assam hills with a passion.

Yet she shared her father's worry over the estate. The terrible earthquake of seven years ago had ripped up acres of hillside and they had had to replant at great expense. The tea trees were only now reaching maturity, while the market for their delicate leaves appeared to have vanished like morning mist. The insatiable British palate now demanded the strong, robust teas of the hot, humid valleys of Upper Assam. She wished there was someone she could turn to for advice, for her father seemed intent on self-destruction.

Clarrie glanced at him. He had dozed off. She got up and fetched a blanket from the camp bed in the corner. Her father had slept in here for the past seven years, unable to enter the bedroom in which his beloved Jane had died. Clarrie tucked it around him. He stirred, his eyes flickering open. His look fixed on her and his jaw slackened.

'Jane?' he said groggily. 'Where've you been, lass?'

Clarrie's breath froze in her throat. He often mistook her for her mother in his drunkenness, but it shook her every time.

'Go to sleep,' she said softly.

'The bairns.' He frowned. 'Are they in bed? Must say goodnight.'

As he struggled to sit up, she pushed him gently back. 'They're fine,' she crooned. 'They're asleep — don't wake them.'

He slumped under the blanket. 'Good,' he sighed.

She leaned over and kissed him on the forehead. Her eyes smarted with tears. She might be only eighteen, but she felt weighed down with a world of responsibilities. How long could they go on like this? Not only was the tea garden failing, but the house needed repairs and Olive's music teacher had just put up her fees. Clarrie swallowed down her panic. She would talk to her father when he was sober. Sooner or later he would have to face up to their problems.

Returning to the sitting room she found Olive crouched in a chair hugging her knees, rocking back and forth. Kamal stood by the carved table in the window guarding the silver teapot.

'He's sleeping,' she told them. Olive. stopped her rocking. Kamal nodded in approval and poured Clarrie a cup of tea while she went to sit beside her sister. She put a hand to Olive's hair and stroked it away from her face. The girl flinched and pulled away, her body taut as piano wire. Clarrie could hear the tell-tale wheezing that preceded an attack of asthma.

'It's all right,' Clarrie said reassuringly. 'You can carry on playing now if you like.'

'No I can't,' Olive panted. 'I'm too upset. Why does he shout like that? And break things. He's always breaking things.'

'He doesn't mean to.'

'Why can't you stop him? Why can't you stop him drinking?'

Clarrie appealed silently to Kamal as he set her cup on the small inlaid table beside her.

'I will clear it all up, Miss Olive. In the morning all will be better,' he said.

'It'll never be better again! I want my mother!' Olive wailed. She broke off in a fit of coughing, that strange panting cough that bedevilled her during the cold season as if she were trying to expel bad air. Clarrie held her, rubbing her back.

'Where's your ointment? Is it in the bedroom? I'll fetch it. Kamal will boil up some water for a head-steam, won't you, Kamal?'

They rushed around attending to Olive's needs, until the girl had calmed down and her coughing had abated. Kamal brewed fresh tea infused with warming spices: cinnamon, cardamom, cloves and ginger. Clarrie breathed in the aroma as she sipped at the golden liquid, her frayed nerves calming with each mouthful. The colour, she noticed thankfully, was returning to Olive's wan face too.

'Where's Ama?' Clarrie asked, realising she had not seen the woman since lunchtime. She had been too busy in the tea garden supervising the weeding to notice.

Kamal gave a disapproving waggle of his head. 'Swanning off down to village doing as she pleases.'

'One of her sons is ill,' Olive said.

'Why didn't she say anything to me?' Clarrie wondered. 'I hope it's nothing serious.'

'Never serious,' Kamal declared, 'always toothache or wind. But Ama flies off like mother hen.' He made a squawking noise.

Clarrie snorted with laughter and Olive smiled. 'Don't mock,' Clarrie said. 'She fusses over you as much as any of us.'

Kamal grinned and shrugged as if the ways of Ama and her kind were beyond his comprehension.

Soon after, they all retired to bed. Olive snuggled up close to Clarrie between chilly damp sheets. On nights when their father was fuelled with alcohol, the thirteen year old always begged to share Clarrie s bed. It was not as if Jock ever barged in and woke them, but any night noise — a hooting owl, the scream of a jackal or the screech of a monkey — set Olive trembling with unfathomable fear.

Clarrie lay awake long after Olive's noisy breathing had settled into a sleeping rhythm. She slept fitfully and awoke before dawn. There was no point lying there stewing over problems; she would go for an early morning ride. Creeping out of bed, Clarrie dressed swiftly and left the house, making for the stables where her white pony, Prince, snorted softly in greeting.

Her heart lifted as she nuzzled him and breathed in his warm smell. They had bought him from Bhutanese traders on a rare holiday in the foothills of the Himalayas, after her mother died. Her father had found Belgooree intolerable for a while and they had trekked for several months, Olive being transported in a basket slung between poles, her anxious face peering out from under a large raffia hat. Clarrie had fallen at once for the sturdy, nimble pony and her father had approved.

'Superior sort, Bhutan ponies. Of course you can have him.'

Clarrie had ridden him almost every day since. She was a familiar sight around the estate and the surrounding forest tracks. Hunters and villagers called to her in greeting and she often stopped to exchange news about the weather, information on animal tracks or predictions about the monsoon.

She saddled Prince, talking to him softly, and led him out into the sharp air of pre-dawn and down the path that snaked away from the house through their overgrown garden. Once through the tangle of betel palms, bamboos, rattan and honeysuckle, she mounted, flung a thick, coarse blanket around her shoulders and set off down the track.

In the half-dark she could see the spiky rows of tea bushes cascading away down the steep slope. Columns of ghostly smoke rose from the first early fires of the villages hidden in the jungle below. Around her, the conical-shaped, densely wooded hills stood darkly against the lightening horizon. She continued through the forest of pines, sal and oaks, the night noises giving way to the scream of waking birds.

For almost an hour Clarrie rode until she reached the summit of her favourite hill, emerging out of the trees into a clearing just as dawn was breaking. Around her lay the toppled stones of an old temple, long reclaimed by jungle creepers. Beside it, under a sheltering tamarind tree, was the hut of a holy man built out of palm leaves and moss. The roof was overrun with jasmine and mimosa and he tended a beautiful garden of roses. A crystal-clear spring bubbled out of nearby rocks, filled a pool and then disappeared underground again. It was a magical place of pungent flowers with a heart-stopping view that stretched for miles. There was no smoke issuing from the swami's hut so Clarrie assumed he was travelling.

She dismounted and led Prince to drink at the pool. Sitting on a tumbledown pillar carved with tigers she gazed at the spreading dawn. Far to the east, the high dark green hills of Upper Assam came rippling out of the dark. The mighty Brahmaputra River that cut its way through the fertile valley was hidden in rolls of fog. Beyond it, looking north, Clarrie watched the light catch the distant peaks of the Himalayas. They thrust out of the .mist, jagged and ethereal, their snow-capped slopes blushing crimson as the dawn awoke them.

Clarrie, wrapped in her blanket, sat motionless as if caught in a spell. Prince wandered off to graze as the sunlight gathered in strength and the remote mountains turned golden as temple roofs. At last, she sighed and stood up. This place always stilled her fractious thoughts. She left a pouch of tea and sugar at the swami's door and remounted Prince. A soft noise made her turn. At the pool a graceful fallow deer stooped to drink. Clarrie was entranced that the animal had crept so close to them without showing fear.

A moment later, a deafening shot exploded from the surrounding trees. The deer's head went up as if yanked on a harness. A second shot passed so close, Prince reared up in terror. Clarrie clutched frantically at the reins to calm him. A third shot hit the deer square on and its legs folded like collapsing cards.

Horrified at the brutality of the moment, Clarrie slackened her hold. Prince danced in crazy, petrified circles, slipping on wet leaves. The next instant she was tossed from the saddle, thumping on to damp ground. Her head hit a stone and her vision turned red. She was aware of men's voices shouting and footsteps running towards her.

'You madman!' a deep voice thundered.

'Just a ruddy native,' another blustered. 'I fired a warning shot.'

'It's a woman, for God's sake!'

Clarrie wanted to carry on listening but their voices were fading. Who were they talking about? Before she could decide, she passed out.

Janet welcomes comments and feedback on her stories. If you would like to do so, you can contact her through her website:
www.janetmacleodtrotter.com

Lightning Source UK Ltd.
Milton Keynes UK
UKOW03f0242060914

238130UK00004B/65/P